Suddenly the little girl understood: There was no safety in the unburned forest — only in the dead zones where the fire had already burned itself out. She let the dog tug her into a patch of cinder no larger than the inside of a car. There was one ghost of a tree, charred and black and naked as a lamp post.

The smoke was beginning to roll in thicker. The dog yapped at her crazily, tugging her down to the ground.

She obeyed, lying on her side, curling up, making herself small. Two seconds later heat slammed down. Above her there was a hissing roar and when she opened her eyes the smoke had closed in and high above she could dimly make out a canopy of surging red.

The sky was on fire.

THE GREAT LOS ANGELES FIRE

EDWARD STEWART

FAWCETT CREST • NEW YORK

For Avonia Bunn, starmaker and true pussycat;
not to mention Nora, Vaslav, and Herbie.

A Fawcett Crest Book
Published by Ballantine Books
Copyright © 1980 by Edward Stewart

Library of Congress Catalog Card Number: 80-13550

ISBN 0-449-74526-8

This edition published by arrangement with Simon and Schuster

Manufactured in the United States of America

First Ballantine Books Edition: August 1982

Before

THIS is the way to see it, the way *he* saw it when he conceived the thing the city will never forget.

It's a simple thing, and a wonder no one saw it before.

Los Angeles is a city with a forest inside it. See it as hills and canyons and mountains and woods in and all around an urban and suburban complexity that is vast and never lets up. There are no boundaries to go by: housing and commerce thrive anywhere here—even on the dreary desert scruff. So forget anything that comes close to exactitude and settle instead for an impression.

A crescent—that's the impression. That's what Los Angeles is. See it as a crescent. See it as a crescent that has turned its back on the rest of the continent. See the points of the crescent touching the Pacific, water filling the concavity from top to bottom.

Keep your eye on that crescent, on the sea caught in its scoop. It's like a skinny man all bent over, and heaped up there against his back is mountain and forest from top to bottom.

If you start up there at the top, it's the hills and mountains they call the Los Padres National Forest. Down around the neck you've got more hills and mountains, and these they call the Angeles National Forest. Next come the hills and mountains they call the San Bernardino National Forest. They shove from midback on down to behind the knees. At that point Desert State Park takes over, finishing off the work the continent has undertaken in its ancient push to dump the whole business into the sea.

And there, going straight up the middle of the skimpy crescent like a spike cleaving the stooped man from feet to belly, is a vertical shaft of mountains and woods that shatters everything apart. They call that shaft the Cleveland National Forest.

Like all the hills and forest that thread through and around the city, it is dry kindling—for the drought is in its ninth week. But this is not ordinary kindling: it contains its own fuse, the flammable resin of the pines.

There you have it: the kindling, the fuse; the city surrounded and penetrated.

Today, September 7, at 6:00 P.M., with the hot dry Santa Ana wind lashing across the hills, there is only one thing missing.

The spark.

That spark is four hours in the future, and once it touches the kindling and the fuse, the thing that the city does not yet even suspect will become the horror that it will never forget.

1

EDWARD K. CALDWELL, Jr., owned the house, but he slipped into it like a thief, careful not to let his keys jingle, careful not to let the screen door slam, careful not to let that floorboard by the stairs squeak as he tiptoed across the front hall to the downstairs bathroom.

He shut the door behind him, careful not to let the latch click; he gargled soundlessly, head back, mouth shaped into a voiceless "ahhhhh"; he opened the faucet just a dribble so there'd be no telltale humming of water in the pipes, no telltale splatter of red mouthwash in the sink. He blew into his hands, cupping the breath back into his nostrils. When he was satisfied that there was no smell of Scotch he went to the garage to get what he needed.

He stooped and hefted the charcoal sack under one arm. With the same arm he reached down and hooked his fingers through the handle of the gallon can. It was commercial napalm, a lazy man's way of getting the barbecue going. He pushed through the screen door to the backyard.

He saw her there, the whole brilliant bikinied length of her oiled and gleaming on the lawn chair. Her feet were poised on the footrest so that her calves sloped, their shape perfect. The dying evening light flashed across her skin and the suntan lotion she'd smoothed over herself sent out sharp glints like sparks from a flint.

Her name was Trish and he had picked her up six months ago in a singles bar.

"Eddy?" she called, stirring at the twanging slam of the screen door. She rolled over and lifted her sunglasses, perching them in her hair. "You been home long?"

"Hour or so," Caldwell said as casually as possible. "Didn't hear you."

"You were dozing. Better watch it. You'll get burned."

She squinted. He was a big man, six-two or better, all density, his massive torso seeming to hurtle at you even when his feet were planted. Sometimes when he was tired something went wrong with the power his burly motion suggested. Sometimes there was a hint of a limp, a hesitation in the right foot.

She saw that he was limping now as he came toward her. Her mind toyed with the limp and the late hour, toyed with connections.

"I didn't hear the car," she said.

"I parked it in front."

She didn't ask why. She couldn't expect him to have a reason for everything, at least not a reason he'd tell her. He bent down and kissed her. She tasted cinnamon. Her mind toyed with that too.

"I'm thirsty," she said.

"You've been in the sun too long. It dehydrates you."

She reached down and lifted an empty glass from the lawn. "Refill me?"

"In a minute," Caldwell said, taking the glass from her with his free hand, not slowing his stride to the grill.

He dumped the sack of charcoal and let the can of igniter fluid slip from his fingers. He hunkered down and yanked open the fire door. He shoved his hand inside and scooped out ashes, fine white ash that he shoveled into a pile between his feet. With his other hand he held her glass. Even with the ashes and his sweat he could smell it—iced tea laced with lemon and mint.

"Honey, I'm parched," she called.

8

"Just a minute." His voice was almost stern. He was not a man to be rushed. He was a man used to the high throttle of command, a fire boss, an absolute force among forceful men. He'd spent his life fighting fire. Fire was his enemy and his career and whether he was fighting a six-alarm blaze or laying the charcoal to grill two steaks he took fire seriously.

So he concentrated now, his deep chest centered over a cone of white ash, and when he had the placement of charcoal perfect and the distribution of fluid perfect he struck a match, and when he was satisfied that the fire was going perfectly he went to the kitchen to refill Trish's glass.

He saw the platter she'd set out with the steaks and the big barbecue fork, the salt and coarse pepper and garlic powder and the English mustard she knew he liked. It pleased him that she knew the little things he liked.

He put fresh ice cubes in her glass and poured tea from the pitcher in the refrigerator. He wanted to do it right for her. He sliced lemon and found mint in the vegetable tray and arranged them so the glass looked pretty.

Then he dropped ice cubes into a second glass and filled it to the top with Scotch. He added a lemon slice and a mint sprig and to complete the deception he took the pitcher and poured what he estimated to be a glass of tea down the sink drain.

He took a glass in each hand and pushed back through the screen door. It suddenly seemed to him hotter outside, a crushing September heat, as though a thermostat had been turned up.

Trish sat up on the lounge chair when she saw Caldwell coming. Her hand went out to take a glass and he quickly handed her the right glass and she gulped gratefully.

"How do you want your salad?" she said.

"How about with lettuce in it?" Caldwell moved to the grill, pretending to monitor the fire. He intended to have another Scotch with dinner, a real one, and he didn't want her smelling his iced tea.

"Oh, too bad," Trish said. "I was thinking of rutabaga and squash and an undergrowth of eggplant."

"Please, ma'am, just a little bit of lettuce?"

Trish swallowed from her glass. She picked up a tube of suntan cream from the lawn and screwed the cap back on. "Sorry," she said, "I'm putting bean sprouts in where the lettuce goes. Besides there's a strike on and lettuce is luxury food now. Only rabbits can afford it."

She sipped as she said this, and Caldwell looked up from his handiwork.

"So, where will we eat?" he said. "Out here or inside?"

"Please, Mr. Fireman, inside? Too hot out here. And anyway, the wind'll blow junk all over our nice salad."

"Might not hurt," Caldwell said.

"Cynic." She smiled.

Caldwell went back into the kitchen and got the steaks. He seasoned them and seared them and cooked them eight minutes on one side and four on the other. His mind kept skipping back to other nights in this backyard, other barbecues. He was glad when they went inside.

He poured himself a real Scotch.

"Bad day?" he heard her say.

"Only when I laugh," he said.

"Peters again?"

He didn't answer. He stiffened slightly. She had a way of reading him. It had been one of the qualities that had drawn him to her. Six months ago there'd been no words in him—only pain and loss and panic and guilt. Her intuitiveness had been comfortable then but in small ways it had started grinding at him; what had been comfortable then was turning into pressure. He didn't want to be understood; he didn't want to be read.

"Then dump him," Trish said. "Get rid of the guy if he bothers you so."

"The man does his work," Caldwell said, and he swung around to face her. "You don't fire civil servants who do their work. There's a union."

"Then you live with him." Trish worked as a ward nurse at L.A. General. Her ideas ran to definites: life/

death, either/or, work with him, fire him. At first he'd liked that in her too.

"He's gunning for me."

She shot him a glance that was instant and sharp as a reflex. "Gunning for you how, Eddy?"

"He's trying to drown me in paper." He gestured toward the briefcase, bloated with documents and memoranda.

She gave him a look. Six months ago he'd liked that look.

"Eddy, you're chief. The head of any department has to cope with a little paperwork."

"I'm a fire fighter, not a goddamned bookkeeper."

"I know, honey, but sometimes you have to face the realities of a situation."

"You want to know the realities of the situation? I'll tell you the realities." He took a swallow of Scotch, set his glass down, then took it up to drink again. "Peters wants my job."

"Oh, Christ," Trish said. She stared at this man who had been her lover for six months, this man whom she had loved for three of those months, stared at him as though she were seeing something about him for the first time. "Every kid who ever saw a fire truck wants your job."

In the silence that slammed down, the words seemed stuck in the air above them, nailed to the ceiling, ugly as neon, too high to reach and take down.

"I'm sorry," Trish said softly.

"Forget it." Eddy Caldwell held his glass out in front of him, studying the depth of the amber liquid inside.

Trish knew this man. She knew his silences and she knew the accusation that festered in them, and this time she could not bear it. "We've got to be able to talk," she pleaded. "People have to talk, Eddy. People can't censor every word before they open their mouths. Sometimes you're talking and things about kids just come up."

"I said forget it." His voice was a slurred growl and he was staring at his plate.

She could tell his mind was somewhere else, his vision fixed on something far from the oak-paneled walls of this dining room. She knew the pain in him and she knew it was a normal reaction. She also knew it was killing him. She got up from her chair and went to him and kissed him gently on the forehead.

"I'll forget it, Eddy, if you will. Let's forget it together, really forget it."

His eyes flicked up at her dully and she could tell he was gone. He was back there at the accident, back there in the burning hell she'd never been able to pull him out of. Dimly, he seemed to be aware she'd touched him. His hand groped for hers automatically, not really caring.

He squeezed but it was a dead squeeze. "It's okay," he said. He had the smile of a hurt boy trying not to cry. "It's really okay, Trish. We've just got to relax, is all." He drank from his glass again. "See? It doesn't matter. I'm relaxing."

"That's no way to relax, Eddy."

He forced a smile and it came out lopsided. It made her sad to remember that once upon a time she'd found that smile handsome.

"Any doctor will tell you, alcohol relaxes you. It gets your mind off things. Come on, I'll fix you a drink." He was slurring now, faintly but unmistakably. "What'll it be—bourbon or Scotch?"

"No," Trish said firmly and gently.

"Oh, come on," Caldwell said, trying to raise himself but quickly settling back into his chair. "Have a drink. We'll both feel better."

"It's not making you feel better, Eddy. Not this time of year."

"Nothing special about this time of year."

"It's the dry season, Eddy. The forests out there are kindling. One lightning bolt, one tossed match could do it. You're chief, Eddy. What if there's a fire, a real fire? What if they need the chief, and you're like this?"

He gazed at her with a wounded, uncomprehending defensiveness. "Like what?"

He honestly doesn't know, she realized with a sudden shock. *He doesn't know he's drunk. He thinks he could handle a twelve-alarm blaze like this.*

"Eat something," Trish said, coaxing. "You need food, honey. Just the meat. Just a little protein."

The mahogany table could have sat six. They sat at one corner, two silent people holding hands, two people drifting apart and lit only by the soft light from the kitchen. Eddy Caldwell turned the glass in his hand so that he could peer straight down to its bottom.

"I used to say that to Mickey," he said.

Trish froze. He had that singsong in his voice, that sadness on his face. She recognized it and she knew he had slipped back into the past. She realized he must have stopped at a bar on the way home.

"No." He shook his head. "It was Joyce that was always trying to get him to finish his meat. Me, I—" He stopped and threw his head back to empty his glass. "Vegetables."

She wanted to look away. The life was spilling out of him and he reminded her of the accident victims that came ripped and bleeding into emergency. She wanted to look away, but her training wouldn't let her. It was her job to help. Even the suicides.

"Vegetables," Caldwell said suddenly.

A jolt of alarm went through her. "What are you talking about, Eddy?"

"His mother made him eat his meat. I used to make him eat the vegetables. Don't know why." He gazed at the table. He moved the glass a little distance across it, leaving a glistening trail. "Sometimes when you're raising a kid it works out that way. The mother's good at one thing, the father's good at something else. She was good with the meat, I was good with the vegetables."

He tried to get to his feet, and it pained Trish to see how he had to make the effort in stages. He pressed his elbows against the table, then his wrists, then pushed himself up with his fists. But still he was not quite standing.

"Stuffy in here." He was looking in Trish's direction but it was an odd look and it chilled her. She didn't think he quite recognized her or anything else in the room. She'd seen it happen with alcoholics in the ward: the memory cut off, as though a guillotine had dropped.

Dear God, she thought: *He's not one of them, not yet. He's barely past his thirtieth birthday.*

"You could choke to death in here," Caldwell said, and he reached for his empty glass.

"You're right," Trish said. She took the glass, letting him think she was going to refill it for him. She rose from the table. She stood there watching him, waiting to see what he would do.

"Air," Caldwell said. He staggered a little, managed to check himself, and then bent an arm up to open his collar. "I can't breathe," he said. "Can you open a window, Joyce—please open a window."

I'm not Joyce, she wanted to scream. *I don't sound like her, I don't even look like her. But you don't see me—all you see is your ghosts.*

Something—maybe the nurse's training, maybe a woman's instinctive gentleness in the face of pain— made her bite back the rage. Instead she made her hand soft and put it to his face. He kept to his place, standing almost his full height now, and she was aware of the physical bulk of the man. It was a good bulk. Six months ago it had been sleek and strong as an athlete's. Gradually it had turned shambling and stooped like a bear's. His still-handsome face was closing down now, sagging toward sleep.

"Drink," he said.

Trish did not move. He started past her, his motion uncertain. She shifted to block his way.

"Eddy—you've had enough."

She turned her hand back and forth, feeling the day's beard growth on his jaw, the thick brown hair in need of a trim at the back of the neck. She could hear him begin it now, the first tortured exhalation. She pulled his head against her shoulder.

"Cry if you want to. I'm here, Eddy."

He let her hold him for a while. He reached down and tried to pry the glass from her hand. *So it's just another act,* she thought. She didn't let him get the glass. She ducked away from him and began clearing the table and went past him into the kitchen.

She busied herself at the sink, stacking dishes. He had touched none of his food. She tucked a sheet of

14

Saran Wrap around his plate and slid it into the refrigerator. She knew his patterns and she knew he'd be hungry at three in the morning.

Eddy Caldwell stayed behind in the dining room, leaning his weight on the table, holding himself on the heels of his hands, his heart...roaring. He tried to draw breath. He pressed his molars together and sucked air through his nostrils.

A thunder began in his gut and rolled up and out in long crashing waves through his chest. After a terrifying instant where he almost lost control the spasm passed. The light came back and the room came back and he saw the woman standing at the kitchen sink, the smooth fall of her naked back ending at the black band of the bikini bottom, the elastic lightly pinching the curve of her hips.

The feeling began to move through him again and he gripped the edge of the table as he felt the hammering begin to rise.

He watched her.

For a long time he watched her rinse glasses and slip them into the washing machine, and then he watched her rinse dishes and knives and forks. Her movements were swift and competent and each movement had its precise purpose. It seemed to him there was something vaguely miraculous in her ability to bring purpose to every movement, glasses in the upper rack, plates in the lower.

It seemed to him he needed miracles.

He needed another drink too.

He went into the kitchen, stood behind her, fumbled with the straps of her halter. She froze. Her gaze fastened on the window that gave onto the backyard, onto the hills to the west, the mountains beyond that had slipped into night.

He had the halter untied now. He let it hang there, riding on the thrust of her astonishing breasts. He fitted his hand against her, the smooth delicate skin oddly cool in his palm. With his other hand he circled her waist, and pressed gently on her belly.

She'd told him she'd never been pregnant.

The halter fell to the floor and lay at her feet.

15

"I need you," he whispered. "My God, I need you."

She did not break his grip but she leaned away from him, putting a sliver of space between them. Her lips parted, and her breathing was tentative, testing, as though cyanide were spreading through the room.

For a long moment he waited for her to answer.

She stood there, her back to him, her gaze fixed. Finally he felt a sigh lift her breasts. She took up the stacked dishes again.

He touched her hair, lifting little sections of it and stroking them back, trying to coax some answer, some reassurance from her.

"Eddy," she said in a very low, very controlled voice, "this is no good. We're going to have to have a talk."

He backed off. "Sure. We'll have a talk."

He drew back to the counter. The bottle that had been full two hours ago was half empty.

He poured himself another glass.

She turned. She watched him drink. Her gaze was hurt and her breasts were velvety in the quiet light.

"Eddy—it's time to call it a day."

"Sure—sure." He belted back the Scotch and poured a refill. Her voice stopped him before he had the glass halfway to his lips.

"Eddy—put that down."

He blinked, not believing he'd heard her right. She was a playmate, not a wife. Playmates didn't have a right to criticize.

"You're killing yourself," she said. Fact. No emotion.

"Come on"—he said, trying to make his voice light—"I had a hard day."

"And Peters is gunning for your job and you're still killing yourself."

He lifted the glass again and again her voice stopped him.

"Eddy, pull yourself out of this." Her voice was cold now and each word was like the thrust of a scalpel into a wound. "Your wife's dead and your son's dead and if you think a fifth of Scotch a day can change that you're a goddamned fool."

He felt sobs coming and he didn't try to hold them back.

"I killed them," he blurted.

"The shit you killed them. But if you don't get off that bottle you're sure as hell going to kill yourself. And, Eddy—I've got news for you. You're a great guy and I used to think I loved you, but I've been watching this funeral for six months. I'm not staying around for the burial."

Sobs broke out of him now, but they weren't sobs, they were heaves, an eruption that gushed up from his stomach and out of his mouth. He slumped against the counter and when the heaves didn't stop he was down on his knees on the linoleum, tears blinding his eyes, hands clawing for some kind of purchase on the cabinet door.

"Get it out," he heard her whisper, her lips soft against his ear. "Get it all out."

He gasped once, twice, seeking breath, then heaved again. *This isn't me,* he thought. *Eddy Caldwell is not puking on his kitchen floor.*

Gradually the convulsions subsided. She helped him to his feet, sponged his mouth with a damp cloth.

"It's better to get it out," she said. "You won't have such a bad headache tomorrow. Come on. Let's go upstairs."

She guided him up the stairs to the bedroom and helped him out of his clothes. He clutched for her hand.

"You didn't mean that, Trish, did you? You're not going to leave me. Not yet. Please?"

He saw something in her eyes far worse than anger or hatred.

He saw pity.

He saw a twenty-two-year-old nurse pitying Eddy Caldwell. Writing him off like one of her terminal patients. He couldn't believe it.

"Get some sleep, Eddy. We'll talk tomorrow."

"He's been missing since Tuesday," the woman said.

"Monday," the little girl said vehemently.

"Okay," Sid Bender said, his peacemaking manner a little worn by now. "Monday or Tuesday isn't a big deal. Where did you lose him?"

"The backyard," the woman said. She was thin and

17

dark-haired and her blue eyes seemed to take in everything.

"Front yard," the girl contradicted. She didn't look at all like her mother. She had Raggedy Ann eyes and blond bangs and a pudgy seven-year-old cuteness.

Cute, Sid Bender thought, *is someone else's little girl.* He'd had two of his own and he knew. He raised his hands, less patiently this time.

"You're telling me he disappeared from home, right? Now where's home?"

The man, speaking for the first time, gave an address on Mulholland. He wore a neat green uniform with Forest Service insignia and in his hand he held a broad-brimmed ranger's hat.

Sid Bender nodded. Nice address. Not ritzy, but nice. "Did he have an ID? See, our funds come out of the county budget and food costs—even dog food. If they have an ID we make damned sure to get them home before mealtime. So if your West Highland terrier had an ID, I can tell you right now—he's not here."

The man and woman and child exchanged glances.

"He could have lost it," the woman said.

"You trained this Westie to take off his own collar?"

"It could have come off by itself. That happens sometimes."

Never wanted to give up, these people. In his thirty-two years with the Los Angeles pound Sid Bender had dealt with ten thousand owners of missing pets and every damned one of them was the same: my dog is special, my dog is different, stop the world right now and find my dog, what the hell else do we pay you taxes for?

"Lady, I've been listening for five minutes and I'm hearing you clearly. Your little girl's dog ran away *and* he had an ID. I understand you're upset, but try to hear *me* clearly: your Westie is not in this pound. Not here. Period."

"But if the collar came off—"

"Collars don't come off. People take them off."

"Couldn't we just *look?*"

"What's the point? I'm telling you, he's not here. Anyway we closed up two minutes ago." Sid Bender gestured with his thumb toward the wall clock. "Come back tomorrow if you want to waste your time—but you're not going to waste mine tonight."

The woman's mouth opened for one more plea, but the husband cut her short. "Come on, honey. Mr. Bender's right. Nipper had a name and address tag and that collar was solid. He's not here."

The little girl was crying again. Sid Bender could tell from the way the father glanced at her that five days of tears was too much. The man was getting fed up with Nipper and the kid and the whole damned crisis.

"Thank you for your time, Mr. Bender," the man said. "Come on, Angie. It's not the end of the world."

Wrong psychology, Sid Bender thought. *You don't tell a kid it's not the end of the world when they lose a pet. It's the end of the universe.* He watched the man put an arm around the woman and an arm around the weeping child and steer them toward the door. He could see they were arguing now, the woman's hands and face suddenly animated, and then she had broken away from the group and was marching straight back to Sid Bender's desk.

He braced himself.

"Mr. Bender, we're going on vacation tomorrow. It's my husband's first vacation in over fourteen months. My daughter's very upset, and that's a terrible way to start a vacation."

"Believe me, I'm sympathetic. There's nothing I can do."

"Couldn't you just let us look in the cages? Even if Nipper's not there, maybe there'll be a dog like him that we could take. It would make all the difference in the world to our little girl."

Ordinarily Sid Bender would have told any woman who made a request like that to go get stuffed. But this one was pretty and she had a gentle voice and her eyes met Sid Bender's openly and frankly.

And her husband worked for the government.

That was tough.

Sid Bender worked for the government and he knew how it was in this era of Proposition 13 and cutbacks

19

and triplicate forms. Against his better judgment, he relented.

"Okay. But make it fast."

Carolyn Miller hurried back to her family. "He'll let us look."

Steve Miller glanced again at his watch and grimaced.

"Steve, it'll only take a second. We'll drive you direct to work and I'll pack your bag, okay?"

He shrugged, giving in but not liking it, never liking it when Carolyn packed his bag for a trip because she always left out some essential and vacation time then had to be wasted tracking down razor blades or Kodachrome film.

Mr. Bender opened a door and let them into what looked like a zoo and smelled like a hospital and sounded like a vivisectionist's ward. It was an entire city block of cages and every cage seemed to have three or four unhappy mutts scrambling and barking inside it.

"It would be faster if we split up," Steve Miller suggested.

Carolyn took Angie by the hand and went to search the cages to the right of the main corridor. She had never seen so many unhappy-looking animals in her life. While one dog alone could look cuddly and lovable, there was nothing cuddly and lovable about five hundred jailed, baying strays. She shuddered and walked faster, her heels echoing like the sharp ticktock of a clock off the naked gray walls.

"Do you see him anywhere?" she asked her little girl.

Angie shook her head glumly.

It seemed to Carolyn that there must be some order or system to the way the dogs were locked up. She wished there was someone to help them.

And then she saw the dark silhouette of a man. He was pushing a cart from cage to cage, stopping to unlock bars and change bowls.

Feeding time, she thought. *That's why they're all barking.*

"Excuse me!" she called brightly.

The man whipped around and faced her.

She gulped.

He wore dark glasses, not the outdoorsy kind that keep sun out of your eyes, but the blind man's kind that keep other people from seeing you. And he wore a gauze mask, the sort you saw photos of Japanese wearing to work in Tokyo smog. He looked like a giant insect. She could feel Angie gripping her hand tighter.

"We're looking for a West Highland terrier," she said. "He ran away five days ago."

The man shook his head and she had a sudden conviction that the thing on his head wasn't hair, it moved all wrong: it was a shaggy brown wig. It struck her that everything about this man was dark glass and gauze and synthetic fiber, that she was looking at a human being and not seeing a single square inch that was really him.

"No West Highland terriers," he said. "Haven't had any of those all summer." His voice was bleached of any sort of expression. It could have been a tape machine speaking from under his denim work shirt.

"His name is Nipper," Carolyn said lamely, not knowing why. She felt she had to say something, not just...*stare* at the man with her mouth hanging open in a dumb-stricken *oh*.

"We get mongrels mostly," the man said, "know what I mean?"

"Well, if you see a Westie that answers to the name Nipper, he's my little girl's."

Something behind the glasses seemed to shift and she sensed the man staring at Angie. *I don't want him looking at her*, she thought. *There's something creepy, something child-molesty about him.*

"Come on, Angie, Daddy's waiting." She pulled the child firmly behind her and ignored the tears that, predictably, began gushing.

Steve was waiting at the door. He took one look at Angie and the tears and he knew.

"We'll find Nipper," he promised, tousling her hair. "He'll show up."

Three minutes later the Millers were seat-belted into the Pinto and because anything was better than Angie's tears they let the child play her transistor radio.

Aunt Nora had given it to her for her birthday and Steve Miller had never heard so many decibels come out of such a small chromium package. Angie kept the radio set to a disco-rock station, and throughout the ride along the freeway and up into the Santa Monica Mountains they were serenaded by the Top 20 latest hits. Every three or four numbers the disc jockey kept plugging the same record and finally Steve Miller asked, "What the hell is *that* song?"

"Melinda Mars' new single," Angie said.

Steve exchanged glances with Carolyn. He wouldn't have thought it possible, but they'd finally come up with musical porno. It sounded like the woman was being *screwed*. And his seven-year-old daughter liked it.

The Pinto pulled to a stop in the clearing. Steve Miller kissed his wife and daughter good-night. "Get a good sleep, you two. See you tomorrow, five thirty sharp, okay?"

"Five thirty sharp." Carolyn nodded. She watched her husband stride toward the lookout tower. Halfway across the clearing he stopped and turned.

"Blades," he called. "Don't forget razor blades."

"I'll pack them," she called, and waved. Instead of slipping the car back into gear she sat a moment.

The sun had set and an evening cool had begun to fill the forest. She closed her eyes and breathed deeply, filling herself with the smell of pine and clean air.

If only life could be like this, she thought, *clean and peaceful and safe.*

When she opened her eyes again a star was blinking just beyond the lookout tower. She nudged her daughter.

"See that star, Angie? Make a wish."

Carolyn Miller made a wish too, an impossible wish. She wished for a perfect vacation.

2

"CAN'T get away from her," Steve Miller said.

"Huh?" Ron Fowler, his co-lookout, glanced up from the logbook. Ron had a long Swedish face that exaggerated every expression, especially perplexity.

Steve nodded toward Ron's radio, going full blast. "Melinda Mars. Here we are on a sixty-foot tower on top of a mountain in the middle of a forest and there's no getting away from her."

Ron frowned. "Why, you don't like her?"

"Do I have a choice?"

"I'll turn it off if it bothers you."

"Forget it, I was only joking." Steve lifted his binoculars again. The night sky and the distant ridge leaped closer. Despite himself he hummed along with Melinda Mars.

Damn, he thought. *They drum these songs into your blood.*

Slowly, he scanned downward across the forest. Nothing to report in that quadrant.

And then his ear caught something wrong. It was a faint, high wailing, and he'd heard the record often enough to know it wasn't Melinda Mars' backup group. It came from out there in the dark. Steve reached over and snapped the radio off.

Ron's head jerked around. "Why'd you do that?"

"Shhh—do you hear something?"

Ron cocked his head and listened.

A wind gusted. The steel tower flexed with a twanging sound. The glass walls of the lookout swayed slightly. The wailing sound came again, fainter this time.

"Just somebody's dog," Ron said.

"You think it's a dog?"

"Couldn't be anything else."

Steve wasn't certain. He decided to check it out. He pushed up from his stool. The damned thing had glass balls on its feet; supposedly you could stand on it in a lightning storm and not get electrocuted. It was a great idea, but the glass balls squeaked.

Ron Fowler put his hands over his ears and grimaced.

"Sorry," Steve said, "but they'll save your life someday."

Ron gave him a good-natured finger; at least Steve hoped it was good-natured. He slid the screen door aside and stepped out onto the narrow platform.

He walked to each side of the lookout in turn, stopping to peer down over the railing into the dark forest. Light specks played fitfully in the shadowy shapes of cedars and firs. A breeze blew a sweet smell of pine up to him. A branch creaked restlessly. He breathed deeply, inhaling the sensation of unending space and boundless peace.

He loved these woods. He'd told Carolyn how much he loved them. He loved every canyon and peak, every stream and ridge. Above all he loved the trees. In their beauty and defenselessness they called to some protective instinct in him. Sometimes, gazing out on the forest like this, he knew he would gladly give his life for the trees.

He hadn't told Carolyn that.

She wouldn't understand and besides it would frighten her.

He heard the sound again. "Sure sounds like a dog," he muttered. But there was something strange about it. He raised his binoculars, adjusted them in the direction of the sound.

His eye followed shiftings in the mysterious tracery of leaves. He couldn't find the animal.

The sound came again. It was a dog all right, but where?

He sharpened the focus. His eye picked out a swarm of fireflies. He followed their flight a moment, then shrugged and went back into the lookout tower.

In the warm half-darkness of the pup tent, the girl pulled away from the boy. "Go brush your teeth first," she said.

"Screw that." The boy's lips were at her neck. With one hand he pushed her hair up and out of the way. His lips began working on her ear.

"Come on, Ronnie, you stink!" The girl jerked away from him. She pulled up her knees and sat naked on the rumpled sleeping bag.

The boy stared at her. He could see a pout pulling at her face. He bent to whisper against her neck. "You know what your problem is, Allison? You're frigid."

"I mean it, Ronnie. You're not coming near me with that mouth of yours."

"Jesus, what a hard, frigid bitch you are." He pulled her back down onto the sleeping bag. "Come on. Relax." He reached his hand between her legs, squeezing at her, massaging her, trying what little he knew.

She strained to force herself up again. "Christ— what a fucking baby. Gimme, gimme—Christ! Why don't you grow up?"

"You want to feel something grown-up, feel this." The boy pushed his hips against hers. He tried to clamp his lips on hers.

She shoved him away hard. "Brush your fucking teeth first. Besides, I've got to pee."

"Shit." He rolled away from her. "You know what's wrong with you, Allison—there's not *that* much romance in your soul." He held up thumb and forefinger, indicating a length of half an inch.

She fumbled to her feet. The tent shook as she collided with the pole. She lifted the canvas flap and as she stepped out into the open she turned and stared back at him. She mimicked the gesture of his hand.

"There's not that much to your dick, either."

The boy gave her the finger. He scratched himself

and yawned. His eye wandered about the dim interior of the tent, vaguely inspecting for the stash of pot and the water pipe.

The girl fumbled over a rise and started down the grade on the other side. The incline was so sharp she had to lean back in the opposite direction to keep herself from falling headlong. She found a clearing in the brush, screened by a stand of baby pine. Satisfied that the spot was private, she crouched down to pee.

A branch snapped somewhere nearby with a quick ripping sound. Her eyes darted up.

"Ronnie—that you?"

There was no answer.

She reached for the toilet paper, realized she'd forgotten it, grabbed a fistful of leaves instead. She made a face. Leaves hurt worse than those old newspapers they hung in the johns in French towns. She'd spent her college junior year in Bordeaux, losing her virginity and learning how to roll joints.

"Ronnie, I'm not kidding—don't try to scare me."

Again there was no answer, at least no human answer. But a dog barked somewhere behind her. The sound was so unexpected it actually scared her.

Allison jumped to her feet and ran. She must have taken a wrong turn, because the tent just wasn't there.

The dog barked again, only this time it was more of a howl than a bark. The thought flashed in her that someone was torturing that animal.

She veered in the opposite direction, up an incline. Brambles tore at her and she veered again. Her foot hit something damp and she skidded and fell full length in a damp patch.

She heard Ronnie laughing and when she looked up he was standing there naked at the top of the rise.

"Fuck it, Ronnie, help me up."

Instead he held out the water pipe. There was a cozy pink glow of pot in the bowl.

She brushed it aside and staggered to her feet. Moist leaves were clinging to her. She slapped them off as though they were maggots. She glared at the laughing face that was trying to grow a beard.

"Didn't you hear that sound?"

The pipe made a bubbling sound as Ronnie took a deep drag. He shook his head. "What sound?"

"There's a dog out there—it sounds like someone's torturing it."

"Maybe it's caught in a trap."

"There aren't any traps in a state park."

He offered the pipe again and this time to steady her nerves she took a long inhalation. The sweet, tangy herb filled her lungs and buoyed her up. Slowly she released the smoke. She took Ronnie's hand, suddenly wanting to make sure she was close to him.

"Ronnie, I'm scared."

"Just your imagination."

The sound came again, a long arc of muffled howl that was suddenly cut short.

The boy stopped, one hand on the tent flap. His face screwed up.

"Want to have a look?"

"I'm scared, Ronnie."

"Okay, I'll have a look."

"I think we should get out of here," she pleaded.

"Allison, you're chicken shit. It's only a dog." He hunched down and reached into the tent for his jeans. He slipped them on in a single quick movement then twisted his feet into his sandals. He groped under the sleeping bag and found the flashlight.

"Ronnie, don't."

The boy waved his hand dismissively and didn't even look back at her.

Her eyes followed the wavering puddle of light moving through the trees. She sighed and bent down and picked up the water pipe. It had gone out. She struck a match and lit it again.

Ronnie stumbled three steps into the forest. He stopped, hearing something. He squinted an ear. As closely as he could make out it was a low mechanical purring just at the threshold of audibility.

Instinct told him it was some distant automobile, its sound carried by a fluke of the night wind. But something else—some stoned certainty—told him whatever it was, it was not distant at all: it was here in the forest with him, an automobile creeping on tiptoes.

He flicked off the flashlight. His eyes scanned the darkness for some flicker of headlights.

Nothing.

After a moment the sound faded down, impossible to distinguish now from the rustling leaves. He chalked it up to imagination and Colombian red. He flicked the flashlight back on and moved forward through the forest. After ten steps he stopped again. Another sound caught his ear: heavy, labored breathing.

Good grass had a way of switching perceptions around, and it occurred to him the breathing might be his own, projected by some cannabis quirk out there into the trees. He stood absolutely still and held his breath. Dimly he could make out the muffled drum of his heart. More clearly, unconnected to the drum, he heard the breathing—a pathetic, windy gasping as though someone or something were struggling for air.

It was there.

It was real.

He played the beam of his light in the direction of the sound. Branches and leaves leaped into dazzling, intricate patterns. Behind them something threw off a sparkle, like a highway road sign catching a sweep of headlights.

He moved toward it. He pushed aside a low-hanging branch and there it was: a beautiful Afghan dog, fast asleep.

Ronnie crouched down and tousled the fur of the animal's head. "Hey, pooch, what are you doing here?"

The animal did not stir.

Ronnie felt along the neck for a name tag, some kind of identification. He felt something else and he saw what it was that had sparkled in the dark. A canister had been attached to the animal's collar. It was steel, unlabeled, the size of a commercial aerosol bomb.

Ronnie shook the animal. "Hey, pooch, whose pooch are you?"

There was no response, no break in the deep, labored breathing.

He held his flashlight close to the canister and squinted, trying to make out if there were any markings. His nose caught a sharp acrid whiff of something

28

like the smell of electric wiring about to short. He realized the canister had a stringlike tail and the tail was destroying itself, changing into glowing ash. It took him a moment to realize that his flashlight had something to do with the ash, in some way had triggered the transformation from wire to pulsating cinder.

Before he could recoil there was a hiss and one blinding instant of white smoke and then as a wall of thunder rolled over him he pitched violently backward. Suddenly there was fire, nothing but leaping yellow flames, and as the pain hit him he screamed.

Something changed in the silence out there, like the intake of a breath before a sneeze. Alerted by his ranger's sixth sense, Steve Miller whipped his head around just as the sound came.

It was like a single beat on a deep bass drum. Answering echoes rolled softly through the hills. Steve counted three heartbeats and the part of him that prayed almost burst: *Dear God, don't let it be...*

Suddenly a narrow geyser of white light ripped up through the forest. It towered one instant over the treetops, then umbrellaed out and collapsed. There was darkness, and for a breath-held moment Steve did not know whether he had actually seen the thing or not.

Then the flicker began, the flicker of a hundred little flames dropping down through the trees, spreading out like a circle of dancers reaching to hold hands.

The pines with their store of flammable resin caught at once. Fire whooshed out from the epicenter of the blast and suddenly an acre of forest was ablaze.

"Holy God!" Ron Fowler gasped, lunging for the phone and punching three digits. His voice was shaking. "This is Sierra Alta lookout—we got a burn, she's mean."

Steve worked rapidly now, not wasting a movement.

He swung the telescope of the firefinder, sighted the pillar of flame, centered the cross hair on it. The sighting apparatus was mounted on a calibrated table with the zero direction oriented due south. He called off the clockwise angular distance of the burn, "Two seven point five!"

An instant later Ron was shouting it into the phone.

By now the fire was edging eastward from its origin. Steve took a quick vertical sighting.

"Estimated distance one and one-quarter mile."

"One one-quarter!" Ron relayed.

Steve Miller stared disbelievingly. Where fifteen seconds ago there had been a smooth ripple of skyline there was now a bleeding chunk of conflagration. He fought to keep tears from blinding him.

"Let me catch the bastard that did that!" he screamed. "Let me catch that bastard!"

The explosion ripped through Allison's pot haze. *That was not in my head, that was out there.*

She crawled to the flap of the tent and peered out. Through the trees she saw a strange brightness. It came to her dully that it was not sunrise, it was not a movie company on location...it was *fire.*

She jumped into her jeans. She didn't even button her shirt. She ran, calling Ronnie's name.

Now she could see the fire roaring upward in a gust of wind. A blast of air caught her in the face, whirling a cloud of tiny black specks into her eyes and nostrils. At first she thought they were cinders and then she realized they were insects. She gagged and spat and stumbled another ten steps forward.

The fire was as tall and tilting as a two-story building about to topple down on her.

She crept as near as she dared till she felt the heat singeing her eyebrows, and then she stood screaming his name, "Ronnie! Ronnie!"

He didn't hear her. The fire was in his ears. It had taken hold of his clothes and fastened on the hairs of his arms and face. It bit into his flesh, scorching the skin from the raw sinew beneath.

He opened his mouth to cry out. He couldn't scream. He couldn't breathe.

He made the mistake of trying.

It was as though a quart of scalding water had been poured down his throat into his lungs. He fought the pain and the disbelief and the pot and everything that urged him to give up consciousness. He made one last effort.

He lunged dizzily. He crashed through the flames into the clear. He dove to the ground. He twisted and writhed in the dirt, trying to smother the fire that was devouring him.

Sparks scattered into the dry brush. Some of these died and some found fuel to burn like tiny candles.

Allison rushed to the writhing thing that she could barely recognize as Ronnie. She ripped off her shirt and tried to blanket out the flames in his hair and clothing. A sickening, burned rubbery smell rose from him. She fought an instinct to retch.

She patted furiously with the shirt and then she saw an edge of raw bone jutting above his blackened cheek. She stared at the shirt in her hand. There were fragments of flesh and hair sticking to it.

"Oh, no, oh, my God," she gasped.

As the vomit pushed up from her stomach she remembered to turn her head.

"You should have held out for a fee," Toby Gladstone said, his voice still at a speaking level but his usually handsome face twisted into a raw shout.

Melinda Mars stared at this man, this lover, this manager-manipulator six years her junior who had made her the top bankable female in films, the top grosser in records, the top Nielsen draw on the occasions when she condescended to do a TV special. She wondered if she needed him. She wondered if she needed these nightly screaming battles. She wondered if it was him or the dope he took that was doing it to him.

She sighed impatiently. "Toby, we've been through it."

"It's taken me three years to build your fee to a quarter million, so what do you do, you volunteer to sing for free. In the Hollywood Bowl, of all the goddamned places."

"Let's not get into this in front of Loren," she said.

After all it was dinnertime, family hour, Mommy

and Mommy's lover and Mommy's kid were supposed to be a Norman Rockwell painting. And here was the lover banging his fists and Mommy glancing toward the kitchen wondering about the caterer's men with their big ears and big tongues; and the five-year-old child just sat on his chair and let the argument blow over him like the spillover from a bad dream. His mouth was half open, his eyes glazed and somewhere else, cool blue wounds in the blond perfection of his face.

Melinda was proud of the child, prouder than of any of her songs or gold records. She viewed him as her biggest hit, music *and* lyrics *and* orchestrations by Melinda Mars. She didn't think these arguments were doing him any good. Dr. Lucius Berman, the kid's $130 shrink, had said life experience was life experience, but Melinda wondered.

"You should have let me do the negotiating," Toby said. "You've never known how to negotiate. You should stick to singing."

"It's for charity. You don't negotiate for charity!"

"It's for a bunch of goddamned cops and firemen."

"They happen to need bulletproof vests and they happen to need fire trucks and for your information the concert might just save a couple of hundred lives—maybe even yours."

Ten years ago she'd been a teenager waving kill-the-pigs placards at SDS rallies, and now she was crusading for cops' widows and didn't even see the contradiction. Toby shook his head, disgusted.

"They conned you. With that very line. That's how they did it."

"Nobody conned anyone! I was proud to be asked. It's an honor. They could have asked a dozen people but they asked *me*."

"Because you're a crusading sap who thinks she's Jane Fonda and they knew you'd say yes."

"It happens to be my fucking duty and I don't want to go into this shit in front of my son—if you don't mind!" Melinda bunched up her Irish linen napkin and threw it down into the dish of catered gazpacho.

"I do mind," Toby said. "You make me look like an

idiot that can't even negotiate for his one goddamned client!"

"Well maybe you should get a different goddamned client!"

"Maybe I goddamned will!"

She looked again at the child, there but not there, turned off inside some secret chamber in his own head. She felt more embarrassed about the child than about the two men from Chasen's hovering in the kitchen, soaking up every word to telegraph to the columnists. Her fights with Toby had driven away eight servants in three months and now they had to get caterers to do their hamburgers. Melinda realized that at least a percentage of it had to be her fault. She made her voice gloved and apologetic. She smiled her forgive-me-I-forgive-you smile.

"Come on, Toby. Let's not argue. We'll only say a lot of things we don't mean."

"You cut off my balls and when I scream you say it's arguing."

"For Chrissake, Toby, the concert will *help*—it's exposure!"

"Sure it's exposure—with your stomach out to *here*. You'll look like a cow."

She shifted irritably, and Toby recognized the instinctive pulling back, not just from him but from the argument, the situation.

"There is nothing wrong with looking pregnant," she said. "Some people happen to think it's beautiful."

Fixing his gaze and his accusation on her, he could see her reflection suddenly appear in the elaborate Louis Quinze, twenty-four-carat gold-leaf mirror. There was an odd perfection about her profile in that mirror: even the bulge of pregnancy seemed in its way perfect, an eighteenth-century note in a sleek twentieth-century room of deep white carpeting, chromium and glass tables, black leather club chairs and oversized couch, a room where Brancusis and Arps and Braques, all signed, all appraised, all totaling over three million dollars, dotted the walls, casually mixed in with pen-and-inks by the kids in Matawan State Hospital.

He watched her in the mirror, saw that with dance

class and diet she'd kept the smooth, supple body of a teenager, athletic and lightly tanned, no bathing suit marks to mar the tan: and then that bulge. Yet he didn't hate the woman in the mirror, didn't hate the bulge, didn't hate anything about her.

It was only the woman in the room who drove him up the wall.

"I'll tell you how *you* look pregnant," he said. "You look fucking ugly. And you know why you look fucking ugly? Because that kid you're carrying is illegitimate and there is nothing beautiful about an illegitimate kid, not one goddamned thing!"

She glanced at her son, cool as an angel in a painting. *What does a child make of this?* she wondered. *Even a five-year-old must get that there's something very, very wrong here.* It dawned on her that she and Toby were the five-year-olds and Loren the only grown-up in the house.

"We're not living in the Middle Ages," she said, forcing the cool. "People don't think that way anymore."

"Maybe people don't but the public does—and in case you forgot, it's the public that's paying for your white Rolls-Royces and your heated pools and hot tubs and your signed Picasso dinner plates—*and* your kid's catered birthday parties. Why the hell does he need a catered birthday party?"

Every now and then Melinda got this flash that Toby was jealous of her kid. She drew herself up to her most simple and dignified. "Because I'm his mother and I care."

"You don't care! You don't care about one fucking thing! You make me look like an idiot, you call that caring? You make yourself look like a tramp in front of the whole Hollywood Bowl, the damned thing will be televised, you call *that* caring?"

"I call it caring very much."

"I call it telling the whole world that Melinda Mars is going to have a bastard. Which is the equivalent of telling them to fuck off. Which is the equivalent of flushing your career down the john."

"Toby, what are you on?"

He was pounding his fists on the table, and signed Picasso butter plates were jumping.

"I am on the *truth*."

"Uh-uh. I hear Quaaludes talking. How many'd you take, or don't you remember?"

And now he was crying, tears running down his face. She wondered if the caterer's men were peeking around corners, snapping candids with hidden miniature cameras.

"Why couldn't you let me handle it? Why do you have to screw yourself singing for free and having that bastard?"

Rage shot through her: not just at the word *bastard* when it was his kid, too, but at the whole timing of the implication and at the implication itself. "What do you expect me to do—have a miscarriage before the concert? Well, since the concert happens to be the day after tomorrow I'm afraid that little idea is *out*."

He dropped his head on the table. His hands flexed as though reaching toward her across an abyss and when he spoke his voice was clogged and rough. "Why can't you marry me?"

Now she felt mean and tiny. He was only being a shit because he loved her.

And then she felt manipulated and wondered if it was worth being loved by a shit when after all love was love and shit was...well, shit; and there was too much of it flying around the Mars-Gladstone ménage these days, why there'd been three very bitchy blind items in the *L.A. Times* gossip column last week alone.

"I've *been* married," she said.

"And you married a prick. You trust me enough to have my kid, why can't you trust me enough to marry me?"

She reached to place her hand around his. She squeezed. She made her voice gentle, the Melinda Mars chest tone that had won seven gold records in three years.

"I do trust you, Toby. I trust you more than anyone else in this world. I just don't trust marriage."

"You're killing me, Melinda. And you're killing yourself."

"Drugs are killing you, Toby. Not me." She stretched her arms overhead, twisted her legs, contracting and releasing the muscles to relax all the tense nerves in her limbs. She rose. Enough yammering. Time to get going.

"I wouldn't need drugs if we were married."

"Jesus, you'd need eight times as many. Toby, I don't want to get into it. And I haven't got time. I'm going to be late for natural childbirth class."

He was up and following her into the living room.

"Another class?"

"It's not another class, it's my weekly class. And do me a favor, don't turn on in front of the kid."

Melinda snatched up her purse from the Mies table in the hallway. Passing the kitchen, she tossed a thank-you nod to the caterer's men and swept on to the garage. She rummaged in her purse and realized she'd brought the wrong keys—the keys to the Rolls.

She wasn't in the mood for the Rolls. You couldn't drive a Rolls to a class of housewives in Pintos and Vegas. Better to take the Jaguar, she decided.

She swept back into the house. Toby and Loren were sprawled on the puma skin in front of the fireplace, and Toby was smoking a joint. An electric shock of anger went through her and she snatched up her son.

"Come on, Loren, you're coming to natural childbirth class."

In the mirror she saw Toby stick out his tongue at her. She whirled.

"You're a kid!" she screamed. "You're not even as mature as my five-year-old!"

"Your five-year-old doesn't screw you," Toby shot back through a cloud of Colombian gold.

Melinda realized she was at a crossroads: She could murder him or she could go to her class.

She chose class.

Loren Mars sat in a steel chair tilted against the gymnasium wall. With his faded shorts and tan face and summer-blond hair he reminded Melinda of an angel shaped and colored by the sun. He was gazing earnestly at her, eyes fixed, face tensed with the effort of understanding all these women and the contortions they were putting themselves through.

There were twelve of them on the high-school gymnasium floor. They wore maternity slacks and floppy sweat shirts and they huffed and puffed and bent and stretched as the instructor called out exercise routines.

Breathing was the important part, the instructor kept saying: right breathing to make things easy for mother and baby when baby finally came. All the women were about as far along as Melinda was, but it was only Melinda who could make it through the ten repetitions of each movement that the instructor called for. Melinda breathed *and* breathed *and* breathed. That was because, as an entertainer, she had to keep in shape. *Thank God ballet lessons are good for something,* she thought.

There was a fine mist of perspiration just under her wide brown eyes when the instructor called, "All right, ladies!"

The women all came to a sitting position. There were snorts of relief and, here and there, some groaning.

"No baby's worth this!" one woman declared loudly enough for all to hear, and another answered, "Mine is!"

It was a running joke, this exchange, a bit of teasing that had lasted through the whole course of prenatal instruction and exercise; by now everyone was tired of it, and just as tired of the course.

"Questions?" the instructor called.

"Yes," a woman behind Melinda called back. "I checked with my obstetrician about this, and he says that even though I don't want anesthesia, there has to be an anesthetist in the delivery room anyway and that I'll have to pay his fee even if I don't use him. I don't get it, but is this fair?"

"No," the instructor said mildly, "it's not fair, but neither is having a baby." Laughter spread among the women seated Indian-style on the gym floor.

Melinda raised her hand.

"Yes, Melinda," the instructor said. Everything was scrupulously first name in the course. It was dumb and sisterly and Melinda loved it.

"Well," Melinda started, looking around and smiling now, "a few days ago that Cameron woman, the one who does that TV program *Newsbreak,* she was carrying on about how dangerous it is to go into a hospital nowadays, that they just don't maintain the sterile conditions they used to."

The instructor smiled and delicate little half-circles formed on either side of her lips. "Come on, Melinda, VV Cameron makes her living scaring people—she's an entertainer."

"Like me, hey?" Melinda shrugged and the others laughed good-naturedly. She knew she was being silly, but this was the one place in the world where it didn't matter. Here she could drop the mask of the supercool superstar; here she was Melinda Mars, mother-to-be, free to act as klutzy as she felt. In a way this gym and these classes were her asylum. No one had begged her for an autograph, no one had bugged her coming on nasty or coming on oozy-nice. They were just a roomful of mothers, God bless them, and Melinda Mars was an insecure mother just like the rest.

"But seriously, is there anything to it?" she persisted. "Something she said did make some sense, about there being staff cutbacks because of labor costs and therefore fewer people to keep things shipshape."

"Well, Melinda, good luck to you, but I don't know where else you could have your baby."

"How about in Paris?" someone called.

"Make mine Venice!"

"No baby's worth a ticket to Venice!" a third woman shouted.

"Mine is," someone answered, and at this there was general groaning and laughter until the instructor blew her gym whistle and announced that class was over.

"See you next week, ladies, and till then remember the two thou shalt nots: no drinking, no smoking."

Afterwards, as Melinda and Loren walked through the deserted parking lot, she heard footsteps hurrying alongside them. Instinctively she took her son's hand and looked around.

A man in a conservative three-piece suit was pacing her. "Miss Mars?" he said.

His voice matched the keenness of his darkly saturnine features. Melinda slowed but did not stop.

"Could I have a word with you?" he said.

A warning alarm went off in Melinda's brain. *Plan ahead* was her motto, and she planned ahead now: thirty seconds ahead. Not much time but it gave her a lead.

"I don't give autographs," she said.

"It has nothing to do with an autograph."

"I don't give interviews."

Both the passenger door and the driver door of her custom-built Jaguar had keyholes in the handles; Melinda let herself into the car by the passenger door. As she slid into the seat she wound the passenger window down. Loren climbed in after her. That gave the stranger only one window to talk through, and it put the boy between him and Melinda.

"I have some property of yours, Miss Mars. I was asked to return it to you personally."

Melinda and the man stared at each other in the dark. The man had one hand on the lowered window; the other hand moved up from his pocket. Melinda sucked in a breath and prayed her instincts were right.

They were.

The hand held an envelope and now the envelope jutted into the air space over the front seat.

"Loren," Melinda said, "take that." She purposely changed her voice, snapping the words out to take the man unawares.

The tactic worked. Loren took the envelope and before the man could snatch it back it was in Melinda's hands.

"Miss Mars," the man said, recovering himself, "you have in your hands a subpoena to appear in Municipal Court on the third day of—"

"Just can it, will you?" Melinda cut in. She ripped the envelope in two, opened the driver's window, and dropped the halves out.

The man sucked in his breath as though she'd socked

39

him in the belly. "Refusing acceptance of a court subpoena is a felony."

"Hey, nitwit," Melinda spat back, "the only felony I committed is littering. And you can tell my schmuck of an ex-husband *if* he wants to share custody of our son he can stop sicking court-appointed goons on me, okay?"

"Miss Mars, by destroying that subpoena you are in contempt of court."

"Go back to your lawbooks, kiddo. Your subpoena was wrongly served. A minor accepted the papers, not me. And if you don't believe that's wrong service, look up the 1968 Supreme Court decision in State of Louisiana versus O'Hara." Melinda wrenched the ignition key and gunned the motor. As she tore out of the parking lot, she glanced in the rearview mirror.

The man was stooped over the pavement picking up the confetti of his legal papers.

"Mommy," the boy asked, "who was that?"

She looked down at the child with his big blue wondering eyes and she took her eyes off the road for just a minute to lean over and tousle his hair and kiss him.

"That was no one, honey. Just an idiot that works for your dad."

"Do I have to go back to Dad?"

You'll never go back to that junkie bastard, she thought, and then she remembered Dr. Lucius Berman saying, *Never disparage your ex, not in front of the boy.* Dr. Lucius Berman cost $130 for a forty-minute hour. *So what?*

"You'll never go back to that junkie bastard again."

Eddy Caldwell tried.

But he could not do it. He could not sleep. The nightmare kept cutting in, the movie flashes of trees exploding in flame, the slow motion of the little boy hurled with a pressure of two hundred pounds per square inch against the steel-mesh fence, the stop frame of skull fragments ripping through freckles and blond hair like bullets coming the wrong way.

It was the scream that shot Caldwell bolt awake, a

scream so tight in his throat he thought it must have been his own.

But the flaming image faded and he came back gradually to the dark cool bedroom with the air conditioner purring in the window, the double bed with its brass headboard and the sleeping woman curled beside him. He realized it had not been Eddy Caldwell who had screamed, it had been the thing in Eddy Caldwell's memory that no amount of time or distance would ever erase.

He gripped his knees to his chest, hunched forward to steady the shivering. There was a pressure in his head like the tightening of a winch.

Must be the booze, he told himself. *Memories can't hurt; not physically—can they?*

He gazed down at the woman beside him, so serene and safe in her sleeping world. He wanted to touch her, wake her, say something to throw a lifeline between him and her, something to anchor him in here and now.

But there was nothing to say.

Besides she had a double shift coming up at the hospital; she needed her sleep.

He turned to the night table to see the time—four eighteen.

He wanted to turn back this clock and every other clock in the world. He wanted the world to go back. He wanted it all to go back to a day just over a year ago, the day he had killed his wife and son.

He wanted a second chance.

The thought drove Caldwell off the bed as if the sheets were crawling with vermin. He moved barefoot across the carpet, his right foot a little slower than his left, with the suggestion of a lag before it responded to the directions of his brain.

He snapped on the bathroom light and ran the cold water in the sink. He drank from the tap and then splashed water over his face. He wet his hands again and furrowed his fingers through his close-cropped hair, its coppery highlights glinting in the fluorescent shaving light.

He snapped off the light and went downstairs. The bottle was still there on the kitchen counter. He unscrewed the cap. He held the bottle to his lips. He swallowed and kept swallowing and then he ripped a sheet of paper from the message pad and took a pencil from the antique shaving mug jammed with stubs.

He printed in large block letters: I KILLED THEM AND I KILLED THIS BOTTLE TOO.

He licked the back of the paper, slapped it against the bottle, and slid the bottle toward the sink. He switched off the kitchen light and went to the front hall and got his briefcase from the table.

The house was old and large, a California Tudor with oak paneling in the major rooms, arches everywhere, heavy double doors. The house had been almost beyond Caldwell's means, but Joyce had begged for it. They'd had to budget: only one car, a lot of hamburger and not much steak, public school for Mickey, the same cheap furniture they'd had in Barstow because it was all they could afford: Sears, Furniture City, manufacturers' closeouts. It looked odd, porch furniture in a Tudor living room. Joyce had tried to pretty up the wicker sofa with a chintz cover.

"We'll get real furniture one of these days," Joyce had said. "The important thing is the house. It's an investment. It's a house we can grow old in, Eddy."

They'd bought the house the year before Mickey was born, the year Los Angeles brought Eddy Caldwell in to make him chief of the department, the youngest chief in county history.

"Don't be afraid of the mortgage, Eddy. You've got a future. Things are going to get easier."

And she had been right. Joyce had always been right. He'd had the doubts but she'd had the courage.

There had been two raises the first year, because Eddy Caldwell fought fire as if fire were a thing with a knife at his throat. He fought it with a hatred that was so blind it was almost personal. The blind hatred had made his fortune. It had paid for the house.

And it had cost him too. It had cost him his wife and child.

Caldwell did not stop in the living room. He passed through another arched doorway into his study. For a time he left the room in darkness and just stood there, touching his fingers to each of the pipes racked in a stand on his desk.

He found the meerschaum he wanted. But he did not take it from the rack. He just touched it. He felt the bowl. He caressed the pattern of the carved wood. He remembered the wrapping paper: out-of-season Santa Claus. He remembered the note:

> *From Mom and me. Happy Father's Day! Love, Michael.*
> P.S. *It really is from me. But Mom helped me pick it out so it is from her too. She also helped me write this. Love and kisses, Michael.*
> P.S. *Happy smoking! You are a great dad!*
> P.S. *But please stop calling me Mickey. That was only okay when I was a baby. Happy, happy Father's Day! Your son, Michael.*

Eddy Caldwell could have cried, and he could have let the tears come and no one would have known. But he stood there, not crying, just wondering how it was the happiest memories could hurt the most.

Finally he dropped the briefcase onto the desk, turned on the lamp, and went around to swing himself into the swivel chair. It was an old thing, all scrubbed oak and iron fittings, a gift from Joyce when he'd taken over the Barstow Fire Department.

He skidded the chair closer to the desk and undid the straps of the briefcase. He slid everything out: personnel ratings, safety studies, violation reports, scheduling revisions, efficiency comparisons, turnout summaries, specifications data, systems abstracts, community-relations projects, complaints, commendations, charts, printouts, reviews, investigations, this for consideration, that for action, initial this, sign that, paper, paper, paper...

Peters' face bobbed up in front of his mind's eye, Peters with his jazzy sideburns and meant-to-be-sexy mustache and aviator glasses that were probably the latest rage but looked to Caldwell ten years out of date; Peters with the "yes, sir" always on his lips and the veiled cunning in his eyes.

Caldwell thought, *The eggless wonder's trying to choke me with this shit.*

He glanced through the week's turnout summaries. He scanned for any mentions of fires in the hills. The hills were the danger zone, the powder keg of dead bark and pine needles and combustible resin that had been building throughout the long dry season.

He flipped through sheet after sheet. But his mind could not connect with the paper. His attention wandered to a folder labeled *Luncheons and Dinners: October.*

He slipped out the single sheet of paper. He wanted to see how often he could be rid of Peters in the months ahead. But he could not focus on the names and dates. The liquor was thudding too hard in his temples and just below consciousness was the image of that head shattering against the steel mesh.

Caldwell tossed the paper aside and reached for the red phone. He dialed two digits.

The response was immediate.

"Yes, Chief."

"Who's this?"

"Ryan, sir."

Caldwell put his fingers to his forehead. Suddenly he had lost the thread of what he was about to say.

"Yeah, well—listen, Ryan." Caldwell pushed the briefcase aside and took up a pencil. He began drawing circles around each of the items entered on the schedule of October luncheons and dinners. "How's it look out there? Anything jumping?"

"We had a paint store in Culver City about two A.M. Otherwise, all quiet. Federal had nothing up to half hour ago. CDF reported a little brush fire in the Santa Monica Mountains. No more than a quarter of an acre."

The California Division of Forestry reported fire in the Santa Monica Mountains—the heart of the powder keg. Caldwell's pencil stopped in midcircle.

"What's the title on it?" Caldwell asked.

"Pretty small to title, Chief. Give me a sec to check the scan against the map, okay?"

Caldwell waited, pencil tapping the uncompleted circle.

"Corona," he heard Ryan say. "I'll get it into the log right now."

"You're damned right you'll get it into the log right now. And you'll call CDF to tell them—you hear, Lieutenant Ryan? And you'll leave a note on your board that everything in the hills from now on gets titled until we've had forty days and forty nights of rain—you read me? And I don't care if it's a single blade of grass cooking, I want a goddamned *name* on it—understood, Ryan?"

A silence gushed from the phone and Caldwell realized he had just exploded.

"I copy, Chief," he heard the man say.

"You *copy,* Ryan? Look, Lieutenant, just do it and keep the fancy language for the girls, okay?" Why am I shouting at him? Caldwell wondered. What's wrong with me? "Look, Ryan, I didn't mean to bark. I'm just jumpy, is all—just tired. Up all night and getting a little squirrelly. These months, you know? Until we get some goddamned rain."

Ryan cleared his throat uneasily. "Yeah, well, we're bound to have rain before the weekend, Chief. Nothing's going to get out of hand. We're on top of things."

It hit Caldwell like a slap across the face that Ryan was trying to calm him down, the greenhorn lieutenant was telling the chief not to worry. Caldwell's voice was very measured when he finally spoke.

"Listen, Ryan. This is the fucking company fire boss speaking, and I say we're on top of *shit.* We don't know one thing more than we did when we were just a bunch of jerkoff monkeys beating at burning bushes with sticks. Good night, Lieutenant."

Caldwell slammed the red receiver back into its cradle. He sat a moment, willing his heart to stop slamming into his ribs.

It's the Scotch. Must be the Scotch. Gotta cut down. Didn't need that last drink.

He reached forward and took the carved meerschaum from the rack. He held the bowl in his hand, turning it, feeling it, running his thumb against the ridges forming in the wood.

P.S. Happy smoking! You are a great dad! Caldwell

jerked forward to yank the receiver off the black telephone. He dialed the Weather Bureau. He listened to the recording.

Continued dry northwesterly winds. Temperatures in mid-eighties. Probability of precipitation, zero percent.

When the tape came full circle he hung up.

On the sheet of October luncheons and dinners he wrote the word *Corona*. He gazed at it a long moment and then he scribbled over it.

He shoved everything back into the briefcase. He switched off the desk lamp, grabbed the briefcase by the handle, and carried it back into the front hallway.

He was halfway up the stairs when a thought occurred to him. He turned around. He did not need to put on the kitchen light. The glow of false dawn humming through the window was more than enough for him to see by. He took the empty fifth of Scotch and plunged it into the trash can, deep beneath the garbage.

Just to make sure, he crumpled the note first.

3

IN her kitchen, forty-five minutes before dawn, Carolyn Miller groggily dropped eggs, milk, and concentrated orange juice into the blender. She pushed a switch and let the mixture whip for thirty seconds.

She walked to the hallway, yawned, and called Angie for the third time.

There was still no answer. She went to investigate. The girl was sprawled across her bed sobbing. Carolyn sat beside her and smoothed her corn-silk hair.

"What's the matter, honey?"

"I want Nipper."

Carolyn drew a deep, patient breath. "Nipper will show up."

Angie's cries redoubled. "He'll show up and no one will be here."

"The neighbors will look after him while we're away."

"I don't want to go away without Nipper."

Carolyn Miller sighed. "Come on. I've made your favorite breakfast drink."

"I'm not hungry."

One of *those* moods, Carolyn realized. She glanced at her wristwatch. They had forty minutes to wolf down breakfast, load up the car, lock up the house, and drive to the state park to pick up Steve. Knowing Steve, he'd be in no mood after a long night shift to put up with a wailing child.

All of which added up to a hell of a way to start a vacation.

Carolyn kissed the child, pondered options, and finally went to the family medicine cabinet. She took down the bottle of green-and-black tranquilizers. She hadn't had to use them in four years, since her miscarriage. She didn't suppose they'd lost their strength, and the doctor had said they were a perfectly safe sedative.

She weighed the pros and cons. The pros won.

She plucked a capsule out of the bottle, took it to the kitchen, and separated the two halves over the blender. Carefully she emptied all the powder into the breakfast drink, then whipped the mix another thirty seconds.

She dipped a finger in and tasted to make sure there was no bitter giveaway.

"I'll make a deal with you," Carolyn said, setting the glass of breakfast drink down on the table in front of her daughter. "You can take your radio with you if you'll promise not to cry anymore about Nipper."

Angie's face screwed up thoughtfully. She dried her eyes and took a swallow of the drink. "What did you put in this? It tastes funny."

"No, it doesn't. Just drink it up, it's good for you." Carolyn watched the child gulp down the mix and she felt like a wicked witch in a fairy tale. *At least the drive will be peaceful,* she thought.

She clapped her hands. "Okay, on the double. Let's get those bags into the car."

Seven minutes later the house was locked up and Carolyn Miller was backing the red Pinto out of the garage. Angie blasted her radio all the way to the Santa Monica Mountains and Carolyn wondered if bringing it along had been such a brilliant idea.

As the car nosed up the winding trail to the lookout, it was nearing sunrise, but there was still enough night for the headlights to throw wavering filigrees of light through the pines.

Carolyn brought the car to a stop in the clearing near the tower and yanked the hand brake on. Her eye was caught by a fire truck parked thirty yards farther up the road. Her heart skipped a beat and then she told herself, *It's nothing serious, the truck wouldn't be just*

48

standing there empty if a fire were raging, whatever happened is under control now....

"Wait for me here, honey, okay? I'm going to get Daddy."

"I want to go up the tower," Angie said.

"No, you don't. Just stay in the car and if you're a smart girl you won't waste the battery in that radio."

Passing the fire truck, Carolyn noticed pine needles and dirt sticking to the loosely rewound hoses. She frowned, and once again a light finger of fear touched her. She turned to make sure Angie was still in the car. The little girl was there. Carolyn waved.

Angie waved back to her mother. Alone in the car now, and bored, she fiddled restlessly with her radio. She couldn't find anything she liked. She snapped the radio off. Craning her head out the window, she stared at the lookout tower above the pines. In the distance a dog barked. Angie pricked up her ears.

The sound came again.

Nipper? she wondered—but what would Nipper be doing here in the mountains?

She slipped the radio strap over her shoulder, then slid out of the car. She stood a moment, listening to the barking, straining to match it to the barking in her memory. It was so much like Nipper—it could be! And it didn't sound far off. Her heart thumped.

She glanced again at the tower. Her mother and father had not yet appeared on the part of the stairway that showed above the trees. There was time.

Angie made her decision.

She set out quickly in the direction of the barking. Every ten yards or so she glanced back over her shoulder, making sure she still had the tower in view to guide her back to the car.

Day was beginning. Only a few last holdout stars were still visible. A restlessness stirred the forest. Light was creeping up above the tops of the trees. An odor of dust and pine hung in the already warm air.

She came to a ravine. The daylight was strong enough now for her to see down into the shadows where something white was moving. She crouched and with one hand moved aside the branches.

49

A dog stood quietly in the bottom of the gully. It eyed the little girl, waiting, whimpering slightly, tail tentatively fanning.

"Nipper!" she cried—for it was a West Highland terrier and it could have been Nipper. The dog barked and pawed the brush, moving its body eagerly now.

Angling her feet carefully sideways, Angie began the steep descent. The dog strained toward her, barking, and she saw it had been leashed to a tree. She slid the last few feet to the bottom of the ravine and bent down beside the animal.

It made a whining sound that wasn't Nipper's. It licked her hand and she bent its head up and saw it didn't have Nipper's marking, the little diamond of darker fluff under the chin.

Still it was a friendly dog.

Quickly, she untied the leash. The animal began bounding in circles around her. But she saw there was something else attached to its neck. A can like Daddy's shaving cream. She caught the animal and felt in its fur for a catch. She couldn't find any.

"Come on, Nipper," she said—she had decided that was the dog's name. "You're coming with me." After all, if someone had left a dog tied up in the woods overnight, they couldn't want the animal anymore, could they?

She found a part of the ravine less steep than where she'd slid down. She scrambled up the slope. The dog bounded up alongside her.

She got to her feet, brushed the dirt and twigs from her clothes. The dog was frisking and barking happily. She reached out to pet it and then, glancing out into the woods, she froze.

There was no lookout tower. The pines were tall, mysterious, unfamiliar. She couldn't see a trail, or even a ghost of one.

She gulped a breath of air. Panic stirred in the pit of her stomach. She was lost.

When Steve and Carolyn Miller got back to the car there was no sign of their daughter. Carolyn raked a hand through her nut-brown hair. It was not like the child to disobey and run off.

"Damn," she said, glancing around the forest, "I told her to wait right here."

Steve cocked an eyebrow. "So much for discipline."

He went to the edge of the clearing and called Angie's name. After a moment, feeling impatience, he walked back to the driver's door. He leaned through the open window and pressed three short jabs against the horn.

The echoes came bouncing back through the forest.

Steve and Carolyn remained silent, listening for some other sound. There was only the twitter of birds, the skitter of some creature dashing through the brush, a last distant echo of the car horn dying down to silence.

Carolyn's eye fell again on the fire truck, mute witness of danger. "Steve," she said, "there isn't a fire anywhere near here, is there?"

"Small fire last night."

She could tell he was irritable when he spoke at her in telegraphese.

"Two hippies dropped a joint."

"But the fire's out, isn't it?" Carolyn said.

A scowl formed on Steve Miller's handsome face. "It's out," he snapped, as though she were some kind of fool for asking.

He's angry, she realized. *Damn it, we're not going to start a two-week vacation with bad tempers!*

Steve pressed the horn again. This time he did not release it. Carolyn covered her ears against the blast and when she could take it no longer she yanked Steve's hand off the horn.

"For goodness' sake, Steve, she's probably just gone to take a pee!"

"How long does it take a kid to pee?" Steve glanced at his wristwatch, then up at the sky where dawn was beginning.

Carolyn could see irritation flicker across his eyes. "All right, we'll look for her," she said. "You go back down the trail and I'll go on ahead. She can't have gone far."

Steve shook his head, looking ever so slightly martyred. Carolyn decided against saying anything more. She turned and walked briskly up the sloping trail.

"Angie!" she called, and then again, cupping her hands to her mouth, "Angie!"

A moment later she heard Steve's voice, baritone and sonorous, mimicking her through the trees. *We sound like yodelers,* she thought. She stopped a moment, listened, then quickened her step.

"Angie! Where are you?"

For five minutes Carolyn followed the deer trail east, calling Angie's name. There was no answer. She told herself not to panic.

Angie's safe. She just went to the bushes to pee. She went the other way. Steve will find her. But she couldn't stop calling and she couldn't stop the lump of fear from pushing up against her lungs.

"Angie!"

An echo bounced back to her through the trees, eerie, mocking, distant.

Angie couldn't have come this far, she thought.

She stopped, uncertain whether to go forward or back.

What if Angie fell down a ravine, what if she hurt herself? What if she can't answer?

Terrifying pictures flashed before Carolyn's mind. She glanced back over her shoulder and with a jolt she realized she'd lost sight of the lookout tower.

At that instant the air flashed.

Carolyn's eye was yanked to a break in the brush. A bolus of flame exploded outward from the center of her vision, a rush of flying spume. There was a roar of angry surf crashing in all directions. For one disbelieving moment she stopped dead in her tracks. A wall of blinding fire leaped up twenty feet in front of her. A gust of wind swept it toward her. Flames hopped from shrub to shrub with horrifying rapidity, sealing off any exit to the west.

She turned to run toward the car. The wind-driven flame was outflanking her, and she realized she could not outrun it. She had no choice but to make a break for the east, away from the trail.

She lurched forward. Her dress caught in the brambles. She lunged a hand to free herself. A thousand tiny needles jabbed into her flesh and a dense cloud of black specks exploded around her, buzzing and swarming and clogging her eyes and mouth and nose. She gulped for air. A clot of tiny insects went down her throat and she had to struggle against a retching contraction.

The hiss and crackle of fire were so deafening she could not even hear her feet crashing through the brush. A crushing mass of heat pressed down on her. The ground seemed to pitch and roll.

She stumbled and when she picked herself up again it was as though she were trying to run with a hundred-pound weight on her back.

The air was darker now, like a gathering eclipse. Ten feet ahead of her, as though it had been booby-trapped, a manzanita bush burst into flame. She veered around it, and then as a sapling ignited, she veered a second time.

Now she had completely lost her sense of direction. She stumbled again. A searing pain shot through her ankle. She huddled on the earth a moment, fighting back tears. A voice commanded, "Get up," and when she raised her eyes she saw her husband standing in the swirling gray.

"Did you find her?" she gasped.

He shook his head.

Carolyn could not hold back the tears.

"Oh, God!"

He pulled her up roughly, shoving her forward. "Come on—we have to make a run for it."

"I don't know if I can—my ankle—"

"Yes, you can."

The smoke was rolling in low and black and suffocating, cutting visibility to less than a yard. "This way!"

Eyes to the ground, Steve Miller pulled his wife along a gully that must have been cut two months ago by the last downpour. It guided them to the top of a rise. The wind had cleared the smoke but it had also fanned the fire into a barrier cutting them off from the tower and the car.

Steve saw one chance: a gap not yet closed. He

plunged ahead. Flailing his jacket, he beat back flames on either side of the narrow corridor.

"Come on!" he screamed over his shoulder.

The smoke was coming so thickly Carolyn could no longer see him. She lunged limping behind him, one arm raised to shield her face from showering sparks. A wave of heat surged up from the ground, making her gulp for breath. She broke through into an open space. Steve tugged her forward across a zone of burned-out earth, still smoldering, through scorched trees dripping strips of flayed bark.

Finally they stood to windward of the flames, hearts pounding, trying to catch their breath. Steve Miller put his arm around his wife. He gazed back at the holocaust.

He wanted to weep; not just for the little girl, but for the trees.

At 5:32 A.M., seven minutes after dawn, a ranger in the easternmost lookout in the Santa Monica Mountains sighted a thin wisp of smoke. It was curling up from a pine ridge three degrees west of due south and he put its distance at two and a half miles.

From the narrowness of the smoke and the lack of burn on the windward side he took it to be a spot fire, the child of some tossed match or lightning strike that had lain dormant for days or even weeks. The forest was full of such sleeping beauties, solitary embers awaiting the right wind or fuel to transform them into thousand-acre blazes. They were the dangerous ones.

The ranger leaped for his phone and punched out the three-digit number. As he double-checked the location from his firefinder, it hit him that the smoke was streaking forward with the speed of a coal-burning locomotive.

"Jesus Christ!" he shouted. In under sixty seconds the fire had run a good quarter mile downwind. "Get down here fast—she's traveling!"

Thirty seconds later, in the lookout at the opposite end of the Santa Susanas, two rangers peered out into the dawn that was breaking so beautifully over the mountains. It wasn't till one of them heard the bubbling of water on the hot plate and turned to fix coffee that he noticed a spot glare a mile or so away. It was low on the western skyline, like a giant mirror angled through the trees to reflect the sunrise.

He lifted his binoculars. The ridge of ponderosas jumped into soft focus, backlit by an arc of flickering yellow. In the instant it took him to sharpen the focus, the flicker surged up into a steady pink glow, sending up tongues of white to lick at the still-night sky.

For one hypnotized moment he was paralyzed, not believing the speed at which the flames were spreading. A low whistle escaped his lips.

"We got a nasty one, Larry—real nasty."

Less than a minute later, in a helicopter patrolling a quarter mile above the San Gabriels, a ranger spotted a ribbon of smoke in the southeast swirling up above the treetops. As he grabbed for the microphone of the two-way radio his eye caught a second smoke, this one to the southwest, darker and thicker than the first, streaming faster, with an ugly red pulsation at the base.

"Holy God!" the pilot exclaimed. He glanced toward the east, where a mushroom of thunder-black smoke was sweeping across the scar of the reservoir.

"Three!" the ranger was shouting to fire control. "We've got three burns!"

As he reeled off the coordinates the pilot nudged him and pointed south, where another needle of smoke was reaching into the sky.

"Four!" the ranger corrected, but even as he said it he saw a fifth to the west, and just beyond, the beginnings of a sixth.

"Jesus Christ," he cried, "the whole range is on fire!"

At the sound of the explosion Angie's arm tightened around the radio.

The dog heard the explosion too. The noise brought it up sharply to attention and now, alerted, it was conscious of something nearer, more tangible, more dangerous than the explosions. The unknown thing swept out from the trees, invisible but *there,* a filtering vapor that made its eyes water and reached stingingly down into its lungs with each gulped swallow of air.

And suddenly it knew: smoke!

It barked urgently, warning the girl. She stood motionless, staring in the direction of the explosions.

The crackling sound came first. It was agitated like the rattling of a tambourine. It built to an orchestra of tambourines, an orchestra rushing crazily through the trees, and suddenly she was afraid: the smell of green leaves and clean pines was gone, something sour and sharp had taken its place. She realized the orchestra was rushing at *her.*

Then she saw the flickering light. At first it was just a glow, like the headlight of a one-eyed jeep crashing through the trees. But suddenly it was brighter than any headlight, brighter than anything she had ever seen, and for one panicked, uncomprehending instant she thought the sun was rising out of the forest floor.

When she saw that the light had tongues and fingers of flame she understood what it was, she understood that she must escape. She turned and ran, not seeing, not choosing a path, just lunging blindly.

Thorns and twigs jabbed at her, catching her clothes. She wrenched free, crashed into brush, lost her footing, fell full out.

The dog was beside her, barking.

She got back painfully to her feet. The fire was rushing forward now, cutting off the direction she'd chosen. She began running to the left, away from the flames.

The dog loped beside her, still barking.

The fire was roaring everywhere now, in front of her, behind her, on either side. There were openings but she couldn't tell which was the safe one. She screamed: "Mommy! Daddy!"

The dog wheeled to a stop and turned and barked. Angie understood that it was a command but it took her an instant to grasp that the dog wanted her to stay exactly where she was, not to move. She obeyed, trusting the animal and whatever instinct it was that guided it.

The dog bounded up a short slope and from the ridge

stared into the valley beyond. Through the trees the dog could see a clearing and on the far side a great semicircle of flame sweeping toward it.

The dog sniffed, testing the air, and somewhere in some suddenly thinking part of its head the equation formed itself: high terrain equaled smoke and heat, low offered the only chance of escape.

The dog bounded back to the clearing where the girl stood. It barked, indicating the way, and after one backward glance to make sure the girl was following, it was running.

She plunged after it.

They ran forward between two ridges. There was smoke in the brush on their left and the bulletlike exploding of pinecones on the right and as they ran fragments of burning bark showered down on them. Angie whimpered. Her throat began to tighten. She couldn't get air.

The dog turned and barked, then edged forward, crawling on its belly. The girl crept behind. A spark fell on the sleeve of her dress and she screamed, slapping it out.

The dog circled behind her, barking, whimpering, nagging her forward.

And then it was too late.

The ravine had held the fire momentarily at bay but now the fire, searching for a way across, found its bridge: rushing along the branch of a half-dead toppled pine it met the branch of a living pine on the other side. A great arm of flame leaped out and seized the younger tree. Like water breaking through a dam, flames raced across the gap, spreading out into a surging wave.

Angie wheeled around. Fifty yards behind them a second wall of fire was sweeping forward, blotting out sky and forest.

The dog dropped to its forepaws, sniffing along the forest floor, peering into the gap between the still unburned duff and the thickening cloud of smoke. Straight ahead, beneath the bridge of fire, the ground dipped and there was one last, quickly shrinking tunnel of escape.

The dog gave one sharp bark, a signal to the girl to follow. The animal lowered its head and plunged ahead. Through squinting eyes Angie could make out the tiny white shape wriggling forward into the sweeping flames. The dog sensed she was hanging back. It turned and barked again.

Angie swallowed. Scalding heat seared into her lungs. Fear paralyzed her. She glanced again over her shoulder.

The fire had moved twenty yards closer.

Still the dog dropped to its belly and slithered forward. Dimly, Angie grasped that it was showing her the way out.

She dropped to her hands and knees. Closer to the ground the air was merely hot, not scalding. She gulped a breath, groped her way forward, eyes squinting through the smoke to make out the little white shape.

A low-reaching branch gouged into her cheek and she whimpered in pain. The dog paid her no attention. It kept wriggling forward and suddenly she could no longer see it.

Angie reached a hand along the ground in front of her. Without warning, there was only space. She cried out, plummeting through empty smoke, rolling across earth dotted with jagged rock.

When she was finally able to break her fall, the dog was beside her again, barking, nagging her up and forward. She glanced at her skinned knee and bleeding forearm and registered, with surprise, that they didn't hurt.

She pulled herself to her knees and then, seeing that the smoke was thinner here, to her feet.

There was no longer the solid wall of fire. There were wavering gaps and these were of two kinds: patches of unburned forest and islands of smoldering ash. Through layers of smoke she sighted a clearing that was still green. She dashed forward.

Barking, the dog looped in front of her. She felt a sudden pain in her foot. The dog had gripped her ankle in its mouth and was tugging in another direction.

Suddenly she understood: there was no safety in the unburned forest—only in the dead zones where the fire

58

had already burned itself out. She let the dog tug her into a patch of cinder no larger than the inside of a car. There was one ghost of a tree, charred and black and naked as a lamppost.

The smoke was beginning to roll in thicker. The dog yapped at her crazily, tugging her down to the ground.

She obeyed, lying on her side, curling up, making herself small. The dog curled up against her and she could feel its little heart thumping even more furiously than hers. She put her arms around it and buried her face in its fur.

Two seconds later heat slammed down. Above her there was a hissing roar and when she opened her eyes the smoke had closed in and high above she could dimly make out a canopy of surging red.

The sky was on fire.

Eddy Caldwell climbed the wide stairs to the bedroom and to the woman who was sleeping there. She had thrown off the sheet and now she lay on her stomach, sprawled on the diagonal, as though she had reached for him in her sleep.

Caldwell stood just inside the doorway. He stared at the long line of her naked back, the furrow low down that divided the strong fiber to either side of her spine. The sinew there seemed tensed and expectant even in sleep.

For a long while he did not move. He stared at this woman in his wife's bed, so different from the wife who had once slept there.

It occurred to him that the air conditioner had been on all night; she must be cold without the sheet. He crossed to the bed and bent down to cover her. He could see her face, turned to the side, contented in sleep.

A rush of tenderness swept over him.

His hand touched her hair, sorting out sleek strips of it and drawing them back behind one ear. Then he touched her where the back narrowed. His hand was large, and—fingers stretched—it covered the woman there from side to side. The hand moved down to her flank and suddenly he felt that thunder again, rolling and spreading upward into his chest.

His hand froze.

He tried to trace the current flowing into him, choking off his air. He tried to understand this dread. And then in a dull, hung-over flash, he realized: *it comes from her*. He was afraid of this woman, afraid of this smooth, faultless wash of tanned flesh, of the shallows and billows of her legs and buttocks. He was afraid because he had once loved a woman and there had been a child and he had killed both of them. He was afraid because it could happen again.

He sat a long time and the hangover came in waves, pushing against his temples and gut. He did not know how long he had sat there, not moving, when the bell ripped the silence in two.

The fire fighter in him recognized *the long ring*. It was a sound Eddy Caldwell had heard only once before in his life. He lunged for the night table, gripped the red telephone receiver.

"All right!" he shouted. "Let's hear it!"

He was aware that the woman beside him had stirred, pulled herself to a sitting position, gathered the sheet up around her nakedness.

"Chief! Jesus Christ!" a voice from the receiver was shouting back at him. "We got a burn! Six! Six mean little shits! My Christ, we got something going out there you would not believe!"

Caldwell clenched the receiver so tight his fingernails dug into the flesh of his hand. He was thinking of the forest out there, waves of timber cresting in the raging flames. He shivered. He realized he'd been waiting a year for this. He needed this fire, he needed it badly. This was his chance. If he could lick a big one he could show the world Eddy Caldwell wasn't licked. Maybe, with luck, he could even show Eddy Caldwell.

When he spoke his voice was very quiet. He didn't let the excitement show.

"I'll be rolling in two minutes. You call me on the car radio and give it to me as it comes. All right, Ryan, go to work. I'm sliding now."

Very calmly, very deliberately, he hung up the telephone. Then, moving quickly now, he grabbed his clothes. He was still buckling his belt as he took the stairs two at a time. He was halfway out the front door when he realized, *I didn't kiss her. I didn't even kiss her good-bye.*

But there wasn't time. He kept going.

He didn't say good-bye, she was thinking. *It was as though I wasn't even here.*

She got to her knees. Holding the sheet to her bosom, she angled to see out the window. A door slammed and she saw Eddy Caldwell double-timing it to the red car waiting at the end of the handsomely curved driveway.

She saw something else too, and it helped her make her decision.

I'm going to leave him. I've been going to leave him for three months, but today I'm going to pack my bags and do it.

It wasn't just because of the mornings he hadn't said good-bye or all those times he'd called her Joyce when her name was Trish or even because of the drinking. It was also because she'd been the right nurse for him at the right time, and though he might not always expect his woman to nurse him, she knew he would always expect it of her. And she knew too there was a time when a nurse was a hindrance, not a help.

She knew he would make it without her, because the thing she saw, the thing that decided her, was the way he ran to the car.

His limp was gone.

4

"KEELAN!" Eddy Caldwell shouted. "Ross!" Where the hell were his bouncers? His office was at the far end of the corridor, and he saw he'd have to shove through the mass of radio and TV people, newspaper and wire service reporters, all jamming the way, all screaming to get his attention.

"Keelan! Ross!" he shouted, elbowing through. "Clear this hallway! I want these clowns out of here!"

"Hey, Chief!" A young guy in jeans and a Kiss-Me-I'm-Italian T-shirt had jammed his face two inches from Caldwell's. With one hand he tried to hold a microphone steady under Caldwell's chin and with the other he jiggled the settings on the tape recorder strapped to his hip. "Do you have any comment on the rumors of arson?"

"My comment is stand aside or I'm going to take your leg off."

But Caldwell didn't need to take that particular leg off; someone pushed from behind. The young man lost his footing and was swept to the side.

Caldwell ignored minicams and shoulders and microphones pressing against him. He forced his way forward, hard. The crowd pressed alongside him. A man with a goatee waved a mike in his face.

"Fletcher," he shouted, "KNX-TV! Is it true the first report came in from a Western Airlines pilot flying over the area?"

Chivalry was dead and Caldwell was using his elbows now, not caring if the obstacle was male or female. "Does it matter?" he shot back over his shoulder.

The man pursued. "Chief Caldwell, don't you think that says something frightening about our fire-defense system?"

Another voice chimed in, a woman, mid-forties, breathing hard. "The *Times* says it took Western more than fifteen minutes to get through to you here. Tell me, Chief Caldwell, does that sound to you like the fire protection we're paying for?"

Caldwell would have liked to give her a crack about the journalism we're paying for, but a bullhorn cut in. It was Ross, at last, standing on a chair, 220 pounds of muscle with murder in his face and veins straining in his neck.

"Ladies and gentlemen, will you please remove yourselves! There are coffee and doughnuts in the pressroom! Fire Chief Edward K. Caldwell will hold a news conference just as soon as full appraisal of the situation has been made!"

A voice called back: "Hey, you with the bullhorn— just tell us if a firebug did it!"

The reporters were driving little maniacs, sharks hungry for blood, and with that shout "firebug" they'd had the first taste of it. They surged forward now, flashbulbs popping, cameras grinding, tape recorders whirring.

Caldwell braced himself, but the tide hit harder than he'd been prepared for. He slammed into the water cooler, lunged a hand to recover his balance, and found himself hanging onto a coolly smiling redhead.

"Good morning, Chief—work got you up early today?" There was mischief in the voice and it matched the mischief in the green eyes. "VV Cameron—Station KLIC."

She was holding out a hand, as though this were a cocktail party instead of a riot, and unthinkingly he took it. He'd heard of her, an up-and-comer with her own chitchat show on local TV. Her hand lingered in his and the smile lingered on her lips and both smile and hand were challenges. He tried to size her up: no tape recorder, no camera, not even a pad or pencil—just a very direct stare and a slender body oozing confidence at every pore. Trouble.

"Chief, do you honestly think you can handle this fire?"

"It's my job to handle it."

"Wasn't it your job to handle the Laurel Canyon fire?"

Caldwell stiffened.

"Didn't nineteen people lose their lives in that disaster? Didn't you blow it, Chief?"

They were hedged around with reporters and spinning tape recorders. Caldwell fought to keep his voice civil.

"As far as I'm concerned, Proposition Thirteen blew it by cutting back our resources. We had to go into Laurel Canyon with less than seventy percent manpower and equipment."

Her smile never once wavered. "You're blaming the people of Los Angeles for the Laurel Canyon disaster?"

"I blame the people who let politicians gut vital services for the sake of phony economy."

An arm cut in, physically separating Caldwell from VV Cameron. It was an experienced, agile arm, and it belonged to Marty Siegel, public-relations manager for the Los Angeles Fire Department. The arm went around Caldwell in a powerful buddy-clamp and began pulling him toward his office door.

"What Chief Caldwell means," Siegel explained, "is that thanks to the Laurel Canyon tragedy manpower cuts have been restored. The Los Angeles Fire Department is more than prepared to handle the present situation."

"Situation, Mr. Siegel?" VV Cameron smiled. "That's your word for this potential holocaust? Situation?"

Caldwell had known Marty Siegel to talk faster and fabricate faster than a White House press secretary, but he'd never seen Marty duck a question as fast as he did now.

"Thanks for your time, Miss Cameron, and thank the rest of you, ladies and gentlemen, but Chief Caldwell has an urgent meeting."

Siegel quickly hustled Caldwell through the office door and shut it hard behind them.

"You got a short fuse, Chief," he warned. "You have to watch it with those barracudas."

Caldwell pushed through the next door. The room was mobbed and the mob was in an uproar. An attempt had been made to put out folding chairs but there were more fire fighters than chairs, and men were crushed three deep against the walls.

Heads turned at Caldwell's entrance. Someone shouted, "All right, stow it, everybody!"

Silence rippled out and a path cleared for him. Caldwell strode to the front of the room. Several of the men patted him on the back.

A voice shouted, "Chopper's standing by, Ed!" It was Keelan, head poking through an open door. "Ready when you are!"

Caldwell glanced toward the communications room on the other side of the glass wall. The big Western Union timer centered over the control panel said 6:48.

"Okay, Jack," he called back. "We'll go up at seven thirty—from here, from the roof."

He took a position in front of the display map that spanned the front wall. He tried to focus on the men waiting for him to speak. They were a sea of faces—excited, revved up like a football team needing only the coach's peptalk before they stormed out to whip the opposition. He tried to hold his attention on them, but his mind flashed an image of that TV woman, her hand lingering in his. *Get with it, Caldwell,* he told himself, yanking himself back to this room, these men, this fire.

"Gentlemen," he said, "what I heard on the way in sounds bad. But so far we're on top of it."

There were knowing nods, knowing grumbles.

"Let's have a look at the slides."

The lights went down and there was only the glow from the communications room next door. The first slide clicked on, hitting Caldwell full in the face like the headlights of an onrushing car. He ducked aside.

It was Peters who spoke, invisible in the dark, his voice smooth as a radio announcer's. "These were taken at approximately thirty-second intervals."

They were helicopter shots of the early stages of one of the burns. It began as a pinpoint in a stand of ponderosa pines, then in the following five slides shot out in an almost perfectly straight hundred-yard line.

The slides shifted to a second burn. "This one was already going when we snapped it."

The first shot showed a semicircle of flame. In the second and third it became a slightly egg-shaped circle. In shots four through eight, the circle grew a tail and the tail became a second circle looping back into the first, a distorted but recognizable figure eight.

That's crazy, Caldwell thought. *That's skywriting, not fire.*

There were shots of four more burns, all taken within nine minutes of sunrise. Peters narrated unemotionally, spinning off locations, times, present status.

The slide show ended with a seventh burn. "Don't know if this adds anything, but it came in at ten twenty-seven last night. It's under control."

Caldwell frowned. Compared to the others, this one was a pinpoint, but it was a pinpoint fifty feet high.

There's no such thing, Caldwell thought, *not in the forest, not in dry season. You don't get fifty-foot pinpoints. They spread before they go that high.*

The lights came back on. Faces in the room were grim. This wasn't just a football game anymore.

"How about speed?" Caldwell asked.

Peters shuffled through a sheaf of papers. Even at seven in the morning he was groomed like a male model. He looked like a man who didn't even sweat.

"Four of them are moving like rocket engines are on them," he said. "The other two—fast, but nothing sensational. Anyhow, looks like there's going to be coupling in no time."

Caldwell saw one of the captains signaling for attention. "What is it, Rizzo?" Rizzo had been with the force twelve years. The mayor had decorated him twice for bravery.

"I had an early look at two of those burns," he said, "and I tell you, Chief, in all my years I've never seen fire as fast and wild as what I was looking at."

The man was trembling. Al Rizzo had faced down

holocausts, he'd made headlines rescuing twin babies from the twentieth floor of a burning high-rise, and he was trembling because of two brush fires in the Santa Monica Mountains.

That told Caldwell more than all the slides and printouts in L.A. He was able to keep his face and tone matter-of-fact.

"What's the update on weather?"

"No change," Peters answered. "More of the same for at least two days."

"Wind?"

"The same. Santa Ana all the way."

"You got a maximum temp for the day?"

"They're saying it'll make ninety-eight."

In short the fire had everything going for it: fuel, temperature, wind—and head start. Caldwell's movements became brisk. He pulled the four-foot pointer away from the magnetic wall-clip. He turned to the map, tapping out the fire zones, christening—just as he'd christened Mickey, he couldn't help thinking.

"Okay—name of this fire is Stone. Here's Simi. Up here Granada. Notice how they're lining up in a shallow parabola. Here's Laurel."

He skipped a beat. *Why did I say Laurel? Laurel Canyon's where I killed them.* He felt as though he'd just jinxed himself. He yanked his thoughts back, moved the pointer into the San Gabriels, was about to name the next blaze when he heard someone call out.

"We should be getting new maps any minute, Chief."

Caldwell recognized Jamie Cuddon, one of the new men. Cuddon was a college grad. He carried a slide rule in his pocket and he figured out differential equations for heat loss through smoke. He struck Caldwell as an armchair fighter.

"That's great," Caldwell said, "but you don't kick over a fire with paper."

Cuddon flushed and instantly Caldwell regretted the sarcasm. *Easy there, Ed,* he told himself, *don't start snapping yet. Before this is out you may need Cuddon and his differential equations.*

Caldwell named the two remaining burns. "Our response to this point is adequate. I want to double the response immediately. And I want standby force to quadruple it if we aren't knocking the fires down by noon. For the time being, until I get a look at these mothers, we're going to divide our forces by seven. That means twenty-eight more engine companies rolled in there right now, four to each burn."

Caldwell turned. "Captain Rizzo—how many tankers you have out there?"

"Three!" Al Rizzo called back.

"Can you double that right away?"

"I can triple it right away!"

"Do it!" Caldwell barked. "And whoever's handling the bulldozers, let's get four times as many out there pronto! Now I want the alert to go out to Civil Defense, Red Cross, Salvation Army. I want police choppers working the Beverly Glen and Bel Air residentials and calling those people out. And I want the mayor's office informed. And the governor's."

Peters shot back: "I informed them both. Half hour ago."

For one instant Caldwell's glance locked with Peters'. He felt an electric surge of antagonism. *The bastard's trying to get ahead of me; it's not the fire he's fighting, it's Chief Eddy Caldwell.*

"Good thinking, Peters," Caldwell said neutrally, ashamed of his pettiness but wondering if it was just pettiness, if there wasn't some truth to his intuition. He missed a beat and then he was barking again.

"CDF and the Federals are going to run their own show until we really know what we're up against. I estimate by nine thirty we'll have the picture. If it looks like a double feature, I'll have the mayor name me fire boss on all seven, and we'll run their forces. If the mayor gives me any trouble, I'll go to the governor. But one thing I promise you, men—this one is ours! And if there's a fuckup, I don't want to have to look any farther than my mirror to know who's responsible. So when I give an order, I want you to haul ass and *do it now!* Let's knock those seven mothers down and take them out before that wind gets any worse. We're in front of this one and we're going to stay in front—do I make myself clear, everybody?"

He looked around the room. All eyes were on him.

All right, I can still deliver a peptalk. Now let's see if I can still put out a fire.

He looked toward the clock above the control panel next door, then at his watch, making sure they were synchronized. He said, "All right, men, that's it. Let's go to war!"

There was a shoving of chairs and a confusion of voices and the room began emptying out. Caldwell went to his desk. He wanted to check those weather reports before going to the roof. He saw Peters at the door ushering the men out, shaking hands with a few of them. *Jesus Christ,* he realized, *the man's campaigning.* But then he saw Peters step suddenly to one side as a woman tried to get past him.

Peters turned and shouted, "She says she's coming in!"

"The hell she is!" Caldwell shouted back.

Too late. She was in. VV Cameron, sleek and slender and moving with quiet determination, had pulled her arm from Peters' grasp and was gliding toward the desk.

"Come on, Chief. I could make you look good and you could use the public relations. Just two questions." Those smiling green eyes bored into him, turning his mind toward things that had nothing to do with fire.

"Lady, I'm fighting a fire, not giving interviews."

"Either you give me some answers, Chief, or I'll find some answers of my own."

"That's what you're paid to do, isn't it?"

"You might not like my kind of answers."

"Keelan," Caldwell signaled. "Clear the room. Personnel only."

Apologetically, Keelan took VV Cameron by the arm. All the way to the door she kept smiling, as though Eddy Caldwell's fly were unzipped and no one saw it but VV Cameron. "Your funeral, Chief," she called.

He glanced down at his lap. It was zipped. He heard the door close and Peters and Marty Siegel were coming toward him.

"You'd better hit it, Chief," Marty Siegel said. "Seven thirty—a little past."

Siegel had the kind of face Eddy Caldwell trusted. There was assurance in it, something seasoned and very knowing. It was a face that went with seeing things and never being surprised.

Caldwell got to his feet. He fumbled in his pockets for his pipe. "Did you see the pictures, Marty?" he asked.

"Saw the slides."

"What do you make of them?"

"Got to be man-made. But how the hell it was done I don't know. Not a guess. Never seen a damn thing like it."

Caldwell handed him the glossies, still slick and smelling of developing fluid. Siegel flipped through them. The eyes crinkled but there wasn't a flicker of surprise. Siegel pointed to one of the prints.

"You'd say maybe a power line if you had just one of these. Or a tight cluster of them, maybe. But when you've got seven—spread out like these, all over hell and gone—no way. It's a firebug, all right. There's just not a whole lot of question about it."

For a moment the three men were silent. Caldwell was aware of Peters' after-shave lotion, something cinnamony and supposed-to-be-masculine. He felt in the side pocket of his jacket. No pipe. The others were looking at him.

"I was looking for my pipe," he said. "Must've left it home." Mickey's pipe: *Happy Father's Day.* "I was really rolled this morning, I can tell you. You hear that long ring and you really roll, you know?"

What the hell am I explaining? he wondered. *What the hell am I apologizing for?*

Marty Siegel handed him back the glossies. "Eddy," he said, and there was a gentleness in his voice that disturbed Caldwell, "you got any theories?"

Caldwell exhaled. He touched a finger to the ache in his temple. "That second burn—Simi. It's a figure eight. Like figure skating. Doesn't make sense. If it's an arsonist, he's running back *into* the fire to close that second loop."

Siegel took out a cigarette and tamped one end

against the back of his hand. "You're saying it's not a bug?"

"I can't figure it. Six fires, spread over all that distance. They all go off within five minutes of one another. Either we've got one bug in six places at once, or we've got six bugs with walkie-talkies. Six crazies? I don't see it."

"Six time bombs," Peters said.

"Time bombs do not walk in figure eights," Caldwell said coldly.

Siegel must have caught something in the voice, because his eyes flicked up curiously and fixed on Caldwell.

"Then what the hell have we got?" Peters said defensively. "If it's not bombs and it's not six crazies, what have we got?"

"We have fire!" Caldwell snapped back at him. "We have got goddamned fire, Mr. Peters! We do not have the goddamned torch that set it off and we don't even know how he did it. So we fight what we've got out there to fight—fire!"

"Can't agree, Chief." Peters was shaking his head. This was a show, Caldwell knew: Peters putting on a show for Siegel, second-guessing the boss, and the worst thing Caldwell could do would be to lose his cool and tell him to shut the hell up.

"It's a bug," Peters was saying, "and however he's doing it, he could set more. He could be at it right now, and chances are he is. No pyro ever gets enough of it, so why the hell should he quit when he's just begun? And consider something else—any bug that could fire up six burns as vicious as these, could just as easily—"

"When hasn't that been the case?" Siegel cut in. "With all the wackos we're recruiting to make up the population, that's a risk you run every day of the week. So what's to get dramatic about?"

"I say we put out an alert," Peters said.

Sure, Caldwell thought, *go public, panic the city.* He didn't like the way Peters was trying to manipulate this.

"I don't want this on the street," Caldwell said. "Not

yet. Marty, put out a press release. Tell the public the fires are normal for the season. And for God's sake cut them down to three."

"I'll handle it," Siegel said.

Caldwell got to his feet and reached for Siegel's hand. "Thanks."

He was halfway to the door when a thought made him stop short and whip around. "What about that fire last night? Think it connects with the other six?"

"We know who set that fire," Peters said. "Two stoned potheads. Besides it was seven hours earlier than the others."

"But it fits." Caldwell went to the map and pointed. "These aren't just isolated burns. They make an arc. And that first fire is smack in the dead center. Part of the design."

Peters shook his head. "Those kids couldn't have set the others. They've been in the hospital since eleven last night."

Caldwell frowned. Usually he had an instinct when it came to arson. But he couldn't get a mental fix on this one. Either there was one torch with the ingenuity to set six fires at once or there were six torches working in a precision team. Plus that seventh. And either way it was ugly news for Los Angeles.

A grim thought nagged at him. "Marty, can you check with the police—see if there've been any threats from terrorist organizations, any demands for money or amnesty for prisoners, anything like that?"

Siegel clasped Caldwell's hand and looked hard into his eyes. "I'll do it."

They moved toward the door and when they were far enough from Peters, Siegel said in a low voice, "Keep your ass on the leather, my friend."

"Sure," Caldwell said, and he thought, *What's going on, I'm getting a peptalk from my own PR man.*

"A fire's just a fire," Siegel said. "There's no meaning in it beyond that. No meaning at all." Siegel's hand was on the doorknob and he swung the door open. "I'm talking about Mickey and Joyce," Siegel said. "You hear me, good buddy?"

Caldwell stared, amazed. It came to him with a jolt

that Marty Siegel was sorry for him. *Jesus Christ, do I look like some kind of invalid?* "Sure," Eddy Caldwell said. "Sure I hear you, Marty."

The rotaries topside and aft, double sets, kicked into high spin, and the pilot shouted, "Ready?" over the roar of air wash and machine.

Caldwell looked at the man, his face chalky in the hard light, and at Peters behind him, skin pink and glowing as though he'd just come from a thirty-dollar facial massage. "Ready!" Caldwell shouted back, snapping into his safety belt.

Beside him he heard the answering click of Peters buckling in.

The pilot grinned and shouted, "Okay, and away she goes!"

With what began as a curt, lurching heave up and back, the spidery aircraft rushed aloft in a great shaking leap that presently gave way to a long dipping slide to the north.

Caldwell gazed down at the city. It was beginning to hit its waking stride. Orderly lumps of traffic backed up at the red lights and less orderly lumps of traffic crammed the throughways. He could see people on foot down there going about their daily run-of-the-mill routines, shopping and hustling and walking the dog and handing out parking tickets, and when he shifted his gaze ten degrees to the north he saw what they could not, the thing that they took to be a bad dose of smog, the fire that was already stripping the outer skin of the city.

Stone was the fire closest in. Police and news helicopters were already churning back and forth along Stone's southernmost front when Caldwell's pilot pointed and Caldwell saw what he needed no man to point out for him. How many sleepless nights had his heart seen what his eyes saw now boiling up at him from the hills and canyons ahead? How many times had he killed this thing that rose to be killed again?

Caldwell gestured for the pilot to take them in close. This was his fire. Day after day he had waited for it. Night after night he had dreamed the roar and the heat

73

and the blazing light of it. Now the fire was here, exactly as he had dreamed it, as though his mind, not the forces out there in the universe, had called it into being.

He was ready for this fire. This was his rematch, his chance to win back the crown.

The aircraft craned momentarily to the west and then spilled east and onward toward the billowing, broken haze. Tongues of flame darted upward as though to swallow the sky. Through drifting layers of smoke Caldwell counted one, two, three...four bulldozers cutting a firebreak, and now he saw trucks, at least a dozen fire trucks, clinging to the berm on either side of the San Diego Freeway.

Despite all the technological advances, there were only two basic ways to fight fire, and they were both as old as fire itself. One was to choke it; that took water or chemicals or a rival fire; the other was to contain it till it burned itself out; that took fire lines. There was no way you could use the first method against a forest fire, so you fell back on the second. You sent teams of men and machines to strip the ground of brush and duff and trees. You created a fuel-less zone two to three feet wide running the length of the fire and then you prayed that wind or renegade sparks or low-hanging branches wouldn't screw you up.

Caldwell prayed now.

And what he saw next sent a tremor of wild sensation through him. It was a feeling that had terror in it—but there was exhilaration in it too. Because it was happening. Before his eyes, the nightmare was materializing.

On the far side of the line, pines and firs were engulfed in a sea of flame. The line would hold so long as the fire kept to ground level. But a hundred yards within the line, a fluke updraft ignited a 150-foot ponderosa. It took only seconds for the tree to burst into a 250-foot torch. The branches began writhing like the arms of a giant being burned alive.

The flame and heat thrashed out in the direction of the gusting wind and the crown of the next pine caught and then the next, and like a ritual lighting of flames on a candelabrum the airborne fire swept tree by tree

74

down toward the fire line that had been meant to contain it. The fire crossed the line as easily as a child stepping over a gutter, and now it swept on toward the undefended highway.

"Holy Christ!" he heard Peters gasp beside him. The voice was edged in boyish eagerness and it irritated Caldwell. It struck him that for Peters this was TV holocaust, war played from the safety of a game room.

Caldwell gazed down. A part of him was sickened and another part, the fighter, was fascinated.

The eight lanes of superhighway would have been the perfect, impenetrable firebreak but for one fact: the fire line had been expected to hold, the highway had not been sealed, and there was still traffic. The drivers did not even see the wall of flame racing through the trees until it was thirty yards from them.

By then it was too late.

Some drivers accelerated, trying to outrace the fire. The highway became a paralyzed jumble of smashups and pileups. Other drivers abandoned their cars and tried to escape on foot.

The bombing of Dresden must have looked like that, Caldwell thought, a tide of humanity trapped between tangled metal and sweeping flame. For there was nowhere to run; the fire slammed down in a solid wall.

A flaming branch landed on the trunk of a car. The gas tank exploded. A rush of flame shot across the gap to the next car and the next. A U-Haul van went up in a spray of white light, made a quarter turn in midair, slammed down on the divider. The wind-lashed flames hurled themselves westward onto the southbound lanes. The line of exploding gas tanks rippled out like a single wave from a stone dropped in water.

In little more than a minute Stone had done it, done what few fires could do: it had jumped the eight lanes of concrete and fastened on the fields to the west. Those fields were now snarling knots of flame throwing off spot fires of their own as far as Caldwell's eye could see.

"Call Communications!" Caldwell shouted to the pilot, and he took the headset when the pilot offered it.

But he said nothing when the microphone was placed on his chest—because now the heat was enormous and then it was suddenly, incredibly worse, a blast of scorching air surrounding them as a rogue thermal slammed the helicopter and hurled it into a shuddering sidewise skid that did not want to stop.

Like a swimmer caught in an undertow, the flimsy aircraft was sucked back in the direction it had come from. Without warning it succumbed to a deadfall—dropping fifty, a hundred, two hundred feet in split seconds as crazy quilts of fire-generated air drafts suffocated the machine's power to purchase altitude.

"Goddamnit, Chief!" Peters cried in a pinched falsetto that was barely recognizable as male, let alone human. "Call in a Mayday! Goddamnit, man!"

But Caldwell did not do it.

For one sudden instant all motion stopped and then the machine took a glassy headlong swoon forward, as if the air had turned to syrup. But this did not last either. A giant fist of heat rammed them from below and sent them skyrocketing upward.

"Jesus, Jesus!" Peters was screaming, only now it seemed less a scream than a prayer. Caldwell heard the man's panic. But it did not interest him even to the extent of arousing contempt. Nor was he interested in wasting so much as a glance at the man who might be his partner in death.

Because there was only one thing worth looking at, there was only one thing worth being afraid of, and it was down there spread out below them.

A mass of flame had obliterated all distinction between highway and field and forest. Destruction whirled and twisted and leaped and sent flaming chunks of debris as big as a man's head spiraling up into the air. Smoke gushed up like the black vomit of a volcano.

Caldwell thought: *There is nothing that has the power of that.*

And aloud he said, "I see you, you son of a bitch. I know you. I know where you are."

"Can't hear you!" the pilot shouted. "What is it?"

"Nothing," Caldwell shouted back. "You're doing fine! Stay with it!"

"I think I can hold it!" the pilot shouted. "You okay?"

"No sweat!" Caldwell shouted. His eyes saw nothing but the inferno flooding the earth below.

The pilot seemed about to shout something else when the aircraft slapped into a wrenching sidelong descent that twisted the machine first left and then right and then whipped it all the way to the right so the nose was facing where the tail had been three seconds ago.

"Mayday! Mayday!" Peters screamed hysterically. He clutched at Caldwell's shoulder and Caldwell flung him off.

And then, just as abruptly as it had seized them, the agonized air let them go. The helicopter righted itself, skimmed briefly along the tall dark wall of smoke rising to starboard, and then soared smoothly aloft and a safe distance south.

"Sorry about that," the pilot called out, grinning like a college jock who'd almost fumbled a play in football.

Peters slapped Caldwell's knee, hearty now. "Ought to add on a cabaret tax for that one!" he shouted.

Ought to add on a cabaret tax for you, you gutless wonder, Caldwell thought. "Yeah," he acknowledged, still looking off to the north. Then, to the pilot, "Nice work. Now take it back."

"Take it *back?*" Peters echoed. He was grinning broadly, as if to deny that Caldwell could be serious.

"That's what I said. Take it back."

Peters' face tautened and the grin died.

Wordlessly, the pilot swung the aircraft around to the north again.

Caldwell adjusted the microphone and brought it closer to his mouth. When he finally spoke his tone was level and matter-of-fact. *I'm doing it,* he thought. *I'm holding.*

"Central, Central," Caldwell said. "This is Leader airborne southwest of Stone. Central, this is Caldwell. Patch me into the battalion bosses in the zone. Let me know when you're ready, Central. I'm listening. Let me know when to go ahead, please."

There was a blast of static and for thirty seconds it hopped through different pitches like a Moog synthesizer gone berserk. Finally Central came on.

"You're there, Chief."

Caldwell took a deep breath that tasted faintly of the charcoal on a grilled steak.

"This is Caldwell, friends and neighbors. It's a bitch from up here. But I guess you don't need me to tell you. I'll tell you some other things I imagine you already know—but just in case you don't, listen up. You have major burn west of Dago Freeway, and you have spotting, fast spotting—I count nine, ten, eleven spot fires going off on a westerly vector from the big one. The farthest one out looks to be about two miles off. Smoke column to my right, east of Dago, I estimate close to two thousand feet deep—and it's carrying firebrand material right on up to the top."

Caldwell let his eye glance again through the Plexiglas. There was something eerie about the free-floating chunks of flame: they glowed like disaster flares sent up in a black fog, they moved like the airborne spores of some luminous, deadly plant, seeking a place to root themselves and spread.

It hit Caldwell that nature was on the side of this fire.

"Lower down you've got incendiaries sailing off to the west at a pretty good clip. There's an overall westerly progress to the general show I'm getting from up here—so move that rig on Dago out of there, please. Get in front. You've got Topanga Canyon Boulevard to take your stand on, and you better start taking. There and on Mulholland north. The picture looks like ten to twelve acres of involvement a minute on a west to northwesterly course."

His eye traveled, anticipating the path of the fire. The fields were thinly dotted with bungalows, swimming pools, tennis courts. *Fuel,* he thought: *a hundred thousand an acre and still fuel.*

Then he craned forward. Far to the northwest he saw what seemed to be a deserted tennis court with a ball-pitching machine still hurling balls across the net, one every five seconds.

"Central, let's clear it out in there now. If anybody's still in there, I want them out—*now*—west to Topanga, north to Mulholland. Another thing, Central, if we have our choppers here, I don't see them. No tankers, either."

Caldwell heard the narrow whine sounding in his ear, a voice like metal drawn into wire:

"Leader, FD airborne assigned to Stone is situated on Stone's northern front per earlier instructions ordered by Assistant Chief Peters. We have three choppers and two tankers deployed in that position and working a pattern between fire Stone and fire Laurel to the north. Hold on, Leader, I have Deputy Chief Keelan waiting to speak to you. He wants it private, Leader—I'm taking off the men downstairs. They're off now, Leader."

"Ed?" Caldwell heard. "Ed, this is Jack. Better come on back, Ed. We got trouble, Pappy. Fires Simi and Stone are estimated to fuse in less than an hour. Battalion chief out of Santa Monica reports no way to stop it and CDF's saying the same thing. Now get this—the other four are going crazy too. What we've right now got is already a whole lot worse than what we had in seventy—and anything else I know about."

Caldwell glanced down again. To the west the fire had fanned out to a front that was at least a mile wide. It seemed to have slowed its forward movement, but that could have just been the distance throwing Caldwell's calculation off. He wiped a trickle of sweat from his face.

"I'm putting out a general alarm. We've got an alert condition all along the northern perimeter and that's with burns that are only about three hours old. We're told CDF and the Federals have already committed everything they've got—and our people are running close to sixty percent of all hands as of *now*."

"Jack," Caldwell cut in, "I don't need those figures. I've only been out forty-five minutes."

Now a subtly shrill note came into Keelan's voice. Caldwell recognized the knife edge of hysteria. "Ed, I'm talking about what's developed since then! This thing is *moving!* If we get much leapfrogging or a big new burn anywhere, we are going to be seriously in the soup on manpower and rig. Ed, there is talk down here we got a bug out there, a real nasty one. He hits us a little more, Pappy, we've got nothing much to *draw* on. We're on the horn to military now. We need all the backstop we can get alerted right now—!"

"All right," Caldwell said. "I'll talk to the prison people. We'll get a few hundred trusties. That'll take time, though. Call the reservations. Get all the able-bodied Navajos and Zuñis and Hopis that want to sign up. They're the best in the business."

"And, Chief…"

"Do it, Jack."

"We need you back here, Chief. We got to get in line down here and start marching."

"I'm on my way, Jack. Just do it and hang in there."

Caldwell held the dead microphone a moment. He gazed down at the holocaust below and he thought, *Oh, yeah—this is the one.* He turned to the pilot.

"Let's take a spin over to Simi." About to fuse, Jack had said. "I want to have a look."

5

VV CAMERON screeched her Karmann-Ghia to a stop in the KLIC-TV parking lot. One wheel and fender were slightly over the diagonal lines of her reserved space, and she didn't give a damn. She sniffed, glanced up at the grimy overcast sky. There was something in the air. It was not smog and it was not her imagination.

Anger thudded in her blood as she strode into the building, nodded a curt hello to the guard, and went directly to Studio 3. She tossed her purse onto the desk with the nameplate VV Cameron. The *Newsbreak* set with its flimsy picture window and panorama of L.A. vibrated as though a wrecker's ball had struck it.

The two cameramen were lining up their shot. VV exchanged hellos. She saw her producer through the control room window. He looked hung over. She waved.

"G'morning, love." Alan Martin, VV's assistant, planted a kiss on her cheek. He looked disgustingly healthy and as usual sounded disgustingly cheerful.

"How does the fire look? Think L.A. will pull through?"

"I wouldn't bet money on it," VV said. "Not with that gang of politicians manning the fire trucks."

"Temper, temper. What happened, they wouldn't let you wear a fire helmet? Wouldn't give you your own personal tour of the hot spots?"

VV had worked with Alan for three years. He was gay and a bitch but they were friends and once or twice

81

they'd even listened to each other's troubles. She let it pass.

"Tell me, Alan, could you see the sun rise this morning?"

"No—but that wasn't the sun's fault. I had a busy night and wasn't exactly up with the birds."

"There *was* no sunrise this morning. It was blacked out by flying soot from God knows how many acres of incinerated trees. And they're calling it a brush fire."

"Maybe it *is* a brush fire, love. And maybe all that black up there was just your ordinary par-for-the-season soot."

VV jerked her head angrily. "There are cinders as big as my thumbnail floating over North Hollywood. The air smells like a barbecue pit. They've closed off twenty-one miles of throughway. That is not a brush fire, my friend. That is the Santa Monica Mountains going sky-high. And that valiant fire department of ours is saying there's absolutely no danger."

"Fire *is* their business, love."

"And exposing liars is mine. Did you get the stuff?" She'd phoned from the fire department, asking Alan to hop it to the *Los Angeles Times* morgue and unearth every inch of newsprint they had on the Laurel Canyon disaster—and on Chief Edward K. Caldwell's role in it.

"Sure I got the stuff." From a brown paper bag Alan produced two slightly dented Styrofoam cups and an unpromising lump of something wrapped in waxed paper. He thumped them down by VV's nameplate. An earthquake seemed to rock the picture window. "Tell me, love. How come you diet on the coffee and binge on the Danish?"

"The stuff, Alan. *Did you get it?*"

"Oh—you mean *that stuff.*" Alan drew a long, bulging business envelope from the pocket of his denim work shirt. He handed it to VV. She shook it empty over the desk. News clippings fluttered down to the Formica.

"Do me a favor," he said; "keep your prune Danish off the clippings. There was a waiting line at the Xerox so I borrowed the originals."

"You stole these?"

"You said it was urgent."

"Alan, they could revoke our privileges."

"Then you'll do a VV Cameron special on the *L.A. Times,* right? In the meantime, there are your basic facts."

VV unfolded a clipping.

Los Angeles (AP)—Scorching wind-lashed flames took the lives of at least 18 and consumed 23 lavish hillside homes in Laurel Canyon before finally being brought under control by 360 fire fighters. Entire blocks of the luxury enclave were reduced to smoldering rubble, with only brick chimneys and gutted automobiles left standing. Police's evacuation plans were foiled by a sudden shift in the wind which according to Fire Chief Edward K. Caldwell "turned a bush fire into a holocaust. You've never seen fire move down a canyon so fast."

VV scanned the column of yellowed print; her eye tallied the inventory of death and damage, pedigreed pets and Picassos lost to the inferno.

"Who was that rock star, she was just making it big, she refused to leave her home?"

"And went up in flames and won her first gold record posthumously. Cindy Jenkins—how quickly the world forgets." Alan unfolded the Cindy Jenkins clipping.

VV skimmed. It seemed a promising angle: star snuffed out by blaze—and by Los Angeles Fire Department's incompetence. "Do we have any footage on her? A concert or the Grammys?"

"You are unscrupulous, love," Alan said. "She was an addict. It was *not* the fault of the Los Angeles Fire Department."

"Just a shot of her. Maybe the Chandler Pavillion concert. It would give a little depth."

"If it's depth you're looking for..." Alan snapped open a third clipping, like a waiter in a three-star restaurant unfurling a diner's napkin.

VV glanced. It was a list: names in heavy black caps, capsule obits in tiny gray type.

"NG," she said. "These are nobodys."

Alan's finger swooped down to tap two of the names. "Joyce Caldwell—wife of our fire chief. And Michael Caldwell was their six-year-old son."

VV Cameron sucked in a deep breath. "I knew he was widowed, but..." Now she understood Caldwell's face, understood what it was in that face that had struck her. Beneath the politico's smile there was a man beaten and haunted; behind the lying facade there was the truth of pain endured.

All right, she told herself. *He's a suffering SOB like all the rest of us—he's still a lousy fire chief and it's time someone blew the whistle.*

"That doesn't make sense. The Caldwells couldn't have lived in Laurel Canyon. The homes start at three hundred thousand dollars."

"Maybe they were just visiting," Alan said. "Maybe Chief Eddy Caldwell bought a home with embezzled county funds. The bottom line is, he lost his family in *that* fire."

"And seventeen other innocent people lost their lives because of his bungling! I'm not wasting any sympathy on Chief Eddy Caldwell."

"Good for you, VV. Hang tough. If it's some real dirt you want, try this."

The dateline was seven weeks after Laurel Canyon. Edward K. Caldwell—no mention that he was fire chief—had been arrested for running a red light, sideswiping a child on a tricycle. Miraculously, no injuries. Blood analysis indicated that E. K. Caldwell had been drinking. Two weeks' suspended sentence.

"The papers didn't play it up," Alan said. "Seems they wanted to give Caldwell a break. You know how sentimental newspaper reporters are—not like us TV folk."

VV steeled herself against a rush of sympathy. "If he's incompetent, he's incompetent. If he's a lush, he's a lush. I don't care if his grandmother and his pet canary were barbecued in Laurel Canyon, the man stands or falls on his record—not on his political pull."

"In that case, why don't you look at his record?" Alan suggested.

The article had not been set up in print; it was typed,

double-spaced, with proofreader's corrections inked in. Eddy Caldwell had been born in Marshalltown, Iowa; he'd served in Vietnam, been decorated twice for heroism; graduated third in his class from Midwestern; was a linebacker in varsity football; joined the Evanston, Illinois, municipal fire force; served with heroism. ..

VV skimmed. It seemed that in his rapid ascent Eddy Caldwell had rescued everything from invalid grandmothers to Rembrandts from burning buildings. The man had guts; VV had to grant him that much.

"Where'd you get this?" she asked.

"It's his obituary. The *Times* keeps it updated—just in case he dies in the line of duty. Which, by the way, he might—this very day."

"Forty-thousand-dollar-a-year bureaucrats do not die in the line of duty. They send underlings to do it for them."

"You really want this man's blood, don't you?"

VV had to admit in a way Alan was right. She was gunning for Caldwell and she had no reason for it except her gut reporter's instinct.

"He's holding back," VV said. "If you want my opinion, he's an outright liar—and instead of protecting the city he's protecting his ass. And if I can't get the truth out of him—sure, I'll settle for blood. Blood sells as well as truth."

Something very much like concern flashed through Alan's face. "You're not making things easy for him, are you?"

"It's not my job to make things easy for anyone."

"Come on, VV. You're a reporter. Look at the facts. Life has crapped on him and he's at the breaking point."

VV didn't want to hear it. "That's his problem," she shot back. "Not L.A.'s."

The other ranger and the pilot had been instinctively considerate. They understood Steve and Carolyn Miller's silence and the terror that lay barely contained beneath it. They did not attempt conversation.

Carolyn Miller leaned sideways to stare anxiously down through the Plexiglas panel. The helicopter had reached the beginnings of the foothills now. The fire had not reached here, and the air was still almost clear. She could see the shadow of the helicopter two hundred feet below, slipping across wooded slopes and crests like a cloud in sped-up motion.

How peaceful the trees look, she thought, *how unaware.*

The craft began to climb. Its vibrations took on a more jarring rhythm and the safety belt dug into her side. The smoke began to wisp up more thickly.

She glanced down at her husband. He was sitting rigidly in the seat in front of her, his gaze fixed on the forest below. From time to time a toneless grunt escaped him. She sensed him probing, not just with his eyes but with the mysterious inner mechanism that some rangers seemed to have, a sixth sense that could read the meaning of leaf and shadow and movement.

Find her, Steve, she silently begged him. *Find Angie while there's still time.* Dimly, through the gathering smoke, she could make out the watchtower. Steve's old tower. It was listing crazily to one side like a smashed birthday cake candle. *That's where it happened,* she thought. *That's where I lost Angie. Me. My fault.*

She stared at the raging flames, flames that could melt metal. Dully, she thought how beautiful they were shimmering through the smoke like schools of goldfish in a night sea.

And then in her mind a picture flashed of a little girl lost in the inferno. Her fingernails dug into her palms. She bit back a scream. A pounding numbness filled her. *Me. My fault.*

She felt helpless, useless, unable to perform the slightest act that could affect the fate of her child.

The smoke was billowing up faster, black now as the heart of a thundercloud. Through the soles of her shoes she could feel the hot updrafts beating against the floor of the copter. The motor made a choking, wheezing sound. The pilot shifted gears. There was an instant of absolute silence and the plane began to drop sickeningly and Carolyn's stomach had the death-sensation of free fall.

Then, with a cough like a generator kicking over,

the motor came back to life and the copter jerked to a standstill. They shot upward, back to where the world was visible.

There were soot tracks on the Plexiglas now. Carolyn stared at them curiously. They reminded her of a child's finger drawings on a dirty window.

And then it hit her. "Oh, my God!"

Steve jerked around. "What is it, honey?"

"I gave her a tranquilizer!"

Steve's face wrinkled in bewilderment. "You *what?*"

"For the trip—to make her sleep."

Steve's gaze slashed at her for one disbelieving moment and then he looked away. He didn't say anything but she could feel his thoughts going on in the silence, grimmer and darker than any spoken word. Something wet began inching down her cheek.

She blotted it with her fist.

By the time Caldwell's helicopter got him there, Laurel and Stone had married, propagated, and launched a dynasty. Together they put out so much heat that a layer of rippling vapor pushed the smoke twenty feet above the fire itself.

Caldwell had the pilot take him around for the grand tour.

Everything was working for the fire: wind, terrain—and least predictable of all, the caprices of chance. To the south there were acres of spot fires, thrown off by the main fire but now separate and independent entities; to the west the fire stretched long fingers, extending its perimeter tenfold at a cost of less than one percent of its area. The fire was like a conquering army thinning out its troops to occupy maximum territory. But while that was risky policy for an army, it was sound strategy for fire. Troops needed support and material, fire needed none.

There was nothing to do, Caldwell realized, but to give the fire the land it wanted and even more land than that to throw up fortified flanks well ahead of the surging front. The amount of land that would have to be sacrificed would depend on how fast the fortifications could be set up. And to that end Caldwell barked orders into his microphone, dispatching troops and armament, laying down the battle lines, and always knowing, in the back of his mind, that it was still a gamble. The wind might shift, the fire lines might not be built in time, a single wind-borne spark could undo in one second what a thousand men had labored twelve hours to accomplish.

It was a gamble but it was Ed Caldwell's gamble.

And Ed Caldwell was going to win it.

The pilot glanced over at him. "Wish I knew what you thought was so funny, Chief."

"Funny?" Caldwell growled, still moving men and trucks and bulldozers in his mind. "Nothing's funny."

"You should see the grin on your face."

And Caldwell realized it was true, he could feel it in the set of his face muscles: he was smiling, happy to be back in his element, back in command, fighting the big battle and fighting to win, happy because the past was dead and all that counted was *now*—this moment, this fight, this fire.

This victory.

Carefully, by sheer force of will, he peeled the smile from his face. But the happiness was still in him, strong as a drug.

Till the radio call came in.

The pilot handed Caldwell the headset. It was Marty Siegel from headquarters. "How about getting your ass back here, man?"

"Sorry, Marty. Too much to take care of up here."

"Some big honchos want to talk to you."

"Put them on the line."

"It's not the kind of talk that can go out on the public airwaves."

"Who are these big honchos?" As Caldwell said the words he sensed Peters stiffen alertly in the seat beside him. And he sensed something else: whoever they were, Peters had set it up.

"His Honor, the mayor, and His Honor, the governor. They want to see you at twelve sharp here at headquarters. That's a big concession, Ed. They're coming to your turf."

"Damn it, Marty, I'm fighting a fire." Caldwell's eyes

flicked to Peters, his hair so expensively cut it looked like a woman's wig. *And I'm fighting my own assistant too.*

"If you don't get back here you're going to be fighting City Hall and Sacramento too."

Caldwell yanked the headset off and threw it down in disgust.

He gazed at Laurel and Stone and all their children. He gazed almost yearningly. *My fire. My chance. I'm the best damned fire fighter they've got and they want me to play politics.*

The pilot was eyeing him, waiting for the command to turn around.

"Shit!" Caldwell yelled. "Take her back!"

The girl and the dog huddled together in the cinders. For almost three minutes they had heard the deafening approach of the fire, but now they felt it.

The air turned from warm to hot to scalding. In ten seconds the temperature climbed to the boiling point of water. The underbrush surrounding their patch of graveyard reached ignition point. There was a sound like a whipcrack and a blinding white flame raced through the brush. Behind it the branches glowed like electrified Christmas trees.

Then, seeking a higher target, the white fire rushed toward a lone fir tree. There was an overpoweringly sweet scent of pine and a hiss like steam escaping a ship's boiler. For one instant the tree was outlined in flickering red and then, with a thundering roar, every inch of it burst into flame and sparks showered down from writhing branches.

The white fire swept on, leaving ragged skeletons of brush and tree, leaving the child and dog terrified but still alive. As the wave of fire receded, the streaming smoke above their heads thinned. The sky flickered darkly, eerily. Angie and the dog lay still, not daring to move, braced for the warning crackle of the next wave.

Instead a sudden splash of cool air rushed along the ground. The dog raised its head and sniffed alertly. Another pocket of cool, smokeless air swept past.

The dog got to its feet, gulping the clean air, searching out its source. The animal barked and tugged at Angie.

She pushed herself up weakly. She gasped for air. The smoke had so parched the membrane of her throat that the first deep breath felt as though her lungs were cracking.

The animal moved forward at first unsteadily, warily, then with growing confidence. It broke into a run.

Angie struggled to keep up, still clutching her radio, lurching and pitching through the charred dead underbrush. Smoke drifted in layers cutting off her vision. There was no sunlight, only a shimmering false night. She could not see where the dog was leading her. Panic clogged her throat.

She realized she had lost the animal. She called out. A bark answered her. It seemed far away. The air was so dense with drifting ash she couldn't see where the sound came from.

"Nipper!" she called. Her voice came out a croak. She lunged forward and suddenly she was in the clear. Ahead of her she saw a stream and rock outcroppings and on the far bank pine and brush untouched by fire.

The dog was splashing in the middle of the stream, barking to her. When she hesitated, the animal came bounding back, urging her forward. She stopped to take off her sneakers, then balancing shoes and radio, she followed the animal into the cool water.

The stream was shallow. It did not even come to her knees. She made a cup of her hands and bent to scoop water up into her mouth. The water was sweet and cool and she felt a sudden wave of sleepiness. She closed her eyes and imagined she was in the bathtub at home, sinking down into the water.

The dog barked sharply. She opened her eyes and, following its lead, stumbled up onto the bank. She searched the sky anxiously. Her heart sank. There was no sun, no blue, only a dome of flickering red sliding down into black.

The dog tugged at her skirt. It had found something. "What is it, Nipper? What's there?"

She followed the animal up into the rocks and

stopped. The dog had led her to the opening of a cave. It made a begging sound now, pawing the earth, bounding in a circle around her.

Angie peered into the dark tunnel. A coolness seemed to pour from inside, inviting her. She hesitated only one moment, then lowered her head and, one hand outstretched, crept forward. The dog ran ahead of her, barking.

It was a small cave and after twelve careful steps she came to a rock wall. Carefully, she set her radio down on the ground. Then she knelt and patted the dog. It licked her hand gratefully.

"Thank you, Nipper. You saved my life."

Then she began crying. She couldn't help it. And when there were no tears left she lay down on the earth. The soil was soft and warm and dry, like a bed sheet that had just come out of the drier.

She curled into a ball and tucked her hands between her thighs. She forgot fear, forgot fire, and slipped down into an all-enveloping drowsiness. She didn't have to run any farther. She could stay here forever. She was safe. She exhaled a long sigh and turned her face toward the wall of rock. She shut her eyes and slept.

For the next hour the dog stood guard over the child, watching the slow rise and fall of her little chest. From time to time the animal stalked to the mouth of the cave. It stuck its nose up in the air and sniffed, measuring smoke and heat and listening to hear if there was any change in the distant crackle of fire. It heard something else: the clattering of a motor, the swoosh of branches whipped in a funnel of wind.

The animal looked up into the gray smoky sky just as a helicopter dipped beneath the haze. The animal barked.

The helicopter did not reply.

The animal dashed into the cave. It pawed the child, it tugged and licked and growled and even pretended to bite, but the child would not stir.

Desperate, the animal bounded out into the brook and stood barking up at the gleaming metal thing in the sky.

* * *

"There!" Carolyn screamed. Her finger jabbed at the Plexiglas. "Down there! I saw something!"

She was certain of it. Through the smoke she had seen something white, something moving—something alive. *Dear God, let it be Angie!*

"Take her back, Harry," Steve told the pilot. "Let's go down for a look."

The copter banked and swung sharply around, then dropped through eddying smoke. Carolyn's eyes raked the swirling gray, searching for a second glimpse of that white thing. Gradually the gray resolved into masses of color, a black and a green divided by a zigzagging scar of dull brown.

Carolyn squinted. Where was it, where was the white thing? "I know I saw it."

"Take her down farther, Harry, can you?" Steve asked.

The copter dropped and hovered. Carolyn searched. The black was burned-out forest and the brown was the bed of what must once have been a stream and the green was a stand of pines that had somehow survived and—there it was, the white thing!

"There!" Carolyn banged her fist against the Plexiglas.

Steve raised his binoculars. After a moment he lowered them. "It's a dog, honey."

A sudden emptiness gripped Carolyn's stomach. She grabbed the binoculars.

"Just a little terrier," Steve said. "Somebody must have lost it."

"Poor mutt," the pilot muttered.

A little terrier like Nipper, Carolyn thought.

"It doesn't stand a chance." The pilot shook his head. "The fire's going to take those pines out like kindling."

"Steve," Carolyn blurted, "can't we—save it?"

Steve smiled sadly. "No way. It's only a dog, honey."

As long as it could see the helicopter, the dog dashed up and down the stony bank, barking furiously into the air. When the helicopter soared out of sight, the dog scampered to the top of the rock outcropping. It opened its mouth and stopped midbark. It sniffed. Its ears pricked.

From the far side of the stream came a groaning, screaming sound. A wind rushed along the forest floor, lashing a mass of superheated air before it.

The dog sensed the wind; even at this distance it felt a sudden parched dryness in its nose and eyes. It heard the faraway explosions of rocks cracking, of air pockets in trees heated to detonation.

Dimly, through thickening smoke, it could see the flickering approach of fire: not one fire but two, each racing the other. At ground level, flames tore through the underbrush. In the treetops, exactly mirroring the holocaust below, flames whipped through the leafy crowns.

The dog knew what the fire wanted, it wanted to cross the stream. It wanted to devour the still-green forest on this bank...and every other thing that lived or moved here.

The dog picked its way down the rocks. It ran barking into the cave. The child lay there, her face and arms covered in scratches and blood.

The dog nudged her with a paw, licked at her face, barked. The child did not stir. The dog bounded back to the mouth of the cave.

Stiffening into an attack position, it faced the approaching inferno.

6

VV CAMERON looked up at the studio clock. Three seconds to go. She darted a hand toward her hair, fluffing it out a bit on one side, then, restoring symmetry, on the other. She glanced at her notes, composed her face into a newscaster's mask: grim but friendly.

The red light flashed on camera one.

"Top of the morning to you, innocent bystanders! This is L.A.'s own VV Cameron with the first of today's editions of *Newsbreak,* KLIC's thoroughly independent round-the-clock coverage of and comment on what's local enough to worry yourself sick over. Did I say this morning's news is hot? Listen, Los Angeles—how does forest fire grab you?"

She aimed a nod at the control booth, signaling the engineer to roll the archive footage. The film unreeled on the monitor, highlights of the last big Bel Air fire, with teasing glimpses of Lancaster, Taylor, and Novak look-alikes, uncorseted and un-made-up, running for dear life.

VV supplied the voice-over.

"While you slumbered, Los Angeles, your backyard was going up in cinders. Yes, it's happening right up there in the Santa Monica Mountains, *and* the Santa Susanas, *and* the San Gabriels. Film notables are this very minute running for their lives and leaving their million-dollar bungalows behind for the insurance companies to fret about."

The red light flashed on camera two and VV subtly reoriented herself.

"But it's not those pampered prima donnas and Donalds of Tinselwood that are the stars in my book. It's you, the card-carrying Californians that care about this city—because you're the ones that have got to live here and make this city work. You and me, Los Angeles, we're not hopping a Concorde to Rome or Acapulco when the whole kit and caboodle burns down. We're stuck with L.A., holocaust or not, it's ours! So here are a few questions I want you to consider:

"Is there any city in the world that has battled as many blazes as many times as we have? The answer is no, my friends, and you know it. Yet what are we doing about it? Are we protecting the lives of our families and loved ones? Are we building more fire stations? Are we putting in hydrants where there are none for blocks and blocks and blocks? We are not, my friends. And why?

"Because your elected political leaders have the idea that fire stations and fire hydrants are unsightly! Oh, no, innocent bystanders, your political leaders don't want those unsightly fire stations and fireplugs that could save the lives of your children! And here's one more fact: cities all over the world, cities everywhere in these United States, have passed laws against roofs made out of flammable material—but have we, my friends? *We have not.* In sixty seconds I'll be making a phone call you won't want to miss—after these happy-making words from William Bill's Town and Country Chevrolet!"

VV waited a count of two, glanced up, and saw she was off the monitor. She hit the talk-back button on her mike.

"Alan?"

"Yes, love?" The voice came back over the studio speaker.

"When I signal, roll the stills. Just the three on top. Any problem?"

"No problem—all set to go."

VV gulped a mouthful of prune Danish, washed it

down with two swallows of tepid coffee, then slid her breakfast out of camera range.

Alan signaled three seconds.

VV checked the fluff of her hair. Camera one blinked red.

"Hello, Los Angeles, VV Cameron here. I'm dialing the headquarters of the Los Angeles Fire Department right now, and in just a few minutes I'll have Chief Edward K. Caldwell on the air."

VV lifted the receiver of her desk phone and dialed. There were two buzzes before a man answered.

"Good morning, this is *Newsbreak,* with VV Cameron, you're on the air on KLIC, and who is this I'm speaking to please?"

"Lieutenant Hannah."

Lieutenants on the switchboard? She wondered how much he drew in pay.

"May we speak to Chief Caldwell, please?"

"He's unavailable right now."

"All right, Lieutenant, we'll speak to someone else who's in charge and who *is* available."

There was another buzz and then a smooth masculine voice saying, "Captain Keelan."

"Hello, Captain? This is VV Cameron, with KLIC's *Newsbreak,* and you're on the air. Tell us, Captain, is there an arsonist out there? And if so, can you tell us what effort is being made to apprehend this madman or madwoman? You're on the air, Captain."

"We have no reason to believe these fires are manmade."

"All right, Captain, we won't pursue *that* particular question. Here's my next: Is your department equipped to fight the terror that has already swept through the hills north of the city?"

VV signaled to the control booth. The monitor flashed a still of a Chicano baby burned to death in its crib. "Isn't it true that we're dangerously short of manpower and equipment to meet the holocaust that threatens to engulf us?"

"Equipment and manpower are adequate to the situation."

"And just what is that situation, Captain?"

The monitor flashed a shot of three women in night-gowns jumping from the window of a burning tenement.

"The situation is a seasonal brush fire. We're containing it and with luck we'll have it under control by sundown."

The monitor flashed a night shot of the Watts riot, entire city blocks going up in flame.

"And yet you *are* evacuating the posh communities of Bel Air and Beverly Hills, are you not? Can you tell us which celebrities chose to stay by their homes and fight it out with the flames racing at them?"

"At this moment I have no such information."

"Thank you, Captain. Thank you for your cooperation. And for your zeal in informing the public."

VV disconnected. She pushed the button that was flashing on the call box.

"Hello, there, you're on *Newsbreak* live. Go ahead, please."

There was a one-second delay on incoming calls. It gave the producer time to break the connection in case a caller turned obscene. It was also a damned nuisance because it confused the callers.

"You mentioned those fire hydrants?" This one sounded like a lulu: a drawling, creaking Southern belle transplanted from 1863.

"Well in my neighborhood the little Mexican boys open the fire hydrants and play in the water, and if you build more fire hydrants you're just going to encourage that kind of abuse."

"Thank you for expressing your opinion," VV said coolly.

She hit the disconnect button. Another light was flashing on the call box. "Hello, there, you're on *Newsbreak* live."

There was static on the voice box but no voice. She slapped a smile over her impatience and spoke louder, as though to a very stupid child. "Can you hear me?"

"Yes, hello. I worked in tactical fire strategy during the war and I'm really concerned, you know what I mean?"

It was not so much a voice as the shadow of a voice,

97

a hissing, expressionless whisper. VV poised a hand over the disconnect button. *Weirdo,* she thought.

"I think they're making a real error in judgment, you know what I mean? I worked in tactical fire control and I know a flash-point situation when I see one."

"Excuse me, sir—" VV sat forward in her chair, every nerve suddenly alert. "You are a fire-fighting professional and you say L.A. is facing a flash-point situation?"

"You have to remember, the Los Angeles region has the fastest-burning ground cover in this part of the hemisphere. What with wind and drought, like we got now, fire could go through that grass and brush at sixty an hour easy. See, when it comes to fire, it's the speed that counts, you know what I mean? The faster the fuel burns the hotter it gets and more people are killed by heat than by fire itself. The heat scalds your lungs, know what I mean?"

"And it is your professional opinion that L.A. is about to get its lungs scalded?"

"Unless they evacuate Bel Air and North Hollywood. You got eight fires in one hour, and half of the Santa Monica Mountains are going up, but the fire department calls it a routine brush fire. They got to be kidding, you know what I mean? You don't get that many fires spaced like that; I mean look at the map and tell me that's routine. Those fires are spaced. I mean those fires are tactical, the timing, the spacing, that's not routine, that's tactical."

VV tried to keep the excitement from showing in her voice. The man was giving her pay dirt: facts, hard-core figures. This could be a hot one, she told herself, an insider. He could even be a defector from the L.A. Fire Department, fed up with their lying handouts. *Easy does it, VV, you've hooked him, reel him in slow.*

"Now let me put this in layman's terms. You're saying that, in your opinion, your professional opinion, these fires are being set by an arsonist?"

Throughout the call there had been something wrong with the connection, a sort of static that kept crowding the voice signal. Now the noise surged up and practically drowned the man out.

"They couldn't happen any other way, you know what I mean?"

Hell, VV thought, *I knew phone service had gone downhill, but this call is coming in like a relay off a dead satellite.* She had to shout over the interference. "And I take it you work with our own Los Angeles Fire Department?"

Suddenly the static was gone. She heard silence and then the man's labored breathing before he answered. "Well, I'd rather not say, because they're handing out one story and I'm saying something else, you know what I mean?"

"Yes, Mr. Concerned Citizen, I know exactly what you mean! Did you hear that, Los Angeles? This man, who is a professional fire fighter, says that the L.A. Fire Department is full of bull guano and we are eyeball to eyeball with holocaust!"

From the corner of her eye she caught a motion in the control booth. On the other side of the glass wall Alan was signaling her to wind up. She glanced at the studio clock and saw she was running slow.

"Sir, you will be watching this situation as it develops?"

"Sure. That's what I'm here for, you know what I mean?"

"Then will you please, for the love of God and your fellowman, keep phoning in and share with Los Angeles your analysis of events? Because frankly you make a hell of a lot more sense than those so-called experts cluttering up the city payroll."

"Sure, I'll stay in touch."

VV disconnected. She faced camera two for her sign-off, her expression a womanly frown of compassion. "That's it for now. This is KLIC's VV Cameron, saying, Be vigilant, my friends, because if you don't watch yours, it'll be theirs next time you look!"

From the booth, Alan gave her a World War II V-for-victory sign. The monitor blanked off and VV dove for her coffee.

As the technicians filed out of the studio, VV found herself alone with Alan. She placed a cajoling hand on his arm. "Alan, I know it's your coffee break, but could you play back just a teensy bit of that phone tape for me?"

"You want to hear the drivel again?" His eyebrows arched. "Why, scared some naughty words got on the air?"

"There's something I want to check. Please, Alan."

"Okay," he sighed, "let me find it."

VV followed Alan into the control room. He searched through a stack of canisters, located one marked *Kooks—Incoming,* and lifted out an eight-inch reel of magnetic tape. He glanced up at VV curiously.

"Is it your period or have you been giving blood to burn victims?"

"How sweet of you to care, Alan—please just play the tape."

"You're white, baby. You could stand in for the sheet in a bleach commercial."

"It's been a busy day. And unlike some of my co-workers, I didn't have time to sunbathe—or put on makeup."

"You're a bigot, VV. I may have a wild life-style but I never touch makeup."

"Then I'd like to know where you got those eye-lashes." She'd spent many a commercial break envying them: they were long, black, and they curled.

"Genetics, love."

"It's not fair."

"All's fair. Here, you need a pick-me-up." He removed the pendant and gold chain from around his neck. The top of the pendant unscrewed, became an inch-long hollow tube. It ended in a bulb designed to fit snugly into the nostril. The bottom half of the pendant held what looked like a generous pinch of powdered sugar. "On the house, sweetheart. Put a little pizzazz back into those cheeks."

VV knew her assistant and she knew it wasn't powdered sugar. She rejected the offer with a quick shake of the head. "Honestly, Alan—I don't touch that stuff. Not at work."

"Why not? The boss lives on it." Alan placed the

inhalator tube in his nostril and took three snorts of the white powder.

VV grimaced her disapproval. "How can you afford it? You earn less than I do."

"Priorities, love." He reassembled his pendant and slipped the chain back around his neck. "Without a little chemical reinforcement I'd go bats in this madhouse."

"No wonder you wear denim. Your clothing budget goes to coke."

"I wear denim because it's sexy. You should try it sometime, VV."

"I'm sexy enough, thanks."

"You can never be sexy enough. Why with the right jeans you might get whistled at—you might even get laid."

Cheeky bastard, she thought, *cheeky and accurate.* She tried to keep her tone to a light bitchy banter. "I have more important things to do—like listening to that tape, if you're straight enough to put it on the machine."

"At least that straight, love. Any particular segment?"

"That man who said he was a tactical fire strategist. The last one."

Alan nodded. "Dr. Strangelove—coming up." He threaded the tape around the soundhead, adjusted dials, clicked switches. A screaming like a panicked chipmunk shrilled from the speaker. He slowed the tape, landed partway into the last call, backed up, caught VV saying, "Hello, you're on *Newsbreak.*"

"Yes, hello," came the oddly toneless reply.

VV listened closely. When the rattling sound came she still couldn't identify it. "Alan, could you go back just a bit?"

Alan pushed the reverse button. There was another spatter of chipmunk panic, then the toneless voice. And then the rattling again.

"Stop the tape," VV said. "Right there. What's that noise? Static?"

Alan ran the tape back and forth over the spot. He dropped to a lower speed and the rattling became thunder. "If it's static we should be able to filter it out—or down." He adjusted switches, reran the segment, tried another switch setting, and another. He shook his head. "'T aint static. Whatever it is, it's live sound. Coming from his end of the line."

VV frowned. "It sounds like he's crunching old newspapers into the phone."

"Maybe that's how tactical fire strategists get their kicks," Alan said.

VV weighed alternatives in the calculating balance of her mind. It took her exactly three seconds to come to a decision. "Alan, can you make me a copy of that phone call?"

"I won't be able to take the noise out without losing the voice."

"Just copy it as is—on a cassette tape. I want to play it to somebody."

Alan shrugged that shrug that said, *See how you exploit me?* "Can do."

The helicopter touched down at one minute after noon on the roof of the Los Angeles Fire Department. Marty Siegel was waiting, hair flapping in the propeller wind, as Caldwell and Peters lowered their heads and ducked out of the cabin.

"Escort service?" Caldwell grinned.

"Come with the salary." Siegel grinned back.

"You mean I'm two minutes late and His Honor's pissing in his pants?"

His Honor wasn't the only one. Peters had vanished into the building, not even waiting for them. In the elevator, alone with Caldwell, Siegel asked about a smudge on his forehead.

"Must have banged my head. You get some pretty rough air currents over those updrifts."

"It's not a bruise, it's a smudge," Siegel said.

"So? I caught a flying cinder."

Siegel took him by the elbow and steered him into the men's room.

"Hey, what is this?" Caldwell protested. "Who said I had to pee?"

Siegel pushed him to the sink, dipped the tip of a

hankie in running water, and worked over the smudge like a makeup man getting Johnny Carson ready to go on-camera.

"We want you to look good, Eddy."

"For who?"

"The press. They're waiting. You're going to pacify them."

"The hell I am—what am I going to tell them they don't know already?"

"Mayor's orders, Eddy. Tell them the good news—only the good news. Keep it short, keep it bright."

Siegel steered Caldwell down the hall into a conference room. The table had been pushed to the wall and extra chairs had been brought in. The room was packed with three times the people it could comfortably hold, all chattering, all turning to stare at Caldwell, and half of them seemed to be standing in aisles or sitting on the floor.

Caldwell threaded his way through the tangle. A speaker's lectern had been set up in the front of the room and Siegel snapped his fingers in the mike to make sure it was alive. There was an eardrum-shattering click and the room lapsed into silence. It was a hungry silence, and Caldwell didn't like it. Someone coughed in the rear.

"Ladies and gentlemen," Siegel reminded the gathering, "Chief Caldwell will take questions, but this is background, not for attribution." As Caldwell stepped to the mike, Siegel nudged him in the ribs, pointing to a work-shirted youngster who'd leaped up in the second row. "Him first," Siegel whispered. "He's friendly."

Caldwell nodded, and the kid identified himself as McLaren of the *L.A. Times.* "How are we doing out there, Chief?"

"Fine, just fine," Caldwell said sourly, wondering why he had to waste precious time being a ventriloquist's dummy. He pointed to a woman on the other side of the room.

"Patterson, *New York Times.*"

Shit, Caldwell thought, *we've gone national.*

"How is this fire going to affect the smog situation and do you have any plans to enforce car pooling?"

"It'll make the smog worse and car pooling is not this department's business." Siegel shot him a glance and Caldwell tried to rein in on the bad temper.

The *Oakland Tribune* wanted to know if there was any suspicion of arson.

"At this point, none whatsoever." Caldwell smiled.

The *San Jose Mercury* asked about campers in the state forests.

"Campers have been evacuated from the danger zone," Caldwell said, careful to keep that *zone* singular.

It seemed he stood there a good half hour taking flack from disaster-starved muckrakers, but his watch told him it had only been seven minutes. It struck him as curious that questions from the local papers were matter-of-fact, almost friendly, while questions from out of state were more probing, more suspicious, like a lawyer's cross-examination at a trial. Caldwell wondered what the hell kind of exaggerations had gone out on the wire services.

A hand went up in the third row. With a nod, Caldwell recognized a man in a dark three-piece suit, and the man stood. He had a pencil-line mustache and the bearing of an affluent undertaker. There was a hint of French accent in his voice, like a dash of liqueur on a serving of crepes suzette.

"Pierre LaChaise, *Le Monde,* Paris." The room fell silent. Caldwell glanced at Marty Siegel and he could see the same thought flashing through both their heads at the same instant: There was no way Monsieur LaChaise could have jetted over from Paris on three hours' notice, so he had to be a Los Angeles-based correspondent. But it was still unheard of for a foreign paper to cover a routine three-alarm brush fire in the L.A. hills. Obviously word had somehow leaked out that this could be the big one. And, in a case like this, a leaked word could be as ultimately destructive as a dropped match.

Caldwell put on his international-goodwill smile. "Yes, Mr. LaChaise?"

"You say these three unrelated blazes broke out at five thirty this morning?"

Caldwell did not like the Frenchman's emphasis on

that word *unrelated*. It seemed to him the mustache arched ironically, like a raised eyebrow.

"That is correct, Mr. LaChaise."

"And twenty-eight companies were dispatched within the hour?"

"Correct."

"Is the response not excessive?"

"This is the dry season, Mr. LaChaise."

"In other words you have reason to fear catastrophe?"

"In other words we're preventing catastrophe." The Frenchman smelled like trouble. Caldwell turned and quickly recognized a man waving his hand in the back row.

"Akiro Takamoto, *Tokyo Times*."

Caldwell glanced again at Siegel. He wondered how many other members of the international press were in that room. Taking a quick count of suit jackets and white shirts, he estimated a good dozen.

"Yes, sir," Caldwell said. Already he'd lost the Japanese's name.

"Your westernmost fire began just northeast of Oak Pass?"

"That's correct."

"And you have two companies holding a fire line farther west at Hidden Valley?"

"North of Hidden Valley," Caldwell corrected.

"But then your westernmost fire has spread?"

"Fire spreads, my friend. It's the nature of the beast."

Siegel shot a quick glance and Caldwell read the warning: *Don't get sarcastic with these sharks. Keep them friendly.*

"I understand that fire spreads," the Japanese said. "I do not understand that one fire spreads three times as far and as fast as the other two."

Caldwell drew a deep breath, wondering how the hell he was going to talk his way out of this one. "It's a question of terrain and duff. Other conditions being equal, fire moves more quickly uphill than downhill, given the tendency of heat to rise. The duff there happens to be especially flammable, due to the resin stored in the pine needles."

Siegel aimed Caldwell a look not so much admiring his erudition as his balls.

Caldwell quickly pointed to another waving hand. The man was six feet when he stood; every inch was clothed in tweed and he spoke with a clipped Oxford accent.

"John Sanders, *London Times*. What sort of pine?"

"Sir?" Caldwell said, not grasping the question.

"What is the especially flammable pine in that region which is tripling the spread of your fire?"

My fire, Caldwell noted; *they're sticking me with the blame already*.

"Second-growth ponderosa," he answered, grabbing the first thought that came to mind.

The Englishman made a careful notation on his pad and Caldwell knew he'd be in trouble on that one.

A woman raised her hand in the front row. Caldwell nodded.

"Sarah Jennings, *Sacramento Bee*." She lifted a tangle of blond hair out of her eyes. "Any danger of these fires spreading down to the populated areas?"

"There's always that danger, Miss Jennings."

"Will you order an evacuation alert?"

"If necessary, but so far we're on top of the problem."

A man in the fifth row identified himself as Harris of the *San Diego Union*. "If you're on top of the fires, why have you asked for state help?"

"When you're dealing with state parks and national forests, it's standard operating procedure for the state to be involved. It does not signal an emergency."

"Are you going to need federal help?"

"If federal land is involved we'll damned sure get it."

Caldwell pointed to a woman on the aisle. As she stood he realized it was VV Cameron with a pair of tinted designer glasses. "Chief Caldwell," she said, "what do you know of a man called Casimir Lovenko?"

"Not a damned thing."

She pushed the glasses up to nest in her hair and her gaze nailed his. "Then why is the mayor bringing him in over your head?"

Caldwell had dealt with hundreds of irresponsible journalists in his career. He'd dealt with some who'd been downright dishonest. The tactics of VV Cameron still took his breath away. His gaze nailed hers right back, hard.

"No one comes in over my head, Miss Cameron. I'm the chief and I'm in charge."

Marty Siegel cleared his throat and slipped a hand over the mike. "We'd better wind up, Ed," he whispered, pointing to his watch. "His Honor's waiting."

"Fine by me," Caldwell muttered. "I'm not loving this any more than you are."

Marty Siegel leaned into the mike and thanked the ladies and gentlemen of the press for their time and attention. He promised to keep them informed of all developments and estimated there'd be another briefing in three hours or so. The reporters began crowding toward the two rear doors.

Caldwell heaved himself to his feet and stood fuming at VV Cameron and her rumor slinging. He stood fuming a moment too long, because she pushed through the crowd and caught him by the arm.

"Let's have a private talk, Chief."

He was irritated, too tired not to show it, and he didn't have energy to waste on TV troublemakers.

"Lady, I've got lives to save." She wouldn't let him go. Her hand clamped down on his shirt cuff and for an instant, before he pulled angrily away, he was aware of her fingers grazing the skin of his wrist.

"Mister, maybe some of us know something you're not admitting—like there are eight fires this morning, not three."

Caldwell froze and he could feel Siegel freezing beside him.

"Miss Cameron," Siegel broke in, "Chief Caldwell has an appointment with the mayor. Now if there's anything I can—"

"You can watch my afternoon telecast." VV Cameron smiled. She slapped the Japanese tape recorder hanging by a strap from her shoulder. "Because I have evidence—right here on these two little spools. It'll blow this fire department and your press handouts sky-high. I wanted to give Chief Caldwell a chance to reply. After all, fair's fair. But if he's too busy—"

Eddy Caldwell stared at this red-haired woman with the flush rising in her narrow face and the manic sparkle in her green eyes, and he realized she wasn't bluffing: rightly or wrongly, she believed she had something on that tape.

"What kind of evidence?" Caldwell said evenly.

Marty Siegel pointed again to his watch. "Eddy, we're late."

"You go ahead," Caldwell said. "Give me three minutes."

VV Cameron unstrapped the tape recorder, set it on the desk, and pressed the start button.

The voice began. VV Cameron settled comfortably against the edge of the desk, watching Caldwell.

What chilled Caldwell most was not what the man said, the times, the locations, the facts, but the way he said it. The voice had no expression, no tone, none of the fallibility of a human voice. It was like something put together by a computer to announce the time of day over a telephone.

The tape wound on for one minute and fifty-four seconds and when VV Cameron reached to click off the recorder Caldwell said, "Give that to me."

VV Cameron stared at him. A smile seemed to flicker around her eyes. "Then it's true?"

"I didn't say it's true. I said give it to me." He lunged a hand for the recorder. VV Cameron whisked it aside and all he caught was the slender bone of her interposed hip.

"Not so fast, Chief. There is a little thing called the First Amendment."

"The First Amendment does not protect evidence of a crime."

"If there *has* been a crime and *this* is evidence then your three unrelated fires are bullshit, is that what you're saying, Chief?"

Eddy Caldwell swallowed. "Where did you get it?"

"One of my loyal fans phoned in. I have a lot of loyal fans, Chief. They would not take it kindly if you mauled me to get this cassette. So let's negotiate—like civilized enemies."

"What do you want for that tape?"

"I want the truth."

"I don't know the truth."

Her eyes took measure of him. "You do know how to count, Chief. He says eight, you say three. Who's nearer the mark?"

Eddy Caldwell hesitated. He knew there was no trusting this woman. She was a boob-tube gossip columnist. Disaster, distortion, and slander were her stock-in-trade and from what he'd heard her stock was rising fast. If he gave her even two percent of the truth she'd parlay it into a citywide panic by midafternoon. On the other hand, even though her "loyal fan" had his fire count wrong, there was too much accurate information on the tape—damn it, too much *inside* information—to dismiss. A torch was stalking L.A. and that tape was the only lead to have turned up so far.

Caldwell decided to risk it. He decided to throw her a grain of truth. "Your friend is a bit nearer the mark than we are."

VV Cameron drew herself up, her eyes flashing vindication. "In other words the Los Angeles Fire Department has put a lid on this story?"

"Those are your words, lady, not mine."

"You're deceiving and endangering the public and you're doing it premeditatedly and cold-bloodedly to save your bureaucratic skins."

"I said I'd negotiate, Miss Cameron. I'm not interested in trading insults."

Her eyes narrowed. "What are you offering for the tape?"

"The truth—when I have it."

"That's not good enough, Chief. I need something for my afternoon show. I need to know what you've got so far."

"So far we have a fire that we're holding and a bug we haven't got a clue on. And that's off the record or I'll personally wring your neck."

"You've downgraded the danger and you've said the fires were natural. I find that despicable."

"And I find arson despicable," he shot back.

Something happened in her face. He couldn't quite

read it. Something shadowy and soft flicked across her features.

"Miss Cameron, war's news, but you don't ask the general to publish his strategy, do you? Well, a fire is a war too."

"Go on," she said.

Her eyes were boring into him with an odd sort of coldness.

"We can win, provided we accomplish three things: We have to contain the fires. We have to stop the bug. And we have to prevent panic. If we fall down on any one of those, at the very least the cost of victory's going to skyrocket—and at worst we might just manage to lose the war. Now so far—God and weather willing—we're ahead of the fires. We haven't got a lead to the bug, but that tape could be the breakthrough. And, with your cooperation, we might be able to stave off panic just long enough to get the job done. It's up to you."

"That's nifty blame-shifting, Chief, but I'm not the firebug."

"Until you give me that tape you're helping *him,* Miss Cameron—not us."

A flush rose in her cheeks. He could sense the calculator inside her ticking off pros and cons down to the tenth decimal place.

"And you have my word of honor, Miss Cameron—when *I* have the facts, *all* the facts—you'll be the first to get them. And you'll get them from me. Personally."

An eyebrow arched. "A private press conference, Chief? Just you and me?"

"Any way you like it. Just *give me that tape.*"

"Chief, I hope I'm wrong. In my experience ninety-nine percent of all government employees are liars who'll do anything to save their ass. But maybe you're the other one percent."

She stared at him but this time there was no defiance, only a disturbing sort of curiosity, as though his face were written in code and she was beginning to decipher it. He wondered what he read there: thirty-one-year age crinkles, lack-of-sleep lines, booze pouches, the fact that he hadn't shaved for thirty-six hours?

"No reporter in her right mind would do this," she said. "But I trust you, Chief. I maybe even like you. You pay your dues."

She handed him the tape machine.

"See you, Chief."

She was halfway to the door when Caldwell thought to call out, "Miss Cameron—whether it's a bug or not—that's off the record."

She turned. "Chief, I said I trust you. That's a two-way street, okay?" She seemed to remember something else. "Oh, and by the way—my source is confidential—but they *are* bringing in a man called Lovenko. He'll be at your meeting and he's a real heavyweight. Good luck."

Marty Siegel intercepted Caldwell in the hallway. "Got a second, Ed? There's someone I want you to meet."

Before Caldwell could protest that they were very late now, Marty Siegel steered him into the snack bar. At a glance Caldwell's eye took in the food and drink machines and the lone occupant of the room, a man at the corner table hunched over a plastic cup of doubtless plastic coffee. Marty Siegel bustled Caldwell over and the man glanced up at them. He had shaggy uncut hair and a shaggy uncut beard and there was a sleepy sort of alertness to his eyes.

Caldwell wondered what the hell was so important about this superannuated hippie. He also wondered why the hell Marty was suddenly acting like the social director on a Caribbean vacation cruise. He got his answer.

"Eddy—meet Casimir Lovenko. Cas, meet our chief—Eddy Caldwell."

The man pushed up clumsily to his feet and held out a monster of a hand. He was a huge man, craggy and slouchy and built like a bear. He dressed like a bear too, a bear that had raided a tourist cabin in Yosemite Park: jeans, sneakers, sweat socks, no tie, blue work shirt scrambled at the collar with one corner sticking up as if starched the wrong way.

His handshake and his voice were oddly gentle. "I've

111

heard a lot about you, Chief Caldwell. It's a pleasure to meet you."

Eddy Caldwell knew then and there: this man was the enemy. "I've heard a little about you," Caldwell said coolly, staring hard at him. *Think you're going to get my job, do you?*

The man's eyes did not flick away.

Marty Siegel cleared his throat. "Cas is with the University of Colorado School of Mines."

"That so," Caldwell said.

"Cas's field is fire," Marty went on. "He knows all there is to know and then some. He's done a lot for the federal government."

"I didn't know the Feds were in on our act this early," Caldwell said.

Still the man's eyes met his, cold and steady and unembarrassed.

"I'm observing," Lovenko said politely. "In a private capacity. There's nothing federal about it."

"If you're observing the fire, Mr. Lovenko, go out the front door, head north, and follow the smoke. You can't miss it. In the meantime, I'm late for a meeting. So please excuse me."

"Eddy," Marty Siegel said, "Cas is coming to the meeting too."

Caldwell's head jerked around. He didn't know what the hell was going on, but he was beginning to get the impression that Marty Siegel was playing both sides of the fence. He beckoned Marty to the door and lowered his voice.

"What's he doing here?"

"Like he said, Eddy, consulting."

"Consulting for who?"

Marty's eyes were all skitter and confusion. "The mayor, Eddy. The mayor wants him."

Caldwell glanced toward the man in the corner unconcernedly stirring his coffee. "Since when does the mayor need a consultant to do *my* job?"

"Take it easy, Eddy. It wasn't my idea."

Rage was pushing out of Eddy Caldwell so hard he could barely keep his voice under control. "Whose idea was it? Come on, Marty. Who contacted him, who did the big-sell job, who brought him in over my head, and who leaked it to the press?"

"Peters did it. He said you've been under a strain. You *have* been under a strain, Eddy."

"What else did Peters say?"

"You know how Peters makes a pitch."

"Tell me how."

"He said Lovenko's the best in the business."

"Better than me?"

Caldwell could see the swallow ride down Marty Siegel's throat.

"Better than me."

"The hell he is."

7

CALDWELL slammed into the conference room, pushing the door so hard the handle hit the plaster wall like a wrecking ball.

A surprised mayor of Los Angeles bounded up from his seat. "There you are, Caldwell. I see you've already met Cas."

Caldwell mumbled acknowledgment of this and the mayor introduced Lovenko to the others. They were sitting in chairs that had been arranged in a circle in the center of the room, and one by one they sprang to their feet to shake the stranger's hand. It was an all-male gathering. Keelan was there, and Peters, and the governor, and three of those pinstripe, button-down, fifty-thousand-a-year notetakers who seemed to follow like Bo-peep's sheep anywhere the governor went.

In a way that was almost fawning, the mayor itemized Lovenko's Ph.D.s in physics, meteorology, ballistics; Lovenko had stockpiled degrees in every discipline conceivably related to fire except—Caldwell noted sardonically—*cordon bleu* cooking.

Lovenko dropped comfortably into a chair and the mayor asked how his flight in had been.

"Excuse me, gentlemen," Caldwell said, "but what we've got outside isn't waiting for us." He ignored the mayor's glance and looked over at Lovenko.

"Now does Mr. Lovenko here know anything, or is he starting cold?"

Lovenko clasped his fingers behind his neck and slowly crossed his ankles. "I know what you've got in the way of fire, yes. Had a pretty good look on the way in. You started with six bachelors and now you've got three happy couples, right?"

"Right," the mayor said. His voice was oddly out of key with the situation, a voice making an impression at a social gathering, not a voice at a crisis conference. "And the couples are spawning pretty damned fast. We've got plenty of fire, all right." He made a nervous little laugh.

Lovenko hunched forward. "What's the position on manpower and material?"

It was Keelan who answered. "As of now, we've got everybody out—all hands and all rigs, including U.S. Forestry Service and California Division of Forestry. We started pulling out military and honor prisoners midmorning. There's anywhere from two to four hundred Indians due off the reservations this afternoon."

"How long can you hold your regulars on the line?" Lovenko asked.

"They'll stick," Caldwell said. "They're fighters."

Lovenko's eyes flicked a challenge up at him. "And they'll tire too." A silence went around the room, an admission that Lovenko was right. "What about chemical retardant?" he asked.

"At our current rate of consumption, two hours wipes out our supply," Keelan said.

Lovenko nodded, like a surgeon who had known the patient would be in no better shape than this. "Water and pressure?"

Keelan was about to answer, but Peters cut in. "A lot of homeowners have plugged into the hydrants to hose down their roofs. Pressure's way down in some sectors."

Maybe it was just a feeling, but Caldwell sensed Peters giving the situation a twist for the worse, playing up the panic angles for the benefit of Their Honors, the mayor and the governor.

"Weather?" Lovenko said.

"Couldn't be worse," Peters answered. "And more of the same is projected. Ground winds in the fire zones are gusting up to fifty, sixty knots. The Santa Ana's giving us a steady generally westerly action at about thirty-five knots."

Lovenko steepled his fingers together, face grim. "What's it costing so far?"

"In life?" Peters shrugged. *Nice shrug*, Caldwell thought: *hinted at all sorts of unspoken disaster*. "So far not much—one volunteer dead of burns, about thirty civilian casualties, mostly campers. Add about an equal number of our people down. Property? That's another story."

"Evacuation plans?" Lovenko asked.

"We're clearing people out well ahead of time," the mayor said with that same goofy cocktail-party brightness in his voice. "There's no serious push on that score yet—and it's a police problem, not yours."

"It could be everybody's problem by nightfall," Caldwell cut in.

"Night's when we'll get ahead of the fire, though," Lovenko said. "Let's all bear that principle in mind and communicate it to the troops. If she wants to lie down at night, that's when we're going to scoot in front of her. I want your men to get the message. Night's the time to fight hardest. I don't want them thinking just because the fire's lying down it's okay for them to lie down too."

"A Santa Ana doesn't always ease off at night," Caldwell said.

Lovenko glanced across at him shrewdly. "But fire sometimes does. There's no explanation for it, but she does. I've seen fire stop halfway across a field an hour after sundown. Abundant fuel in front, stout wind to her back, not a reason in the world to quit, but she *does*. Go figure it."

"She's a bitch, that's all," Keelan muttered.

Lovenko nodded in agreement. "They don't come any more capricious than fire. You've got a block of houses, but does the bitch run right through them like science says she should? No, not this lady. She selects. She takes this house here, that house there—skips the house in between."

Jesus, Caldwell thought, *he's talking like a god-*

damned theater critic admiring some star's performance!

"Now I want you to have your battalion chiefs begin convincing the men." Lovenko socked one hand into the other. "I want those men believing that when the sun turns off, it's going to cool those burns right down."

"I can't lie to seasoned fire fighters," Caldwell said quietly.

"You won't be lying," Lovenko shot back. "There's no lie in this. There's faith. For the time it takes to choke this thing, I want you to marshal the faith that we can do it!"

The mayor had been darting his eyes nervously between Lovenko and Caldwell, like a spectator who'd bet his life savings on a tennis finals match. "She'll burn out," he said hopefully. "I mean, don't they always in the end?"

"Positively," Lovenko said. Caldwell caught the irony but didn't think the mayor did. "When there's nothing left to burn. So let's concentrate on choking her." Again he socked one hand into the other, like a baseball catcher limbering up his glove. "Okay, I need a blueprint composite of the burns at discovery—and a composite of your most recent update."

Keelan handed Lovenko the large paper sheets and Lovenko spread them on the floor inside the circle of chairs. He peered from one to the other, nodding, and in a voice that seemed more thinking aloud than statement, he muttered, "It was the fuel all right. What he loses on account of the water, he makes up for in fuel and land configuration."

Lovenko leaned forward to turn the blueprints around so that Caldwell had compass-point South at the bottom of the frame. Lovenko pointed to the sheets.

"These are man-made."

So what the hell else is new? Caldwell thought angrily. *We're paying money for this genius?*

"Fucking *nut*-made," Keelan said.

The mayor was nodding wisely. The governor hadn't flicked a muscle.

Lovenko drew a finger along the composite of the early-morning scans. "The arsonist is not improvising, gentlemen. The design is right here—and it's evident. He would have done better to choose Tucson or Denver, but the fuel's better here."

"What's your point?" Caldwell demanded.

"Your man intends to create a line of fire running from *here*"—and with this Lovenko placed his finger on the coast north of Los Angeles, traced a curve that arched inland behind the city, and swooped back to the coast south of it—"to right down here. He's already raised fire on one-third of that line. And I might add that—for the purposes of his design—it's not at all necessary that he fill out the line."

Lovenko looked up from the sheets as though measuring the impact of his speech in the faces of his audience. Then turning to Peters, "How about offshore weather conditions—was there a cold front out there this morning?"

"There was." Peters nodded.

"And are they predicting a continuing offshore cold front?"

"They are."

It was running as smoothly as a rehearsed skit and His Honor, the mayor, was lapping it up and Ed Caldwell didn't see why he had to take another minute of it. "Would you mind getting to the point?" he cut in.

Lovenko threw him a look that was halfway between forgiving and pitying and Caldwell felt like slugging him on the spot. Lovenko sighed and got to his feet. His great height was now apparent to everyone in the room, and most of all to Ed Caldwell, himself a big man, a man very conscious of size and of the advantage it conferred.

"The point," Lovenko said, "is February 13, 1945. On that night fourteen hundred of our bombers unloaded six hundred fifty thousand incendiary bombs, hundreds of two-ton blockbusters, and scores of four-ton blockbusters on the once-glorious German city of Dresden."

Caldwell began squirming in his chair. There was a fire out there, real fire *now*, and the visiting expert expected them to sit still for prehistory.

"We did this in three stages over fifteen hours. We

achieved a smoke column that topped out at better than three miles, a flame display visible as far as two hundred miles away, and the deaths of over seventy thousand persons. By ringing the city in explosives, we created an ocean of fire—with ground winds of one hundred forty miles an hour."

Lovenko's long arms began moving, acting out the flames, as though he'd been there in person. *Goddamned performer*, Caldwell thought. *Wonder how many times he's done this number?*

"Now on that night in the city of Dresden, gentlemen, the air became flame. Literally. It was either exhausted by fire or vacuumed from ground level by a giant thermal rushing straight up. You've all seen this occur in a fireplace—we call it the Venturi effect—the flue drafts the fire. Now consider a leviathan fireplace. Because that's what the Los Angeles basin is. Now consider the draft. Skyward. All one has to do is house the effect. And that, gentlemen, your mountains and hills will do."

The mayor looked puzzled. "What about the ocean? There are no mountains and hills in the ocean to house anything."

Lovenko nodded, as though congratulating a sharp student on making a good point. "You're forgetting the cold front, Your Honor. That cold front, for all practical purposes, might just as well be a wall. It has the power to drive hot air up—exactly the same power as the mountains. And between that cold front and those mountains you have a flue of truly gigantic suction. Look at Los Angeles, gentlemen. Add it up. That fire—plus that gigantic flue—equals *fire storm*."

The word went off like a gunshot, creating a stunned silence.

Caldwell jumped to his feet in fury. "Fire storm's a bunch of bullshit. There's talk about them, but who can prove there ever was one?"

"Granted," Lovenko conceded, "at Hamburg and Dresden we had no measuring instruments. And certainly no informants to furnish us with objective accounts. The point is, we tried to create a fire storm. And I believe this is precisely what your man is trying

119

to do in L.A. And he has a decidedly better chance of bringing off a fire storm in this setting than the Allies had in Hamburg or Dresden."

"This is horseshit," Caldwell said. "I have fire out there. That's what I'm paid to fight—and not any goddamn theoretical theory!"

"But if you accept my theory and I'm wrong," Lovenko said mildly, "you're out nothing. Whereas if you accept it and I'm *right,* you're prepared for a catastrophe that could level this city and incinerate its inhabitants. Because once that storm gets going, gentlemen, you have a hurricane. Try to imagine a *wind* going at hurricane speed—could you outrun it? Could you outrun *flame* blowing at that speed?"

Caldwell couldn't read the governor's face, but one glance at the mayor told him that His Honor was thoroughly enthralled by Lovenko's science-fiction word picture. Caldwell knew he had to knock Lovenko down but he decided to do it Lovenko's way, sly, not shouting.

"Now let's just follow this out a little more," Caldwell said. "Assuming the bug is aiming to do what you say, which direction would he try to run it from? What's his next move? Seems to me he could show up anywhere along here." With his foot Caldwell indicated the unburned arc of the hypothetical crescent. "And here." Lovenko leaned forward to run his finger up and down the Cleveland National Forest. "Now that's a sizesome piece of territory," Caldwell said. "Would he try to move the fire line on down from north to south—or would he come in with his next number somewhere down here?"

Every man in the room looked to Lovenko, awaiting the answer.

"What would *you* do?" Lovenko said.

Clever bastard, Caldwell thought, *he's parrying me.* "Well, going by your theory, I'd let the fire do as much of my work as it could. So if I started up here, the top third of the arc, I'd go for the bottom third next. That way there'd be two big fires sucking toward one another and with a little bit of luck they'd join up."

Lovenko nodded, neither agreeing nor disagreeing. "But of course," he said, "our man might in point of fact be *many* men. In that case they could complete the ring around the city without waiting for the fires to join."

"But if there *was* a gang," Caldwell countered, "wouldn't they get the whole ring going at once while they had this cold front that you say is so important? Otherwise they might lose the fourth wall on that flue."

Caldwell thought he'd trapped his adversary. But instead of agreeing or disagreeing, Lovenko went on smoothly. "In that case our job's even harder. It's much more difficult to hunt down one man and interdict him than to discover, say, some clutch of lunatic radicals bent on destroying the city. So if Chief Caldwell's right, we're searching for one man among millions."

Caldwell had to admire the dexterity of that one: *if Chief Caldwell's right.* All he'd done had been to point to a contradiction in Lovenko's theory and Lovenko had turned it around and tagged the whole thing Caldwell's theory.

Caldwell decided to bait a little trap of his own. "Dr. Lovenko, is there any particular reason you think the firebug's a man?"

Lovenko skipped just a beat, eyes measuring Caldwell, and then he smiled. "I'll have to admit to a little sexism here. I'm assuming it's a man and I have no evidence. Sorry about that." It was a nice mood-lightening admission, and the others chuckled tolerantly. "But the fact remains," Lovenko went on, "that finding one man *or* woman in a city of three million is close to an impossibility. If that man or woman wants to burn the town down there's no stopping him or her—right? So what do we do?"

No one spoke. Lovenko let the question fall into the silence and send out rhetorical ripples.

"I'll tell you what we do. We can't stop the arsonist, so we stop the plan. And here's how. The bug's trying to ring us. He's going for three arcs to make a ring, with the ocean giving him the cold front he needs to form the fourth arc and close the circle. Circle equals fire storm; that's his plan." Lovenko glanced up ironically at Caldwell. "Excuse me, Chief. *Her* plan."

The mayor smiled and Caldwell caught the smile. Lovenko went on.

"So we interdict the circle. No circle, no fire storm. Get it?"

The mayor nodded.

"Now we can't shove against the cold front. So we break the arcs and we shove against the breaks. In practical terms, that means we don't push against the movement east or west. We push north and south. You see what I'm saying?"

Caldwell saw and he didn't like it. He didn't like it one bit.

"We let the fires come in and go out. What we don't let them do is go up and down. This means sacrificing property. We give up the parts to save the whole."

"What you're saying," Caldwell said coldly, "is we give away suburbs to save the city?"

Lovenko nodded. "You're following me. We don't go up against the fire from street to street. We go up against the plan, against the configuration the torch is trying to establish. We're fighting his *strategy*. What we're *not* fighting is small battles from block to block. Now I realize this represents a radical shift from what your people are used to. It's not exactly traditional fire fighting."

"There's no goddamned tradition where fighting fire is concerned," Caldwell said. "There's only good sense and bad sense. This community expects good sense from me, which is why I'm wearing this uniform. My job is to protect life and property. Not to go around fighting *ideas*. And so far this idea of yours is nowhere except in your head."

"*His* head," Lovenko corrected, and then, grinning, corrected himself again. "Excuse me, Chief. His or *her* head."

"What makes you so goddamned sure?" Caldwell studied the man's face, expecting to find arrogance written there, but finding only the engrossed expression of a man absorbed in a problem, of intelligence stalking its quarry.

"I can't be one hundred percent sure," Lovenko said. "Nothing's one hundred percent sure in this universe."

"You're guessing," Caldwell said.

Lovenko's eyes met his in dead earnestness. "And guessing is what I'm good at. I miss, Caldwell, but not that often."

"I say you don't know any more about how to put this fire out than you know about how it started."

It was the mayor who spoke. "And you do, Mr. Caldwell?"

Caldwell whipped around to face him. "Damned right I do. We attack those fires head-on! To hell with north-south east-west—fire's fire!"

"And the firebug?" the mayor said, eyes meeting Caldwell's levelly. "You have a theory about him as well?"

"Or about *her*," Lovenko put in, and everyone but Caldwell chuckled.

"I have more than Mr. Lovenko does," Caldwell said. "I have the firebug's voice." There was a stir in the room and the mayor said, "Would you care to clarify that, Mr. Caldwell? You have the voice?"

Caldwell turned to Marty Siegel. "Marty, how much information did we give out on the fires?"

"Up till ten o'clock we held to the story that there were three unrelated burns."

"Three," Caldwell emphasized.

Siegel nodded. "One in the Santa Monicas, one in the Santa Susanas, one in the San Gabriels."

Caldwell faced the others. "I'm going to play you a tape. It's a recording of a call made to a local phone-in TV program at nine o'clock this morning."

Caldwell pressed the start button on VV Cameron's cassette machine. For one minute and fifty-four seconds the room listened in silence. Caldwell pressed the stop button. He let the impact sink in a moment before speaking.

"He has the locations. This department did not give out *that* information. He has the times. This department did not give out *that* information."

"But he has the wrong number of fires," the mayor objected. "He says eight, and there were only six."

"Seven," Caldwell corrected, "if you count the fire

last night—and we can't rule out that they might all have been connected."

"He's still inaccurate," the mayor said. "He says eight started at once—but only six started at once."

"And *that* information was not given out," Caldwell shot back.

"Then he works for the fire department," the mayor said. "Or he has a contact here."

"Wrong," Caldwell said. "If he worked here or had a contact here, his information would be seven fires—not eight."

"Then how do you explain the discrepancy?" Peters said. "There were seven fires in fact, but your so-called firebug says eight. He couldn't be the man."

Caldwell turned to face Peters. "On the contrary. His saying eight means he *is* the man, because the eighth fire exists only in the firebug's head."

"Would you mind going through that again?" the mayor said, frowning.

"Look!" Caldwell cried. "He's not giving us the facts, because he doesn't *know* the facts. We sat on the facts! All he knows is the plan, and *that's* what he's giving us, *his* plan! Eight fires were planned to go off this morning at dawn. That means eight timing mechanisms were used. Of those eight, one went off early—the fire last night—and one didn't go off at all. Which leaves six fires. Only he doesn't know that. All he knows is that we gave out three fires. We cut his eight little babies down to three and he's angry. He wants credit for those other five. So he goes public—on VV Cameron's phone-in show."

Lovenko had contributed nothing to the discussion of the tape but now he spoke up. "Funny way of talking—'know what I mean, know what I mean?' all the time—that phrase seems to be his trademark."

The mayor turned. "Do you agree with Chief Caldwell?" he asked. "Think he's our man?"

Lovenko nodded. "He's our man all right. Ninety percent probability. And he's a professional."

"Professional fire fighter?"

"Fire setter."

The mayor looked even more baffled than he had by Caldwell. "A mob torch?"

Lovenko shook his head. "The mob does not buy four-thousand-acre fires. Only one outfit does that: the military."

The mayor seemed incredulous. "A torch for the military?"

"They exist. We used them in Korea and Vietnam. Hell, we used them as far back as World War Two. We're not using them now, so he's gone free-lance. But it's a lead—and a damned good one."

"I don't want this getting out," the mayor said, wiping his forehead. "Not one word of it. We'd have panic if the public heard one whisper about military arsonists or fire storms. No one talks to the press except Marty Siegel, and all press releases go through my office."

"It doesn't take a fire storm or an arsonist to panic people," Caldwell said. "All it takes is what we've got up in those hills right now."

"We have to accentuate the positive," the mayor said. "That VV Cameron woman—she could be a useful link to the firebug. Let's use her."

Caldwell didn't agree. "Technically, Your Honor, VV Cameron's the enemy. She wants to get this story and spill it across the airwaves. She doesn't care if she panics the whole city so long as she has a scoop."

"Then feed her some tidbits—harmless inside stuff. Keep her talking to that so-called expert and put a trace on that line."

"It's not our phone—and the station will scream freedom of the press."

"Then get her permission."

"How?"

The mayor flicked a glance at him. "She's a woman, Caldwell. Use your charm."

"With all due respect, Your Honor, my job is to fight fire."

"With all due respect, Caldwell, your job is what my office says it is. I want the identity of that caller. And I want you to take Dr. Lovenko up in a helicopter and give him a good look at those fires."

* * *

The copter dipped toward the west ridge. Caldwell looked down again. The front was moving rapidly here. A surge of wind hurled the advancing edge of fire across a stand of giant cedars. One minute they were there and living and green. The next instant flames shot up and there was only ash and scorched trunks.

It took less than thirty seconds.

Caldwell brought his gaze back into the plane, back to the man beside him. He said nothing for a time. And then he said, "It's my fire. You understand, Lovenko? You stand behind me. Whisper in my ear. But it's got to be me that stands up next to the fire."

"Of course," Lovenko said expressionlessly, still staring down below.

"I'm good," Caldwell said. "I'm good at this business. I'm a fighter. All my life I've been a fighter."

"I'm trying to help you," Lovenko said. "That's all I'm trying to do."

"You're asking me to let things burn." Caldwell tried to keep his voice from rising, tried to rein in on the anger that was building inside him. "You're asking me to let people and homes go to hell. You're asking me to forget good sense and common decency—and you're not giving me anything better to go on than a guess. How the hell do I get away with calling the suburban population out of their homes so fire can have them free and clear?"

"Life's a risk, my friend," Lovenko said evenly. "You have to take gambles and you have to make judgments. You're supposed to make judgments—that's one of the reasons you're wearing that uniform. I'm giving you a chance to make a judgment while there's still time. Look, Caldwell, you can go stand up to those burns the routine way. Win or lose, there's no flies on you. Whatever happens, they can't stick it on you. *They* can't. But *I* can. Because I'll know. We'll both know: it was your responsibility and you flubbed."

"Listen, mister," Caldwell exploded, "don't you come in here and tell me what my responsibility is! Now maybe I never wrote any papers or played with matches in some laboratory—but I've been a fire fighter all my life! It's cost me, mister, it's cost me plenty—and I'm maybe a lot of things you'll never want to pin a medal on me for, but irresponsible is one thing I'm not! You hear me?"

Caldwell was shouting now. He heard himself shouting and he knew he should stop this, stop this right now before he said things that couldn't be taken back. For God's sake, the pilot was there in the front seat taking in every word!

But what stopped Caldwell, what cut his shout short was the absolute calm of Lovenko's reply.

"My friend, if that firebug closes his ring and this city blows away, in hell you're going to know that Cas Lovenko knows. In hell you're going to know that in another man's head there's a finger pointing at you."

And suddenly Caldwell heard his own voice, odd and tight and quiet. "I can do my own pointing in my own head, thanks."

Lovenko looked at him a long moment. "Caldwell, I'm sorry I said that. It wasn't necessary. It's only necessary to say your way won't work."

The first thing VV saw when she stepped into the studio parking lot was the white Bentley. The second was a tanned Adonis, striding toward her with arms spread.

"VV, baby!"

"Toby, love," she mumbled back through the embrace, then pushed him far enough away to get air.

"Haven't seen you in a long time," he said.

"That's true," she agreed. She fished in her purse for her car keys and wondered what the hell Toby Gladstone wanted this time.

"Been catching your shows, though."

"All of them, Toby?"

"A lot."

"You should phone in sometime."

A smile skittered across his face. "Yeah, well, sometime I will. Hey, look, there's no point standing here in the sun."

VV glanced up at the sky. A second veneer of soot seemed to have been pasted over the first. The sun was definitely...*dingy*. "What sun?"

"You know what I mean." Toby Gladstone touched her arm, touched it in such a way as to remind her that they had been to bed together four, count 'em, four times, and one of those times, when Melinda had done that concert at the Vatican and couldn't take a lover along, for the whole night. "Might as well be comfortable."

Toby pulled open the passenger door of the Bentley and nodded VV in.

Air conditioning whooshed out and she didn't need a second invitation. She settled herself on the seat, curious to know what he was hustling for now, knowing damned well it was not, never had been, VV Cameron's delectable ass. She didn't fool herself: she was a minor-league TV contact for him, nothing more.

Her thigh felt something gorgeous through the panty hose and her fingers went down and confirmed that she was sitting on white kid upholstery. *Jesus.*

His face was two inches from hers, a street-hustler's face made handsome and smooth by Malibu sun and salon facials and caps and—just possibly—ninety thousand dollars' worth of surgery. She wondered if that hairline was an implant.

"VV, you could do me a terrific favor."

"That so, Toby?"

"That disaster footage you used on your morning show? I need it."

She felt the stirrings of a refusal. "I didn't know you were doing documentaries, Toby."

"I just need it for tonight. You'll have it back tomorrow in mint condition—scout's honor."

Honor, scout, and Toby Gladstone just didn't go together. "It's against regulations to let film out of the studio," VV said.

"Who's going to know?"

"And the Malibu footage isn't ours, we got it from NBC."

"And you can give it *back* to NBC—tomorrow. Come on, VV—old times' sake?"

"You can't lay a thumb on the film. Not one frame of it. You can't even splice new leader on."

"All I want to do is *run* the film! I swear, just run it!"

"Okay, Toby. I'll loan you the film."

"VV, you're a doll."

"*If* you give me an interview with Melinda for tomorrow's show."

His face went sour as though vinegar had been splashed in a light coffee. "You know she hates interviews."

"That's the deal." VV pressed a button and the goddamned door opened itself. She glanced back at Toby's tanned face working furiously. "Take it or leave it, love."

"Thank you." Carolyn Miller took the black coffee from the volunteer and sat a distance away from the first-aid station. In the east she saw a crimson flare bloom up out of the trees and send out a canopy of black and float gently back to the skyline.

My little girl is there, she thought. *There.* And she seemed to be staring down into an abyss that had no bottom. Behind her were voices of Red Cross nurses and wounded men. She felt her husband watching her as she watched the burning mountains.

Steve touched her face with his hand. "Don't. Please don't," he said.

She pressed the palm of her hand to her lips to still a sudden quaking.

One of the volunteers must have switched on a portable radio, because suddenly a woman was singing behind them: not a real woman, but the electronic ghost of one, a sensuous whimper gliding and skipping over a thumping, marching disco beat.

Steve stiffened. Carolyn was aware of something whirling and working in him and then soft as the click of a mercury switch a light went on in him. He grabbed her arm.

"That song—that damned song!" He jumped up and she thought she was looking into the face of a madman. "Angie was playing that thing!"

"It's Melinda Mars," Carolyn said gently. "It's a big hit."

129

"Does Angie have her radio with her?"

Carolyn reflected a moment, rerunning a movie film of memory in her head. She saw the seat of the car, the wrapping of a frozen raspberry yogurt popsicle, Nipper's rubber bone, and she *thought* and she saw the chrome glitter of that terrible little transistor radio, and then she definitely saw that last image of her daughter, fidgeting on the seat, twisting around to reach something in the back.

"Of course she had it," Carolyn suddenly remembered. "I told her she could bring it if she stopped crying about Nipper."

Steve's face was flushed and eager. "And where's the radio now?"

"I haven't seen it."

His head was bobbing up and down.

"That's it—that's it!"

"Steve—what are you talking about?"

"It's only a chance, honey— You wait here." He was already three bounds away from her, running.

"Where are you going?" she cried after him.

"Up in that copter again!"

VV Cameron arrived at the Melinda Mars house on the dot of three. Toby Gladstone came running to the gate and from a distance she thought he was naked under that terrycloth robe. At ten feet she saw he was wearing a peekaboo bikini.

"Start rolling," she whispered to her sound man and cameraman. "Don't wait for setups. Get everything you can."

Chatting and gesturing, Toby led them to a glass-walled building behind the bathhouses. VV could see Melinda Mars inside, pushing control buttons on a monster tape console, glaring at her sheet music, lips shaping a very distinct four-letter word.

Toby knocked on the door and pushed it open.

"Hey, Melly, here's VV Cameron—she wants to get some film of you for *Newsbreak*."

Melinda pretended to be absorbed in her sheet music; at least it struck VV as pretending.

"Melly," Toby tried again, "you got a sec?"

"I don't like that bass," Melinda said, killing the sound, barely glancing up to throw an icy frown at VV. "Sounds like he's hitting a washtub with a broom."

"We'll rerecord the bass."

"I can't practice without a bass." Melinda threw down the sheet music and came to the doorway. VV couldn't help thinking that the woman was radiant in pregnancy. She wore a long loose shirt of deep violet silk and beneath it French jeans that must have been cut below the abdomen. Her face and arms were tanned, with that extra creamy smoothness that only maternity can bestow. Her hair was sun-streaked and she wore it in a sort of ponytail fastened with a bracelet that looked like twenty thousand dollars of Cartier's best.

Toby did the introductions. Melinda glared VV straight in the eye. "I don't give interviews."

"Honey," Toby pleaded, "I explained. It's not an interview. VV just wants some footage."

Melinda tossed a nod toward the sound man with his shoulder-slung, battery-driven tape kit and his four-foot collapsible sound boom. "Then what's that?"

VV smiled what she hoped was a disarming smile. "My producer hoped you'd say a few words."

Melinda fixed her with a squint. "I've seen your program. You're a scare show."

VV held the smile. "Anything to keep the ratings high."

Melinda shook her head. "Toby, if I don't talk to Barbara Walters why the hell should I talk to *Newsbreak?* They're not even national."

"It's exposure," Toby said, "for the concert."

"Okay," Melinda sighed. "Three minutes. Toby, will you see if you can dig up another bass track for 'YWCA'?"

Toby nodded and shambled toward the pool.

"You got your sound level?" Melinda asked the sound man.

VV signaled the cameraman to start rolling. They strolled across the lawn. VV asked the usual questions. She did not get any of the usual answers. Almost desperately, her eye swept the Melinda Mars compound, inventorying the bustle and rush for vignettes that would look good on TV.

Preparations appeared to be raging for a party. Men from Chasen's were setting up elaborate buffets. Groundsmen were putting up striped marquees. There was a stage with a cyclorama for rear projections. Gardeners were tying orchids to trees.

"Things seem to be in quite a flurry around here, Miss Mars. You're obviously preparing some kind of celebration. What's up?"

"My son's birthday."

"It's certainly going to be a birthday to remember. Who are you inviting?"

"Friends."

VV realized Melinda Mars was going to give monosyllables for answers and screw up the interview. "What are you serving?"

"Food. Booze."

VV sized her interviewee up as moody, flamboyant, a pain in the ass, and a ferocious talent. The woman had revolutionized pop music, bringing together blues and rock and disco and veneering the mix with the old Jerome Kern schmaltz that had never been far from Middle America's heart. She'd reached back to medieval music for her instrumental tracks just as she'd reached forward to electronics and synthesizers. She'd grabbed anything and everything in the supermarket of sound and thrown it into the Melinda Mars processor, and what had emerged had kept her on *Billboard*'s top ten for six spectacular years.

I am going to get this interview, VV vowed. *There's got to be some way of opening her up.*

Just beyond the glass studio VV spied a gnarled freestanding tree that could have been an oak or gingko. At first she could not understand why anyone would have riveted chromium bars to its trunk, and then she realized that the bars were a ladder and that the Frank Lloyd Wright-looking *thing* poking through the leaves was a tree house.

"And is that where your son plays?" VV asked brightly.

"Sometimes."

"Could we get a shot of the birthday boy?"

"No photographs. He's too young."

Melinda sniffed. She peered up at the gathering haze. The sky had a poorly focused look, like a color photograph printed out of register. The sun was an orange amoeba twisting through restless gray currents.

"Toby!" she shouted, and from his deck chair Toby acknowledged her with a shrug of one well-muscled shoulder. "You said this place was above the smog line."

"It *is* above the smog line."

"Then what's that?" Melinda Mars jabbed a finger at the sky.

The man glanced up and readjusted his terry-cloth robe. "So? The smog's above the smog line."

Melinda Mars strode to poolside. VV motioned the cameraman and sound man to follow, to get it all down for the viewers. This could be hot.

Melinda Mars stood hands on hips, feet firmly planted on the travertine marble of the pool deck. "We're not going to have smog at my son's birthday!"

Toby Gladstone arched an eyebrow and squinted up at her. "Then why don't you complain to the Weather Bureau—or to God—wherever you have better contacts."

He rolled over onto his stomach. Melinda reached to jerk him back around.

"Phone the studio. Get three wind machines up here and three technicians to run them during the party."

"Wind machines," Toby marveled. "You're always the firstest with the mostest, Melly love."

"And charge it to studio overhead—not my percentage!" Melinda whirled on her heel and glowered at VV and her crew. "You got enough footage." She jerked a thumb toward the gate. "Scram."

Angie Miller stirred. A smell of charcoal and a crackling sound pressed in on her. Groggily, she pulled herself to half-consciousness. Through slitted eyes she made out flickering silhouettes on the wall.

It hit her that the house was on fire.

She staggered to her feet and was baffled that her legs didn't want to stay straight. The wall was jagged and slanted and that baffled her too. Fear shivered through her like the buzzing of a fly against a window screen.

And then as suddenly as the clap of a bell it came back to her: the forest, the fire, the cave...

The dog was whimpering at her feet. The dog that wasn't Nipper. She petted it and it licked her hand gratefully. She took another step, almost managing to stand steady this time.

A grayish-white smoke was puffing in through the mouth of the cave. She staggered toward it. The dog barked and tried to block her way but she pushed it aside and stood peering out into what had been forest. Through the sifting layers of haze she could see a line of trees burning as evenly as the flames on a kitchen stove.

A roar in the air made her look up. Far above the whirlpooling smoke she made out the bobbing shape of a helicopter. A spasm of coughing seized her. She tried to cry out. Her throat was parched and only a dry rasping came from it. Helplessly, she watched the helicopter bob up and down and up and down like a toy in a bathtub of dirty water. She waved her arms violently. The movement threw her off-balance. She took a stumbling step backward and her foot struck something.

Her eye fell on Aunt Nora's radio. An idea came to her. She gave the on/off knob a clockwise turn. Sound came spilling from the tiny speaker. It worked!

Radio in hand, she crawled forward toward the stream. The heat of the fire had evaporated all but a dark trickle of water, and bodies of tiny fish and insects studded the rocky bed.

The dog came barking after her, nipping at her heels. She shooed it away.

Carefully, she balanced the radio on a flat rock in the center of the streambed. She gave the volume knob a final twist as far clockwise as it would go. The voice of Melinda Mars came screaming out of the speaker. Angie threw a glance up at the canopy of smoke, searching for the helicopter, wondering if the sound would reach, wondering if *anything* would reach.

Five feet away, a flaming branch crashed to the streambed. Angie jumped and ran.

The copter, one thousand feet above the burning forest, tipped into a ninety-degree turn. There were three men inside: the pilot, Steve Miller, and Al Harrison, a bugging expert who free-lanced for big business, the CIA, and—at the moment—for Steve Miller. There was numbness in their faces, a sense of disbelief that what they saw below them was really happening.

Harrison, a stocky, black-haired man in his late twenties, wore earphones. A wire connected them to the twenty-pound control box that rested in his lap. Another wire ran from the box out through the open crack in the canopy. Though whiplashes of heat came stinging through the opening, Al Harrison didn't move his hand an inch. Even when a live spark landed on his thumb he didn't jerk or wince. He slapped it out, holding the mike boom steady through the crack.

The mike was an M-34 long-distance directional. It represented state-of-the-art high CIA technology. Using filters, frequency suppressors and boosters, a laser carrier-wave, it could pick out the sound of a human voice a quarter mile away and disentangle it from an astonishing amount of surrounding din. It had been pioneered for eavesdropping on foreign embassies and later had been used to locate stranded mountaineers and shipwreck victims. The catch was that it needed an unimpeded line of sight and, of course, the operator had to know where to aim it.

Harrison's strategy was the only possible one under the circumstances: he scanned with the mike, hoping to catch some random human sound and then home in on it. So far, the M-34 had isolated the whimpers and skitters of panicked forest animals, it had brought the crackles and pops of fire as close as a burning match held to the ear, but it had detected nothing resembling the radio that Steve Miller said had to be there.

Yet the radio *was* there, perched on a rock in a stream, and it was blasting. Four times in as many minutes the M-34 had come within three minutes of arc of picking it up. By now the approaching fire had

135

evaporated most of the water in the stream, and the radio sat in a whirlwind of hissing steam. As the heat began to melt the antenna the sound changed subtly, losing its higher partials. But it was still recognizable as a human voice, the voice of Melinda Mars belting her latest hit.

That was the only link to Angie Miller: the disembodied voice of a pop singer in the depth of a flaming forest.

And it was enough.

Al Harrison heard the brittle crack as the glass window over the dial popped. He didn't recognize the sound, but his ear immediately caught the tinkle of technology and he knew it did not belong in a forest.

And then he picked up the voice: Melinda Mars screaming her climactic *Don't ever hurt me again.*

Actually the *again* was cut short as flames ripped through the radio circuitry, but the second and a half of Melinda had been enough to give Al Harrison his fix. Whipping ultrahigh-resolution binoculars to his eyes, he caught a flashing light, and with a sharpening of focus he made out what was left of the chromium-decked radio.

"Down there," he said unemotionally. "That's the radio."

Steve Miller jerked his binoculars in the same direction. It took him a moment to see the chrome corpse of Aunt Nora's gift. And then, panning to the right, he saw the mouth of the cave. And he knew where his little girl was.

"Take her down!" he screamed.

"You'll never get in there!" the pilot shouted.

"The hell I won't! Take her down!"

Steve Miller let himself down the swaying ladder. Ten rungs from the bottom he jumped. He landed in a crouch, in spiraling layers of smoke that gave him flickers of visibility.

He saw the cave and ran for it. He heard something howl and thought it sounded like a dog. He groped through smoke into the cave. The air became breathable but there was no light and he had to squint to see the lump of torn dress huddled on the ground.

"*Angie!*"

Her face was black and bloody and her clothes were shreds but her eyes opened and she made a rasping sound in her throat. He scooped her up in his arms. "Put your arms around my neck, honey. Hold on tight and close your eyes."

The smoke was eddying thicker. He pulled in one last deep breath and ran. The air was searing outside the cave. He could hear the helicopter roaring above him but he had to wait for a pocket in the smoke before he could see the swaying ladder. He freed one hand and lunged it but the ladder swayed just out of reach and he missed.

A wind gusted along the streambed. Heated air shot upward. The helicopter rode the updraft, then dipped. Its position now was lower than an instant before and the pilot didn't have time to adjust. The spinning blades chopped into outstretched branches of dead pine. The motor's roar became a scream and the copter heeled sideways.

Steve Miller grabbed again for the ladder and almost made contact but something threw him off-balance. A dog was barking at his feet.

There was a deafening crackle—not flame, but the snapping of a thousand matchsticks—as metal shredded wood and sawdust rained down and ignited and soared up again in blinding spirals. The copter struggled for purchase, shuddered, shot up, came to an almost stationary hover.

Steve Miller adjusted Angie's weight against his shoulder. The dog was tearing at his trousers again. He kicked it away angrily. Angie whimpered something and his arm tightened around her.

The copter dropped again, this time cautiously. The bottom rung of the ladder swayed through the smoke, barely within range. The propellers were whipping smoke and heat and burning wood particles into Steve Miller's eyes and nose and mouth.

He grabbed again and this time his hand caught metal. He gripped and the heat came stabbing through his glove. He yanked twice and the helicopter lifted, taking him and the child he held pressed to him.

He felt that his arm was being ripped from its socket but he held on, not releasing the burning metal, not releasing the child. Together they lifted up through smoke and finally into the clear and then as the helicopter veered back toward safety they swung out in a wide arc and the muscles in his arm screamed.

He closed his eyes, not looking down, pretending he was riding an amusement park loop-the-loop on a hot summer night. *Dear God, don't let me let go,* he prayed, feeling the child's heart thud against his. *Don't don't don't let me let go.*

The helicopter sent a blast of burning wind shooting along the ground. The barking dog recoiled.

And then the helicopter was gone and with it the humans.

The dog was alone now and afraid. Its heart thudded against its ribs and its matted, blackened coat trembled. A battle was going on in its lungs as the demand for oxygen fought the searing pain of each inhalation.

The animal knew it could not hold out much longer. The fire was closing down its senses, its last avenue of survival. It could not see through smoke, through the tears that smoke brought to its eyes. It could not hear through the hisses and crackles. No smell reached its nose through the blanketing stench of a world that was turning to carbon. The heat surrounding it had risen to such a pitch that it could no longer feel gradations, only agony and the certainty that death was near.

The animal turned again to the cave. Whimpering, it crawled to the very back. It lifted its head to blink once more at the sinister red glow, then curled up on the ground and shut its eyes.

The fire drew nearer.

The dog howled once.

Then it waited.

8

CALDWELL pushed the buzzer and didn't hear a ring. He knocked. In a moment the door opened and VV Cameron stood there in a pale blue T-shirt and very faded jeans. He didn't think she'd had them on very long.

"Hi, there, Chief. This *is* a surprise." She motioned him in. At a glance he could see she liked vivid wall hangings, plants, and minimal furniture.

"Didn't mean to barge in," he apologized. "I tried phoning. The line was busy for a hell of a long time."

"Off the hook. I was taking a hell of a long bath. I do that after a long day. Don't you?"

"I never have time for anything but a shower."

She smiled and suddenly there were little smile brackets around her lips. Her hair fell naturally to her shoulders. The bath had made it wavy, almost curly. Caldwell found something comforting and unexpected in that smile and that face, in the wide eyes that so relaxedly took him in.

"You should make time," she said. "You don't work twenty-four hours a day, do you?"

"Today I do."

"Then this is not a social visit?"

"No, Miss Cameron—I'm sorry, but this is not a social visit."

"I'm sorry too. By the way, after hours the name's

VV—not Miss Cameron. And it *is* after hours. For me, at least. I'm having a drink. Can I offer you one?"

"I'd better not."

A look came into her eyes that he couldn't quite decipher, as though she knew something about him that he did not.

"Iced tea? And I promise not to booby-trap it with vodka."

"Sounds good."

She vanished into the kitchen. He followed her with his ears now instead of his eyes. There was a running of water, the slamming of an ice tray against a sink, a muttered mild profanity as something tinkled against the floor. He smiled. Silence, and then she reappeared with a tray. The pitcher was beaded with condensation. Ice and mint and lemon were waiting in the glasses.

She poured and handed him his. They sat on the sofa and toasted each other.

"What's the VV stand for?"

"Vanessa Victoria. When I was in school they used to call me Nessie. It sounded too much like the Loch Ness monster, so I switched to VV."

"Good nickname. Stays in the mind. Like a trademark."

"Glad you think so. It's supposed to."

He tried to think how to ease into the subject that had brought him there. He couldn't.

She stared into her glass and then at him. "You said you're here on business, Chief. If you're waiting for me to get out my tape recorder, don't. I never use one."

"I need your help, VV."

There was a change in her expression. Nothing moved in her face, but something shifted behind her eyes. "Chief, you've had my help. I want my story. That was the deal, remember?"

"We have to know the name of the man on that tape."

"Can't help you, Chief."

"Yes, you can."

Smiling, she shook her head. She raised her glass and took a long swallow. "We don't take their names. They don't have to give their names. That's the way it works. Sorry, Chief. Couldn't help even if I wanted to."

"If he's the man we want, he'll phone in again."

"Possibly."

"You could let us put a trace on the line."

Her gaze came up at his, a cool blaze of outrage. "I could also tell you to take a running jump into Hades."

"We need his name, VV."

"Not from me." She got up from the sofa. Her feet marked out three careful steps. She whirled. The face was defiant now.

"I'm a reporter, Chief. I don't play those games. I don't betray my sources."

Caldwell could smell what was coming. He didn't need it. Not the Joan of Arc act, not the lecture on the U.S. Constitution. He didn't need any of it. "Crap on your sources. We need to find him."

"Crap on you!" she screamed. "The Supreme Court has stated that TV journalism enjoys the same safeguards as print journalism, and I suggest you review your Bill of Rights!"

"I'm not abridging the freedom of your press, Miss Cameron."

"You sure as shit are. What you're asking is the equivalent of divulging my sources and turning over my notes. You came to the wrong Judas, Chief. I will not betray my profession. Civil liberties have been eroded enough in this so-called democracy."

"Lady," Caldwell sighed, "this so-called democracy is on fire and that psycho you're protecting could be the firebug. If you don't wake up and help us, you and your civil liberties and all the rest of this city could be cinders tomorrow."

Her eyes came up at him. There was a sudden slyness in them, as though she'd caught the scent of something. "Then you're admitting it. You're admitting that story you put out is a crock of whitewash. There *is* a pyromaniac and L.A. *is* on the verge of disaster and you're keeping it under wraps so we can all burn up in our cozy little beds!"

He slammed his glass down on the table. "I'm admitting there's a psycho torching L.A. and your phone pal is very probably him!"

"My phone pal could also be a concerned citizen who

doesn't buy the bureaucratic crap and deception you people are handing out!"

He sprang to his feet. "My men are risking their lives and if you call that crap I swear I'll slug you."

"Your men are risking *our* lives, and I *do* call it crap, I call it the same crap that took nineteen lives at Laurel Canyon—or did Laurel Canyon slip your memory, *mister?*"

Caldwell didn't have time to think. His hand went back and came forward. He heard the slap and saw her rubbing her cheek but it took him an instant to make the connection between his hand and her cheek and the iced rage in her eyes.

"Get out—now."

"Look, I'm sorry. It's been a crazy day, I—"

"I said now, Mr. Caldwell." She opened the door and stood aside, holding it, her T-shirt rising and falling with the rapidity of her breathing. "And if you want my sources, get a Supreme Court order. That's the only way I'll cooperate with your kind—ever!"

She slammed the door after him. Hard. The blood was thudding so hard through her veins that the image of the room trembled before her eyes.

When her hands had stopped shaking she took the glass he'd drunk from, emptied it down the kitchen sink, scoured it by hand, and stuck it in the dishwasher with the dirty dishes awaiting a full load.

She paced and then she poured herself a stiff Scotch, jabbed on the TV, and sat staring at the evening news. The top story flashed before her: fire in the Santa Monicas, fire in the Santa Susanas, fire in the San Gabriels, fire the color of blood, pulsing like a raw wound, and above it, framing it, smoke the color of charred flesh.

Her breath stopped short as it suddenly hit her that that *was* blood, that *was* flesh, the newscaster was describing two volunteer fire fighters caught in the Santa Monicas.

A contraction began in her stomach and she barely made it in time to the john. As she puked Scotch a voice behind her continued calmly: "The mayor has announced that twenty percent of the proceeds from tomorrow's Hollywood Bowl concert for the police and fire departments will go to emergency care for burn victims. In a related event—"

VV staggered back into the living room and snapped the set off.

A new slide flicked onto the screen. Caldwell sat forward in the darkness, frowning. It was a daylight shot, an aerial view of a fire line. A scar of raw earth separated flame from forest. "Where's this?"

"Laurel," Peters answered.

In the next slide the fire had jumped the line and a patch of red showed to the south of the scar. Caldwell estimated the burn had a four-foot diameter. In the following slide it had elongated into a twenty-foot worm. He didn't see a single human being in the picture.

"Where the hell are the patrols?" he exploded.

"We're short of men," Lovenko said quietly.

"What the hell's the point of a fire line if there's no patrol?"

Peters turned around in his seat. There was not a hint of strain in his face or voice. "Ed, do you have any idea how many miles of front we're holding right now?"

"Damned right I have an idea! And fuckups like that don't help! When did that fire jump? Who was in charge?"

At that moment a door opened and Marty Siegel stepped into the room. He bent down and tapped Caldwell on the shoulder. "You have a call," he whispered. "Personal."

"Can't take it," Caldwell snapped back. His eyes didn't bother to leave the screen.

"She says it's urgent."

"She?" Caldwell's eyes flicked around. "Who's *she?*"

"VV Cameron."

Caldwell hesitated. He was aware of Peters' and Lovenko's sudden attention, their faintly ironic interest. He pushed up from the chair.

"Hold that slide. I'll be right back."

"You can take the call over there." Marty Siegel indicated the phone with the blinking light.

Caldwell lifted the receiver and pushed the button. He lowered his voice to a toneless neutrality. "Ed Caldwell here."

"Chief, it's VV." She sounded clogged up, as though she'd caught cold and needed to blow her nose. "I just wanted to say I'm sorry."

He exhaled. He remembered that face and the comfort of that smile, and a little of the tension went out of him. "It was my fault, VV—not yours."

"Let's not get into another argument. You're trying to save lives and I was a self-righteous girl scout. Chief, I want to help you catch that bastard. I phoned the studio. You can put a trace on the line any time you want."

Carolyn Miller turned to glance one last time at the bed where Angie lay, thin and pale and asleep, cuddled with Teddy bears and Raggedy Anns, peaceful and dreaming and home safe. *Thank God,* Carolyn Miller thought. *Thank you, God.*

She pulled the door behind her and heard the latch tap softly into place. For a moment she stood in the hallway motionless. Her nerves felt as though they were still stretched on winches. She wanted to cry, to collapse, to dissolve into a blob of nonfeeling.

She went into the living room and sat down in the easy chair. She hung her head forward and concentrated on relaxing the muscles at the back of her neck. Her heart was racing, pounding at her ribs like a prisoner shaking the bars of the cell. She willed it to slow. Gradually the beating leveled off and she was able to draw a normal breath.

There was a footstep. She looked up and saw her husband. He had put on a fresh ranger's shirt. He had his cap in his hands.

She leaped to her feet. "Steve, what are you doing?"

He put his hands on her shoulders, held her firmly at arm's length.

"Sweetheart, I have to."

"You're not going back out there!"

Apology and confusion were written all over his face,

but she saw something else too, tiny grim lines of determination.

"They need me," he said quietly.

"But we need you too—*I* need you. Steve, don't go— not tonight."

"The fire won't wait, honey. They haven't got enough men."

"But—it's your *vacation. Our* vacation." The plea sounded lame even before the words were out.

"Angie came back to us. Don't you see, honey? That's a debt."

She felt ashamed of herself, ashamed for needing him, for wanting at this moment to be the only thing in his life that mattered.

He kissed her. She followed him outside and silently watched him get into the car. He backed out of the drive. The headlights wavered through the haze. He drove slowly, glancing back at her. He waved just before the car turned to the left at the bottom of the hill.

She waved back, but too late: he was gone.

What if he doesn't come back, she thought. *What if there's an accident. What if the fire . . .*

She didn't finish the thought. Darkness and silence pressed in on her. She started back toward the house, and then she stopped, startled, as though she were seeing the building for the first time.

The low white clapboard structure seemed to hug the land on which it sat, as if it had to hold tight to keep itself from slipping down into the quiet, courteous street below. It was dwarfed in front by an elegant row of high white elms. Tonight Carolyn Miller saw the house as a votary, a being bent to its knees in prayer before the spires of the trees.

It was not a large house, but it was adequate to the Millers' needs. With ingenuity and dedication, with plaster and electric saws and sanders and savings, they had added little touches over the years, making it comfortable and hospitable to their needs. It was a house that had taken everything they had—their money, their energies, their love—and it had returned to them the most any house can give: it had become their *home.*

Carolyn Miller hurried into her home. She locked the door behind her.

It was a little after 10:00 P.M. when Sid Bender heard barking on the other side of the dog shelter. He took his flashlight and crossed the compound to the building that housed the cages.

A station wagon was parked at the door. The lights had been turned on inside the building, and a man stood in one of the cages. He held a lasso.

"Oh, it's you, Defino." Sid Bender flicked off his flashlight, saving the battery. He raised his voice to be heard over the barking. "Didn't know you were working tonight."

"I'm not," came the answer.

In the three years he had worked with the man, Sid Bender had never quite gotten used to that voice. It reminded him of the old Edison cylinders he had heard in museums, not so much a human utterance as the mechanically contrived ghost of one. There was no emotion to the voice, no range: instead of the octave or so a normal human voice could play over, it seemed to have only one note. But for Sid Bender the oddest thing was that it was a ventriloquist's voice: it seemed to come not from the man but from the empty space *next to him.*

He watched Defino. Lasso trailing on the cage floor, the man circled toward the German shepherd. The animal barked and growled and snapped, but it did not even attempt to bite. It went down cowering on its belly.

Something in Defino seemed to inspire obedience in dogs, and Bender had often wondered precisely what it was. Did the animals see the man as other men did—an object of terror and instinctive revulsion?

It had taken Sid Bender a long time to master that revulsion. He still had a vivid memory of the afternoon he'd stepped out of the cubicle in the men's room to find Defino bent over the sink. Defino must have thought he was alone in the john, because he'd taken off the mask and the glasses and the wig and placed them in a neat pile on the shelf. As the face—if you could call that residue a face—had come up and whipped around,

Sid Bender's breath had been sucked out of him so fast the only thing he could say was, "Ohhhh—" the long toneless gasp of his lungs clutching for air.

Defino had scrambled the wig and the glasses back on and Sid Bender had mastered the vomit urge gathering in his stomach and he'd forced himself to look, not to avert his eyes, not to show by his reaction that Defino was a monster.

And he forced himself now, staring straight into the dark glasses that masked the eyes. *See? I can look you in the face, Defino, I'm not prejudiced against scar tissue and purple skin grafts, why to me you're just a man like any other man, see, I'm not even puking.*

But why the hell hadn't he had plastic surgery? Bender wondered.

Defino got the lasso around the animal and then, when the animal still wouldn't move, he stooped down to squeeze its testicles. The animal let out one little whine, tiny and ridiculously high for such a brute, and then went along obediently, right into the back of the station wagon.

"Adopting more strays, Defino?" Sid Bender asked.

"Somebody has to," Defino said. "You know what I mean?"

He pulled the gauze mask down from his lower face, exposing the lipless hole that functioned as a mouth. He used his fingernails to tweeze a cigarette from the pack in his workshirt pocket. Sid Bender watched the operation closely, because while it revolted him it fascinated him too.

Defino poked the cigarette into the hole that had been a mouth, and in one swift motion, snatching a match from under the fingers of the same hand, he flicked it into flame, lit the cigarette, and put out the match by pinching the burning nipple between thumb and forefinger. He tossed it to the floor.

Sid Bender had seen Defino do this thing with fire and for a long time he had wondered where the fire came from. By watching the man very closely he had finally understood how it was done.

The last two fingers of the right hand were always curled against the palm. No matter what kind of work

147

the man was doing, no matter what time of day it was, the fingers were curled and there were always matches there. With just a jot of friction, a scratch, Defino produced heat enough to make them flare.

It always looked to Sid Bender as though the flame came from Defino's fingers, from the man's very flesh. It gave Sid Bender a disturbing tingle in the pit of the stomach to watch the fire that came from this man's body.

"How do you feed them?" Sid Bender asked. "I mean, how do you pay for it?"

Defino inhaled on the cigarette. Without lips, the inhalation was an effort, an intense pulling of lungs and diaphragm. It made a high whistling sound, and again the sound seemed to come not from the man but from the space around him.

"It's not that expensive," Defino said. "Not when you buy in bulk. You know what I mean?"

Sid Bender strolled back to his office, where the other night man and a can of beer were awaiting him. He picked up his hand of poker. "That poor bastard." He shook his head.

"Defino?" the other said. Sid Bender nodded. "Well, I suppose somebody's got to love him. With a kisser like that, it might as well be those dogs."

It took Defino the better part of forty minutes to drag the other seven dogs into the station wagon. He slammed the rear door and got in behind the wheel.

The little terrier that had been waiting at its post on the front seat went mad with delight to see its master settle into place. It teased at his sleeve, tearing at it with its tiny teeth, sniffing at the faintly burnt odor of matches that clung to the man's right hand.

Defino smacked the dog away. He jabbed the key into the ignition, gave it a sideways wrench, and then with a tap of the gas pedal fired up the motor. He kept the car in low gear. It moved smoothly, slowly, almost noiselessly away from the compound.

In the rear, eight dogs struggled for position in the cramped space behind the heavy wire.

Once it was off county grounds, the station wagon

gathered speed. It took an easterly route, along the throughway where the night air was pooling in umber pockets beneath the streetlights.

It headed toward the mountains.

Loren's birthday party went into high gear early. By eleven o'clock, after she'd put Loren to bed and turned up the air conditioner to blanket the sound, Melinda knew she had another smash.

The place was crawling with two hundred film and TV and recording glitterati. The drive was jammed with Rollses and Bentleys and Mercedeses parked five and six deep. The coat racks in the study and the brass bed in the master bedroom were loaded down with designer wraps and shawls as expensive as furs and far more sparkling. The two indoor bars and the three outside were doing standing-room-only business. The buffet tables were piled with pots of Caspian caviar and roasts and delicate finger sandwiches and the food was going like a Melinda Mars single.

Melinda circulated smoothly, accepting kisses and congratulations on her new hit, never spending more than sixty seconds with any one guest.

The night was thick with laughter and gossip and the rich smell of pot openly smoked and the music of strolling violins and accordions. Sex was in the air, as obvious as the vented blouses and décolletage on some of the women, and as always in Hollywood it shaded over into money, with deals and adultery often arranged in the same breath.

The cokeheads had discovered and taken over the bathhouses; the orgy lovers had swooped instinctively on the sauna and the recording studio; and even Loren's Neiman-Marcus tree house was bobbing on its moorings a little more than the breeze warranted. A rumor was making the rounds that two top agents and the foulest-mouth bitch in network TV were up there having a ménage.

Melinda had to smile. Maybe it was true.

From time to time, through the weavings of the guests, she spotted Toby. He looked a little too exuberant, kissing too many women and hugging too many

149

men, but she chalked that up to speed. At least he was steady on his feet.

There was a light in the eastern sky like a line of glowing coals, and Melinda heard whispers that the brush fire—some said two or three fires—was far more serious than the press or TV had admitted. But this was said as a matter of interest, not of concern, a mere fact far less important than who had signed with whom and who was getting in on whose. Anyway, the wind machines, aimed into the air above guests' heads, kept the smoke at bay. And they added nice ripples to women's and men's hairdos.

A little after eleven thirty the rented butler whispered to Melinda that she had visitors waiting in the study.

"Tell them to come on out," she said.

The butler bit his lower lip. "I don't believe Madame invited them."

That sounded weird enough to be interesting. Melinda apologized to her TV producer; showering excuse me's and smiles, she pried her way through the laughing, chattering mob into the study.

A man in a dark suit was leaning against the mantelpiece. A gray-faced woman, sitting stiffly on the edge of a chair, rose as Melinda came in. They were like a morgue in the middle of a fair.

"We've met before," the man said, and Melinda recognized the court officer who'd tried to serve a subpoena in the school parking lot. She felt her face go into an angry burn.

"This is Estelle Murdoch," the man said, "of Family Court," and the woman held out a hand that Melinda simply ignored.

"What do you two want?" she snapped.

"Miss Mars," the woman said with pained primness, "do you understand the meaning of the term 'reckless endangerment of a minor'?"

"Out." Melinda jabbed her thumb toward the door. "Now."

"Miss Mars," the woman persevered, "the court has the power to make a determination as to the moral fitness—"

150

Melinda cut her short. "The Supreme Court has determined that you two goons are trespassing. Helmholtz versus Louisiana, 1957."

"We are not here to trespass," the woman said, "but to make a determination."

"It's a pretty shitty hour to make a determination," Melinda shot back.

Nothing seemed to faze the woman. "I must say, this is hardly the atmosphere to raise a minor in."

Melinda flipped out an empty hand. "Your warrant. Let me see it. You got three seconds." Melinda gave her four seconds, then went to the door and signaled the nearest security guard. "Be a doll and get rid of these two, will you?"

Schmucks, Melinda muttered, they'd made her miss the first part of the live entertainment, an act called The Disasters that Toby owned a share in.

Melinda caught the tail end: four leather punks gyrated on the stage and bowed earsplitting shrieks from electronic violins and violas. The vocalist, a girl in a fifties Balenciaga slashed along the thigh, used a technique Melinda had never heard before: she screamed into a handheld mike, literally screamed like a rape victim, but she modulated the head-jangling racket to actual notes.

"A-flat above high C," Melinda marveled to her neighbor, last year's Academy Award for best script adapted from another medium. "Better than Queen of the Night."

"It's awful," the writer said. He shook his head. "And what's that film behind them?"

Melinda shrugged. "Rear projection. They use some kind of mirrored lens to increase the throw."

"But what's the footage?"

"Newsreel. Toby borrowed it from one of the TV stations."

The writer looked pained. Writers, Melinda had noticed, always looked pained.

"But isn't it the Santa Monica brushfire?" he said.

"It was on television this morning," the wife of a studio vice-president volunteered. "I recognize those dead birds. I'm into ecology."

Melinda saw the writer's lips move, and she thought he said, "That's disgusting," but she couldn't be sure. Recorded explosions and gunfire came ripping from The Disasters' megawatt speakers, and the stage was blanketed in jets of colored smoke.

There were cries of "Wow!" and "Wild!" Melinda smiled the smile of a proud hostess. There was no question.

Loren's birthday was a success.

The shack in North Hollywood was tumbledown and sparsely furnished and the air inside was stagnant with fumes of dog excrement and urine. That did not bother Defino. He was busy coaxing a mongrel with a biscuit.

The dog, initially suspicious, retreated to a corner, hunkering down into the pile of strewn newspapers to stare balefully at this stranger bearing strange gifts. "Here, doggy, here, honey!" The man, still crouching, inched forward, waving the biscuit gracefully from side to side as though it were a flare sending out smell instead of light.

The dog sniffed and smell prevailed over suspicion. It crawled toward the biscuit, eyes and head moving to track its motion. The man put the biscuit down on the newspaper. The dog began licking at it, at first hesitantly, and then as the first chemicals penetrated its saliva, with almost frenzied relish.

The man's hand lunged and in one stabbing sweep the hypodermic dug two inches below the loose skin of the neck. The dog let out a panicked squeal, grotesquely treble coming from an animal the size of a husky. The man pressed the plunger slowly, ignoring the animal's momentary pain, emptying all the green liquid in the ampoule into the bloodstream.

He removed the hypodermic with a quick jerk. Then, moving with the quick, economical gestures of experience, he attached the harness and the chain and the wonderful arabesquing loops of fuse that his fingers loved to caress and finally the canister itself.

His eyes were flat and emotionless as he watched the animal's pupils dilate. A moment later the head sagged and the front legs buckled and the animal went down on the floor in a puddle of fur and paws and wheezing snout.

The man paused and looked blankly down at the three dogs already harnessed and injected. They had sprawled in various positions on the floor, groggy and disoriented, sleep beginning to pool in their eyes. Across the room four dogs, unharnessed and un-drugged, prowled restlessly. They pawed at newspaper and raised their heads to mewl at him like hungry infants. Defino had begun to bend to load another am-poule into the syringe when a sound caught his ear, a sound he had been waiting for all evening.

He turned, suddenly jerked and took a step forward, alert now, all attention focused on the whispering TV. He reached to raise the volume. He fixed his gaze on the TV screen, on the thing flaming and ripping across the hills.

He settled down in his jalopy of an easy chair. The lipless hole that was his mouth could not smile, but his muscles relaxed like those of an animal being petted by a kindly hand and an almost purring sound came out of him. His shirt fell open. His body was thick and corded with sinew and the skin was a patchwork of red-and-violet grafts and hairless, second-growth white that was eerily reptilian in its shining smoothness.

He rocked back and forth and the purring became almost a buzz. His eyes bulged excitedly from their sockets like a child's blue marbles. The voice on the TV was hard-hitting, unemotional, macho know-it-all. *Four hundred acres in two hours...eight hundred fire fighters and three hundred volunteers...property damage already in the millions....*

A thick strand of spittle beaded the man's purple-white patchwork chin. A hot, bubbling excitement crawled up from his gut into his lungs and throat and finally burst out of his mouth in gurgling, childlike laughter. This was success, this was power: to know without being known, to watch without being watched, to touch and rip and violate *them* without their being able even to touch back.

Thoughts sang in his head. *There I am—on TV! That's me! Hey, look fellas, look Mom, look all you ass-*

153

holes, that's your boy, I did all that, small-town boy makes good with a bang, hey?

He was pleased. The work was good. It was well made. It would have the recognition and awe of millions. It would survive. Men might not remember the maker, but they would never forget the work he had wrought.

Afterward, before getting back to the dogs, Defino remembered to blot his trousers with newspaper and zip his fly.

The men offered to stand aside for him, but Ed Caldwell took his place in the chow line the same as everyone else. The menu was baked beans, stew, pie, and coffee. It was quick-energy food, served around the clock.

Caldwell took a cup of coffee. Nothing more. He walked away from the campsite. He stood gazing down the eastern slope. Far away he could see the flickering light in the San Gabriels, and above it the floating canopy of gray and pink.

Something wrenched inside him. The winds had driven the flames uphill. What had been ponderosas and incense cedars and Douglas firs was now a sea of red. He could see the fire sending out feelers, little scars of light gashing the dark.

He took his coffee to the communications truck. The radio-man silently handed him the latest maps and copter photos sent up from headquarters. Caldwell flipped through them grimly, estimating the burn total. *We're not winning this one,* he thought. *Not yet, not by a long shot.*

Granada and Laurel seemed pretty well contained. In an hour or two they'd be burning down and it might be safe to shift forces away from them. Simi/Stone had expanded its front by three miles.

Caldwell radioed the sector boss at Simi to check on spot fires behind the line. There were three, isolated and under control. Caldwell had a hunch Simi/Stone was going to be the tough one. "Keep an eye out for those spots, Fred. Keep patrolling."

"We're doing what we can, Ed. We haven't got the men."

"I know, I know. But keep patrolling."

Caldwell took a long swallow of coffee. It was cold now. He swished it around in his mouth, wishing it was a shot of whiskey. He realized that he hadn't craved liquor or even thought about it in close to twenty hours. *Maybe I'm going cold turkey,* he thought. *Maybe this fire's going to do it for me.*

"Get me Peters at headquarters," Caldwell said.

"I sure can try," the radio operator said. It took two minutes, and Peters sounded as though he'd been dozing.

"How's the weather looking?" Caldwell asked.

"No change."

"What about the rain from Hawaii?"

"Taking its time."

"Shit." Caldwell rapped a pencil against the empty Styrofoam cup.

"Any new—" Superstitiously, he wouldn't say the word. "Developments?"

"Fire in a jewelry store on Cienega."

"I mean in the hills."

"Nothing."

Neither spoke, and then Peters said, "He set the last six at dawn, Ed. We won't know for another two or three hours."

"Thanks for reminding me," Caldwell said, and almost immediately was ashamed of the tone. Peters might be a backstabber, but he certainly wasn't to blame for the arsonist. *I'm tired,* Caldwell realized. *Look how my hand's shaking. Like an old man.*

"Ed," Peters' voice was saying, "your friend called— Trish. She called six times. Didn't you get the messages?"

"I guess not," Caldwell said. *Butt out, Peters,* he caught himself thinking, and again he had to remind himself, *It's not Peters' fault, what the hell's wrong with me?*

"I told her you're all right, Ed, but I'm sure even if you woke her now she wouldn't mind hearing from you. Want me to patch you in to the switchboard?"

"Sure," Caldwell said vacantly, "do that."

The switchboard operator came on and Caldwell fished in his work-shirt pocket and pinched out the piece of paper with VV Cameron's number. "Right away, sir," the voice said, and there were three buzzes and then a very sleepy, "Hello?"

I'm crazy, Ed Caldwell thought. *This thing's on radio, it's on an open switchboard. There've got to be two dozen people listening in. Including Peters.*

"VV? It's Ed." He didn't want to have to say the last name but there was only silence, no recognition. "Ed Caldwell."

"Ed?" He could hear surprise and disbelief curling her voice up into a question mark. "Where are you?"

"Working a long shift tonight."

"Oh—all those voices and noise—I thought you might be—"

Say it, he thought, *in a bar.* She didn't say it. He liked her for not saying it, not playing those right/ wrong games he got at home.

"This is crazy, VV—I know it's the middle of the night—but you were the only human voice I heard today—and I just wanted to hear a human voice before I kick in."

There was another silence and he wondered if he'd said too much.

"You'll hear my human voice tomorrow, Chief. Now get some sleep. You need your rest and L.A. needs you in good shape."

"I'll do that."

"And, Chief—thanks for calling."

VV Cameron lowered the receiver very slowly into its cradle. She clicked off the bedside lamp and lay a moment staring at the ceiling, thinking of Eddy Caldwell and that haunted thing in his eyes, thinking of Eddy Caldwell thinking enough of VV Cameron to call her in the middle of the night just to say he was thinking of her.

She was glad. She didn't know why, but she liked that. She liked that very much.

It was 4:30 A.M. and Herman and Doryce Atlas were

still there, the last to go—as usual. Nothing seemed to get the message across to them: not yawns, not glazed eyes, not even direct hints. Melinda, dead on her feet, finally managed to maneuver them to the front door.

"When can we have that lunch?" Herman said, fixing her with his hungry brown eyes.

"Gee, I'll have to look at my datebook," Melinda evaded, "but let's do it real soon, okay?" Doryce gave her a look that translated, *Don't condescend to us, bitch,* but Melinda ignored it. She was one of the few performers in Hollywood on whom Herman Atlas had not one particle of dirt.

He had worked his way up from tax accountant to executive in charge of production at one of the conglomerate-owned studios. He'd embezzled and been caught. A gossip columnist who hated his wife had blabbed the story and blabbed it hard. The judge had suspended Herman's sentence. It was whispered that he was snorting over five thousand dollars of coke a week. He looked it and acted it, lurching around parties red-faced and perspiring and talking up deals that everyone knew were hot air. Herman and his wife Doryce were the A set's charity cases, and everyone knew it but Herman and Doryce.

"Charming party," Doryce said, doing her Kate Hepburn imitation.

"Glad you could make it," Melinda said, nailing her good-night smile into place.

"I'll send the galleys up by messenger," Herman said.

What galleys? Melinda wondered. She knew he'd optioned one of the Manson killers' memoirs and she had a sinking feeling she'd said yes just to get rid of him and go mix with her guests.

"Drive safely!" Melinda called; she'd noticed there was no chauffeur in their Bentley.

She waved her fingers gaily, then closed the front door. She dropped the smile and it felt good, like putting down a hundred-pound weight she'd been carrying in her jaws all evening.

She crossed the living room, stopping to pick up the roach end of a joint that someone had dropped on the rug. She flicked it into the fireplace.

The caterer's men were darting around the lawn, packing up crystal and silver and taking down marquees.

"Hey, fellas," Melinda called, "you can turn off those wind machines and leave the cleaning up for tomorrow."

The headman came deferentially around the edge of the swimming pool. "If you don't mind, Miss Mars, the men would prefer to finish up now. Save on driving time, you know."

He smiled. It was a beautifully capped smile and Melinda supposed he'd once tried to make it in films. Once upon a very long time ago.

"I do mind."

She handed him five $100 bills. He blinked and made an awkward, gulping little bow.

"Of course, Miss Mars. Thank you. Thank you very much."

The men filed out quickly, thanking her. Melinda nodded, bolted the front door, then went back to stare at the debris.

The lawn looked as though a carnival had just pulled up stakes. And that, Melinda knew, meant the party had been a smash.

She gazed at her swimming pool, her Henry Moore standing sculpture, her four and a half acres, her Edward Durell Stone bathhouses, her pine forest.

Her mind drifted back to the three-room apartment on the Grand Concourse in the Bronx; the walk home from high school, the muggers who were there even in broad daylight; her mother refusing to cosign a Household Finance Corp. loan to get her into Juilliard for voice lessons; Juilliard turning her down after she'd earned the money hustling tips at a summer job in the Poconos; two years making the rounds of the quasi-gay cabarets in Greenwich Village, two years of sending composites and résumés and announcements to William Morris agents who never showed up for her one-night-only appearances; two years of marriage to the drunk who barfed at her debut at the Duplex and who turned out to be not only a William Morris agent but a junkie.

The only thing she ever got out of that marriage was Loren, and a three-year contract with the Morris people. The Morris people proved she was a star; it took them four years to do it, but they proved it and then she dropped them and went to CMA. Loren proved she was more than just a star-bitch-ego-genius, and she'd never drop Loren, not for all the threats and subpoenas in the world, not for all the stardom, not for anything or anyone.

Her gaze drifted up toward the stars. Only there were no stars: just that odd flicker in the east. She sniffed and smelled a pungent message in the air. She shuddered and went inside and opened the door to Loren's room.

He was peacefully asleep, his hair a spill of pale gold on the pillow. She bent down to kiss him. He stirred but did not wake.

Something bothered her. The room seemed chilly. She went to adjust the air conditioner. Her finger touched the control and stopped.

There were black flakes on the window ledge, flakes the size of moths that had somehow wormed their way through the accordion-fold panels between air conditioner and window frame. She touched one and brought her finger up to her eye.

It was an ash. A large, black glob of incinerated *something* that had sailed here from God only knew where. *Damn.* If ashes had gotten through Loren's air conditioner, then the roof must be covered in the stuff.

She wanted to ask Toby about the roof, but he was fast asleep in their king-sized brass bed. No wonder, with all the Quaaludes he'd been popping at the party.

She undressed. As she was getting into bed she let her weight—and the baby's—fall abruptly on the mattress. The sudden motion brought Toby out of sleep. His eyes still closed, he reached out his hand to rest it on her breast.

"I'm sorry, honey," she said, "I didn't mean to wake you."

"Remember to do your exercises?"

"Too tired."

"Naughty, naughty. Let me feel your muscle." Toby

gently brought his hand closed on her breast. "Some muscle, babe." His eyes were still closed. "Keep up the good work."

She placed her hand over his. "Toby, can I ask you something about the roof?"

"Sure, babe."

"Is it fireproofed?"

"Mmmm—I think so."

"But you don't know?"

Toby sat up slightly and caressed Melinda's breast in earnest now. "I can find out. How about let's talk about it mañana, okay?"

"I'm worried, Toby. There's that fire in the hills and—"

"Honey, as far as that fire is concerned, it could be twenty million light-years from this house. We are in a firesafe zone."

"What does that mean?" Melinda said dubiously. She didn't see how a house could be firesafe with a flammable roof.

"It means I talked to the TV news people and I talked to the mayor's office and there is absolutely nothing to worry about."

Melinda frowned and Toby caught it.

"*And,* if there *were* anything to worry about, you can bet your ass the mayor would be here personally to whisk us away in his limousine—because His Honor needs you very, very much."

"He needs me till tonight," Melinda said. "Till the concert."

"Babe, you are worrying yourself over *nothing.* Now unless you let me feel your other muscle, I'm not going to forgive you."

Melinda sighed. She lifted his hand and placed it on her other breast. "Forgiven?" she said.

The station wagon slowed. The little dog on the front seat, its head resting on the man's lap, gave a start and looked up. As if it'd been pinched, the little dog pulled away from Defino's lap and leaped to its feet. Its round eyes darted from window to window as it gaped expectantly at the big trees marked out in black against the sky. The dog whimpered, its small body squirming. Its toenails caught on the torn leatherette.

Defino steered the car off the dirt road, braked, and then pushed open the door on his side. The little terrier barked once, a high, sharp report.

Defino hurried now. He went to the rear of the station wagon. From the rigging laid neatly out he took a length of fuse, skinny and coiled like a gray snake. At either end there was a U-shaped hook, and at one end a section of translucent yellow plastic.

Defino looped the fuse over one shoulder. He took a flashlight in one hand. Then he pulled a large, drowsy German shepherd down from the car. He began his march.

The dog followed without resistance. The canister attached to its collar clinked as it moved.

Defino headed upland, away from the car and into the tall trees. He stopped. A whistling sound came singing from his chest. He spotted the beam of flashlight along the ground, looking for just the right place, just the right terrain.

He set out again, continuing upland. He was searching for a site just up from where the brush was thickest, the slash deepest. He wanted a route dense with foliage; he wanted thick duff along the runway, a bed of leaf mold, and pine needles.

He noted the forest growth as he went: the mangled branches of manzanita, the tangle of chamiso and sumac and scrub oak, and pines—everywhere the pines, flammable with resin that would set the world to frying.

Fifty yards farther on Defino stopped again. He swept the beam of the flashlight in a slow arc, advanced three steps, and then snapped the flashlight under his arm so that it lit the ground in front of him.

This would do.

He undid the rope from around his waist. He went hand over hand to the dog. He loosened the noose and lifted it from the dog's head, one hand gripping the leather harness. He dropped the rope and slipped the coiled fuse from his shoulder. He felt along the length of it till he found the hook, buckled the hook to the harness, then let go of the dog.

Again he felt along the fuse till his hand came to the translucent casing. He was careful not to expose it to the flashlight. Gripping the yellow cylinder, he advanced three steps to an upright steel marker post set out by the Forestry Service.

He reached into his pocket for a two-headed latch. One head he clipped into the U-hook, the other into a hole punched through the marker.

Now he took the flashlight from under his arm. He directed the beam to where the hook was fastened to the marker. He quickly jerked the light away; it took only a candlepower to set off the fuse. He turned the beam onto the dog.

The animal stood there looking into the light. It strained against the leash. The leash held.

Defino took the syringe from his belt and a blue ampoule from his pocket. He injected the dog in the loose skin beneath the hip. Almost immediately, the dog went stumbling down onto all fours.

Defino smiled. Above him he could hear the Santa Ana, the feverish, malignant wind seeking entry through the crowning canopy of trees.

9

IT WAS a dream, but the place and time were real: Quan Tri, South Vietnam, August 1971.

Cas Lovenko knew they were real because he'd been there. He'd heard the muffled thud of pickaxes breaking ground for tarmac. He'd heard the rattle of privates target-practicing at tin-roofed huts. And he'd seen the sergeant, a handsome young guy, built like a welterweight boxer, with smooth Mediterranean features, instructing the recruits in arson.

Only the sergeant called it fire control technique. "You don't just douse in napalm, know what I mean? You make your material work for you, you make wind currents work for you, whatever's there you make it work for you—and it will. You know what I mean?"

He obviously knew his subject, but he might as well have been lecturing disco fans on Bach's counterpoint. The troops were bored. Several were openly smoking joints.

The sergeant, undaunted, had prepared neat little pieces of rubble for the demonstration.

"Here we have our obvious flammables, you know what I mean? Straw, wood, old rags. Easy."

It took him a flick of a match: ignition. He stood back, regarding his work one smiling moment, proud as a parent watching a healthy child at play.

A breeze ruffled the palms. The sun seemed darker,

the air thicker. Dust rose, swallowing the breeze. The sergeant strolled on to the next pile.

"Okay, here we have the less elementary flammables: rubber, plastic, glass. Notice I say less elementary, because they *are* flammable, only it takes a little doing, know what I mean?"

He crouched, poured neat driblets of kerosene, flicked another match.

Ignition.

"See, with a little effort you can get a gorgeous burn going."

The sun poured out a coppery heat that singed the dirt with a faint continuous hiss. The earth smelled unclean, as though the heat had stirred up fumes of things buried beneath.

Now the sergeant strolled to the last pile. "And these are the impossibles. Concrete, barbed wire, corrugated steel siding. This is the sort of problem you face with tanks or airplanes or trains, so watch."

He worked with paraffin, gasoline, gunpowder, deft and sure, as absorbed in his alchemy as a monk illuminating a medieval manuscript. Finally he lit a match.

Ignition.

Cas Lovenko had never seen such a performance. Out of nothing plus one match, out of the simplest addition of dead material and dead fuel, the boy brought forth living, breathing fire. He had an intuition that reached into fire the way a trainer's does into his animals. He had the gift.

He was an artist.

"The principle, what I just showed you, is that anything burns, even the stuff that doesn't, you know what I mean? Nothing is fireproof; there are only certain materials that are heatproof up to a threshold, see what I mean? So you have to know three things: what are you trying to burn, what's the burn threshold, and what material is going to get you there?"

His eyes swept his audience and he cleared his throat. "Now modern technology has saved us a lot of the work. Instead of walking around with bottles of kerosene and *gas* and nitroglycerin—which could be dangerous, you know what I mean?—science has given us—" The boy hefted it in one smooth motion. It resembled a fire extinguisher except that instead of a hose it had a short, angry-looking snout.

"A flamethrower. With this one device you can achieve any of the thresholds you'll need in hand-to-hand ground warfare, you know what I mean? To use this you don't need to know anything and I mean not *anything* except how to push a button."

The sergeant demonstrated, aiming at the ground, pushing the button and releasing one singing instant of pure white flame.

"Who knows how to push a button, raise your hands?"

A platoon of bored, surly faces stared back at the instructor. Not a hand was raised. He shrugged, philosophical, good-humored about it.

"Okay, who *doesn't* know how to push a button? You."

He thrust the flamethrower at the nearest recruit, a fuzz-cheeked teenager who had just ground the tail end of a joint under his boot and whose glazed eyes should have been warning that he was so stoned his head was on Mars. The teenager backed off but the instructor forced the flamethrower into his hands, then turned to point at a concrete bunker. "Okay, push your button and burn her."

The teenager fumbled and his face turned red and the other recruits began snickering. The instructor smiled sympathetically. He was just reaching for the flamethrower when the recruit found the button.

A jet of piercing white light came hissing from the spout. Flame flowered out of the center of the instructor's chest, a white-red rose of fire that opened and bloomed and gusted up to enclose the arms and shoulders and the screaming face.

In one second what had been a man was a roaring, crackling conflagration, howling and hurling itself into the dirt, rolling and cooking and screaming and cooking and cooking....

By the time Cas Lovenko rushed to him and flung his jacket around the torso and tried to smother the flames, there was nothing human left, only a whimpering howl that rolled toward him, a smear of ash and once-human flesh dribbling down the skull like epileptic drool, two charred clumps of raw finger-bone digging into Cas Lovenko, trying to grasp at survival.

And losing their grip.

With a jerk, Casimir Lovenko awoke from the dream.

He found himself sitting bolt upright on a strange sofa in a strange room. His heart was thumping and his thoughts were spilling in a hot prickle of excitement. He knew if he could just hold on to it, not let it slide away into the waking world, he had it, the clue, the thing his subconscious had been searching for.

His eye took in the lit windows of unappetizing sandwiches, the Coca-Cola logo that seemed to fizz, and he remembered that he had dozed off in the snack bar.

He wiped his forehead and his hand came away dry. He got to his feet, struggling not to be awake but to cling to the sleeping reality of the dream. He fumbled into the hallway and followed the corridor into a thicket of dark cubicles.

He flicked on a desk light. The walls leaped into pale industrial green. He lifted a telephone receiver and, consulting the address book in his pocket, asked the operator to connect him to General Mark Cunningham at the Pentagon.

Waiting, he glanced at his watch. It was barely four o'clock — 7:00 A.M. on the East Coast. In another cubicle he could hear the halting rhythm of one lone typewriter, some poor slob of a bureaucrat hunting and pecking to fill out some county-mandated report form.

A voice came on the line, female and no-nonsense. "General Cunningham won't be in till nine thirty. Can I take a message?"

"This is Cas Lovenko. Emergency. Can you give me his home number?"

"I'm sorry, sir, I can't give out that information."

"That name again is Lovenko, L-o-v-e-n-k-o; would you take my number and have him contact me immediately?" Lovenko read off the number and without waiting for a refusal he hung up.

A minute and twenty seconds later the phone rang.

"Cas, you son of a gun, what's the big emergency?"

"Los Angeles is going up in smoke, that's the emergency. Mark, do you remember that young guy—I think he was a sergeant, Company Q, Quan Tri, seventy-one—he was a fire specialist? He could burn anything—concrete, metal, hell, probably even water, you name it—he got burned in an accident instructing the troops?"

There was a silence and then General Mark Cunningham's voice came three thousand miles. "I have a dim recollection. Didn't he die when one of his men turned a flamethrower on him?"

"That's what I have to find out. Can you get me his name, present whereabouts, everything you or the VA has on file?"

"I can track it down, sure. Present whereabouts is probably Arlington Cemetery."

"And, Mark—if you can dig up any records of his voice—radio traffic, phone taps, anything—can you get me a voiceprint?"

"That'll be tougher—it'll be classified."

"All I need's the voice. Not the words."

"I'll try. How soon do you need it?"

"I need it yesterday, Mark. I have a hunch he's burning down the city."

On Sugar Pine Mountain, at a point not far from the San Sevaine lookout station in the San Bernardino Range, a German shepherd stirred drowsily from a doped sleep and staggered to its legs. After four stumbling steps it was pulled up short by a metallic-gray leash running from its collar to the steel post behind it.

The animal strained but could not break the line. It turned, stumbled back to the post, and sniffed at the U-hook attaching the line. It licked the yellow casing. It curled up again on the ground and waited, resigned to its leash, confident that sooner or later human hands would release it.

The dog was wrong. What released it was not a human, but the sun.

Seven minutes later, at dawn, sun rays poked

through the cover of trees overhead. One of them touched the yellow casing.

The dog stirred as a smell of burning electrical wiring reached its nostrils. A red glow, bright as a live ember, raced from the casing along the length of fuse. The dog backed away from it. Though the animal did not realize it, and did not need to realize it, its situation was radically, rapidly changing.

The length of fuse had done three things: It had acted as a leash, limiting the dog to a five-foot radius. It had bound four loops of steel chain to the dog's collar. It had been wired to the canister attached to that chain.

Now, as the fuse sizzled to ash, the dog was released. The loops of the chain fell free. Finally, as the scorching pinwheel of heat reached the end of the fuse, the canister exploded.

The terrified dog pulled away from the post. This time there was no resistance, nothing holding it back. The animal broke into a crazed run. At the end of the steel chain it dragged a ball of flaming chemical through the tinder-dry duff and slash. Fire sprang up in the path behind it, marking its panicked zigzags. It took a little under four seconds for the canister itself to be consumed.

Now, finally able to put distance between itself and the flames, the dog ran howling through the woods.

The ranger in the lookout tower rubbed his eyes. It was almost the end of his shift. He felt tired and was looking forward to nothing so much as going to bed. He glanced again at his watch and wondered what the hell was keeping his replacement.

He stared out at the deep green canopy of the forest, the treetops tipped here and there with the brilliant red of the rising sun. He yawned.

And then he saw a flare of blinding white rocketing up into the eastern sky. He couldn't see where it had come from; it had been there, already airborne, when it tugged at the corner of his eye. It floated down over the trees and sank into the green canopy.

An instant later he saw the thin line of smoke. In the time it took him to grab for the phone and punch three digits, the thin line had thickened into a smudge and flares were rocketing up across a 180-degree arc of horizon.

"The whole damned range is on fire," he screamed, "the whole damned range!"

At dawn the West Highland terrier came out of the cave. The forest was waiting.

But it was a different forest from before. It was a place where nothing lived: no animal, no plant, not even the fire that had consumed the land. All was death now, carbon and ash and twisted skeletons of what had been living trees and creatures.

The dog hesitated. It sniffed the ground and then raising its nose it sniffed the air. It smelled death, but death without danger. The dog moved into the dead trees. The canister and fuse clanked softly against its collar. The dog wandered through puddles of shadow and light.

There was no tree cover left here, only stripped branches clawing at the sky, hovering pockets of layered smoke. The sun's rays reached down through the naked trees. They touched the blackened earth and the dog that moved across it. They touched the yellow translucent cylinder hanging at its neck.

The heat rise was infinitesimal, but the cylinder was a trigger and it had been precision-tooled to respond to infinitesimal gradations of temperature. The plastic eye within the cylinder ought to have sensed the heat change and winked open. The cornea of the eye ought to have sparked and the spark ought to have ignited the fuse.

But this eye was a mutant.

The machine that had manufactured it had made a mistake. The eye had two lids, one on top of the other. The sun could not get through them both. So, for a while longer, the eye slumbered and the dog wandered.

Within the yellow cylinder, degree by infinitesimal degree, the heat rose, seeking a new threshold.

He was a stocky man in his late thirties with curly red hair and an almost Ozark accent. He had credentials from the telephone company and from the Los Angeles police, and it took him the better part of fifteen minutes to attach the little black box to the cord that ran from VV's call-in phone to the control room.

"You push this button, right on top of the box, the minute you get your caller. Push down hard."

VV nodded. Pushing a button was as easy as—well, as pushing a button.

"Alan," she said, "you push the button. I'll signal when."

"And you," the red-haired man said, turning again to VV, "you keep him on the line as long as you can, at least three minutes, but the longer the better. All clear?"

VV nodded again. It all seemed so simple and failsafe and yet she couldn't shake a feeling that something truly dumb was going to go wrong. Something truly dumb always went wrong when VV Cameron had a chance to bat a home run.

She settled herself into her glass chair. A little drum of nervousness was tapping somewhere at the base of her throat. She tried to ignore it by reviewing lastminute details. Her eye went down to the clipboard in her lap, swept across the small glass table. The white four-button telephone was placed within graceful leaning reach.

"Eight seconds!" Alan called over the studio speaker.

Raising her eyes to the monitor, she smiled her hellothere smile; no crusades today, this was a bait-a-trap day. She crossed her long, slender legs, angled herself toward camera one.

The first call was already flashing on the phone when the red light blinked on. VV leaned forward to push down the button and lift the receiver.

"This is VV Cameron and you're on the air," she said, looking into the camera. No sound. "Can you hear me?"

"Yes—hello," a voice came hesitantly. Not him. A her. *Damn!* "I'm calling about the police?"

VV nodded, her finger poised to disconnect if it turned out to be a superannuated pig-hater left over from the sixties. "I hope you don't mind my calling?"

"That depends what you're calling about. Could you get to the point, dear?"

"I'm a prostitute."

VV's finger almost jabbed the disconnect but she hesitated. *Why not? This could be kicky,* she thought. *The viewers deserve a little soft-core smut.*

"The cops are always ready to hassle us prostitutes, but they're never there to protect. I mean, I pay taxes after all, same as anyone else."

"Do you, dear?"

"Sure—sales tax."

"And how aren't the police protecting you and your sisters?"

"Three prostitutes have been murdered down on the strip this month—same slasher—and the cops haven't lifted a finger."

"How do you know it's the same slasher?"

"Honey, in this business, you just *know.*"

"Well, honey, maybe you know something that the police and the rest of us don't. Thanks for sharing."

Offering the camera a forbearing smile, VV disconnected and took the next call. A bartender with a Chicano lilt to his voice complained that his landlord was racist and hadn't passed along his Proposition 13 savings.

It went on like that: nothing but piddling phone calls. No Mr. Fire Technician. Impatience was gnawing at VV, tinged with growing panic. He *had* to call. This was her story, her exclusive, her chance not only to bag that raise but to step over her skinflint no-nuts boss into the network big time.

And, of course, it was a chance to catch the bastard.

But the piddling phone calls kept jamming the lines, right up to the commercial break. When the little red light on the camera blinked off she let it all hang out, banging her fists in frustration on the table, crying, "Shit!"

"What gives, pudding?" It was Alan's voice on the studio speaker.

"That bastard. Why doesn't he phone? What the hell's keeping him?"

"Patience is a virtue, lovely lady. A watched pot

never boils. Have a cancer stick and work off some of that rage."

VV reached behind her to take one of the three cigarettes she had concealed between her hip and the chair. A technician rushed over to light it for her. She thanked him with a smile, took a deep drag, exhaled, and tried to will the tension out of her.

Her eye wandered from the Pizza Hut commercial on the monitor down to the phone. Two buttons blinking. Maybe, *maybe* one was Mr. Right. *Which one do I push? Eeeny, meeny, miney mo...*

"Ready in eight seconds," Alan called.

"Cigarette somebody." VV took one last drag, held the cigarette aloft; the technician darted back to grab it. She expelled the smoke to the side, waved her hand through it to clear the air, and had her smile ready and in place just as the red light flashed on camera two.

Eeny, meeny, the right button. She snatched up the phone.

"Hello, you're on *Newsbreak*."

"My name is C.T. Bailey, retired?" It was the voice of a little old biddy. "Out here in Los Alamitos? I'm a regular listener?"

Damn, VV cursed, *why didn't I pick the left?*

C.T. Bailey rambled on about civil service pensions and the rising cost of living. VV's eye kept skittering from the stillblinking light up to the studio clock, to the second hand chewing away at the remaining three minutes.

"Thanks very much for your civic interest," VV cut in, jabbing out the call and throwing so much weight so fast onto the left-hand button that the reflection in the glass tabletop visibly buckled. "You're on *Newsbreak*."

"I'm worried, VV, you know what I mean?"

Pay dirt. She leaned to the side far enough to get one finger off-camera and flip a signal to Alan to activate the trace. "What's worrying you, angel?"

"Seems to me the fire department is paid to defend our life and limb, you know what I mean, but all I see them defending is the life and limbs of trees. You know what I mean?"

"No, what do you mean?" *Keep him talking!*

"All the fire-fighting force is up in the forests instead of down in the city protecting hospitals and schools and homes and private citizens. It looks like official policy, know what I mean, the orders must have come from the chief, trees before people. I think the people have a right to be defended and I think they should call City Hall and let the mayor know they're mad as hell."

Alan was making a reeling-in motion with his hands, telling her to stretch the call.

"Now look," she said, instinct telling her to disagree, get him into an argument no matter how dumb, "maybe the fire department knows a little bit more about this fire than you do."

"*These* fires," the toneless voice corrected.

"Maybe if they stop the brush fires and the forest fires," VV said, "maybe they won't *have* to defend hospitals and schools."

"They're defrauding the people, you know what I mean?"

"But maybe the fire department knows a little more about strategy than you do, Mr.—"

He didn't bite, just contradicted smoothly: "I know a little about strategy myself, and theirs stinks. It's criminal negligence."

"But if the fire department defends the city instead of the forests—"

VV felt herself floundering. *Why the hell am I talking to this crazy—literally—crazy idiot? To trap him, VV. Keep going.* "If those forests went up, first of all the ecology of the basin would be thrown out of whack for decades, and second—second—if the city was ringed with fires like that, we'd be stuck like rats in a trap. There'd be a *holocaust*. Is that what you're advocating, Mr.—?"

The man narrowed his lashless eyes at the TV screen. Something was wrong. He'd seen this blabbermouth day in, day out for almost three years, and usually she was a four-star bitch. What was with this sweet act, the "Mr.," the breathy, almost apologetic contradictions when she usually expressed her disagreements

173

with a blunderbuss? She'd chewed out every other nit-wit that called in and she was practically—*coming on* to him, breathing sexy, stretching her words...

Stretching, that was it!

It hit him in a flash. He almost jumped out of the chair. They were tracing the goddamned call! A discharge of electric panic went through him and with it furious loathing for the woman who had almost tricked him.

"Gotta sign off before you trace this," he said quickly, "know what I mean?"

He slammed the phone back into the cradle. The fading shot of VV Cameron's undisguised confusion, the darting eyes, the reaching hand that didn't know where to reach—that almost made him laugh.

But the trace.

That bothered him. He reached down, dug his fingers into the thick pelt of the Labrador pacing at his feet. He squeezed dog flesh, released, squeezed till the repeated movement calmed the wheeling of his mind.

He'd worked for the phone company on one of those preferential hiring "disability" quotas; he knew how those traces worked. They couldn't have changed the system in three years. It took three minutes to trace a call, three fucking minutes.

He was safe.

Hell, he could even call the Cameron bitch again! Tomorrow!

Chuckling, he heaved himself up from the chair and strode into the kitchen. He banged around in the cabinet under the sink, rattling through lids that seemed to have lost their pots and pots that had never had lids.

He found what he was looking for. Cradling it in his hand, laughing now, he brought it back into the room that reeked of dog waste and carefully set it down on the wooden crate that served as a phone table.

He'd call again, taunting, and at the first sound of her voice he'd put it into action. What an invention: high technology and just the thing—an hourglass-shaped three-minute egg timer.

* * *

174

VV Cameron struggled to keep her smile in place and set the dead telephone back into its cradle. The minute her face was off the monitor she muttered a not-very-gentle "Crap!" and signaled Alan through the glass wall. She leaned toward the mike.

"Alan love, how did we do on that trace?"

The voice came back over the studio speaker. "They got the exchange. North Hollywood."

"And that's *all?*"

"That's all, sweetheart."

"Fuck!"

Alan signaled the countdown till live camera, and the sign he gave for one second looked suspiciously as though he were giving her the finger. VV composed herself and delivered lead-in and voice-over for some footage of two fifty-year-old twins, victims of an adoption racket at age six, who'd been reunited through the efforts of station KLIC-TV.

She sat through the sign-off and shuffled papers as the credits on the monitor rolled over a shot of VV Cameron shuffling papers. The station logo came on and she bolted from the chair, skidding it into the backdrop so hard that the L.A. panorama almost fell backward.

"Alan, goddamnit, rerun that tape!"

Alan was standing in the control-room doorway munching a jelly doughnut. "Patience is a virtue, now let's not panic." He wiped his fingers and reversed the tape and set it in forward again. At fifteen inches per second the sound was far superior to the earlier tapes.

VV squinted an ear. That static had definite overtones of...*crunching.* "Okay, Alan, what's that sound?"

"Newspaper. Either the Jolly Green Giant ran out of Charmin, or a couple of dogs are pawing *very* desperately."

VV jabbed a finger toward the spinning reel. "Run it back a sec—there. What's that?"

Alan went back and forward over the spot, playing with filters and dials. "A rather pathetic, distinctly canine *growl,* I'd say."

"A dog!" VV cried.

"I'd say plural dogs, love. Listen to that again."

Alan was right: the growls were definitely an overlapping duet. VV snapped her fingers. "Okay, he's got dogs and newspaper on the floor—what does that tell you?"

"It tells me his place smells like a kennel, love, an absolute *kennel*."

Melinda poured herself another cup of coffee, sipped, set it down on the tape deck. Angling her ear, closing her eyes this time, she played the mix of the instrumental tracks once again.

No. Absolutely not.

She killed the power with a jab of the off switch and forty-three musicians wound down to a basso growl. She flung open the studio door and strode across the lawn toward the pool.

"Toby, I don't like the arrangement."

Toby stretched back comfortably against the deck chair, pulled a joint out of his silver cigarette case, lit it, and flipped the match into the swimming pool. "Which one?"

"America." She had programmed a very, very downtempo "America the Beautiful," a dirge treatment that seemed to suit these times of runaway inflation and the what-the-hell give-up mood of the country. She'd always had luck with her down versions of up numbers, and tonight was the big unveiling of "America." But it felt wrong to her.

"What's the matter with the arrangement?"

"That horn."

His face was squinted up, apparently in concentration on the ember at the tip of his joint. It struck Melinda that there were tiny lines around his eyes that she hadn't seen before, gray hairs at his temples. *He'd better slow down,* she thought, *he's aging*.

"It's a beautiful horn solo," he said.

"It's *my* solo, not some goddamned French horn's."

"It's a very talented arrangement."

"It shits."

The pale eyes met hers. There was implied anger in the unwavering stare.

"Honey, do you know Richard Strauss's 'Four Last Songs'?" he asked.

"No I don't know Richard Strauss's 'Four Last Songs.' Not by heart."

"There's a violin solo in the third song. Elisabeth Schwarzkopf never complained. Kirsten Flagstad never complained."

"My audience is not paying for opera. And I don't pretend to be Schwarzkopf or Flagstad."

He flicked a look up at her. "And don't try."

She gritted her teeth hard. "I'm not going to have a fight, Toby. It's too early. I'm cutting the horn. Just dropping the whole thirty-one bars."

"If you knew what you'd paid for those thirty-one bars you wouldn't be in such a rush."

Sometimes Melinda wondered if Toby got kickbacks from her arrangers. She felt her temper beginning to slip out of control; tiny aggravations were piling up into anger. She could feel the tenseness gathering in her throat muscles, symptom of the desire to scream. At this rate she'd have laryngitis before she even sang a note.

"Where's Loren?" she grumbled.

Toby tossed a nod toward the tree house.

Melinda glanced out over the lawn and saw it was still littered with glasses and napkins. "Those caterers haven't showed up."

"You trying to work yourself into a mood?" Toby asked.

"The lawn's a goddamned mess. What the hell do I pay servants for?"

"Take it easy; the caterers will show up."

Melinda sniffed dubiously. Beneath the smell of pot she caught a hint of burned wood. "What's happening to the air in this town?"

Toby shrugged. "Don't panic. It's that fire over in the hills."

"It smells like a fire over *here*."

"You *are* in a mood, baby." He flipped open the cigarette case. "Have one."

She shook her head in angry refusal. "When are you going to grow up? It's not even noon and you're stoned."

"Not stoned. Just getting a buzz on."

"You don't *need* a buzz on. You have to get over to the Bowl and make sure it's set up for the concert."

"And before that I have to have lunch with the mayor and the governor at the Brown Derby. Therefore I need a buzz on." Toby stood up, nodded with almost crazy good cheer, and nearly lost his balance.

She gave him the finger. He gave her the finger back. She snatched a china plate from the lawn with a smear of gray caviar still clinging to it and hurled it at him with her deadliest Frisbee aim. He ducked and the plate sailed past him into the swimming pool.

"See you at six at the Bowl." Toby waved and vanished into the house.

Melinda felt surplus anger still churning in her. "Loren!" she screamed.

"Yeah?" came a voice from the tree.

"Be careful up there." She stomped back across the lawn into the studio, slammed the door behind her, and jammed the tape into forward.

Toby took the Maserati. It was a Maserati day. As he drove, he kept one eye on his wristwatch. Plenty of time. Coming out of the canyon, he noticed a zebra-striped sawhorse blocking the incoming lane. A highway patrol car was pulled to the side of the road and two highway policemen were sitting in the front seat.

Toby swung near the roadblock so that he could call out to one of the cops: "What's happening?"

The policeman in the driver's seat grinned and threw him a hand signal that seemed to say "Everything's under control."

Toby didn't believe it. He kept going, but when he passed a red Toyota heading into the canyon he slowed again, watching in the rearview mirror. The highway police turned the Toyota back. Toby pulled to the edge of the road and as the Toyota passed he beeped his horn and leaned to the window.

"Say, what's going on back there?" he called.

The driver, a heavyset man with thinning gray hair, slowed to shout back, "Road's out!"

"How come?"

"Rockslides."

A U-turn brought Toby neatly back to the roadblock. "Would you mind telling me what the hell you're trying to pull?"

For a moment the highway policeman was motionless and then he sauntered over to the Maserati. One hand on his hip holster, he stared at Toby, eyes only half-visible behind their sunglasses.

"How come you've blocked this road off?" Toby demanded.

The policeman's voice was polite, but it was the politeness of a man with a gun three inches from his hand. "We're not allowing traffic into the canyon, sir. Orders of the mayor."

And now Toby understood the oily, billowing cloud of gray gathering in the east.

"How near is that fire?"

The policeman's eyes remained fixed and unblinking behind the glasses. "The fire is being contained."

"My girlfriend and her kid are back there!"

"Sir, there is no danger."

"Then what's with these rockslides? I was just up there, there's not even a loose pebble on that road!"

"Please turn this car around, sir."

"Not till I get my girlfriend and her kid out."

"All residents will be evacuated when and if necessary."

"Yeah? And what do you call that smoke up there— it looks to me like when-and-if's right now."

"Please don't make trouble, sir. We can make trouble right back."

Toby peered down the road past the police block. There was no other traffic in sight. He floored the accelerator, whipping the steering wheel counterclockwise. The car went rocketing into the left lane. Toby gave the wheel another wrench and dodged sharply around the roadblock and back into the right lane.

It was a dumb thing to have done. He hadn't seen the other highway patrol car, but it was waiting for him just around the bend. There was no room to pass. He had a choice of crashing or braking. He braked and skidding wheels screamed.

A patrolman approached, gun drawn. There was nothing polite in the voice. "Get out with your hands up."

Shouldn't have had that joint, Toby realized. *Shoulda listened to Momma.*

VV Cameron leaned across Ed Caldwell's desk and pushed the stop button on the tape recorder. His eyes went from her to the machine and back again. He didn't understand her excitement.

"What does it give us, VV? A telephone exchange in North Hollywood. That's twenty square miles and ten thousand numbers. Doesn't exactly pinpoint him, does it?"

"We have a little bit more than a phone number, Chief." VV reversed the tape. She ran it forward till she found the noise again. Caldwell listened. He looked up at the slender freckled face poised over the tape recorder. "Don't you recognize the sound?" she asked.

He shook his head. "Should I?"

"You've never owned a dog?"

"My son had one....I gave it away."

"Haven't you ever heard a dog pawing newspaper?"

"Can't say I've had the pleasure."

"For the record, Chief, that noise is a dog with a very full bladder tearing apart a floor full of newspaper." She picked out another segment of tape and boosted the volume. "And that pathetic mewling is how a dog sounds when it's begging." She raced the tape forward and picked another segment. "And that duet is *two* dogs begging."

Caldwell stared at her. A wrinkle of perplexity ran vertically between his eyes. "Maybe I'm being dense, VV, but I can't see the significance."

"The significance, Chief, is dogs."

"*Dogs?* There must be half a million dogs in this city."

"And at least two of them belong to Mr. Phone-in. *And,* he doesn't walk them."

"How do you figure that?"

"Newspaper on the floor."

"Maybe the dogs aren't housebroken."

"The dogs are begging to get *out*. An unhousebroken dog wouldn't."

"Maybe they're hungry."

"That's not the sound, Chief. They're singing the I-gotta-go song. Which means they're housebroken and not being let out of the house. Ergo, newspaper on the floor. Now why would you housebreak a dog and then not let it out of the house?"

Caldwell bit his underlip. "I don't know. Why?"

"You wouldn't. It's throwing away a very hard-won education."

"I don't follow this. You're saying the dogs are housebroken, or they wouldn't be whining to get out, *but* they're shitting in the house, because there's newspaper on the floor."

"Right."

"So what's your conclusion?"

"They're not his dogs. No owner would do that."

"VV, what the hell does this have to do with the fires?"

"Chief, I don't know *what* it has to do with the fires, but I do know two very curious facts about this very curious phone-caller. One, he's burning down forests. Two, he's mistreating other people's dogs. *At the same time.*"

"I still don't get the connection."

She looked at him, the keenness of her eyes magnified by the tinted glasses.

"Chief, use your imagination. You're a dog. You're housebroken. You're locked indoors by someone who's not your owner and you gotta go and all you've got to go on is a pile of last week's bad news. Now what is your heart's desire? What is your fantasy of fantasies? Where of all places on earth would you yearn to be?"

Caldwell shrugged. "Where?"

"A *forest,* goddamnit. *That's* the connection!"

Caldwell scratched his hairline, looked at her a moment, shook his head. "Sorry, VV—I don't buy it."

"I'm not asking you to buy it, Chief. I'm asking you

to check it out. You had a fire night before last, six fires yesterday, eight fires this morning. Check the reports on those fifteen fires: check the victims, check the witnesses, check what was going on in the vicinity. If a dog shows up in any one of those fires, in any way, shape, or form—that's your lead."

"Dogs," Caldwell muttered, mulling the notion. "VV, that's crazy."

"Chief, what does it cost you to check your own files?"

Caldwell was silent a long moment, listening to the silence of his own thoughts. He flicked a glance up at VV and reached for the telephone, and asked to be connected to Peters. "Pull the records on all the fires in the mountains in the last two days. Give me anything that has to do with dogs."

Peters' voice came across the line incredulously. *"Dogs?"*

"That's right, friend. Dead, alive, mutts, thoroughbreds, German shepherds, Chihuahuas. Anything in those reports with four legs that barks. Get it to me soonest, will you?"

Caldwell hung up and turned to VV. "It'll take awhile."

VV stared at the face lined with fatigue. "Chief, you're wiped out. Take a break, why don't you?"

"A break?" He shook his head. "This isn't TV, my friend. We don't take breaks—not with fifteen fires raging out there."

"You'll be in a lot better shape with a cup of coffee in you."

He nodded toward the electric pot on the corner table. "Help yourself. It's on the taxpayers."

"There's a quiet little coffee shop across the street. You could use five minutes' quiet. Come on, Chief. Get someone to cover for you. The coffee's on me. They make great espresso."

Caldwell considered the suggestion. He liked it. He liked her. He punched Lovenko's number. "Cas, I'm going to take five. I'll be at the coffee shop across the street. Can you cover for me?"

Caldwell sipped and frowned. He looked up at her.

Her eyes were green and waiting and just a little bit guilty.

"Espresso?" he said.

She shrugged. "Tastes like instant. Sorry about that. Guess their espresso machine's on the fritz."

He set down the cup. "VV, why'd you ask me here?"

"Why'd you come?"

"That's not an answer."

"Yes it is, Chief. It's a very direct answer to a very dumb question."

Caldwell pointed his finger at her, then back at himself. "You direct, me dumb?"

"Something like that." VV leaned forward to lift her cup from the table and the sunlight from the window flashed in her red hair. Ed Caldwell was suddenly aware of the fullness at her breasts that dwindled to the narrowness at her waist. It seemed a simple geometric fact, a something that shrank to nothing. Why did it amaze him? And why did he fight it?

"You have a lot of confidence in yourself, don't you?" he said. "And maybe just a little contempt for other people?"

"Chief, right this moment, you'll see my hand's shaking. Look at my coffee cup. Notice those little ripples? Now if that's confidence, okay, I'm confident. As for contempt for other people—at this moment you're the other people. And what I'm feeling I wouldn't exactly call contempt."

"What would you call it?" Caldwell said.

She glared at him. "Are you dumb, or just a shit?"

"I call that contempt."

"It was a rhetorical question. Wasn't meant to be answered."

"You mean I'm a dumb shit."

"I mean I didn't mean it."

"Then what did you mean?"

"Chief, I'm the trained interviewer, not you. I've had three years' experience. In the industry, I'm considered pretty accurate with a harpoon. So please don't try to put me on the spot, because I can turn the tables very easily."

"Turn them."

"Why don't we just enjoy our coffee?"

"Because I don't enjoy instant."

"What kind do you drink?"

"Instant. Milk, no sugar."

"You ever been in analysis, Chief?"

"I went to a shrink for a while."

"Then you know that someone who dislikes instant but drinks it anyway is either very lazy or has very low self-esteem."

"If that's a multiple choice, I can tell you I'm not lazy."

"Then your self-esteem is pretty low and I'd say that's pretty dumb."

"*What's* dumb about it?"

VV stared at the still-trembling surface of her coffee. She wondered why Eddy Caldwell's presence should arouse fear in her. Fear of what? "You're a nice guy, Chief. You should like yourself a little better."

"What's nice about me?"

"A few things. Maybe even a lot of things. I don't know you well enough yet to say."

"The only thing you know about me, VV, is I don't like instant. Beyond that, you're a fortune-teller reading coffee grounds."

"This fortune-teller cheated. The *Los Angeles Times* keeps a file on you. I've read the update." She saw his frown, saw the tension raising ridges at the sides of his jaw.

"Then you know I killed my wife and kid."

She sat forward in the chair, hands clasped tightly around the cup. That was her only reaction. "I know they're dead. That's all the file told me."

"Now you know the update."

She didn't miss a beat. "Why'd you kill them, Chief?"

"I didn't mean to." He hesitated. "Look, VV. There's no way to fight a fire drunk, so I've been sober thirty hours. But for six months before that I didn't have one sober moment. So what I'm going through is politely called withdrawal. My guts are spinning and my head feels very freaky. I can do my job because it's not personal. I'm still good at things that aren't personal. But personal things, like sitting here talking to you, I can't handle worth a damn. Not without a drink."

"Are you asking for a drink?"

"I'm explaining that it's very hard for me to talk to you without spilling all over the place."

"Do you want to spill all over the place?"

He met her eyes, deep green and speculative, and he knew the thing they were speculating about was Eddy Caldwell. He nodded. "Yes."

She sat looking across the table at him, and suddenly there was no tension in her, no fear of being a fool or of being a bitch, no fear of his rejecting her, because rejection and bitchery and foolishness didn't matter. The only thing that mattered was that he trusted her. Without warning, there was someone in the world who trusted VV Cameron and his name happened to be Edward K. Caldwell and he happened to be sitting at this table in this coffee shop.

"Spill," she said.

He stared down at his coffee. "It was Mickey's birthday. Mickey was my kid. It was his sixth birthday. Joyce was always after me, saying I never spent any time with him. Joyce was my wife. She was right. They'd just made me chief, I was married to the fire department. She put her foot down. She said, Eddy, you're going to spend Mickey's birthday with *him,* not the fire department. You're going to take him to Disneyland. Mickey was really excited about Disneyland.

"His birthday came and so did the fire in Laurel Canyon. Same day. I said, Joyce, I'm chief, I've got to go. Mickey was dancing around, all excited, he loved fires better than Disneyland. Take us, he said. Take us along. You know, that Laurel Canyon thing, it looked small. They all look small at the start, but this one— we had it under control, it looked like it'd stay small. So I drove out for a look, took Joyce and Mickey with me. Warned them to stay in the car."

Ed Caldwell was silent, staring into his coffee, remembering.

VV reached a hand to brush the hair off his forehead. "What happened?"

His voice was choked. "The wind changed. That's all.

185

The wind changed. Like that." He snapped a finger. "There was no warning. There was no fire line, there were no men, nothing between that fire and Mickey and Joyce. It was moving at ninety miles an hour. Like a tidal wave. They got out of the car. They ran."

He stopped.

Gently, VV said, "What happened?"

He spoke with his eyes shut, as though memory were a movie unreeling behind clenched lids.

"It was by the country club. There was a twelve-foot fence. Made of sturdy, heavy-gauge wire, crisscross. You know the kind. The wire made diamonds, little diamonds, little so—nothing could get through. So no one could get through. Private club. No trespassing."

Again he slowed.

"Ed—keep going. What happened?"

"No one got through. That's what happened. The fire got through. Joyce and Mickey didn't. They had the fence on one side, fire coming at them from the other."

"But you tried to save them—I know you tried, Ed."

"Oh, sure, we tried all right. With all available hoses. Soon as we saw what was happening. All available hoses. Two hundred pounds pressure per square inch. Eight hoses. You know what killed them?"

She stared at the tightness in his face, the unseeing in his eyes.

"Tell me, Ed."

"The water. The two hundred pounds per square inch. Slammed them against that fence and—they couldn't get through. Pieces of them got through—and then the fire...swept right in and finished them. All the water did was...drown them. Didn't stop the fire. Didn't do a damned thing to the fire. That fire just kept on going. Nothing could stop that fire."

She had a suddenly intense sense of him, not only of his physical male presence, of the breadth and height of him bent over in the chair, but of the grief and the suffering, almost as big as the man, almost as male. At the same moment she had a vivid and sure sense of the courage in him, the courage he did not even know he possessed. She realized she had never known a brave man. She realized Ed Caldwell was the first.

"Ed—it wasn't your fault."

"If I hadn't taken them with me..."

"You didn't know."

"I should have known. It's my job to know."

"But no one could know a thing like that. Ed, you have to be like that fire. Just keep on going. Don't let Laurel Canyon stop you. Don't let anything stop you. Keep burning. Don't go out."

For a long moment they looked at each other. Neither of them spoke. His eyes were grave.

"That's how I got this limp," he said.

"What limp?"

"The limp in this leg. You never noticed I limp?"

"Eddy, you *don't limp.*"

"I tried to get to them and the water slammed me too. That's how I got the limp."

"*You don't limp.*"

He gazed at her and she could see his perplexity. "What are you trying to do, VV—soft-soap me or cheer me up?"

"Neither. Both. Take your pick."

He stared at her a long moment and seemed about to say something. Instead he glanced abruptly at his watch.

"Time's up. Thanks for the espresso. And...thanks."

In the small, square, windowless room that the Los Angeles Fire Department had lent him as a temporary office, Casimir Lovenko shifted the telephone receiver from one ear to the other.

"Virtually a blank wall," the patrician and slightly drawling voice of General Mark Cunningham continued without a break.

"Come on, Mark," Lovenko prodded, "you must have at least been able to turn up his name."

"That much we managed: Franklyn Amory Venice."

"Venice as in Italy?"

"You got it. Frank for short."

Lovenko jotted on a scratch pad.

"After the accident," General Cunningham went on, "he was packed in ice and flown to the burn center in Houston. Records show there were burns over eighty percent of his body. Amazingly enough, he lived. One year and two weeks and twenty-eight skin grafts later he was sent to the veterans' hospital at Arlington."

"Why?"

"Psychiatric tests. Apparently he passed, because three weeks later he was discharged. Now here's where we get to the blank wall. We have no further records on Corporal Frank Amory Venice. None whatsoever."

"That's not possible. What about veterans' benefits? Pension, disability? He must have had disability. What about medical insurance?"

"You won't believe this, Cas, but Frank Venice to this day has not cashed a single government check. Not his pension, not his disability, not his insurance. All were returned, addressee unknown. My guess is, the man's dead. And the VA agrees with me. I wouldn't be surprised if he took his own life. He was a mess, Cas. No man would want to live in that kind of shape."

"I'm not so sure, Mark. What about voiceprint—any luck there?"

"The Veterans Administration has a tape of one of the psychiatric tests. But that's confidential—privileged communication."

"And according to you and the VA the man's dead and the dead do not have privileged communication. Anyway I'm not asking for a transcript, all I want is a print of the voice."

"I'll try, Cas. I'll try my damnedest."

Lovenko thanked the general and hung up. He watched Marty Siegel, seated in a chair across the cubicle, tapping a pencil on his knee.

"All we have is a name," Lovenko said gloomily. "We don't even know if the man's alive, let alone if he's here in Los Angeles."

"Correction, Cas." Marty Siegel's pencil stopped tapping. "If this man's the bug, we know he's alive. *And* we know he has a phone. So we check the phone listings. While we're at it, we check utility records. We check automobile registrations, police records, Social Security, state unemployment. We check every scrap of state and county paper till we turn that name up. By the way, what is the name?"

"Franklyn Amory Venice," Lovenko said. "Frank for short. Venice as in Italy."

The information was waiting on Caldwell's desk. He reviewed it quickly. Peters had made the job easier by marking anything that had to do with dogs in transparent yellow ink.

"What's the news, Chief?" VV asked, watching him.

Wordlessly, he handed her the manila folder.

VV stared at the pages in what at first seemed to be perplexity. For a long while she remained silent.

Caldwell realized he was angry. Angry at his own mind for being unable to grasp the pieces of this problem and put them together. He felt like an ape in an experiment too clumsy to place one building block upon the other.

Dogs.

Dogs on the tape-recorded telephone call.

Two pot-smoking hippies and one dog badly burned in a fire in the Santa Monicas two nights ago.

A mongrel rescued from a burn site yesterday morning.

A crazed cocker spaniel biting a fire fighter this morning.

He willed his mind to be systematic. He went over it again, but it didn't make sense. Something was missing. Suddenly VV took up a pen and began jotting on a note pad. Her teeth were biting down on her lower lip and she seemed to be on the track of something. Finally she looked up at Caldwell. Running her finger along the stiff corner of the file she said in a quiet voice, "In your average dry-season mountain fire, how many dogs usually show up in the reports?"

"None."

"In less than forty-eight hours you've had fifteen fires and dogs have been involved in three of those, three different fires, three different dogs. Does that strike you as statistically significant?"

Caldwell drummed his fingers on the arms of his chair, a nervous habit he had when thinking. He stared at the ceiling, flashing images of *dog* through his mind, images of *fire,* trying to find some point of overlap in the two.

"Definitely significant," he said. But *how?*

"Now if I'm reading these reports correctly," VV said, "two of these dogs are strays. The mongrel and the cocker spaniel. How did they get into those fires? Stray into them? Isn't that stretching coincidence? And what about the dog in the first fire? This report says unidentified man, unidentified woman, hospitalized. *And* unidentified dog. Was the dog theirs, or was it a third stray?"

Caldwell hunched his shoulders in a helpless shrug. He swallowed. His mouth was astonishingly dry. He rose to pour himself a cup of coffee from the machine in the corner. "How about you?" he asked VV.

"Splash of milk, no sugar," she answered automatically.

He handed her the cup. "We still don't know for sure that that first fire connects with the others."

VV peered at him over the rims of her tinted glasses. "Come *on,* Chief. Look at where the fire broke out. It's dead center in your first arc. And look at that dog." VV was silent a moment and then she snapped her fingers, as though something she'd said had triggered an association. "That's exactly it. Look at those dogs."

She jumped to her feet.

"Chief, those dogs were there! They saw three of those fires! They're *witnesses!*"

"*Were* witnesses," Caldwell corrected. "The cocker spaniel was destroyed; the mongrel died of burns."

"And the first dog?"

Caldwell flipped again through the pages. There was no mention of what had happened to the animal. "Search me."

"I'm going to find that mutt."

"VV, you can't question a dog."

"Chief, I'm an investigative reporter. If there is one living witness, I'm going to get that story. Now what hospital are unidentified man and unidentified woman in?"

* * *

190

Two minutes after VV Cameron left fire department headquarters, Lieutenant Harvey Burgett of the Los Angeles Police Department received a telephone call from the Pentagon. He said one word.

"Ready."

He placed the receiver in the electronic cradle and pressed a button. A computer in the Pentagon began talking to a computer in L.A. police headquarters. At the terminal in Lieutenant Burgett's office a printout drum began spinning.

Lieutenant Burgett poured himself a cup of coffee, put his feet up on an open drawer, and leaned back in his chair to wait. As the drum whirred he flipped through the afternoon paper. He paused at the center-fold photos of burn victims and devastated forest. He sighed and went on to the crossword puzzle. He was stuck on 7 down, Hittite deity in three letters, when the drum clanked to a stop.

His feet hit the floor and his hand reached the drum in almost the same instant. He yanked the sheet off the machine, flipped open the manila folder on the desk, and slapped the Washington voiceprint down next to the L.A. print.

His eye told him in one glance what he wanted to know. Nevertheless he took a magnifying glass and went over the two prints ridge by ridge, crest by crest, and valley by valley. When he'd satisfied himself he picked up the telephone and punched out a number.

"Lovenko? Lieutenant Burgett, police headquarters. I think I have something for you."

Caldwell was waiting with Lovenko when a raw-boned grim-faced man of thirty-five or so knocked on the open door of the cubicle. He introduced himself as Harvey Burgett. Handshakes were exchanged all around.

"I brought you the army voiceprint." Lieutenant Burgett produced a manila envelope from inside his jacket. He pulled out two documents that looked like barometric graphs in negative.

Identical barometric graphs.

"As you can see," the lieutenant said, "it matches the KLIC voiceprint."

Lovenko nodded.

Caldwell had an anxious thought. "How reliable are those voiceprints?"

Lieutenant Burgett seemed to be expecting that question. "As close to proof positive as you can get. I'd say there's no doubt about it. The man who phoned VV Cameron and Sergeant Frank Venice are one and the same. Just for the record, the army sent along his photo."

The photograph that Burgett took from the envelope had the low-gloss, inky look of old-fashioned rotogravure. It showed a curly-haired handsome young man with a small dark mustache and large, light-colored eyes.

"That's him," Lovenko said.

He said it so matter-of-factly that it took an instant for Caldwell to register the sudden pulse of excitement in his blood.

"Of course," Lieutenant Burgett said, "this was taken almost ten years ago."

"And one near death by burning ago," Lovenko said. "So he lived after all." Lovenko shook his head. "It's no wonder. No wonder at all."

"No wonder what?" Caldwell said.

"No wonder he wants to burn the city down. America destroyed him, he'll settle for Los Angeles. Let's *pray* he'll settle for L.A. He may have bigger plans."

"What do you mean, America destroyed him?" Caldwell said.

Lovenko described Sergeant Frank Venice's accident. "There's no way he could still look like this picture. I saw him afterward. No plastic surgeon could have rebuilt that wreck."

"Okay," Caldwell said, "so the photo's no good. But we have the name. And we know he's within range of KLIC—hell, that's local. Has anyone tried looking in the phone book?"

"We did that," Lieutenant Burgett said. "We found *a* Frank Venice. He's eighty-nine years old, he's blind, and he's in an old folks' home."

Caldwell slammed one fist into the other. "There's got to be another Frank Venice."

"We checked all the computer records," Lieutenant Burgett said. "Utilities, phone, Social Security, police, auto license. We only turned up the one."

Caldwell's initial excitement had passed but not his certainty. "No. There are two. *Our* Frank Venice is here. The voiceprint proves it. He's here and he's setting those fires."

Lieutenant Burgett scratched his head. "All I can suggest then is that he's using a different name."

Lovenko exhaled a sigh. "Thank you, Lieutenant."

"Anytime. You know where to reach me if you need me, sir. You too, Chief."

10

THE third floor of the hospital was mobbed with visitors. VV went directly to the nurse at the station. "Do you have a Ronald Fairbanks on this floor?" Admissions had given her the name.

The nurse glanced up at her. "We sure do."

"I'd like to talk with him."

The nurse shook her head. "No way."

The woman's eyes lingered on her and VV sensed a spark of recognition. She decided to pull the celebrity angle. Sometimes it worked in these situations.

"Look, my name's VV Cameron. I'm with KLIC-TV and I'm on a story."

The nurse broke into a smile and stood up and shook hands.

"I *knew* you looked familiar. I watch your show every chance I get, but I work such crazy hours..."

VV nodded, cutting short the apology. She accepted the fact that she was not a recognizable celebrity—yet. She worked for a dinky independent station and a lot of her audience were channel hoppers dodging commercials and quiz shows on the networks. Still, most of them knew they knew her and something always tugged their eyes back.

"I'd really be grateful if you'd let me interview the Fairbanks boy. I promise it won't take more than three minutes. Couldn't you just let me sneak in?"

"It wouldn't do any good, Miss Cameron. He's packed

in ice and he's got enough Demerol in him to stun an elephant. Third-degree burns over forty percent of his body. But I'll tell you what. You can talk to Allison Joyce. She was with him. Only she's guarded, so you can't go in like that."

The nurse took VV to a linen closet and handed her a nurse's smock.

"Just button it up over your dress. Room three eleven. Smile at the cop and walk fast."

VV smiled and walked fast. The policeman looked up from his newspaper and let her pass. VV closed the door behind her.

The room was very dim behind closed blinds. It took VV's eyes a moment to adjust. The girl was sitting up in bed, staring at her.

"You're not a nurse," the girl said.

"No. I'm a reporter."

"I've seen your show. You're VV Cameron. I like the way you sock it to those assholes. Do you have any grass?"

VV shook her head. "Sorry."

The girl lit a cigarette and took a long drag that didn't seem to satisfy her in the least.

"How can you light a cigarette?" VV asked. "I mean—doesn't the flame bother you?"

The girl shrugged indifferently. She was very young and very pretty but she wore makeup that would have been excessive on a carnival stripper. VV wondered if it was to cover burns but somehow she didn't think the doctors would allow that.

"You mean the fire?" the girl said. "Ronnie got burned, not me. I told him to leave that dog alone. He wouldn't listen."

VV drew a chair up to the bed. "Allison," she said in a lowered voice, "tell me about that dog."

The girl gave VV a sizing-up look. After a moment she took a deep drag and sighed. "We heard barking. I thought the animal was being tortured, you know, the barking sounded real weird. Then it stopped and Ronnie went to look. Next thing I knew something exploded and I ran out of the tent and Ronnie was on fire and there was fire all around him."

"What about the dog?"

The girl nodded vaguely. VV wondered if the doctors had given her some kind of pain-killer.

"The dog was on fire too."

"Whose animal was it?"

"I don't know. It was just there."

"Allison, how did the fire start?"

"We didn't start it. We were high, but we didn't start any fire. Ronnie didn't even have matches on him when he left the tent."

"Then do you have any idea what *did* start it?"

The girl sucked on her cigarette.

"Allison, I believe you that you didn't have anything to do with it. What I want to know is, was there any connection between the fire and that dog?"

The girl twisted to the bedside table and stubbed out the cigarette in a coffee saucer. Then, slowly, she gathered herself into a huddling posture. Her shoulders hunched and her hands lumped protectively and probably unthinkingly in the region of her groin. Perspiration sparkled on her forehead. For a long moment she was silent and finally the answer came in a whispered monotone.

"You're not going to believe this."

"I will believe it, Allison. Just tell me what happened."

"I'm not trying to get out of anything and I'm not making this up. I don't understand this and I don't know how, but from what I saw—the dog started the fire."

"The *dog?*"

The girl's eyes met VV's. She nodded. "The dog."

VV dialed from the pay phone just off the visitors' lounge. The call went by radio relay from headquarters to the mobile unit in zone two in the Santa Susanas. A ranger managed to locate Ed Caldwell and hand him the headset. VV was shouting.

"Chief, can you hear me?"

"I can hear something that sounds like you," he shouted back over a din of sirens and helicopters. "VV, we know the man's name. The man that phoned in. Frank Venice. Mean anything to you?"

She frowned and tested the name for reverberations. "Not offhand. Have you got him?"

"Can't trace him. Police are working on it. All we've got so far is the name."

"Okay, I'll put my subconscious to work on it. In the meantime, I have some news for *you*. This man Venice may have had a hand in this, but according to my information he didn't start the first fire."

Caldwell grabbed the headset closer. "Do you know who did?"

"I know *what* did. A dog."

"Knock it off, VV. That's crazy."

"Crazy like Mrs. O'Leary's cow and the Chicago fire. I'm going to look for the dog, and when I find it I'll be in touch."

"VV—hold on!"

"Sorry, Chief. Time's up."

Caldwell was left holding a dead line. He glanced over his shoulder at the sound of his name being called.

A pilot was waving to him urgently. "Hey, Chief—copter's ready!"

VV found the third-floor nurse at her station. "There was a dog involved. Do you have any idea what happened to it?"

The nurse nodded. "That poor animal. Let me ring Emergency. They'd probably know where it was sent. That is, if it lived."

Three minutes later VV was striding toward her car with an address in her pocket. Luck was with her. She found a parking place in front of the two-story white-painted brick office building. She pushed the buzzer marked M. MacDonald, Veterinary Surgeon. A blond-haired girl in blue jeans let her in.

"Dr. MacDonald?"

"I'm his assistant."

"I'd like to see the doctor about the dog that was burned two nights ago."

"Are you the owner?"

"No." VV hesitated. "I'm a reporter."

Two women sitting with cat carriers glanced up from their magazines. VV had the impression one of them recognized her.

"Could you wait just a moment?" The girl disappeared behind a louvered door. A moment later a white-haired man poked his head out and asked VV to step in back.

"You're here about the Afghan hound?" His face was grim, but the eyes suggested that under other circumstances it might have been cheerful. VV introduced herself and, twisting facts a little, said she was doing a story on cruelty to animals. She felt guilty saying it but the doctor seemed convinced. And eager.

"Come right this way, Miss Cameron." He led her briskly down a corridor of caged animals. Most were dozing but two or three dogs roused themselves to bark. "This is the animal."

VV bent toward the cage. For a moment she thought she was going to vomit. It must have once been a beautiful creature. There were patches of coat left and VV could see that it had been long and full and white. But most of the dog was bandages oozing salve and harnesses holding the bandages and shaved strips of brown, baked-looking skin.

She reached a hand through the bars of the cage. The dog looked up at her, its eyes yellow and drowsy. A trembling shook it but it did not rise. It remained collapsed on its side, too drugged, too exhausted, to be interested in the life around it. VV turned, baffled and disbelieving, to the veterinarian. "What happened to it?"

"The animal was tortured. Willfully, sadistically abused. See the bandages around its neck?"

VV nodded.

"It had a strip of burned flesh three inches wide going clear around."

"But what could have done it?"

The vet passed his hand along the top of his head where the white hair was thinning. His eyes were remote and angry. "You mean what—or who? Obviously a very disturbed person was responsible."

"But how was it done?"

"A flammable liquid was smeared around the neck and something ignited it."

"But that's a big animal—why didn't it defend itself?"

"Probably didn't know what was going on. They're not bright animals. You see, when the beauty was bred into them, the brains were bred out."

"It's a purebred?"

"Definitely. My guess is pedigreed."

VV's mind clicked. "Then it could be traced?"

"With a little effort, sure."

"Doctor, I want to find out who owns this dog and I want to find out how it got into that forest. How do I do it?"

The doctor's eyebrows worked a moment, moving up and down. "Check the records at the Los Angeles show dog association. I have a hunch this animal might have taken a few first prizes."

From his helicopter, Ed Caldwell policed the growing holocaust. *This is mine,* he thought. *I wished for it.* And now he wished he hadn't. Because the fighter in him that had exulted only twenty-four hours ago was no longer exulting: in fact, the fighter was a little bit...scared.

The fire was surf now. It was an ocean riding over the land, an orange sea that careened down one hill only to course crazily up the next, splashing even faster up a grade than it swam down. And where sea collided with sea, where wind and heat sucked them together, it was a violent welding whose sum was many times the total of its parts.

For there was nothing arithmetic about fire. Caldwell brooded about that. Fire was not this quantity added to that quantity. Staring down at the roaring tide of destruction he could see fire was not even one quantity times another. Fire was the cubing of quantities, holocaust to the third power, volume piling upon volume until the depth was drowning.

This fire had reached that stage now. It was an ocean of gas aflame, surf rushing up and over Cajon Summit and racing to meet the flooding blaze that sprinted up and over Mount Wilson, so that what flooded to the south out of the San Gabriels flooded into the tide washing to the north out of the San Bernardinos, an inexhaustible ocean fed by the infinite fuel of flammable things.

And the people knew.

Caldwell could see it, swooping down over Century City, Beverly Hills, downtown. He saw the uneasy population staring up at the sky, sensing something far worse than smog in the air. He saw them glued to TV sets in store windows, huddled around car radios. He saw them pointing and he saw them running and he saw them hosing down their houses.

From a thousand feet in the air he could feel the mounting skepticism and dread.

They knew.

A refrain started going around in Caldwell's head. *Come out, Frank Venice, wherever you are.*

The blue-haired lady at the show dog association was thrilled, simply thrilled, that *the* VV Cameron of KLIC-TV's *Newsbreak* planned to devote an *entire* segment to pedigreed pooches.

"But why Afghans?"

"My producer makes the decisions," VV lied. "Mine not to reason why."

"Of course. They *do* photograph nicely. Then let's see—you'll want the list of owners in Southern California? Let me copy that for you."

There were forty-two names on the list, running down two pages. VV waved the second sheet in the air.

"Alan!" she screamed.

Her assistant ducked his head into the office. "You shrieked, love?"

"Take this and phone everyone on the list. *Now.*"

Alan stared at the sheet and then, incredulously, at VV.

"Love, what has happened to your divine little brain? Los Angeles is on the verge of going up in smoke. Flames are racing down the canyons and movie stars
200

are fleeing luxury bungalows for their lives. And VV Cameron is organizing a *dog show?*"

"Dear friend, don't ask me to give you the whole story now, but *one* of these dogs was involved in *one* of those fires. And I want to find out *which* dog. So please get on the phone."

"What do I say—Hello, madam, is your Afghan hound a pyromaniac?"

"Try asking if their Afghan hound is missing. And put a check by the name if the answer is yes."

All of them sat staring at the bank of television screens, rectangles of flame twisting and threading skyward. Caldwell rubbed his hand back and forth across his grizzled chin, marveling despite himself. There was almost a beauty to the holocaust, to the surging, deadly power. *God made fire,* Caldwell thought. *He gave it that power.*

It was the governor who held high rank and it was the governor who asked the first question. "Where do we stand, Ed? What's the situation?"

Ed Caldwell shook his head. "Piss-poor."

The governor absorbed this calmly and turned to Lovenko. "Cas? What's your estimate?"

Lovenko exhaled loudly. "We've got two flanks out of three burning. The only way it could get worse would be if the third went up. And that would mean—" He didn't say it; he didn't say *fire storm.* But the silence said it. And everyone in the room heard it.

The governor scratched his chin. "Then where do we go from here?"

Lovenko went to the map. He touched his pointer to the crescent that two days ago had been green and that today was raging red at either end.

"We stop the burns from connecting."

"How?"

The pointer stroked the still-green arc that was the central third of the crescent.

"No choice. We throw our manpower here."

"Have we got the manpower?"

"Not yet. We have to draw all the help we can from

San Diego, Santa Barbara, San Luis Obispo, Bakersfield."

"Will that be enough?"

"I suggest we widen the military draw—we'll work that through your office."

The governor nodded. "And how do you deploy your men?"

Now the pointer drew a line bisecting the central arc. "Firebreak."

The governor squinted. He seemed to be working out a pained mathematical calculation. "Aren't you giving away a hell of a lot of trees?"

"Only if worse comes to worst. There's no way we can hold down arcs one and three and defend all of arc two. We haven't got the men and we won't have them. So we economize. With whatever manpower we can muster, we defend half of arc two."

"Which half?"

"We make an educated guess which side of the fire line he'll strike."

"And if your guess is wrong?"

"We lose. But that's not likely. He's an artist, and artists have their technique—their pattern, if you will. His pattern is to let the wind work for him. So if the wind keeps blowing from the west, he'll strike east of the line."

"Why east?"

"Because the wind will do his joins for him. Fire one, which he has, links with fire two, which he sets. Fire two links with three, which he already has."

"So it hinges on fire two," the governor said.

Lovenko nodded. "But we're there ahead of him. We stop fire two. The fire line stops fire one. No join, no fire storm."

This seemed to satisfy the governor—at least for the moment—but it did not satisfy the mayor.

"I've got citizens to cope with. So suppose you tell me what I'm supposed to tell them about your lines of defense."

"You tell them nothing," Lovenko said quietly, "or you tell them everything."

"Are you *crazy?*" The mayor turned anxiously to the

others. "There are homeowners out there looking to lynch somebody—and *I'm* the man that's visible. Now somebody give me something to defend myself with...or I'm going to have to divert some of our manpower back to routine fire fighting."

Lovenko shook his head. "Don't do it. We're barely holding as is. You take men out of the hills to hose down houses and you may earn a few votes but you'll be mayor of a pile of rubble."

The mayor's eyes came up to Caldwell. They were hungry eyes now, and a little pathetic, eyes of a trapped animal sniffing for a way out. "Ed—you're chief. Now give me something. Give me some line I can hand the people. Something to cover myself."

"Your Honor, I wasn't in favor of the Lovenko plan—as you know. But we're committed to it. If we shift now we're going to lose the forests and there's no way we can save enough houses to justify it. If we were going to go residential we should have done it from the start."

Tiny beads of sweat studded the mayor's well-groomed hairline. Ed Caldwell knew exactly what was bugging His Honor: he had bigger things in mind than staying mayor all his life, and this little foul-up could ruin him.

"You haven't answered my question," the mayor prodded.

Caldwell shrugged, refusing to accept this added guilt. "You're the politician, sir. It's up to you and your media people to deal with the public. That's what you pay your media people for, isn't it? You're paying me to knock down these fires and stop a fire storm. And you're paying Lovenko to show us how. We're all full up with assignments, Your Honor."

There was a visible twitch in the nerve under the mayor's eye. "Lovenko, you're the professor. How the hell do we handle this?"

Lovenko steepled his fingers together thoughtfully. "Our manpower is withdrawing to effect the interdiction of a fire ring. As a result people's homes are going up in flames. Under these circumstances"—his eyes swept the faces of the others—"it will become increasingly difficult—and unwise—to keep our purposes secret."

"What the hell is that supposed to mean?" the mayor snapped.

Lovenko drew a deep breath. "I say if the patient has cancer, tell him. If it's operable, tell him that too. The cancer we're facing is operable—for the moment. It will only become terminal if instead of cutting it out we let it spread. What we're doing now—hosing down grass and trees and not giving priority to houses—that's the surgical method that's indicated. So tell them. Tell your enraged citizenry. Tell them the fire chief and his men are protecting this city from fire storm, from a catastrophe a thousand times worse than the loss of a few hundred split-levels."

The mayor shifted in his seat. He passed a finger under his shirt collar. "Isn't that—a little alarmist?"

Lovenko shook his head. "If the third arc is fired up, if the rest of the burn continues as is, if the offshore front system holds—then we have every good chance of the worst becoming a reality."

The mayor stared a moment at the bank of TV screens. "You're laying a lot of ifs on me, Professor, and I've got angry neighborhoods ready to blow apart. If I even *whisper* fire storm..." He laughed grimly. "I might as well announce we've got King Kong loose in Azusa and Black Death blowing in from Torrance. Look, boys, this is a pretty fritzy city to begin with. It wouldn't take much to panic the whole number right off its nut. *Fire storm?* Why not tell them the San Andy Fault just decided to split its gut?"

"You're not quite getting the point, sir." Ed Caldwell's voice was a whisper now, a raging whisper, raging from the days he had been screaming instructions to deaf men. "As things stand at this very minute the fire is way out ahead of us. We're looking forward to the arsonist's third hit. That third hit could do it. I mean really do it, sir. I'm not talking votes, I'm talking lives. We've got to decide whether or not to inform the people. And if we decide yes, we'd better start evacuating them as fast as we can."

"We *could* evacuate." It was Peters talking, jumping on board, his voice jabbing in eagerly like a schoolboy's hand thrust into the air. "We could implement an evacuation program tonight."

The mayor turned and he stared at Peters as though he were a rabid mouse. "Evacuate an area of this size, a population as dense as this? Even under the most tranquil circumstances, and we're a long way from that, we couldn't get the people out of this city in any orderly fashion without guns at their backs. We'd need the entire U.S. Army."

Peters wilted.

The governor spoke. His voice was coiled and quiet and grave. "We could do that. We could put guns at their backs."

The mayor was shaking his head now, flailing like a man going down in quicksand. "Come on—this city? We'd have a rebellion." His glance went across to the chief of police. "Mac? You haven't said anything, Mac."

Chief of Police McCloskey nodded somberly. The mayor controlled the police department's purse strings, and even before McCloskey answered, Ed Caldwell knew what the gist of the reply would have to be.

"I just don't see pulling off a general evacuation." McCloskey picked nervously at a jacket button. "Not with the time line we've got."

The mayor was braced forward in his chair, the drowning man ready to pounce on his rescuer and drag them both down. "Then how *would* you handle it, Mac?"

"I'd—well, I'd keep that third arc from going up. No third arc, no fire storm, right? So I'd deploy all available forces to nailing the arsonist."

Ed Caldwell slammed a fist down onto the table. The veins in his temple were pounding and his voice was close to a shout. "How the hell are you going to turn up one guy or two or three guys in all that wilderness in eight hours? All it takes is one more burn—one tossed match *anywhere* in that arc—and we've had it! What are you going to do, patrol every square inch? Even if you could borrow ten thousand soldiers, for one thing they don't know the terrain and for another they couldn't get here in time. So that idea, if you'll excuse the term, is fertilizer. There's only one sure way to save lives, and that's to tell the people, tell 'em fast, and start getting them out!"

The governor was tapping out unperturbed piano exercises on the tabletop. "Gentlemen." His voice was soothing, philosophical, the voice of a conciliator. "Hollering *fire!* in a crowded room is a serious act—even when there *is* a fire. Hollering something as mysterious and frightening as *fire storm!* might prove to be an act equivalent to murder."

Lovenko sighed. "Don't you think the people have a right to know what they're facing?"

"The people have a right to be protected," the mayor said, spitting out the syllables like sharp little pellets, "and we are paid to give them that protection. We do our job best by sparing them the riot and mayhem of a bungled, last-minute evacuation attempt."

"We got a problem," the chief of police broke in. His face was awkward, embarrassed, as though he wished he didn't have to bring up the point he was about to. "There's a television show—Station KLIC—*Newsbreak.* People phone in and sound off. Somebody phoned in and sounded off today. Now where he got this information I don't know. He could have been guessing, maybe he was just using his eyes. But he said it's fire department policy to hose down grass and trees instead of houses. He said phone City Hall, raise hell. Anyway, a lot of viewers heard that."

"And a lot phoned City Hall," the mayor added in a grumbling undertone.

"Now if an average Joe figures out the policy," the police chief went on, "how are you going to keep the whole city from knowing?"

"That wasn't an average Joe," Ed Caldwell cut in, "that was the arsonist. Which is why, Chief McCloskey, you had a trace on that line—a trace that didn't work fast enough. What the arsonist wants is to create a political storm that draws fire fighters *out* of the hills. Then he'll be free to complete his fire storm."

"I don't know the motives of this man who called in." McCloskey spread his hands in a gesture of helplessness that was at the same time an implied rejection of Caldwell's thinking. "A mind reader I am not. But I do know the press picked it up and—as they say—the word is now out."

"We'll issue a counterstatement," the mayor said with abrupt resolve. "We'll say it's a bunch of hysterical crap. Yellow journalism. Irresponsible scare tactics."

"That *is* an option," the governor said. "We stake out a position of credible deniability. After all, we do it routinely with earthquake."

"But in this case," Lovenko said, "your credible deniability is a lie."

"We've got to," the mayor said, voice clenched like a fist. "Till we've got the job done, we pacify the public. No matter how big a lie it takes."

"You're assuming we *will* get the job done," Lovenko said.

The mayor's glance flipped up. "All right, Professor. At the moment we have a fighting chance. The moment may come when we don't. If that moment comes—how much warning will we have?"

Lovenko leaned back in his chair. His glance swept out an arc of ceiling and he folded his hands across his stomach, shaking his head. "Mr. Mayor, as of now you're retaining me for my expert advice and opinion on fire fighting. If, however, you wish me to perform as a deity, I'll have to reconsider my fee."

"Gentlemen," the governor said impatiently, "we have very little time and very few options. We appear to be agreed on the basic approach. It involves a certain sacrifice of candor—and of real estate—but it's our best, our only, chance of avoiding panic and fire storm. So let's stand pat on present policy."

Ed Caldwell rose to his feet, wheeling, in the same motion, on the governor. "I want to register a strong vote against official silence. It's fasci—" He bit back the word *fascistic*. "We've got to tell the truth. The truth is the only policy that *works!*"

It felt lame and naive, and the governor tossed a contemptuous glance up at him.

"That's the most damned stupid, boyish eyewash I've heard since Washington and the apple tree."

"Cherry tree," Lovenko corrected. "Newton had the apple tree."

There was laughter at this, but it was only Peters', and when he saw no one joining in he cut it short and pushed up from his chair. "I'll have our press officer issue a denial that we're deviating from routine procedure. I'll go take care of that right now."

Peters moved swiftly to the door. The mayor gazed after him approvingly. There was silence.

"That's a good man," the mayor said. "You've got a damned good man there, Caldwell." And then, to the governor, "Well, Gus, perhaps we'd better shove along. We have a busy schedule. And a late lunch with Melinda Mars' manager. She's singing for us tonight, you know."

"Didn't know," the governor said.

"Assuming the concert goes ahead as scheduled," the mayor qualified.

"Of course it'll go on," the governor said. "That's the best way on earth to reassure the public. As a matter of fact, would it help if I put in a personal appearance—from the stage?"

The mayor nodded thoughtfully. It was a political thoughtfulness. "Wonderful idea. And it might help if I stood right there beside you."

Of the forty-two names on the list, only two reported their Afghan hounds missing. VV Cameron took them in alphabetical order.

Mrs. Hoyt Benjamin III received VV in the garden of her Bel Air mansion. A handsome woman of fifty-three or so, she wore overalls with peat-moss stains on the knees.

"I didn't mean to interrupt your gardening," VV apologized, introducing herself.

"KLIC—are you new?" Mrs. Benjamin spoke with an East Coast finishing-school accent and gestured with pruning shears delicate enough to be cuticle scissors.

"We've had our license three years."

"And have you worked all that time with Father John?"

"I'm sorry—I don't know Father John."

Mrs. Benjamin received the information with a

barely perceptible narrowing of her amber eyes. "But I assumed he sent you."

"No one sent me, Mrs. Benjamin. As I mentioned on the phone, I'm researching a story for KLIC."

"This KLIC—it's a church?"

"No. We're a television station."

"How extraordinary. Felice has contacted your television station?"

"No one contacted us, Mrs. Benjamin."

"But if Father John didn't send you and you're not in touch with Felice, how were you directed to me?"

A notion was beginning to buzz very strongly in the back of VV Cameron's mind that she and Mrs. Benjamin were on two decidedly different wavelengths and possibly in different universes.

"I got your name from the show dog association."

The slopes and curves of Mrs. Benjamin's beautifully manicured face subtly realigned themselves. The voice betrayed just a hint of impatience.

"Miss Cameron, what is your interest in my dog?"

"I'm trying to identify a male Afghan that was found two nights ago in the Santa Monica Mountains. Possibly the animal is yours."

Mrs. Benjamin shook her head with surprising vehemence. "No, that's not possible. Felice entered Larger Life five weeks ago."

It took VV a minute to understand. "Your dog is dead?"

Mrs. Benjamin's lower lip trembled. She blinked hard and a brave smile deepened the lines of her face. "My dog is no longer in the realm of physical being. Except for his ashes, of course. They're under the hibiscus at the end of the garden. It was his favorite place."

VV Cameron felt a flash of embarrassment. She began backtracking toward the driveway where she'd parked the Karmann-Ghia. "I'm very sorry, Mrs. Benjamin. I misunderstood."

"There's nothing to be sorry about. Felice will return as a schnauzer sometime in March. Father John is certain of it."

* * *

Norma Jay, wife of the Hollywood film director Harrison Jay, received VV Cameron in her Beverly Hills living room. Her husband's last three films had been top grossers, and the living room looked it. Beneath one cathedral ceiling, VV counted four Chagalls, five authentic Tiffany lamps, one Aubusson carpet, and two Oscars.

"Excuse the pied-à-terre." Mrs. Jay waved a hand airily. "It's a mess. My husband and I just got back from London. Had to recut the film. Don't ever fly nonstop, it's murder. Care for a drink?"

"Maybe a light vodka tonic, thanks."

Mrs. Jay crossed to the bar. She was barefoot. She moved like an ex-dancer and she handled bar paraphernalia with a speed that was almost professional. She mixed one drink and handed it to VV.

"Don't wait for me, I'm not drinking. Why don't we make ourselves comfortable?"

Mrs. Jay led them to one of the room's four sofas. Sitting, she patted a strand of hair into place. It looked like the sort of hair that took eight man-hours and five hundred dollars a week to maintain.

Mrs. Jay smiled at VV in half-profile. "What station did you say you were with? I'm not much of a television viewer, and while your face is familiar I can't say I place it."

VV smiled patiently. "VV Cameron of KLIC-TV. I have a show called *Newsbreak*."

"Oh, you're not with one of the networks then?"

"We're independent."

"And you wanted to see me about an interview?"

"I wanted to see you about your dog."

Mrs. Jay's expression tightened. Her eyes and mouth were suddenly nested in tight little lines. After a moment she said, "Which dog—Spinoza or Einstein?"

"Your Afghan hound."

"That's Spinoza. Einstein's the poodle."

"You said your Afghan is missing?"

Mrs. Jay lifted the lid of a carved crystal box. She took out a cigarette, lit it, and exhaled a loud sigh of smoke. "Yes, Spinoza vanished."

"When?"

"Five days ago."

It fits, VV thought excitedly. "Where?"

"Downtown. He jumped out of the station wagon."

"Was he wearing identification?"

"He can't stand those things around his neck."

"And you've had no word of him?"

"We offered a reward, and of course that brings in phone calls—there are a lot of sick people in this world, Miss Cameron, as I'm sure I don't need to tell you. Why are you so interested in Spinoza?"

"An Afghan hound was found in the Santa Monica Mountains two nights ago. He was in a fire, Mrs. Jay. He was badly burned, but he's alive. I've checked the records of the show dog association; I've phoned forty-two dog owners. I believe he's your dog."

"Badly burned?"

"He won't win any more shows."

Mrs. Jay angled her suntanned wrist and glanced at a thin sliver of gold watch.

"The reward expired twenty-four hours ago. I'm very sorry, Miss—"

"I'm not here for the reward. I need information."

Mrs. Jay flicked a grim glance out at VV. "Where is he?"

VV gave her the address, then asked, "Do you have any idea how the dog could have got into the mountains?"

Mrs. Jay stabbed her cigarette into a jade ashtray, expertly decapitating it. "Maybe you don't know Afghans, Miss Cameron. They're not exactly homing pigeons and those beautiful narrow faces don't leave much room for brains. When an Afghan starts running, it keeps running. It doesn't stop, it doesn't change direction. I was in the middle lane when Spinoza jumped out the window. By the time the chauffeur found a parking place, he was gone. I suppose he just kept running till he hit the mountains."

"You didn't see anyone stop him or chase him?"

"No, Miss Cameron," Norma Jay said with interview-terminating finality, rising to her feet, "I didn't

211

see a thing. I don't wear my glasses in public."

* * *

The white telephone blinked. Peters jabbed the button and snatched the receiver up to his ear. "Peters...Just a sec. For you, Cas."

Lovenko reached a hand, swiveling away from the TV monitors with their eight different visions of holocaust.

"Lovenko."

The cool, patrician drawl of General Mark Cunningham came up from three time zones and three thousand miles away. "Unearthed another piece of information from the records, Cas. It may have some bearing. Frank Venice was a pretty off-the-wall type to begin with. But those burns did it. When they released him from Arlington, he was borderline psychotic."

"Christ, Mark—we know that! We're staring at the proof right now!"

11

MELINDA MARS sat in the air-conditioned cool of the studio, playing the same tape segment over and over, trying to decide if she could live with the French horn solo, if there should even *be* a French horn solo in a Melinda Mars disco number. Did this new arranger own stock in a French horn factory? And what was she supposed to do for thirty-one bars, hum along, turn cartwheels?

She grinned at the thought of turning cartwheels in her condition, looked out through the glass wall, and caught sight of Loren's foot dangling off the platform of the tree house. Without warning, a sudden, swooping nausea gripped her, spun her. She steadied herself, breathed deeply, and tasted something acrid and sharp in the air she gulped into her lungs.

She rested her hands, fingers clasped, over the great altar of her belly, willing the malaise to pass. "Margaret," she murmured, "Margaret if it's a girl. And a boy—a boy is definitely Sam. Samuel? Or maybe— Oliver. Maybe Oliver Samuel."

The sound of the horn seemed to cut into her. She slammed the tape to a stop. Did she hear someone calling? Did she hear *Mom, Mom!* carrying to her dimly through that impenetrable glass wall?

She felt a powerful drowsiness crushing her, as if sleep were a giant sitting on her chest. She fought the drowsiness, stumbled to the door, and out onto the lawn. She shielded her eyes to look up into the tree house.

"What? Loren, what's wrong?"

"I see it!" the boy shouted down at her. "I can see it from here!"

"What?" she called back, part of her already knowing, already dreading the answer she knew he would give.

"Fire!" the boy shouted happily. "A terrific fire! I never saw anything like it! It's a monster! Mom, you should see it—it's really something!"

She could see her son's feet dancing in delighted agitation as he hopped around the wooden platform for a better vantage point. A deep shudder went through her. She mastered it. She willed herself to be calm. She knew that it was suddenly immensely important that she handle this calmly.

"Loren," she called up into the tree, "I want you to tell me, how far away is the fire?"

"What?" the boy shouted back.

"Listen to me carefully." She surprised herself with the mild tone she was able to achieve. "Tell me how far the fire is from us."

"I don't know. It's in different places, sort of."

"But the nearest part—how far away is it? A mile? Two miles?"

"How far is a mile?" Loren called back.

"Can you see the lookout?"

"What's the lookout?"

"It's the place where people stand to take a look at the woods. It's like your tree house, only it's not in a tree, it's all by itself. It's really high. Can you see it?"

"Oh, *that* thing," Loren said. "No, I can't see it. The fire's in front of it."

"You mean the fire is on *this* side of the lookout? You mean the fire is *between* us and there?"

"Yeah, sure!" the boy called back. "I told you, it's a monster! Come up and have a look!"

For a moment she almost thought of making the attempt. She stopped at the base of the tree and called up again. "Loren, you know we live in a canyon, right?"

"Right!" she heard her son say, and then she saw his feet moving, searching for a new place to look from.

"Okay now. Tell Mom if there's any fire inside the canyon."

For a space of seconds she heard no response. She craned her head. Where was he?

"Loren? Did you do what Mommy asked?"

There was no answer.

"Loren! Please answer Mommy! Are you looking? Is there fire inside the canyon?"

"Oh, sure," the boy called down to her.

Fear slammed through her. She fought to control her voice, to slow the jumbled spinning of her thoughts.

"I want you to come down here now, Loren. No questions. Just come."

"Aw, Mom," the boy said. "It's great. Please, Mom. Just let me stay a little bit more, okay?"

"Now, Loren!" she shouted, shocked at the sound of her own voice almost dissolving into tears. "I want you down here this instant! Or I'm going to spank you!"

"Coming, coming, coming," the boy chanted. One foot poked down below the platform and then the other, then the legs, the knees, all of him gradually materializing with maddening slowness.

As soon as Melinda could reach him she yanked, almost ripping him from the ladder. When she had him safely on the ground she took him firmly by the hand and walked him quickly inside the house.

She slammed the door closed. *Now what?* She tried to think, tried to slam some sort of order onto the panicked rush in her head.

The roof! The roof could be on fire this very minute! If it were, how would she know?

Run!

Wait a minute, wait a minute.

Think!

First the fire department. She moved quickly to the bedroom. There was no dial tone when she lifted the phone, only ghosts of rings and busy signals.

She dialed O for operator and got a dead silence.

She ripped open the telephone book and found the number for fire and emergency but when she dialed nothing happened.

She felt the baby shove violently at her heart.

"Oh, God. God in heaven," she uttered aloud, and then commanded herself, "Think, Melinda—*think!*"

She slammed down the receiver and then she thought: *The cars! Get one of the cars.* She came up off the bed as though fire were already hissing beneath it. She ran back toward the living room.

But she never made it.

One foot struck the doorjamb and the other skidded out from under her and suddenly, with clattering gracelessness, she found herself crumpled on the hallway floor, her legs jutting out at angles that she had never in her life seen.

She screamed: "Loren!" She screamed her son's name just once. And then, with all the strength that was in her, she raised her torso just enough to prop herself against the wall.

She tried not to look at the legs that seemed to have no more connection to her than mangled toothpicks. She tried to make believe they belonged to someone else.

She raised her eyes and, blinking through the waves of pain, she saw her son squinting down at her.

"How come it got dark all of a sudden? Mom? You know how come it did that?"

"Probably just a thunderstorm," she gritted, trying to shift weight off the part of her hip where shards of glass seemed to be cutting into her.

"Rain would be good, wouldn't it?" Loren said. "That way the drought would be over and it would put out the fire."

"But until the rain comes we have to help it. So I want you to go get the garden hose. It's right outside the garage door. And there's another hose inside the garage. Now make sure the one outside the door is attached to the little pipe there. Then carry the other end as far as you can back toward me. Then you go back into the garage and bring the second hose here. Okay?"

"Okay." A little ridge of bafflement creased his forehead. "Mom, are you okay?"

"I just had a fall and I'm catching my breath. So you're going to have to help me. Go get those hoses. It

216

may be very dark outside. Don't worry about it. Just hurry on back here. Be careful now. No falling. No bumping into things. Now get going."

She heard the boy's bare feet moving along the hallway, vanishing into silence. She tried to visualize him in the garage, tried to will him to do it right: attach the first hose, bring the end of it as far back as it would reach...

Dimly, cutting through her thoughts, she heard a voice far above her, booming and yet indistinct, not real at all and yet more real than even the pain in her hip and leg and stomach.

She fought to get a grip on that voice, to sift it from the jumble of impressions churning inside her. Gradually it came to her that the voice was an airborne bullhorn, that the over-and-over incantation was meant for her.

"...south as far as you can. When you see fire, stop and wait for further instructions. When you see the fire line, stop and wait where you are for further instructions. Stay calm. There is no reason to be alarmed. Wear heavy clothing and keep your mouth covered. This is your police department issuing an official evacuation notice. All residents of this area will leave the area immediately. Go as far south as you can. When you see..."

And the voice faded.

The hallway faded.

Even the pain seemed to fade, leaving only a dim sensation that there was something wet underneath her, that something had ruptured.

She tried to rid herself of such thoughts. She knew it was silly to imagine such things—silly and wasteful and distracting. She knew she had a job to do, and she knew that imagining the worst would help nothing, would only hinder, and might even help make the worst a reality.

She told herself that the baby was fine, that babies were the toughest little things, God made them that way so they'd survive. She told herself that her legs might have suffered some bad bruising, a mild fracture or two perhaps, maybe even a minor tearing of tendons.

She tried to tell herself that nothing really very serious was happening inside her, that all it amounted to was a few insignificant coincidences adding up to something damned inconvenient.

A woman falls. She happens to be pregnant. A lot of pregnant women fall. The telephones are out of order for a while.

So what? And so what if there happens to be a blackout?

But now she lost track, now she couldn't disentangle what was going on inside her from what was going on outside: because the blackout could have been her, not the electricity. The blackout could have been her own consciousness coming and going like the coming and going of pain in a shattered leg or a ripped womb....

But it *was* darker in the house, and the humming sound of the air conditioners—hadn't it stopped? Or was she imagining silence just as she had imagined that voice hammering from the sky hours and hours ago—or had it been minutes?

Why was she trying to panic herself?

After all, did she have any real proof that the fire was anywhere near the house?

Of course not. Yes, there *was* a fire. Of course there was. She knew Loren knew what a fire was.

So?

So there was a fire. Weren't there always fires? For goodness' sake, hadn't she lived three years now in Southern California? Hadn't she been hearing about brush fires and grass fires and forest fires since she'd come out here? And wasn't this the fire season?

So what?

Had she ever really been hurt by fire? Did she know anyone who ever had been?

Of course not!

All right, there had been a fire. But that had been a long time ago. It had probably died out by now or been brought under control or taken off in some other direction. For pity's sake, it had been hours and hours and she hadn't seen the least little *bit* of fire!

And yet it *was* dark and she had been alone a very long time....

"Honey," she called, "are you there?"

"Right here, Mom."

"Good boy." She reached a hand to touch his hair but he was too tall for her, she couldn't struggle up far enough. "How far did you get with the first hose? How close back to Mommy?"

"Just around to where the kitchen stops and the living room starts."

"Okay now, that's good. Now give me the other hose so I can feel around on it."

She put out her hands, suddenly needing to protect her legs, suddenly thinking how long it had been since the baby had kicked or punched or taken a glide from one resting place to another.

"Just slide the hose over here easy to Mommy." She found the wrong end first and went back around. "Feel this end?" she said. "This thing that spins here? Feel how it turns? Give me your hand so you can feel. Feel it?"

"Sure."

"Okay. You take this end and you go back to where you left off with the other hose. Then you turn this spinny thing so it screws onto the end of the other hose. You have to match them up and hold the two ends together very carefully. And then you push and turn this spinny thing here and they'll hold together. Can you do that?"

"Sure I can do it," Loren said, a touch of childish condescension in his voice. "I've seen the gardener do it a hundred times."

"Good. And when you've done that, go back in the garage and turn the water on all the way. Do you know how to turn the water on?"

"Mom, for Pete's sake, I know how to take a bath!"

"Okay, hurry now."

She waited, listening to the boy's hurry and clatter. Squinting her eyes, she could see a flickering design in the glass doors, chips of glowing wood being puffed into the garden. There seemed to be a churning motion to the darkness, hints of flashes and splintering light, ripped shadows darting in and out of an orange murkiness.

219

She heard the water whispering from the hose. Her fingers felt the floorboards growing damp beneath her.

"Now what, Mom?"

"Take the hose and spray it all around. The walls, the ceiling, the furniture, everything."

"Why?"

"Oh, it's just a game, sweetheart." *Yes,* she told herself, *it's just make-believe, like the orange glow outside.* "It's just something to keep us busy till Toby comes home."

"He's sure going to holler. When he sees everything wet, he's going to really holler."

"We'll just tell him we had to do something silly to keep busy while the lights were out."

"And because you hurt yourself," Loren said.

"Oh, I'm fine. Just sprained my ankle a little. Just a little twist—that's all."

"Did it hurt the baby too?" she heard her son asking across the black distance that separated them.

"Of course not. Babies are tough little things. You can't hurt a baby." And once she had said the words it flashed to her that she had worsened the odds, dared fate. "Do a good job now, hon. Really get everything soaking wet. Just keep turning around and get everything soppy, okay?"

"I'm doing it, Mom," the boy called back.

She heard lamps and small objects fall as the water from the garden hose washed them over and off tables.

"Hey, Mom," the boy called, "the water's hot—it hurts!"

"*Hot?*" A tremor of panic splintered along her neck.

"Yeah—I don't like this anymore."

"Loren, put the hose down. Just put it down and come on over here and sit by Mommy. I'm getting a little lonesome for my favorite fella."

She heard the freed end of the hose snapping and splashing through the water that had pooled on the living-room floor. When her son was cuddled next to her again, she reached out and touched him, touched her son's chest and shoulders and face, and hugged him hard.

"I love you, honey," Melinda said.

220

"Good mommy," the boy said dreamily, resting his head against her breasts and petting her soft, soft hair.

For a long while they stayed that way. For a long while there was no sound but the dance of the hose flipping through the shallow water. But then she heard another sound, very distantly, the heavy sighing of some enormous thing exhaling its breath.

"Are you asleep, honey?" she whispered.

There was no answer. She could feel her child's fatigue as if it were an ache howling in her bowels. She could feel the water beneath them getting hotter, like the spillover of a sauna. In the reflecting glass doors she glimpsed flashes of familiar objects as the haywire, pulsing light suddenly seized a sandbox, a tricycle, a deck chair—illuminated them for an instant, dropped them back into churning darkness.

She had heard that the smoke killed you before the fire. Maybe it was easier that way.

She sat very still against the wall.

Perhaps the smoke had already gotten to Loren. His sleep was deep and perfect and smiling, the sleep of the safe and well-loved child.

Melinda Mars looked out into the wild snapping light. She preferred the dark. She closed her eyes and held her child close.

A mongrel. A crazed cocker spaniel. A pedigreed Afghan hound.

VV Cameron tapped her pencil irritably against the desk top.

Three dogs. Fifteen fires. Three into fifteen is five.

Where the hell is the connection? Damn it, I need some fresh input.

Alan appeared as if on cue in the open doorway of the office. He was looking thin and dark, haggard yet glamorous, in a male-model way, and VV couldn't help thinking he'd better start getting more in his diet than suntans and coke.

He had brought a sandwich and coffee from the deli and he cleared a space on the desk to set them down. "Nutrition time, VV. Can't run on an empty tank. Eat."

"I'm thinking."

"You look as though you're contemplating suicide."

"It's a riddle."

"Try me."

"What do a mongrel, a crazed cocker spaniel, and a run-away pedigreed Afghan hound all have in common?"

"Let me guess. I've got it. They're all dogs."

"Don't be a smart-ass. I *know* they're dogs."

"Don't jump down my throat, VV. It takes time and skill to crack a riddle." He sat down on the edge of the desk, unwrapped the sandwich, and held up half of it. "Pretty please?"

VV shrugged. "Be my guest. You need to put on weight."

Alan took a mouthful of chopped liver with bacon on rye. He chewed a moment with the expression of a wine taster sampling a choice vintage.

"I'm getting it, VV. The mongrel, I assume, is a scurvy little beast that no one wants. The cocker spaniel is crazed, so it's dangerous to keep him at home. And the Afghan is a runaway. There's some awful pun here, VV, and I'm going to strangle you. It has to do with weights and measures, right?"

"Why do you say that?"

"Because obviously all three of them wind up at the pound."

"Good Lord." VV set down her coffee. "The pound. Of course." She jumped up and kissed him. "You're a genius, Alan!"

"Hey, if that's a riddle, I don't get it. It's not funny."

"You bet it's not funny." VV grabbed her purse.

"Where are you dashing to, love?"

"The pound—and you can have the whole sandwich!"

The cage smelled like a public latrine. There was no window, only the filth-clogged grid of a nonfunctioning air conditioner. Toby Gladstone shook the bars till the desk sergeant came and told him to be a mensh and cut it out.

"I don't think you fellows realize who I am."

"I realize you're a pain in the ass, buddy."

Toby ripped his wallet from his jacket and with a flip tossed out the dangling ladder of credit cards.

The officer peered at the cards and scratched his chin thoughtfully. "Rings a bell. Running a roadblock, assaulting an officer, resisting arrest. You're *that* Toby Gladstone, right?"

"I want to phone the mayor."

"Why don't you try phoning a lawyer first?"

"I don't want a goddamned lawyer. I want to be put in touch with the mayor *this minute!*"

"You'll be in touch with a judge, bubby, and you'll wait your turn." The sergeant reached a finger through the bars to tweak one of the cards. "By the way, you can charge the fine. We take major credit cards."

The sergeant went back to his newspaper. Toby felt the soft footfall of inspiration.

"Officer—sir!"

The sergeant glanced up again.

"I didn't mean to be rude."

"Sure you didn't."

"Is that today's *Times?*"

"It's not tomorrow's."

"Do me a favor and look on page twelve."

"What's on page twelve?"

"Me."

Intrigued now, the sergeant leafed through the paper. He came to page twelve, stared at the photograph of celebrities at Melinda Mars' blowout, squinted across the room at the man in the cage in the torn Calvin Klein shirt.

"So you're a friend of Melinda Mars, hey? My kid's a real fan of hers."

"I'm not just her friend—I'm her manager."

"Could you get her to write an autograph to Cindy? That's my little girl."

"Melinda will do anything I tell her to. And if I'm not on the phone to the mayor in ten minutes, I'm telling her to cancel tonight's concert at the Bowl. You know what that will mean, Sergeant? The police will have to go begging with tin cups to pay for their bulletproof vests."

The sergeant's eyes traveled once more from the

newspaper to the man in the cage. He heaved himself up from the chair, took a key from the ring at his belt, and swung open the cage door.

"Come on, Mr. Gladstone," he said, "let's find you a phone."

"I'm looking for a dog," VV said to the man at the desk. He had white hair and a reddish, oddly naked face. She could see him wondering where the hell he knew her from.

"You're in the right place, lady." He flicked his head toward the double metal door where all the barking and yapping seemed to be coming from. "Take your pick. We got two thousand of them."

She glanced at the nameplate on the desk. "Actually, Mr. Bender, it's not the dog I want. I need some information about him."

His eyes remained on her, neutrally, but she could sense wariness in them. She decided to go the celebrity route, such as it was.

"My name's VV Cameron. I'm with KLIC-TV."

He snapped a finger. "The gal—I mean the lady on *Newsbreak.*"

"Right." She brushed her hair off her forehead and flashed her camera-one smile.

"So—what kind of information you looking for?"

"Can you tell me if a male Afghan hound was taken from the pound any time between last Monday and Wednesday—and who took him?"

"That's assuming we *had* a male Afghan."

"This one ran away Monday. It wasn't returned."

"Your dog?"

"No."

VV realized she had no cover story prepared. "I'm trying to work up a segment on how the pound operates."

It sounded lame and it didn't explain why she wanted the Afghan, but the man seemed to buy it. VV supposed that, like every other public service in the wake of Proposition 13, the pound was hurting for funds and could use some good public relations.

"Tell you what." The man placed his hamlike palms

on the desk and pushed himself up. "Let's go check the records. An Afghan should be a cinch. We don't see too many of those."

VV followed him into another office. He poked through a file of Monday's admissions, found nothing, went to Tuesday's, almost immediately found a male Afghan.

"Adopted," the man said, "three days ago."

VV ran through a quick calculation. The dog ran away five days ago, was brought into the pound four days ago, was removed the following day, and that same night was almost burned to death in the mountains.

The chronology worked.

VV's eye skimmed the printed form with its hand-scrawled, barely legible particulars. She stopped at the name of the adopting party. There were two initials and nothing more.

"F.D.?" she said quizzically.

The man nodded. "Frank Defino."

"Do you normally put initials instead of the name?"

The man smiled. "Not usually. But Frank filled this out himself."

"You mean he just walked in and took the dog? What do you run here, a self-service dog shelter?"

The man laughed. "Frank works here. He's a real dog nut. He's always taking the dogs home." The man looked at her with sudden concern. "You're not going to do an exposé or anything, are you? Sure, he's bending the rules, but it saves the county money. And most of the dogs he takes are mutts. No one would want them anyway. They'd just wind up getting gassed."

VV wasn't certain the animals were doing much better in the dog-loving hands of Frank Defino. But she kept that suspicion to herself. "I'd like to talk with Mr. Defino."

The man studied her like a buyer suspiciously checking out a used car. "Frank's a good guy and the only friends he's got in the world are those dogs. Don't hurt him, lady."

"I'm not going to make trouble for him or the dogs."

The man's eyes were dubious. "He's on sick leave."

"What's the matter with him?"

"Nothing. He just had the leave coming and—you know—he's been taking it these last two days."

The last two days, VV thought. That fitted with the fires. A lot of things about Mr. Defino were beginning to fit.

The man was watching her, his face tensed with doubt. "You sure you're not doing an exposé? Maybe I'm talking too much."

"I promise, all I want is a sixty-second human-interest segment on a man who loves dogs and who's doing something for them."

"Yeah, that's Frank all right."

"Can you give me his phone?"

He pursed his lips and raised his eyebrows. She could feel the indecision whirling in him.

"I won't do anything without Mr. Defino's consent. You have my word of honor," she said.

"He doesn't have a phone."

Disappointment slammed through VV. Her one painstaking lead had suddenly come untied. The firebug had a phone. Defino didn't. Yet Defino had had that dog; his initials on the form proved it. There had to be a connection: Defino and the firebug *meshed.*

"I can give you Frank's address," the man said, not sounding at all enthusiastic at the idea. "But I should warn you—he doesn't like strangers. Especially you being from television—he'll hate that."

"Why? What's he got against TV?"

"You might say he was camera-shy. His face was burned off in Vietnam."

For the last two days Los Angeles had lived in a rising ocean of smoke. Carbon particles were everywhere: in the air, on the buildings and cars, and above all in and on the people, on their skin, in their hair, their noses and throats, their lungs. Every step they took was through smoke; everything they touched was dusted in smoke; every forkful of food they put in their mouths was coated with a layer of it. The waste product of combustion was inescapable.

So far, because the smoke had proceeded by degrees and even now in the sectors away from the fires was no more than one part in ten billion, Angelenos were not especially aware of it. Their eyes were irritated and they blinked and sniffled a little more than usual but the smoke had not yet reached the saturation point where the human animal's instincts would sound the age-old alarm: FIRE!

Yet, though the average saturation was low, the average itself was a statistical fiction; in fact there were varying saturations, some virtually negligible, some so high the air was black to the eye and burned to the nose.

One of these maverick saturations had gathered in the area of the Brown Derby. The foyer of the restaurant was jammed with people awaiting tables. Each time the door opened and a new hopeful entered, the wind drove another surge of smoke inside.

Though the restaurant was air-conditioned, the central units could not cope with the added pollution. The foyer had become a mob scene of coughs, sniffles, and running eyes. As the polluted air was forced into the dining area itself, the coughing spread, like a subliminal plague.

The mayor's table was one of the last to be reached by the smoke. His Honor was aware of an irritation in the sinuses, but he assumed this was a late summer cold. He was also aware of a certain shortness of breath and a decided shortness of temper, but he did not connect the two to a common cause.

Instead he tried to deny the signals of his own nervous system and chatted with his guest, the governor. Occasionally he glanced at the empty place at the table, sneaked a peek at his watch, and wondered what the hell was delaying Toby Gladstone. When a waiter brought a telephone to the table, however, it was impossible to contain further irritation. The mayor exploded.

"No phone calls."

"But, sir—"

"I don't care who or what it is, I'm having lunch."

Many notables dined at the Derby when their publicity was sagging and made a point of having telephones brought to their tables; though the call might

227

be nothing more than a prearranged ring from the cleaning woman, it could *look* as though Sue Mengers or the William Morris office had finally come through with that fifteen-million-dollar package.

Unlike the image-conscious souls of show biz, the mayor got quite enough of the telephone during working hours, and he had left a standing order with the Derby management: no calls, ever, in any way, shape, or form, and especially never in the form of the obsequious waiter clutching the white extension phone with its dangling jack.

And still the waiter refused to vanish.

"Your office, sir. They say it's urgent."

The mayor smiled an embarrassed apology to the governor. "Sorry."

He signaled the waiter to plug in the phone. He lifted the receiver and identified himself in three curt syllables.

His secretary was on the line. "Trouble, Your Honor. Toby Gladstone's in jail."

"What the hell for?"

"Possession. Running a blockade. Assaulting an officer."

"Damned fool. He's kept us waiting almost an hour."

"He wants to talk to you. I have him on the other line."

"Damn it," the mayor snapped. "I can't spring him from jail." And then, smiling as his guest arched an eyebrow, "That's the governor's prerogative."

"He's threatening to pull Melinda Mars from the Bowl concert."

"Excuse me, Gus," the mayor apologized to his guest. Then, "All right, put him through."

Toby Gladstone came on the line, his voice edged in hysteria, screaming something about the homes in Malibu Canyon.

"Now, Toby," the mayor soothed, "the canyon is being evacuated by state troopers with bullhorns. Everything is under control."

"Her goddamned studio's soundproof!" the voice came hollering back. The mayor had to distance the receiver from his ear. "A *fleet* of bullhorns couldn't get through."

The mayor's mind skipped quickly through alternatives. He needed that concert. He needed the publicity, he needed the image as Mr. Stay-Cool in crisis; above all his budget needed the receipts, which through accounting sleight of hand would balance some very questionable red ink.

"Well, Toby, why don't I phone Malibu sector control and make sure they got her out?"

"They couldn't have got her out!" the phone screamed, and again the mayor had to jerk it away from his ear. "She's there and her kid's there! Now you go in and *get* her! And if I'm not talking to her in one hour, you haven't got a concert!"

And you, the mayor thought, *will have one barbecued Melinda Mars for a meal ticket.* The mayor gloved his voice in honey. "I'll get right to it, Toby, if you'll just clear the line, okay?"

He tapped the cradle till his secretary picked up again.

"Mabel, check Malibu Canyon, will you. Find out if they evacuated Melinda Mars and her kid and get back to me soonest, okay?"

The mayor barely had time to sprinkle egg yolk on another melba round of caviar before the telephone blinked again. His secretary told him Miss Mars had not responded to the evacuation alert and was presumed absent from premises.

"She's not absent, Mabel. She's got some kind of soundproof studio and she's in there with her kid. Send a copter and a rescue team in and keep me posted, okay? We'll be here another—say, two hours." After all, it was the mayor's duty to counteract alarmist rumors by presenting a façade of calm and business as usual, and what more effective place to do it than in L.A.'s finest and most-talked-about restaurant?

The governor nodded agreeably, just as a violent fit of coughing seized him.

Ed Caldwell was at sector five fire camp when the call came from the mayor's office. He listened, nodded grimly, and told the radio operator to raise Lovenko at headquarters.

"Cas?"

"What's up?"

"You got a picture of Malibu Canyon?"

"Just coming in now."

"Can you see the north end of the canyon?"

"Sure can."

"You see the last house up in there?"

"No. Hold on. Hold it. Last house? Yes, now I see it."

"Is there fire on it?"

"No, no fire."

"How far's it from the fire?"

"I estimate between seventy-five and a hundred yards. Hard to tell."

"You have any idea how the wind's moving in there?"

"It's not. Not since about early afternoon. That's why we haven't had much burn in the canyon. There's a crazy kind of calm all around it."

"Okay, Professor, think fast. I've got a very pregnant woman in that house. Baby's due in two weeks. I've also got a six-year-old kid in there with her. Now how do I get them out?"

There was an instant of static and then Lovenko's voice. "Chopper lift won't work. Not if she's that pregnant. Unless of course you used a chopper to get in there and could load her right onto it."

"Maybe," Caldwell said, weighing the idea. "But if there's fire around, you've got your fuel ready to blow."

"Listen," Lovenko said, "your trucks outfitted with aluminum reflector suits?"

"Some of them. Blankets too."

"Okay. Here's how you do it. Wrap the tanks. Those suits can handle up to two thousand degrees Fahrenheit without raising the interior temp over a hundred."

"That fuel flashes low, Cas."

"So long as you can stay clear of the actual burn, the aluminum housing should hold the tanks."

It sounded to Caldwell like a hell of a lot of shoulds and maybes and ifs.

"Is that your best shot?" Caldwell asked. He heard

the air beating in the distance and turned and saw copter headlights probing down through the smoke.

"Afraid so," Lovenko said. "No magic."

"Hanging up, Cas. The chopper's here." Caldwell handed the mike back to the radio operator. When he turned toward the field the aircraft was touching down.

Every sane instinct in Caldwell said *no*. But his memory flashed a picture of a screaming woman and child engulfed in flame and his mind wouldn't let go of it. His blood whispered that this was it, this was Ed Caldwell's second chance . . . Ed Caldwell's only chance.

He wheeled and shouted to the men around him. "Go to every vehicle stationed on this field and get every reflector suit and blanket you can find! And wire! And staple guns! On the double!"

And then he was running across the field to meet the pilot.

It took twelve men seven minutes to blanket the fuel tanks. And then the Bell 206B vaulted noisily into an angling flutter forward and up. The youthful pilot, a man named Mendez, strained to see ahead through the false, smoke-made night. The cockpit controls gave just enough light to profile his lean brown face, just enough light for Caldwell to check his gear and see the street map.

"Go!" Caldwell shouted. "Go!"

Mendez answered by opening the throttle all the way up. He ignored altitude and worked for speed, keeping the copter as close to the ground as he dared. Rivers of jittery, sparking smoke ran across his vision, but Mendez did not climb to avoid the hazard of firebrands. He held the aircraft to a steady level course, taking altitude only as he needed it to keep his distance from the ground.

"You think the blankets'll hold?" Caldwell shouted.

Mendez's voice carried clearly above the beating of the rotors and the snarl of the straining engine. His words were crisp, as if they came with edges and corners. "At this speed? No!"

"You worried?" Caldwell shouted back.

"I look it?" Mendez's eyes were fixed on the flaming

obstacle course ahead. "Besides, don't I have this fancy suit on?"

"You're a hard one!" Caldwell shouted.

"Inside and out," Mendez shouted back. "There's iron in them refried beans."

The seconds passed, their cadence running with the crown fire that jumped from tree to tree below. But then there was no fire below, and Caldwell shouted, "That's it! That's Malibu!"

Mendez followed the dipping earth until he had the copter moving in a scooping rush through the long, narrow basin. Fire appeared again in white smeary blotches spattered like flecks of phosphorescent paint against the walls and floor of the canyon below.

"Houses!" Caldwell shouted. "They're catching!"

Mendez gave acknowledgment with a short, tight nod of the head. The Bell 206 covered the course from near to far rim of the canyon in seconds. Mendez turned his fist around and jabbed his thumb down toward the ground. "Malibu!" he shouted.

"Can we get in?" Caldwell shouted.

"Which house?" Mendez shouted back, breaking the aircraft into a steep bank to the left.

"Last one! Big fancy swimming pool in back!" Caldwell answered, shifting in his seat to peer below. All he could see was a sea of flames off to the right, tossing skyward in arching, wind-whipped waves.

The aircraft was slapped broadside by a sudden thermal and shuttled woozily back into the direction of the turn.

"Wind's up!" Mendez shouted. "Hold on!"

"Can you see the house?" Caldwell screamed, for now the fire was screaming too, and the din of struggling machine and erupting air drowned all other sound.

"Fire's on it if that's what you're asking!" Mendez screamed back, cutting back power and leveling out in spasms of strict descent.

"Get in! Get in!" Caldwell screamed. He had flung open the door and was out and running before the copter had even settled to the ground.

The gear he carried was heavy and the aluminum reflector coveralls slowed him. But Caldwell was across

232

the lawn and wasted no more than one try at the front door. The knob was so hot in his hand that, without the mitten, the flesh would have smoked right off.

Locked!

He wheeled to the left and circled the house, scanning through the sight shield for some point of entry. When he saw the sliding glass doors he raised the long ax. He had it in motion as he shouldered to his right and hurled a left-handed chop into the wide-spreading glass.

His weight and momentum carried him through the rainbow of flying shards and into the room. He saw sparks shooting from electrical outlets and the length of garden hose winding lazily across the still-watery floor. He moved forward into the smoke-clogged darkness, dropped the ax, yanked the flashlight from the loop at his hip, and quickly swept the beam through the billowing black clouds.

At the upper horizon of his sight shield he saw flame beginning to root down through the ceiling. He started to run right toward the kitchen. Instinct stopped him, an intuition in his blood signaling him that it was in bedrooms that humankind went to hide. He pivoted to his left, his boots squishing through the water-sogged carpet. The flashlight probed the hallway ahead.

The woman sat on the floor, unmoving, her eyes blinking into the sudden piercing light. Caldwell went toward her, lifting the helmet off his head. When she spoke it was the voice he had heard on the radio, the voice that had won seven gold records, and he had a flash of disorientation.

"Please—can't we let him sleep? I don't want him to see this."

Caldwell did not waste oxygen answering. He bent to the boy. "All right, son—I'm waking you up," and he raised the boy slightly and gently rocked him back and forth.

The boy's eyes opened, but in the way of children he still seemed to be asleep when he spoke. "Mom! It's an astronaut! Look!"

"Here we go, kid," Caldwell said, and then to the mother, "What's his name?"

She seemed to register an instant's surprise that there could be anyone in the civilized world who didn't know the name of Melinda Mars' son, and then she said, "Loren. His name's Loren."

Caldwell lifted the boy till he stood. "On your feet, Loren. You're a good trooper now, right?"

Caldwell did not wait for the child to answer. "Listen now, these are your orders, Sergeant Mars. I'm taking Mommy, and you're taking hold of my pants, and not anything in the world is going to make you let go. Got it, Sergeant? Understand?"

The boy yawned and nodded sleepily.

"Now you just grab onto me as soon as I get Mommy up. Ready?" Caldwell bent to the woman, his lips close to her ear. "This is going to hurt, Miss Mars."

The woman nodded.

"Grit your teeth, Miss Mars. Bite down hard."

He had her, and then he had her up and over his left shoulder, his right hand free to work the high-pressure water unit if he had to.

"Loren!" Caldwell shouted, turning in the darkness. "Get my flashlight there and aim it out in front of me and grab on and don't you ever let go! Hurry, now, son! Come on now, fast!"

Caldwell tried to adjust to the weight of her, tried to relax his left shoulder and pull the bone down under the flesh, as though this might cushion the unborn life that rode upon him.

"Here we go!" Caldwell shouted against the bellowing of the fire. "Aim that light and grab hold good! Are you with me, son?"

For answer the boy tugged twice on the silvered leg. Caldwell turned back toward the living room.

"Hold that light straight out now!" he shouted.

But there was no need for the flashlight: a splash of fire flooded in around the broken glass doors, hissing into steam as it seared the wet floor.

"Move back!" Caldwell shouted, stepping back into the cover of the hallway. "Loren! You see where I've got some silver pads tied to my back? Reach up there fast now and pull that cord! Come on, fast!"

Caldwell took the aluminum reflector sheet that the

boy handed up to him. He threw it over Melinda Mars. "Spread it all over yourself!" Caldwell called. "Cover yourself good now! Everyone all set?"

"I'm fine," he heard Melinda Mars say, and the voice that seemed bent under pain fought back. Again he could feel the boy tug twice in answer.

"Okay," Caldwell shouted. "We're going on out there! Forward, march!"

Caldwell lunged forward. He could feel her weight now, and the boy holding to him seemed like a sack of iron dragging him down. He hoisted the woman, readjusting her, and he fixed his legs for a run.

When he came to the end of the hallway he looked quickly to his right and saw the fire draw back and then flop forward again, like a wide-throated viper striking. Caldwell had the wand of the water unit aimed and spraying off to his right now, holding the flames at bay. He took two quick steps into the living room and checked to his left for the front door.

"My feet!" the boy screamed.

Caldwell whipped his head around. The boy was barefoot on the smoking floor.

"What's the matter?" Melinda Mars cried, trying to thrash around and see.

"It's nothing," Caldwell shouted. "It's okay!"

He wrestled the water unit off his right shoulder and let it thump to the floor. He reached his right arm down behind him to grab for the boy.

"Up you go!" he shouted. "Come on, boy, both hands! Grab up there and hold on tight! You've got to hold on tight so I can use my arm!"

Caldwell crouched until he felt the boy well in place. Then he straightened up, his legs almost buckling under the weight of mother and son and unborn baby.

"Here we go!" he shouted, breaking fast for the front door, hand out to throw the lock and fling the door wide. He had taken three forward lurches onto the lawn when a suffocating thunder began its rumble from below his heart.

"Oh, Jesus, *no*," Caldwell gasped, feeling the sudden sharp pincers squeezing the life from his chest. He shouted, "Son! Son, can you hear me? If I fall down, you

235

keep on going! You see that airplane there? If I fall down you just keep right on going and climb aboard!"

Caldwell staggered. His jaw fell open with pain. He went down on one knee and tried to stand again.

"Run, run, son!" Caldwell groaned, but he felt the small hand still grasping him around the neck, refusing to let go.

"No!" Caldwell shouted at Mendez when he saw the man lunging across the smoking lawn. "Go back! The boy will come!"

But the boy didn't let go and—realizing he would never let go—Caldwell felt new strength billow through him, a strength made of anger and defiance, a *yes* to all the *no's* in the universe, a screw-you to everything that wanted to stop him.

He struggled up again, willing himself erect, standing now, staggering back and then stumbling forward down the lawn under the weight of the woman and boy, his heart as strong as the grip of that boy's hand which would never again leave his.

Yes, the strength in him roared, and he shouldered past Mendez's outstretched arms, flashing brilliant wrinkles of silver light. He forced his way through the suffocating smoke and across the last smoldering distance to the helicopter. He eased the woman in through the open canopy, and Mendez reached in from the other side to shift her to the rear space.

Caldwell hoisted the boy until Mendez had him and pulled him all the way in, and then Mendez leaned across the passenger seat and lowered his arm.

"Grab!" he screamed. "Grab me!"

Caldwell grabbed and Mendez yanked him up and in.

"Come on, Dad," Mendez shouted, "it's time to do a little flying!"

Just as the grass around the aircraft liquefied into a lake of flame, Mendez kicked the topside rotors into high throttle.

"Climb! Climb!" Caldwell screamed.

There was a great wrenching pull as the copter lifted away and jerked straight up, clutching the air for al-

236

titude, then banking sharply as Mendez veered back toward the fire camp.

"No!" Caldwell shouted above the roar of the engine. "San Bernardino! The hospital! You hear?"

Grinning, Mendez corrected his course.

Caldwell twisted in his seat to look at Melinda Mars. He reached back to take her hand in his.

She tried to smile—but tears came instead.

Caldwell squeezed her hand. He searched for something to say to her, something to give her what she needed right now. But when he spoke it was something else that he said.

"You're all right, now, son," Ed Caldwell said. "You're here. You're safe. You're with me."

12

THE ADDRESS was a run-down apartment building with pink paint peeling off the stucco like skin off a sunburned face. VV parked her car at the curb. She made her way to the interior court, stopping at the mailboxes.

There was no Defino, but there were unlabeled boxes with mail showing through and there was a T. Shaughnessy, super, in apartment three.

VV went to the super's door. It was open. A television set was going somewhere in the dimness inside. VV could hear crashes and car skids and an uproar of canned laughter. She leaned hard on the buzzer.

A woman shuffled to the door. She wore a faded tent of a housecoat and the fluff of white hair framing her face showed residual traces of dye jobs. The effect was a ghostly rainbow limited to the blond-red-brown spectrum.

"Help you?"

"Are you the manager?"

"Owner." The lines around her eyes and mouth were as deep as cracks in sunbaked mud and a vein was pulsing impatiently in her forehead. "You looking to rent?"

"I'm looking for a friend. Frank Defino. I was told he lived here."

"Friend of Defino's?" This obviously struck T. Shaughnessy as highly unlikely.

"I need to talk to him."

The woman scowled, piercing VV with a glance of cold skepticism. "You from the Board of Health?"

"No, I'm not. My name's VV—"

The woman cut VV short, jetting cigarette smoke through her nostrils. "'Cause I got rid of those dogs. No pets, that's my rule, and he kept bringing in those goddamned mutts."

"*Is* Mr. Defino here? Could I please speak to him?"

"*Mister* Defino. That's good. No. He's not here. I threw him out two days ago. Say—did he go and hire some kind of lawyer? Is that why you're nosing around?"

"I'm not a lawyer. I'm not from the Board of Health. My name's VV Cameron, I—"

The woman moved her body to block the door. Great stains of sweat smeared the armpits of her robe. "'Cause he owes me two months' back rent. You can tell him he's not getting a thing out of that apartment till he pays up." The woman flipped a nod toward an apartment at the rear of the court, beside the garage door.

"Can you tell me where he's gone?"

"How do I know? He'll be back. All his junk's still there." Again, probably without conscious thought, the woman nodded toward the apartment.

"When are you expecting him?"

"If he's not back today he's paying for another month." The woman went back to her television, and this time she shut the door behind her.

VV hesitated only a moment. She crossed the courtyard and, with one backward glance to make sure no one was watching, she stepped into the flowerbed, careful not to trample the ragged red pansies.

Standing high on her tiptoes, she was able to squint through the window into the apartment. She sucked in her breath and quickly Kleenexed the dust from one of the panes. She could see through the angled slats of a Venetian blind.

The dim rear wall was blanketed in a chaos of overlapping maps and charts and diagrams. Some of them were studded with colored thumbtacks and others bore slashes of grease pencil. The bed wasn't really a bed,

239

it looked more like a cot. There was a bowl of water on the floor and beside it a rubber dish of something reddish and moldy-looking. Carpenter's tools lay everywhere: wrenches and screwdrivers of a dozen different sizes, saws and hammers and pliers. There was a workbench with a vise and what looked like an electric saw, and on the linoleum beneath it, two lengths of sawed-off metal pipe and several links of small-gauge steel chain.

That's not an apartment, VV thought, *that's a war games room.*

She did not hear the footstep behind her. She was not aware of the eyes staring with cold ferocity at her. She was caught completely unprepared by the hand that roughly seized her and whipped her around.

"What the hell are you doing snooping around here?"

A cry aborted midway in VV's throat. The instant of shock was so total she could hardly get her voice out. "I thought I saw a light. I thought Mr. Defino might be in."

T. Shaughnessy was clearly unconvinced and just as clearly enraged. "Look what you did to those flowers! You just get the hell out of here or I'm calling the cops!"

VV got the hell out. Certainty drummed in her now. She hurried to the little cigar store across from the apartments. Late-afternoon sun was slanting down through the smoky sky as she dropped a dime into the pay phone slot.

She was unable to reach Caldwell at the fire department. The switchboard gave her Peters instead.

"Could you tell Ed I'm ninety-nine percent certain I've found the man?"

"What man?" Peters said smoothly, so smoothly she almost answered.

"Ed will know," VV said. She gave Peters the address and had him read it back to make certain he had it right. "Tell him to bring a search warrant. It'll save time."

Dr. Jim Stern glanced up. The orderlies had wheeled two stretcher cases into the emergency room. Dr. Stern looked at them idly. Fire victims, to judge by the faces and clothes streaked with soot. One was a young boy, unconscious. The other was a woman, not at all unconscious: on the contrary, very alert and struggling hard to prop herself up on her elbows. The orderly had to keep pushing her down.

Dr. Stern completed the medication report on the mugging victim whose head he had just stitched. It occurred to him that that woman looked a little like Melinda Mars. As the stretcher approached, the likeness grew into an almost exact resemblance.

Good Lord, it's her, Melinda Mars, he thought, still not quite believing it. The wheeled stretcher squeaked to a stop.

"Okay," Dr. Stern signaled the nurse, "let's get her on oxygen, clean her up, cut her out of this—" He couldn't tell what the garment had originally been, but it was a heap of burned swaddling now.

The nurse wheeled the oxygen tank over.

Melinda Mars swiped the mask aside with one hand. "Where's my son?"

"Dr. Parrish is taking care of your son. He's fine."

The nurse made another try with the mask.

"Nurse," the doctor said, "she doesn't seem to need oxygen." Then, leaning close to Miss Mars so she wouldn't have to shout: "Are you hurt anywhere? Do you have burns, wounds, bleeding?"

The nurse was clipping away at the clothes and an assistant was sponging away the glops of burned cloth.

"There are burns on my lower left leg. Superficial."

As Dr. Stern lifted the cloth she reacted with a violent wince.

"The leg's broken."

Dr. Stern noted the ridge of bone pushing up against the skin. "Demerol," he instructed the nurse.

Miss Mars' hands stayed his. "No narcotics. Clean the burn and give me a zinc-oxide topical solution. Set the bone in a splint, not a cast."

"Miss Mars," the doctor said pleasantly, "I'm the doctor, all right?"

"May I please finish?" She met his eyes unwaveringly. "I'm in labor. The contractions are coming at twenty-minute intervals. I want natural delivery with no anesthesia, but—"

"Miss Mars, don't tire yourself."

"May I finish, Doctor? I have a concert at eight o'clock, so you may have to induce labor. I can miss the rehearsal, but I can't miss the concert."

"You have a multiple fracture," the doctor observed.

"I'm not going on that stage in a cast."

"Miss Mars, you're not going on that stage period."

"The hell I'm not."

"Nurse—Demerol, scopolamine. On the double."

Miss Mars began struggling to sit up. The doctor pressed her down with one hand. "Just relax now."

"I don't want that shit in my veins!"

The doctor slapped her across the face, backhand, forehand, and in the instant of shocked unresistingness that followed he managed to rip the cloth from her arm and swab clean an area large enough for the nurse to plunge in the hypodermic.

Miss Mars tensed and with one last effort tried to sit up.

"She's going to snap the needle!" the nurse cried.

The doctor pushed Miss Mars back with both hands and held her down till he felt the first relaxation of the muscles.

The nurse emptied the hypodermic into the upper arm and withdrew the syringe, staring at it in mild amazement that it had survived.

"Bastards," Miss Mars was muttering.

"That's right, Miss Mars, we're bastards. And fans. Now why don't you have yourself a little nap? I think you've earned one."

Somewhere, drowsily, a church bell tolled the hour. VV looked again at her watch. She realized she had to make a decision. She got out of the car, locked it—she didn't trust the neighborhood—and crossed the street to the cigar store.

A stunning Mexican girl who couldn't have been more than eighteen years old was having an emotional breakdown into the pay phone. In Spanish. VV pulled a ten-dollar bill from her purse, cursed silently that she didn't have a five, and waved it in front of the creamy-skinned beauty.

"*Por favor?*" VV coaxed.

The girl surrendered the phone and VV caught the tail end of what sounded like a mother's harangue. *Perdóname, Mamacita.* She broke the connection, dropped a dime, and dialed the station.

"Alan, I'm not going to make the broadcast. Can you cover for me?"

"Now, love, you know our discriminating viewers will accept nothing but the best, and science has yet to find a substitute for VV Cameron."

"Run the Melinda Mars footage."

"That rip-off white-face Billie Holiday? *Why?*"

"Because I'm on to something very, very big."

"All right, deprive the loyal fans—but *torture* them?"

"I mean *big,* Alan. The fire. We lost the phone lead, but I found another."

"You mean Mr. Concerned Citizen Dog Fancier Fire Expert? Another lead to Jack the Zippo?"

"I'm going to break this story, Alan."

"And when you go to CBS—please, please, take me along?"

"It's a promise."

Since the whole *Newsbreak* gimmick was the hard-hitting female, Alan drafted Patricia, the research assistant, to do the honors. Being a mouse, she naturally refused, and Alan just as naturally refused the refusal.

"Your chance to be an overnight sensation, love."

He scrawled her patter on huge sheets of cardboard, pushed her into the glass hot seat, and had one of the electricians stand off-camera and flash the immortal prose to her.

Three minutes into the telecast the call-in phone rang in the control booth. Alan answered.

"Where's VV Cameron?"

A superextraordinary gulp rode up Alan's throat. The voice was creepy, bad-tempered, and by now very familiar. Alan pressed the trace button and held it down and prayed those idiots at Ma Bell weren't taking a tea break.

"Is this a personal call or a phone-in?"

"This is a personal phone-in. Put her on the line and put me on the show."

Think, Alan, think. Why, oh, why did I take that last snort? He covered the mouthpiece and shouted, "VV, call on line three!"

The engineers flipped astonished looks his way.

Alan was not deterred.

"Take three first, okay? You're on in thirty."

In the shack in North Hollywood the man with the three-minute egg timer in his hand wondered what the hell *thirty* meant.

Seconds, he supposed.

He tilted the timer back and forth, watching the salt spill from chamber to chamber, waited for the sound of VV Cameron's voice when he would start the salt flowing for real. His heart was thumping from the excitement of what he was about to do. He had chosen his words and they were beauts. He'd lifted them from the old Ford commercials.

There's a fire storm in your future.

Chuckling, he rocked back and forth. He shifted the phone to the other ear.

Where the hell *was* the bitch? He reached to jiggle the cradle, then pulled his finger back. Bad idea. His call was first in line and if he broke the connection he might have to wait, he might not even get back on, and this was one chance in a million, don't throw it away.

His eye went up to the television screen. It still wasn't VV Cameron. But it wasn't that librarian type who'd opened the show, either. Hell, it was that singer, Melinda Mars, with a belly out to *here*. She was walking through a garden and he realized it was film footage, they were running *film*, stalling him—*tracing* him!

"*FUCK YOU!*" he screamed, "*YOU'LL ALL ROAST ANYWAY!*" and in a hard, chopping swing he brought the edge of his hand down across the telephone cradle.

The connection broke eight nanoseconds too late. The tracing mechanism at the central switching office had tracked down the eighth digit of the phone number.

The information was automatically fed to the computer housing the Greater Los Angeles telephone subscriber list. Three seconds later the laser-printed name of subscriber and address of same spilled into the printout basket.

Ms. Imogene Picone, a trainee in Bell Telephone special projects, hit the hot line to police headquarters and in her clearest diction read off the information to a man who identified himself as Sergeant Gluskowski.

Defino did not even take the time to punch off the TV. Within twenty seconds of realizing he'd been suckered he was out the door and into the station wagon, trying to start the motor, flooding the engine, cursing, giving it time to unflood, twisting the ignition key again, and flooring the accelerator.

The dogs in back began howling. "Shut yer yaps!" he snapped.

This time the engine turned over, but Defino was so rattled he put the car into forward instead of reverse and bolted into a garbage can. He reversed, not bothering the stop at neutral. The gears screamed like a skinned cat.

He jammed the gas to the floor, righted the steering wheel, and took the edge off a wood gatepost as he looped into the street, slammed back into forward—the skinned cat screamed again—and accelerated with hiccupping lurches to the corner.

Just as Defino's station wagon was turning off the street, an unmarked police car was swinging onto it one block away. The car skidded to a stop in front of the tumbledown unpainted shack. Three plainclothesmen jumped out and dashed across the unweeded, garbage-strewn lawn.

Their guns were drawn as they kicked in the unlocked, unresisting front door. "Police!" one of them shouted, and another, "Hands up!"

They had expected to find an arsonist, but all they found was a television set playing to an empty room and, in the word of the third policeman, groaning with his fingers to his nose, "Dog shit...Christ, the dog shit!"

It was just after seven when Eddy Caldwell's car screeched to a stop across the street from VV's.

"Hey, Chief," she yelled, waving, "over here!"

He had a police car behind him, and the policeman had a search warrant, and VV led the way through the courtyard to apartment three. En route she noticed Ed Caldwell's filth-caked face and clothes.

"What the hell have you been doing, Chief?"

He shrugged and patted her. "Rescuing superstars."

The policeman rattled Mrs. Shaughnessy's screen door. There was a distinct gin smell about the old lady, as well as a gin slowness in her ability to absorb the meaning of a search warrant.

"The premises inhabited by Frank Defino," the policeman repeated.

"Ain't here," Mrs. Shaughnessy said.

"You got a key? This is a search warrant, lady. I can shoot the lock off if you won't let us in."

It was a third-party warrant, the sort of court-sanctioned intrusion on privacy that VV had denounced to her viewers. This time, she let it pass. It got them where they needed to get.

VV flicked on the light switch by the door. For a moment she stood blinking. The walls and ceiling were painted stark, flat white. The bare floor was painted gray that had chipped away in places to let the gray concrete below peek through.

"Need me for anything else?" the policeman asked.

"Nothing else," Caldwell said. "Thanks."

"You better keep this in case the tenant comes back." The policeman gave Caldwell the warrant. "See you."

"See you," Caldwell answered, but already he was inventorying the residence of Frank Venice alias Frank Defino, lover of dogs and forest fires, and certainly no lover of furniture. His eye took in a folding cot, a table beside it, a workbench, and litter.

"It's a prison cell," VV said.

Caldwell nodded grimly. "Except a prisoner doesn't have a choice. Defino does."

"Does he?"

Caldwell's eyes narrowed on her. "Why do you say that?"

"He's insane, isn't he? Aren't insane people driven?"

"That doesn't excuse it." The narrow eyes fixed her and Caldwell was silent just a beat. "What would you do if we caught him?" he said.

Irritation rose in VV. She had been making an observation, not an apology. *This is dumb,* she thought. *We're arguing and there's no point.* It was as silly as a lovers' quarrel.

Remember the date, VV, and the time, and exactly the way it felt. Maybe you'll be celebrating this years from now, along with first meeting and first kiss and first...you know, all the firsts.

"If we catch him, Chief, it's not my job to do anything to him. And it's not yours, either."

There was just an instant when Caldwell's face hardened, and then it relaxed into a grin and his hand tousled her red hair. "You're okay, VV."

They gazed at each other, suddenly aware that they were touching.

"Chief," VV said, pulling away, "maybe we'd better get on with the search."

"Maybe we'd better," he said with a sudden hoarseness in his voice.

VV concentrated on the room now. She could not fathom it any more than she could the sort of man who would willingly live in it. Every object seemed to be chosen not for the comfort it offered body or eye, but for its utility. Except for the wall coverings. These were charts, a riot of abstract colors, green swirls encircling red and blue swirls, crests and waves and ovals of brown and orange, tiny pointillist dots of black and scarlet.

"Maps," Caldwell observed. And he went to study them. A vertical crease came into his brow and his hand went to his chin. His eyes scanned.

They were maps of great beauty and detail, and their makers were identified in small print in the lower-left-hand corner of each: the United States Topographic Command, the United States Deaprtment of the Interior Geological Survey, National Ocean Survey, Defense Mapping Agency Topographic Center.

"What are they?" VV asked.

Caldwell shook his head. "They're everything you ever wanted to know about everything between the thirty-fifth and third-third parallels and the hundred twenty-second and hundred eighteenth meridians."

Puzzlement clouded VV's face.

"They're a portrait of Los Angeles," Caldwell said, and now anger sounded in his voice, still controlled but there. "Planimetry, contour intervals, transverse Mercator projection, reliability variants, magnetic declination for the current year—the works." He slammed a hand against a chart.

A sort of awe came into VV's eyes as she began to understand not only the maps but the meaning of the red grease-pencil marks scattered across them.

"How did he get them?"

"All you have to do is write away," Caldwell said. "He wrote away." Caldwell's breathing was coming rapidly now, his jaw set and grim.

VV crossed to the workbench and stared down at the tools. "What kind of saw is that?"

"It cuts metal," Caldwell said tersely. He bent down to the floor to pick up a quarter-inch link of steel chain. "Like that." He handed VV the sawed link and she stared at it.

"But why? What's it for?"

"If he left it here it's not for anything," Caldwell said. "It's what he sawed it off from that counts."

The only human touch that VV could see in the place were two squat bowls on the floor. They were made of the same industrial red rubber as plumber's helpers. One contained an inch of water, the other several desiccated nuggets of a substance she realized must be dog food.

How odd, she thought, that the only human touch would be a dog's feeding and water bowls. She wondered about the lonely man who had lived here. Had the loneliness caused the warp, or had the warp fathered the loneliness? Or had they worked together in some undefinable, unholy synergy?

"Well, I'll be damned." Caldwell was staring at the

little table next to the cot. All VV saw was a cheap drugstore alarm clock, a box of kitchen matches.

"What is it, Chief?"

She tried to see the thing that had caught Caldwell's eye. The alarm clock was set for six thirty. There didn't seem to be anything extraordinary in that. Then she peered closer at the table. She saw some strands of what looked like brown hair. She picked them up, rolled them between her fingers. There was something wrong with them, some quality at once brittle and slick.

"A wig," she said. "He wears a wig. A cheap wig."

But then she realized it wasn't the wig either that interested Caldwell.

He held up the box of matches. "These are a real collector's item."

VV stared but she didn't get it.

Caldwell pushed open the box and offered it to her, like chocolate bonbons after dinner. "Take one."

"What is this, a match trick?"

"Take one."

She took one.

"Light it."

She reached the match head toward the friction board on the side of the box, but Caldwell whisked the box out of reach.

"Not that way," he said.

VV frowned and suddenly she understood. She stooped and scraped the phosphorous head against the bare floor. The match sizzled into flame. She stared at it a moment and then extinguished it with a quick wrist-snap motion.

"But—these aren't sold anymore."

Caldwell nodded. "They're illegal—in the United States."

"Then how did he—"

Caldwell showed her the box. The writing was in two alphabets, and the Latin alphabet looked like Portuguese.

"He went to a lot of trouble," Caldwell said. "Looks like no trouble's too great for our friend. Not him. He's dedicated."

Caldwell crossed the room now and swung open the

door of one closet. There was very little in the way of clothes. Three neatly pressed animal shelter uniforms hung on the rod. Two pairs of large high-top sneakers were carefully aligned on the floor. On one of the shelves was a supply of canned dog food with an opener laid next to the cans.

Beneath was a shelf of toiletries, and VV looked carefully at these. The mouthwash and shaving cream and deodorant were ordinary enough for any American male indoctrinated by TV commercials, but the skin softeners and emollients and wrinkle vanishers were decidedly unmale.

VV picked up a jumbo jar of twelve-hour skin moisturizer. "Chief, it doesn't make sense. If he's so vain about his skin, why the hell would he lay in an el cheapo like this? It's pig fat and coconut oil."

"Maybe it goes with the wig," Caldwell said.

"Wig and skin cream," VV said, working through the addition, seeing what he meant. "Drag queen?"

Caldwell shrugged.

"No way," VV said. She swept a hand across the closet. "Where are the dresses, the shoes, the jewelry? Padded bras? Drag queens have *style*. It may be style that makes you barf, but it's not municipal uniforms and sneakers."

"Well," Caldwell said, "what's the other reason people wear wigs?"

"He could be disguising himself, or—he's *bald*." Like someone who had rheumatic fever and lost all his hair, she thought. *I once knew an eight-year-old kid like that, and he wore a wig*.

"Then the skin cream..."

"He's got real shit skin," Caldwell said. "The kind you have to keep underwater twenty-four hours a day."

Something tugged at a corner of VV's memory. There *was* something about the man's skin, something she'd heard only today.

"He doesn't like to be photographed," she said. "He was...*burned*."

"Bald and burned," Caldwell said. "Sounds like a beaut."

250

"He sounds pathetic," VV said. "No friends but dogs, no home but—this."

Caldwell didn't comment. His hand explored the shelf of woolens. Beneath the soft socks and heavy sweater he found a stack of lab books with stickers pasted to their speckled covers. He opened the top one, flipped through the yellowed pages of tiny, exact script.

"You want to feel sorry for him?" Caldwell handed her the book.

VV turned to the first page. Centered there, like a printed title, were the block capital words THE FIRES.

Two pages on was the subtitle, "Our Lady of the Angels School," followed by a hand-lettered report, apparently copied from or based on news items, of ninety children and three nuns who burned to death when their school caught fire. Twenty-four of the children, obediently awaiting their teacher's instructions, were turned to ashes at their desks.

An item on "The Great Chicago Fire," in the same meticulous lettering, reported that the heat of the conflagration ranged for three days between two and three thousand degrees.

Another page: Forest fires in 1894 destroyed nearly two dozen Minnesota towns. People tried to save themselves by huddling in ponds, but the flames evaporated the water and then—mercilessly—the helpless people.

There was a report on "The Coconut Grove Nightclub," November 28, 1942, detailing the panic, the two-minute gutting of the pleasure dome that left 492 dead.

As VV skimmed pages a nausea pushed against the lining of her stomach. This was pornography, the very special pornography of a very special man. The book contained fire after fire, lovingly printed out, the number of victims dead, of victims scarred, the damage done, the ground covered, the cost in everything that could be measured, how great the heat, how high the flame, how fast the fire—and the velocity of the wind. It was this last that was always underlined. *Wind.*

"Why wind?" VV asked. "Why's it so important to him?"

Caldwell was engrossed in the next lab book, and he

barely turned his head to answer. "Because wind is what makes a fire work."

He was squinting at what was evidently a diary. The first entry was dated May 12, 1968, the day the diarist had been inducted into the army. Caldwell riffled through the pages. There were entries on basic training, on drillmasters hated and drillmasters endured; entries on technical schools: a month at the Applied Physics Laboratory at Johns Hopkins University, a month at the Fire Research Station in Bomarton Springs, Texas, three months at the United States Naval Research Laboratory.

Astonishingly few of the entries were personal. Most listed facts learned, experiments conducted with success or failure duly noted; one or two entries might have referred to amorous adventure or then again they could have referred to deserts with whimsical names. Caldwell muttered, handed the book to VV. And then he came to a lab book that froze his expression and made his heart drop two hundred feet inside him. Hands trembling, he picked it up. The label, with spiderlike neatness, spelled out the title: "THE GREAT LOS ANGELES FIRE."

"My God," Ed Caldwell said. "Oh, my God."

He took the book across to the cot. Weak-kneed, legs shaking, he sat down and began to read. VV watched him ripping through those pages, saw his face telling it all, the shock, the dismay, and anger—the dawning comprehension.

For the first time now she realized the air in the room was stagnant, the heat stupendous. It was as if the tatterboard walls with their washed-over white were the reflecting walls of an oven. She had an overwhelming impulse to scream and run.

"It's all here," Caldwell said finally, and his voice was almost a suffocated moan.

"What is it, Chief?"

"Everything. How he's doing it, when, where. That chain you were wondering about—there's a fuel bomb on one end. There's a dog on the other."

VV's stomach contracted.

"He's leashing the dogs with light-sensitive fuse. The

sun comes up, the fuse ignites, sets off the bomb, releases the dog. The dog runs in panic and the bomb gets dragged ten yards or so before the fuel's used up. By then the forest's on fire."

VV sat down on the bed beside him. "Does the book say—why?"

"Lovenko had him pegged, all right. *He wants to start a fire storm.* The biggest, the bestest fire storm any fire school grad ever unleashed. His doctoral thesis. His masterwork. His forget-me-not to the human race."

"But why, Eddy? Why does he want to do it?"

Caldwell sighed. "I have a theory, but why don't we just ask when we see him," he said with heavy irony. He got to his feet, paced grimly a moment, then turned to face her.

"VV, I need your help."

"Sure, Chief."

"You got a pencil?"

"That's easy. Settle for a ball-point?" She ferreted the pen out of her purse and handed it to him.

He ripped a blank page from the back of the speckled lab book. Bending over the workbench, leafing back to earlier pages, he copied out a rapid string of figures. He folded the paper and handed it to her.

"I'm going to give this to you fast, VV, because there's no time. I want you to telephone headquarters. Ask for Lovenko, Cas Lovenko."

"Lovenko," she repeated. "Cas."

"Give him the coordinates on the paper. They're latitudes and longitudes. Have him read them back, make sure he's got them. Then tell him this: we're on the wrong side of the fire line. You got that?"

She nodded. "Wrong side of the fire line. Okay."

"Tell him the bombs are being placed at these coordinates and they're being placed *now.*"

Biting her lower lip, she nodded again. "Now," she repeated. "Being placed now."

Caldwell jammed the lab book into his pocket. He broke into a forward lunge.

"Chief—where are you going?"

"He's out there now, VV. There's no time. He's got to be stopped. Looks like I get the job."

She jumped up. "I'll come with you."

"The hell you will. My goddamned car radio went on the blink this afternoon. Someone has to get word through to headquarters. So get on that phone—fast."

VV nodded. "Lovenko," she said.

And Caldwell was gone, slamming the door so hard behind him that it rebounded open.

VV stood only a moment, staring at the figures on the piece of paper. And then she snapped open her purse and scrambled for a dime.

13

THEY wouldn't put VV through to Cas Lovenko, but made her talk to Assistant Chief Peters instead.

"I'm calling for Ed Caldwell. Do you have a pencil?"

"Just a sec. Okay, shoot."

"Take down these coordinates in exactly the order I give them to you." She read off all eight sets. "Defino is setting his fire bombs in those places in that order. He's out there now. Caldwell's heading him off at fire site one, but you have to send men to back him up."

"Where'd you get this information?"

VV didn't trust Peters. He'd leaked that story about Lovenko coming in over Caldwell's head and intuition told her he was gunning for the chief.

"We found Defino's notebooks. You're on the wrong side of the fire line."

"Okay. I'll pass it on."

She wanted to say, *Pass it on fast, creep,* but instinct warned her not to antagonize him. He was a man, she sensed, who would put his antagonisms ahead of all else, including the survival of Los Angeles.

She hung up the pay phone and came out of the cigar store onto a sidewalk now littered with whores and drug pushers and the spillover of massage parlors. She crossed to her car and started the motor.

VV Cameron, a hot little voice whispered in her ear, *you're sitting on the story of the decade. You have the facts, the names. You even have the latitudes and longitudes. You can break this on television right now.*

They'll cut into the programming for you.

Boy, will they ever. This is the scoop of your lifetime. Barbara Walters, move over.

She thought about that. She thought about it very carefully and then she made up her mind and slipped the car into gear.

Ed Caldwell shifted down to low. He steered off the road and into the brush. When he judged he had gone deep enough into the forest to hide, he pulled to a stop. He spent a moment looking at the map, double-checking that he'd come to the right place, then glanced again at his watch.

I'm ahead of Defino. Provided he keeps to his schedule, I have a ten-minute lead.

He slipped from the car and eased the door shut behind him. He stood a moment in the dark, listening to the night sounds of Cleveland National Forest. The wind boiled overhead, like a great crazy winged thing raging through the treetops.

He snapped his flashlight on. The beam revealed trees, gray and brooding now that day was gone. He played the beam upland, searching till he found the spot. He recognized it from Defino's notes and plans. He saw the duff and the incline and the brush ready to kindle into flame, and he knew.

This was the place. Whatever was going to happen would happen here. The thing that had to be faced would be faced here. He knew he would face it alone, unaided.

And a part of him was afraid.

He moved stealthily uphill toward the spot. He stopped dead in his tracks. He had the sense that something had stopped at exactly the instant he had, that out there in the darkness something was breathing and the only reason he didn't hear it was that it was breathing at his cadence, using him and the flurry of his lungs to mask itself.

He cut the flashlight. He clutched at his breath, held himself rigid, tensed, as though the slightest motion would shatter him in two. He could see nothing but the black gradations of the forest growth. He listened. He heard only the wind, no human sound but the beating of his own heart.

But there was another sound. Not human. Animal. The hoarse breathing of a...*dog,* a sleeping dog not more than five feet away.

Unthinkingly, Caldwell flicked the light back on.

Then he remembered the bomb blueprints and the light-sensitive fuse.

He cut the flashlight, groped blindly toward the sound of breathing. He found the animal, a warm puddle of snoring fur beneath a manzanita. He clenched his memory, trying to recall how Defino had wired the bomb. The fuse had to be around the animal's neck, doubling as a leash....

Feeling through the fur, Caldwell found the fuse. He yanked hard, separating it from the canister. Then, exploring along its length, he tracked it to the tree where Defino had secured it. He gave another yank, untied the knot, groped along the ground for stray fragments. When he was certain he had all the fuse safely in the dark of his pocket, he turned on the flashlight and went back to the dog.

He stared down at a tranquil, tranquilized gray-and-brown mongrel.

This doesn't make sense, he thought. *I'm supposed to be here ahead of Defino, but Defino's been here ahead of me...*a good twenty minutes from the look of it.

Then it hit Caldwell.

Something must have alerted Defino. He'd caught on to the phone trace. He'd jumped the whole schedule up. He was rushing it, getting as many dogs into the woods as he could before he was stopped.

Caldwell went through a rapid mental calculation. It was no good lagging behind Defino. The only way to catch him was to get ahead of him. But Defino had to be at burn site two this very moment. So two was out. Caldwell would have to leapfrog, go directly to burn site three.

He gathered the sleeping dog up into his arms and hurried back to the car.

* * *

By eight o'clock excited crowds had begun to gather at the Hollywood Bowl. At the intersection of Highland and Hollywood traffic had to slow for the ingathering. There were supporters of the fire department, supporters of the police—but above all, there were the legions of Melinda Mars fans.

Mars was more than a star, more than an event. She was a state of mind that brought out all the secret brightness and brashness in those who loved her. The sidewalks and parking lots that night sparkled with constellations of the jeweled rich and the sequined unrich. They chatted and they laughed and they kept alert eyes peeled for celebrities. More than a few smoked preconcert joints or sneaked snorts of coke to heighten their musical awareness.

They came singly and in couples. They came in club groups and tour groups and chartered busloads. They came not just from Los Angeles but from all over the world, from wherever disc and tape and film and electromagnetic waves had carried the Mars voice and magic.

Among the ticket holders that night there were five exchange students from New Delhi, India, and two honeymooning couples from Kalgoorlie, Australia; and there was an attractive young secretary from Toledo, Ohio, who was to play a small but pivotal part in the tragic events of that evening.

Her name was Wilma Boborovsky. She was vacationing in L.A. with her husband Clarence, a lawyer. The Boborovskys joined the crowds filtering through the entrances and took their seats early. Wilma had bought tickets at the next-to-last moment and they were far from choice; in fact, they were in the back row.

"Well," Wilma remarked, eyeing the distance to the stage, "we've got a helluva view all right—better than Mount Lookout. Let's just hope we can hear."

"The Bowl's supposed to have the best natural acoustics in the world," Clarence said. He'd read the guidebook.

Wilma was not cheered by natural acoustics. The concert was a benefit and she'd paid fifteen dollars a seat to hear her idol.

"And the best sound system too," Clarence added.

The sound system cheered Wilma. She smiled and settled back in her seat. "I'm glad we came," she said, squeezing Clarence's hand. "Tonight's going to be special. I just know it."

She looked up at the sky. It appeared odd to her, stained with something darker than mere nightfall. The air was heavy, as though the atmospheric pressure had mysteriously doubled. It was hot too.

Wilma squirmed out of her jacket.

"Let me help," Clarence said, and he reached over to arrange the jacket on the back of her seat.

"Thanks," Wilma said. She gazed around the amphitheater. Even this early it was beginning to fill up. Voices made a sound like the sea. The mood of the crowd seemed to shimmer.

"I hope she sings 'Battle Hymn of the Republic,'" Wilma said dreamily.

"Me too," Clarence said.

Elbows propped on her knees, Wilma Boborovsky gazed at the empty stage, waiting for the moment when it would burst into light and produce the shining miracle of Melinda Mars.

At 8:07 P.M. weather satellites flashed word that the Hawaiian low-pressure area had finally started moving east. Los Angeles could expect rain within six to eight hours.

"Six to eight to fourteen hours," Lovenko grumbled, all too familiar with the maddening imprecision of long-range meteorological forecasts. He'd sooner rely on horoscopes and chicken entrails. His eye scanned the local weather update.

"That wind's shifting," he noticed. "Coming from the east now."

"Only a breeze," Peters said. "Dominant wind's still westerly."

But Lovenko was conscious of a disturbing new factor. He glanced over the updated burn charts, now almost an hour old, then toward the bank of flickering TV screens.

"Simi/Stone's heading for the fire line."

"So?" Peters said with a nonchalance that was unbelievable.

Lovenko's eye was taking Simi/Stone and driving her straight on through that fire line. "Evacuate the Bowl," he said suddenly.

Peters's head jerked up, his eyes huge and for one instant goggling. "You're crazy."

Lovenko whipped around in his seat. "Twenty thousand people are sitting in the path of that fire. Get 'em out of there!"

Peters chuckled, shaking his head in cool, firm denial. "The path of that fire stops *here*." Peters touched a finger to the line on the wall chart that represented the Santa Monica firebreak. "No way Simi/Stone's going to hop across that."

"No way it was going to hop an eight-lane throughway either," Lovenko challenged.

Peters sucked in a breath through his teeth. "Those people," he said, "are safe."

"Those people are hostages!" Lovenko jumped to his feet. His finger jabbed at the map. He was shouting now and the veins were standing out in his face and throat. "Between that fire line and those people you have two thousand acres of *kindling!* If those hills were sprayed in *napalm* they couldn't be a better candidate for flash fire!"

"The fire line will hold," Peters said quietly, as though calming a hysterical child.

Lovenko stared unbelievingly at this man in the sixty-dollar tapered shirt, this picture of tailored, manicured cool so smug under pressure. "All it takes is one spark—one rogue thermal—one dangling branch!" Lovenko snapped his fingers. "One *cigarette butt* west of that fireline could do it! Not to mention one fucking firebug!" Even as he shouted, Lovenko could see the monitor image of the fire reaching tendrils toward the west. "For God's sake, Peters, that fire's *moving!*"

"Lovenko," Peters said firmly, standing, "I'm second in command. Which means at this moment I'm the one who has to answer to the mayor and the governor, not you."

Rage and terror swept Lovenko. Suddenly he understood the priorities of this man Peters, the priorities of all the men like him. Peters wanted to advance. This was his chance. He was betting his career against the fire.

And for chips he was using twenty thousand lives.

"You're worried about *the mayor and the governor?*" Lovenko cried. "You're worried about those two penguins and their dumb speeches?"

"They're counting on me, Cas. We could have a very bad panic situation if I ordered an evacuation."

"If you don't evacuate and if Simi/Stone blows to the line and if that fire jumps—you'll have *real* panic!"

"There are some mighty big *ifs* there, friend. Mighty big."

"Listen, you idiot!" Lovenko was screaming now. On the other side of the glass wall heads turned curiously. "You don't bluff fire, you don't wait to see the whites of its eyes! Pull your goddamned macho act with the politicians but don't pull it with *fire!* Get those people OUT while there's still time!"

Peters put a hand on Lovenko's shoulder. Lovenko flung it off like a reptile.

"Don't you worry, Cas. I'm keeping an eye on the situation."

Lovenko whipped his head around. He stared at Peters out of a face that was a motionless mask of fury. For one savage instant he was on the verge of spitting out all the contempt and rage this man inspired in him, spitting it into the assistant chief's bland, smug smile.

Instead he wheeled around, strode to the door, and slammed it like a cannon shot behind him.

The West Highland terrier launched a volley of barks. It was staring down the wooded slope toward the Hollywood Bowl.

Beams of searchlights played in the air, intersecting the layers of smoke that hung in the night. The distant amphitheater glittered with movement and light. The hot wind carried sporadic gusts of sound up the hill, the babble of a thousand competing voices, the electric whine of musical instruments testing, testing, one, two, testing.

The dog whimpered. The fever of exhaustion showed in its eyes. It shivered, and the shiver passed with a metallic clinking along the length of chain that dangled from its collar.

The dog turned. The chain had wrapped itself one turn around the left hind leg, and as a result the animal walked with a limp.

It was a curious sight, the animal limping into the forest pulling ten feet behind it a metal canister that mimicked its every turn and hesitation.

Odder still, the canister had a tail of its own, a six-foot length of what looked like thin gray rope. As the animal moved deeper into the hills, this second tail swished softly across the forest floor, raising ridges into the tinder-dry duff.

In his windowless, industrial-green cubicle Cas Lovenko controlled the angry trembling of his finger long enough to punch out the number. There were two rings. Lieutenant Harvey Burgett of the Los Angeles police identified himself crisply.

"Lieutenant, Cas Lovenko here. How many men can you round up on sixty seconds' notice? We have to evacuate the Hollywood Bowl."

Shit, Melinda Mars thought. *I'm dead.*

There was no other explanation for so many flowers. She'd woken up at her own funeral. She could even hear the fans wailing.

They really loved me, she thought. *Wonder who's crying? Mama? The president of Casablanca Records?*

She couldn't resist a little peek over the roses, even if it *was* bad form to peek at your own funeral. It wasn't Mama and it wasn't the president of Casablanca Records. It was someone Melinda had never laid eyes on before in her life.

Weird, Melinda said to herself.

It was a red-faced, bald-headed *kid* in a blue blanket who didn't even look old enough to talk, let alone know who or what Melinda Mars had been.

And yet when the kid's glance flipped her way Melinda was dead certain they'd met somewhere. She tried to flex her memory muscles but something was paralyzing them.

"Eight pounds, twelve ounces," a man said.

Melinda struggled to angle her head a little higher. She recognized Toby, a very dim and very happy Toby. He was rocking the baby gently back and forth.

"Hey, Oliver Samuel, say hello to Mom." He held the baby up. All sorts of things began filtering back into Melinda's head.

"That's Oliver Samuel? *Our* Oliver Samuel?"

Toby nodded. "No one else's."

Melinda watched him fold back the blue blanket and run his finger under the baby's chin. The baby made a bubbly sound. "He's beautiful."

"You bet." He brought the baby to her.

Hello, you angel, Melinda thought. *Nine months of natural childbirth classes down the drain, but hello, you angel, anyway.*

Some telepathic spark must have leaped from Melinda to the child. He stared at her like an artist-and-repertory man evaluating a demonstration record.

"I don't think Oliver Samuel likes me."

"Sure he does."

"Can I hold him?"

"Sure." Very slowly and delicately Toby laid the baby in Melinda's arms. She braced for tears, screams, some kind of explosion.

It didn't come.

Melinda gazed at the wispy-bald head, the rosebud of the puckered lips, the doll-like eyes of such astonishing purity that stared up at her and seemed to know exactly who she was. "He looks so—*new*," Melinda marveled.

"Brand-new," Toby said. "Hardly unwrapped."

Melinda felt safe holding the baby. That was funny. It was the *baby* that was supposed to feel safe.

"My second gold record," Melinda murmured.

"What's that, Melly?"

"Just thinking. Loren's one, and Oliver Samuel's two."

"Two what?"

She looked at Toby. He was gold too. *I've got a lot*

of gold in my life, she thought. "Where's Loren?" she asked.

"He's doing just fine. A little smoke inhalation, nothing serious. You can see him tomorrow."

Another memory popped up. "That man who rescued us—he risked his life."

Toby nodded.

"Who was he?"

Toby gave her a look that was knowing and, in a teasing way, mysterious. "The fire chief."

"Fire chief!" she exclaimed softly, and it was not Melinda Mars superstar who reacted but the ghost of the girl she had been, the pudgy teenager who'd never been able to get agents to return her calls, who'd never managed to get her composite past the front office, who'd sung to half-empty cabarets in Greenwhich Village without the money to pay a decent pianist, who'd never had new arrangements or a new dress for an opening, the girl whom managers never asked to come back and whom audiences never asked for a second encore.

And now they sent fire chiefs to rescue her from Malibu Canyon!

"How come?" she asked. "Why the chief?"

Toby bent down to kiss her on the tip of her nose. "I had to pull strings."

Her mind couldn't quite put it all together. "You didn't *tell* them to send the chief. You didn't do that, Toby—did you?"

"I told them to send the best."

"And he came—for *me?*"

"They drew lots. The chief won. Frankly, I think he pulled rank."

She shook her head. She could not quite bring things into focus. "We have to do something for him. He could've been killed. What do you do for the fire chief? What does he need—a new engine?"

"Send him tickets to your next concert."

The word went through her like a jolt of electricity. "The concert!" She reached for the bedside clock. "O-migod, the concert!"

She struggled to shift her legs out of the bed and was baffled when they seemed five times heavier and thicker than human legs. She reached down and felt plaster and tape, and then she felt Toby pressing her gently back against the pillow, smoothing the covers of the hospital bed back over her again.

"Forget the concert, Melly. There's no way you can make it."

"But, Toby, it's a sellout."

"You'll have other sellouts."

"But the *Bowl!*"

"It'll still be there."

She let herself sink back into the bed. "Who's going on instead?"

"Not to worry. I'm sending in my new act. The Disasters."

Melinda decided to accept it philosophically. "Oh, hell, they need the exposure more than me." She looked again at the clock. "But, Toby, don't you want to be there to see them?"

"It's all set up. I want to be here with you. And Oliver Samuel."

It was a wise and lucky decision. Because Melinda Mars and Toby Gladstone were in a San Bernardino hospital that night and not at the Hollywood Bowl, they lived.

Melinda relaxed. She wanted Toby with her tonight. That was the way it ought to be. Toby and her and Oliver Samuel.

And still a tiny misgiving wrenched at her. "Toby, I feel lousy."

He shrugged. "You're entitled. You've been through a lot."

"But all those people—they're *expecting* me."

"They'll forgive you."

"I've never missed a date in my life."

"You'll book another date. And it'll give you time to rework those arrangements. The French horn, remember?"

Melinda remembered. She stared at Toby smiling down at the baby. She sighed. She hated to admit she was wrong, but...

"Toby, I've been thinking it over. I'm going to do it your way."

"You're going to keep the horn?"

What kind of idiot did he think she was? Keep the fucking *horn?* She shook her head.

"I'm going to marry you, idiot."

He broke into a grin. "You mean it?"

"Sure, I mean it."

He bent down to kiss her. "I gotta make a phone call. Don't go 'way!"

Steve Miller was armed. He was patrolling the forested hills above the Hollywood Bowl. Like hundreds of other rangers and police, he was on the lookout for the arsonist.

It was almost pitch-black as he crept through the trees, these trees that he loved and ached for. He stepped softly to minimize the crackling of his boots in the dry duff. Smoke had blotted out the stars. The only light in the sky was the eerie reflected glow of the hill fires. Carbon-saturated air prickled into his nostrils and with each stinging breath sorrow and anger mounted in him.

His orders were to shoot to kill. He wanted to kill.

At 8:32 an instinct flashed to him that he was not alone, that something, someone, behind the trees on the opposite crest of the ravine was observing him—stalking him.

A shape moved. A sapling bent, then straightened again. He heard the crunch of a footfall. His hand went to his holster.

"Hold it right there."

Halfway across Los Angeles, Ed Caldwell was still braced, still waiting in the dark.

He had no weapon, only the flashlight, gripped hard in his hand. He had only the strength of his body, now crumbling under the weight of two days' fatigue and the six months' abuse that had preceded.

His boots crunched in the dry brush as he shifted weight from foot to foot. His shirt gave off little scratching noises as it rubbed against the scraggly bark of the tree trunk that hid him.

He could see the vague outline of the narrow roadway and now, moving along it, a stealthy dark bulk that had no color.

The thing was gone.

He wondered if he had imagined it. Perhaps that was what your mind did when you listened too hard, expected too hard.

His eye leaped from tree to tree, sliding over surfaces, inspecting bits of darkness to snatch at whatever it was that might have hidden itself behind them. He sensed something stilled and waiting.

He breathed in quick, shallow intakes of air. His heart rattled like a stone being shaken in the hollows of his chest.

He pulled behind his cover again and lowered himself into a squat.

"And now," the governor said, winding up a seven-minute speech that had—among other topics—touched upon his decision to run for another term, "the bad news."

His tone was somber, as though announcing a death in the family of man.

"And very, very bad news I'm afraid it is."

A hush swept through the capacity audience.

"Melinda Mars will not be singing for us tonight."

The audience groaned. The Bowl's stunning natural acoustics shaped that groan into a collective outcry from the very bowels of hell.

The governor raised both hands, signaling for silence. "The reason—ladies and gentlemen, the reason—"

The groan died down but resentment flared. A sell-out audience of twenty thousand Melinda Mars fans felt they'd paid a fifty-dollar top and been suckered into this natural amphitheater in the Cahuenga Hills for nothing more than a campaign speech.

"The REASON is that Miss Mars is at this moment...in a San...Bernardino...*hospital!*"

There was a chain reaction of shocked little outcries.

"She is in the *maternity ward...*"

The governor knew his audience and he knew how

267

to feed out a line. A blanket of hushed expectancy fell. He milked the pause.

"...where she has given birth..."

There were handclaps now, and happy screams, and excited faces flashing grins.

"...to a lovely, healthy, eight-and-one-half-pound baby boy..."

The screams and applause crescendoed. The governor had to shout.

"...and that baby's name, ladies and gentlemen, that baby's name is—*Oliver...Samuel...Gladstone!* And, my friends—"

Joyful pandemonium spilled over the amphitheater.

"Friends, friends, may I have your attention *please!* Hold ON to your ticket stubs! Because Miss Mars...Miss Mars *personally*...requests...the honor...of the presence of *each* and *every* one of you here at the Hollywood Bowl one week from now...AT HER WEDDING TO MR.—TOBY—GLADSTONE!"

In one spontaneous wave the audience rose to their feet, screaming and cheering and stamping.

For 812 men, women, and children in that audience, it was the last standing ovation they ever gave anyone or anything on earth.

Steve Miller heard a rustle in the brush and turned.

Just visible in the dark, a small white dog was standing ten feet away. The animal was whimpering. It was in some sort of pain. It was a West Highland terrier.

Exactly like Nipper, Steve Miller thought. *Exactly like my little girl's dog.*

Steve Miller snapped his fingers. "Here, doggy. Come here, doggy."

He whistled and crouched down. The dog stared up at him, panting, tongue hanging out. Its coat was smeared with leaves and mud and ash. Steve touched the animal gently. It yelped and bounded away.

There was something off in its gait, a suggestion that the left hind leg was wounded. Steve Miller followed the tiny bobbing figure with its curious, unsymmetrical lope.

Now the animal stood in the thicket and it seemed

to be waiting for him. There was a sort of defiance in its stance, as though it had retreated as far as it was going to.

Steve Miller reached a hand and whispered. "Come here, pal. Don't be afraid. What's wrong with your foot?"

Cautiously sniffing, the dog took a step toward him.

At the same moment a sound in the bush made Steve Miller whirl. The dog barked and leaped back. The bush fluttered and Steve Miller saw the glint of something metallic, cylindrical.

He did not see the chain. He did not see the connection between the metal thing and the dog.

An image grabbed at his mind and it was the shape of a crouching man with a gun. Steve Miller drew his revolver. He fired three shots, aiming for what he took to be the gun barrel.

The first shot severed a link of the chain, and dime-sized bits of metal rained down on the brush.

The second shot went wild, ripping a seven-inch strip of bark from a pine.

The third shot was right on target. It found the bomb.

A yellow flame spat upward, igniting dead leaves and dried pine needles. Fire tore along the forest floor like a surgical scar ripped open. In less than ten seconds the thicket was ablaze.

Steve Miller aimed the spout of the extinguisher strapped to his shoulder. The fire was spreading too fast. He whipped up the aerial of his walkie-talkie. He shouted his location, the size and speed of the burn.

A voice crackled back, "Can you hold the fire?"

"No way, not by myself," Steve Miller shouted back. "Send a team!"

"Buddy, there ain't no team. Save your ass!"

Steve Miller backed away from the spreading flames and the searing heat. He sprayed chemical extinguisher till there was none left. The fire didn't care. It ignored the sprayed areas, ate around them, kept coming.

Steve Miller shucked the dead extinguisher and grabbed the little white dog in his arms and ran.

14

UP UNTIL 8:42 P.M. Peters actually believed he had the situation under control. And to tell the truth he was enjoying his moment of authority.

Under his temporary command over eight thousand fire fighters—professionals, military, and volunteers—were deployed on seventeen separate fronts. Seven superscooper water bombers were ferrying payloads of salt water from the bays to the burning slopes. Eighteen helicopters and eleven military C-130 transports were dousing the flames in chemical retardants. Fire lines were holding. With nightfall a good half of the burns seemed to be slowing down.

The situation was looking good.

Assistant Chief Peters was looking good.

To be sure, there were scattered difficulties. In residential areas homeowners plugged into fire hydrants to hose down their houses, drastically lowering water pressure; on the larger fire fronts, media people and gawkers actually hindered the fire-fighting effort. But, administratively speaking, these were police problems. Peters would not need to take the blame for them.

At 8:42 Peters was proud of himself.

At 8:43 a helicopter over Hollywood Lake flashed word that the fire was spotting west of the fire line.

Peters shot one glance at the Hill Park monitor. He saw what was coming.

How? a voice in him screamed. *What went wrong?*

Another voice told him to slow down, not to panic. Review the data. Wasn't there some sort of advantage to be wrung from the situation?

Then it came to him.

The fire was moving downhill. The prevailing wind was still against it. That gave him time. That gave him a chance to outflank Caldwell, the mayor, even the governor.

With one act of apparent bravery he would etch himself indelibly into the minds of twenty million Californians. *He would sound the warning in person—from the stage of the Hollywood Bowl.*

Peters hit the radio mike. In a voice so shaking with excitement he could barely control it, he ordered all available forces to the Hollywood Bowl.

The order was too little too late. But what Assistant Chief Peters did next put the seal of certainty on the disaster.

He ordered a helicopter to take him immediately to the Bowl.

By 8:45 the speeches were long finished. Discreet helicopters had whisked the politicians far from the Hollywood Bowl.

The performance had begun. Initially, many in the capacity audience were disappointed. While The Disasters were an adequate lead-in to a star act, they were hardly, at this stage of their careers, stars themselves. In many respects the music was almost dated, a hokey arrangement performed by a period dance band. For all their outlandish getup and gear, The Disasters could as easily have been wearing the short-cut tuxedo jackets and funny hats of an earlier era.

But it was precisely this aspect of their performance that gradually won the audience over: the bumptious gaiety was endearing. And there was an irresistible assertive quality to the pounding, "upbeat" major chords.

By the time The Disasters were ready to play their trump card, the audience was on their side—many were even clapping along. It was during a raucous chorus of "Walking My Baby Back Home" that that trump was played.

The violins and violas, heretofore merely amplified, went electronic, all shrilling different notes. The female vocalist unleashed an earsplitting scream into the mike. Many in the audience were convinced she was in pain, if not torment. The cyclorama background of pastoral greens and blues suddenly became a technicolor photomontage of forest fire, arson, war, volcanic eruption, while dry-ice machines pumped a terrifying volume of colored vapor into the air. At the same instant loudspeakers throughout the amphitheater unleashed a deafening barrage of explosions and gunfire.

The good guys were gone, the punks held the stage.

The effect was electrifying, if not precisely controlled. For a low gray canopy of smoke now billowed in over the Bowl. Many in the audience were amazed that mere stage effects could produce such a suffocating cloud cover, and more than a few were far from amused as their throats began hacking up coughs and their eyes running tears.

Up to that point, annoyance was clear and present; danger seemed only illusion.

And then, shouldering his way through the astonished performers, Cas Lovenko strode onto the stage.

At the same moment Lieutenant Harvey Burgett and his men were taking up positions at the exits; others were sprinting down the aisles. Backstage, an electrician pulled the plug. The Disasters, reduced to unamplified scrapes and squeals, traded panicky glances.

Lovenko waved his arms. Speaking into a handheld mike, he called for attention. "Ladies and gentlemen, there is no cause for alarm. I repeat, no cause for alarm. As I call your section numbers will you please rise, proceed to the nearest aisle, and follow the instructions of the officer stationed there."

In her back-row seat, Wilma Boborovsky turned to her husband Clarence and muttered, "What now?"

Clarence shrugged. "Probably some kind of bomb threat."

Wilma made a face. "Wouldn't you know? Not only

272

do we *not* get to see Melinda Mars, we don't even get to see the stand-ins!"

"Can't be helped," Clarence soothed. "Just listen to the man and do what he says."

"Please do not rise until your section number is called," Lovenko's voice boomed through the amphitheater. "Please do not talk. Please keep calm. There is no cause for alarm."

As Cas Lovenko began calling out section numbers, the fire front was still almost three-quarters of a mile distant. It was moving at a speed in the neighborhood of four and a half miles per hour. Technically, the audience in the Bowl had almost ten minutes' warning. That was more than enough time to complete what began as a model of calm and orderly evacuation.

At least it ought to have been.

But as the tide of flame coursed toward the amphitheater, a helicopter was racing toward the flame, and Assistant Chief Peters was gazing through the Plexiglas, his eyes fixed on the corridor of darkness between the fire and the Bowl. He was translating that corridor into time, planning the moves that would get him to that stage and the words that would make him a hero.

And then the craft banked.

Peters' eye jerked to the pilot. "What the hell are you doing?"

"Going around, sir."

"There's no time. Take her up, not around."

"But, sir, the updrafts—"

"*Up*, buster. You speaka de English?"

The pilot bent over the controls. His face knotted into a tight squint as he peered at the indicators on the panel. Peters watched the boy's hands flutter and grope among a cluster of knobs and short sticks.

The motor roared. The helicopter lurched upward, but there was a sickening wrongness to the ascent, a buffeting tremor like an epileptic seizure. Suddenly the copter dropped fifty feet, caught an instant's immobility, and dropped again.

It came to Peters with a jolt that all experienced hands had been ordered into the field: the boy was a

273

trainee with no more experience than the minimum hours it took to get a license.

"You're losing altitude!" Peters screamed. "Get this thing up!"

"I'm trying!" the boy shot back in a panicky yell.

The aircraft shuddered, took on the uncontrolled shivering of a man in an electric chair. Peters' mind was racing now. He'd never piloted before, but he'd obviously seen a hell of a lot more hours in the air than this frightened kid.

And he knew which stick controlled altitude.

He lunged a hand for the knob and swung it forward with all his weight.

"Get your goddamned hand away!" the boy screamed, smashing Peters in the chest with his elbow.

Peters held tight. The motor's whine jumped up three octaves into a crazed shriek. The spasms shaking the copter now became a lunatic side-to-side wagging.

Peters felt himself yanked painfully to one side as the craft banked.

And kept banking.

He felt the boy's fingernails digging into the flesh of his hand. He heard the motor give a last violent cough and die. He saw earth and sky change places; he saw the flaming inferno come loop-the-looping toward his unbelieving eyes.

But Assistant Chief Peters held on to the knob.

Waiting for their section to be called, Wilma Boborovsky squirmed back into the jacket that her husband had hung over the rear of her seat. Clarence turned to help her. His eye was caught by an astonishing flurry of activity in the woods uphill from the Bowl. He nudged his wife and pointed.

Like a rush of lemmings, whole flocks of rabbits and coyotes were scampering down the hills. And then Clarence and Wilma Boborovsky saw the thing that was driving the animals from their homes.

A spray of sparks, high and fast, skittered along the upper reaches of the treetops. Small capering flames were leaping in jagged patches downhill toward the Bowl. Before the Boborovskys' incredulous eyes, a cluster of trees detonated into a cloud of fire. The cluster next to it was set off, and the next, as though the fire were playing a lethal game of tag with the wooded slope.

Wilma Boborovsky screamed, "FIRE!"

That scream brought the process of orderly evacuation to a halt as swiftly as a machete severing a head from a man's body. The eyes of those within hearing jerked in the direction of the cry. A ripple effect carried the alarm far beyond the sound of Wilma Boborovsky's voice. Three thousand eyes turned in one wave toward the rear of the Bowl.

What they saw was like a page from the apocalypse. A helicopter came bobbing wildly through the flames—not above them, but *through* them. It was a helicopter like none that anyone in the audience had ever seen: in the instant before the flames detonated the fuel tank, the craft appeared to be flying at a crazy tilt—almost *upside down.*

After the explosion, no one could be sure. No one took the time to look. Besides, the light was as blinding as a sun touching down to earth.

In her panic, Wilma Boborovsky dropped her jacket.

The fact that neither she nor Clarence stopped to pick up that jacket no doubt saved their lives. They were among the survivors of the Bowl disaster, and—as Wilma was later to tell interviewer VV Cameron of KLIC-TV—they survived it the only way possible: "We *ran!* Sweet Jesus, we HOTFOOTED IT!"

In the seven minutes before Wilma Boborovsky sounded the alarm, Cas Lovenko came close to achieving the impossible: he almost evacuated twenty thousand men, women, and children from the Hollywood Bowl.

Almost.

He had not reckoned with Assistant Chief Peters and his helicopter.

That flaming helicopter did more than incinerate the assistant chief and his young pilot. It sparked panic. What had been a disciplined if nervous crowd became a terrified, clawing mob. The Hollywood Bowl victims, in their desperation to save themselves, became one another's murderers.

People were trampled in the aisles. Cars tried to ram their way out of the parking lots. Fire trucks jammed the lanes. Tie-ups and collisions multiplied in geometric progression.

Two human waves smashed into each other: the panicked remnant of the audience, stampeding for their lives, and the fire fighters, desperately struggling to contain the holocaust.

Each wave canceled the other. Neither achieved its objective.

Eight hundred and twelve human beings were trapped. Eight hundred and twelve died.

Needlessly.

I figured it right on the nose, Ed Caldwell thought. *Or maybe just took a lucky guess.*

There was no dog at burn site three.

His eye picked out a tree that would give him cover. He cut sharply through the brush and hunched down in the darkness to wait.

Seven minutes later, his vigil ended—with a whistle.

The phosphorescent hands of his watch pointed to 8:53 when he heard it. The sound was so high and tiny that at first his ear could not locate the source. It seemed to come from everywhere, from nowhere. Not in front of him, not behind him. To the side.

Which side?

He tensed. He waited to see if the sound would be repeated.

It came again, the same whistling, still faint.

He could not tag the sound. It matched nothing in his experience, nothing in his memory. It was distant and whining and eerie and an involuntary shudder went through him.

Slowly, his muscles contracting by millionths of an inch, Caldwell reoriented himself. He turned until he was facing what instinct told him had to be the direction of the whistling. His eyes worked at sorting out sections of the night, sifting through them for some-
276

thing that might be part of a face, a patch of clothing, a portion of an arm.

A spear of light suddenly lanced the black frame of his vision. At first it was a spark winking in and out of the foliage and gradually it became a ray sliding through the trees with an odd up-and-down jagging motion.

He held his breath.

It was difficult to judge, but the light source seemed to be thirty or forty yards away. At first he could not tell exactly which way the light was moving. He could not tell anything about it except the brightness and the bobbing, up-and-down, side-to-side dance. His first impression was that the light was flitting without aim or purpose, a twelve-volt butterfly caught up in the sheer pleasure of movement and exploration.

But gradually an underlying drift showed, a slow curving bend through the woods and toward the road.

Straining to see, he could dimly make out a human shape. The shape detached itself from the murky waters of the night.

Caldwell did not move. He watched the dancing beam. He could see the forward edge of the hand from which the light's length shot into the night.

And now he could hear the excited barking of a small dog. The barking was coming straight at him, and with it the crackling commotion of a small animal cutting swiftly through the brush.

Now he heard footsteps—heavy, uneven, as though one leg were dragging a weight. And it came to him what the whistling was: the effort of lungs grabbing for air.

There was no mistaking the shape now: it was the lumbering form of a limping man. Several feet ahead of the shape, a little terrier scooted back and forth through the beam of bobbing light.

The animal looped back to the man, whimpering and sniffing at his trousers, pawing at the cuffs. The man dropped the flashlight. For an instant the forest was black. Caldwell heard what sounded like a curse. When the light reappeared it was in the hand of the stooping man.

The man stood again, came forward slowly. The bobbing light borrowed some of the lopsided rhythm of his step. It scanned from side to side, searching.

Caldwell understood. Defino was looking for his burn site.

Anger surged in Caldwell, cutting off his wind like a golf ball in his throat. He wanted to twist the man and pummel him and snap him apart. He fought to control the fury and loathing that writhed in his hands.

Defino found his burn site.

He set his flashlight on the ground beside him. The beam caught a lopsided brunette slash of store-bought hair.

Caldwell watched the man bend to his work. The little dog jumped at him, playfully snatching at his loose trousers, taking the whole thing for a game. The man slid what appeared to be a grease pencil out from his belt loop. He twisted the top off, and Caldwell saw that it was a hypodermic.

Now Defino took something else from his pocket. He jabbed the needle through the rubber cap of a blue ampoule, extracted the liquid, then—holding the dog tightly by the scruff—emptied the hypodermic into the loose skin at the back of the neck.

He withdrew the needle with a quick jerk, sheathed it, and slid it back beneath his belt loop.

Caldwell gripped his flashlight hard in his hand. As a weapon it seemed pitifully inadequate. But it was all he had.

Defino worked rapidly, with practiced care. From his belt he unhooked a coil of steel chain, a looped length of fuse, a canister shaped like an aerosol of shaving cream. He set them down neatly on the forest floor.

The dog's mewls became questioning now. Its forelegs buckled and then the hind legs and then it was down on its side.

Defino pulled up one of the animal's eyelids. Satisfied that it was unconscious, he placed a collar around the dog's neck. He attached the loop of chain to the collar, then the fuse.

Slowly, so slowly that the muscles of his thighs were almost screaming in pain, Caldwell straightened to his feet. He inched around the tree now, soundlessly, pressing close to its bulk. He flicked on the flashlight and in the same movement straightened up and stood out from the tree.

"Defino. Venice. Whatever you call yourself."

The head jerked up. A face that was puckered into scars and bruises stared at him with black, glowing eyes. It was the bare, wrecked rudiments of a face, a skull with stitched-together skin stretched over it.

Caldwell caught his breath sharply. He swallowed.

"Okay, Defino. I'm armed. Don't try anything. Do exactly what I say."

Without turning his body or letting the light slide off Defino, Caldwell turned his head and called as though he had a platoon of men hidden behind him: "You men stay back there. I'll handle this!"

Then, facing Defino again: "Take that bomb off the dog. Take the whole thing off. Bring it here."

Defino said nothing. His lashless eyes, small and black, stared unblinking across the light.

Caldwell repeated the command. "Come on, Defino. Do it. One false move, and you're dead."

Defino obeyed. With the same meticulous care as before, he undid his work. He stood, faced Caldwell.

A warning bell went off in Caldwell's head. "No funny stuff, Defino."

The man lifted the chain and the fuse and the canister. Slowly, he wound the chain around his own neck. When he had finished winding the chain, he arranged the canister so that it hung down his chest like the pendant of a necklace.

What's he doing? Caldwell asked himself: *What the hell is he doing?*

Defino moved toward him now, so slowly it was as though Caldwell were dreaming it. But he knew the man moving toward him with the chain wound around his neck was no dream, no mere nightmare: this was real, this was happening.

Defino stopped. The muscles of the scarred face pulled back tautly. The mouth twisted into a leering, lipless grin. It was a face stripped down to one emotion: raw, naked, triumphant hate.

He's going to set himself on fire, Caldwell realized. *He's going to take me and himself and the whole forest with one big bang.*

For one instant Defino stood motionless. And then slowly he came toward Caldwell.

Terror jetted through Ed Caldwell, more paralyzing than any terror he had ever known. Every instinct in him screamed: *run!*

His legs would not answer his will, there was not even a twitch of obedience in them. He stood glued to the spot, hypnotized by the specter of his own extinction.

And Defino *knew.*

Caldwell could see the wreck that was Defino's face, and the wreck...*smiled.*

The shock of that smile gave Caldwell back his voice. "Dear God—*no!*"

And God must have heard.

From out of the dark came the whipsnap of a cracking branch and then like stones raining on metal the snapping of dozens of branches and the rising groan of a motor roaring into life. Two headlights snapped on, plucking twin holes out of the dark. With a shrilling of gears they swiveled, caught Defino in profile, locked on him.

A red Karmann-Ghia nosed off the road. The scream of its motor filled the forest like the cry of a maddened animal. The tires spat up earth; twigs and duff and soil showered like buckshot from a gun.

Defino glanced to the side, into the mirrored parabolic lights.

And he understood.

The car wanted him.

He veered sharply away, lunging through brush and then onto the road. The car veered with him, the pitch of its motor now an uncontrolled howl.

What happened next seemed to Caldwell a slow-motion ballet, but it couldn't have taken more than two seconds.

The headlights ignited the fuse around Defino's neck.

The fuse swung out in an arc. A live ember raced

hissing along its flying tail. For the one split second the canister pulsed white light. A deafening *crack* echoed through the trees.

Flame fountained from Defino's neck. Flame rushed along his outstretched arms, crowned his head, billowed out behind him in a wide-flowing cloak. His chest exploded in light.

The Karmann-Ghia came shearing through a sapling and then it sheered through Defino, ripping one limb of fire from the central core, hurling the rest of the fiery human ball up through air and down with a thudding impact onto the road again.

The Karmann-Ghia slammed to a wrenching stop. VV Cameron stumbled from it. She held one instant to the door, steadying herself, then with a staggering step went to Ed Caldwell and clung to him.

Caldwell gripped her shoulder and pressed her to him.

They stared down at Defino. The fire had spent itself now. What had been a man had metamorphosed into a twisted charcoal mummy.

VV was shaking her head, denying the reality of this moment, of this man dead at her feet.

"Stay here," Caldwell said. "I'll be right back."

He went and got the dog. He heard the roaring wind and very faintly the high distant wail of an approaching fire siren. It was the most beautiful wail he'd ever heard.

Good for VV, he thought. *She got word through.*

When he returned she was standing there, staring at the thing on the ground, her eyes glazed and unbelieving.

"Eddy...hold me, please..." VV whimpered. There was a trembling in her voice.

Caldwell smiled to instill courage in that shocked and suddenly childlike face.

"Come on," he said.

He led her to his car. He laid the sleeping dog next to the other animal already snoring on the back seat.

"We have to make one stop," he said. "Defino left a dog at the second burn site."

He eased the car into gear, then looked at the woman

sitting hunched and shocked on the seat beside him. Gratitude overflowed him. He pulled her toward him and put his arm around her.

"You know something, VV?"

She stared at him, blinking.

"I think L.A. is going to be okay. And I think Eddy Caldwell's going to be okay too. Thanks, VV."

They picked up the third dog, a sleeping beauty that must have had more than one Irish setter in its ancestry. They drove back to Caldwell's house because he remembered some dry dog food left over from the days when Mickey had had a pet.

"That stuff keeps, doesn't it?" Caldwell said.

"Anything keeps," VV said, "so long as you don't expose it to light or air."

"What about a wound?" Caldwell said, not knowing exactly why he said it but sensing that small talk could only help VV's nerves.

"What are you talking about?" There was a spark of genuine bafflement in her green eyes.

"If you were wounded and you didn't expose that wound to light or air, it would keep too, wouldn't it?"

VV shook her head. "Don't ever try it, Chief. You'd get gangrene."

Caldwell nodded and swung the car into the drive. "I think that's what almost happened."

VV stared at him. "What's with you, Chief?"

"Nothing. Something. Doesn't matter. Come on, let's get the dogs into the garage. You take the terrier."

There was a note for Ed Caldwell on the hall table by the phone. He didn't see it till he'd dialed headquarters and asked for Lovenko. The operator said it would take a moment to patch him in. He propped the receiver under one ear and opened the envelope.

The note was from Trish. In it she said she had tried for six months to love him. She said other things, too, but the most important thing that she said was goodbye.

Ed Caldwell had trouble digesting the note. He felt it had to do with a time and a man no longer real. In fact, nothing that had happened before the fire seemed real anymore.

Nothing at all.

VV was watching him with an odd intensity. Her face was strained and anxious. *Not anxious for herself,* he realized. *For me.*

He had a sudden sense that she knew, that she'd read it all on his face.

He reached out an arm and pulled her toward him. She laid her head against his shoulder just as Lovenko's voice came onto the line.

"Cas? Ed Caldwell here. How are we doing?"

"How are *you* doing, fella?" It sounded as though Lovenko was riding in a car with a siren.

"Not too bad. I got our man. With a little help from a friend. He won't be setting any more fires."

"So I heard. Nice work."

"What about your end, Cas?"

"It's under control. We're holding the fires. Looks like we'll have rain sometime tonight. The rain should do it."

There was an odd sound in Lovenko's voice: not bent, not broken, something else. It took Caldwell a moment to recognize anger.

"Things under control enough for me to spend ten minutes in the shower? I'm filthy."

"You can spend the night in bed, friend," Lovenko said. "Starting now."

"Come on—things aren't *that* much under control."

"Seem to be. We're on top of the burns. They're beginning to lie down. Like I said, the rain will do it. If anything comes up we know where to reach you."

"Fire lines holding?"

There was a pause. "We had a problem at the Hollywood Bowl."

"The *Bowl*—Jesus Christ!"

VV's eyes flicked up at him, alarmed. He squeezed her shoulder.

"We're on top of it, Ed. It's history. Take your shower and go to bed. I'll tell you all about it tomorrow."

"Are you sure...?" Caldwell wanted to protest, but the idea of a shower and bed and the nearness of VV

283

were much too tempting. This was one time he was ready to delegate authority.

"Ed," Lovenko said firmly, "you're a hell of a fire chief and you did a hell of a job. Los Angeles wouldn't be here without you."

"Or without you, Cas."

"So get your goddamned sleep. You've earned it. Pleasant dreams."

Ed Caldwell hung up the phone. He started to speak.

"Yes?" VV said.

"Nothing."

They stared, holding each other in the cool trembling of their gazes. He felt all the emptiness in the house, all the space waiting to be filled. Slowly, his arms reached and pulled her against him, pulled her tight. Their mouths came together. He had an awareness of the reality of this moment that was so sudden and enveloping he wanted to cry out.

But there was no cry; there were no more words.

Gently, he took her by the hand and led her up the stairs.

Afterward

Toward dawn a noise awakens Eddy Caldwell. He bolts awake. The bed sheet slips off him. He stares down at the woman sleeping beside him.

Something taps at the window. When he squints, a blur is running down the pane. There is a skittering sound of a million tiny feet tiptoeing on the roof and in the tree leaves and on the street. Something in the sky unlocks with a clap and the tiptoes become a dancing, deafening tumult of slaps and stamps.

Eddy Caldwell yells and leaps across the room. He throws open the window. Cool air races into the house. He bounds out onto the balcony. Water spills across his eyes and nose and splashes sweetness into his mouth.

He gazes through the downpour.

Wherever he looks, Los Angeles is still there: the mountains, the downtown skyline, the houses, the street-lights and traffic signals, the trees and grass, and all the growing things that root in the earth and climb to the sun.

"VV! Come quick!" he calls. "Look!"

"What is it, Eddy? What's the matter?"

"Rain!" he cries. "God bless it, it's raining!"

Eddy Caldwell holds out an arm to her. He pulls her beside him, then tips back his face and lets the rain drench them both.